CONNOR

IN THE COMPANY OF SNIPERS

Book 5

IRISH WINTERS

COPYRIGHT

Connor; In the Company of Snipers, 5

Edited by InkTip Editing, Ashley Argyle inktipediting@gmail.com

Cover design and author photo by Kelli Ann Morgan,
http://www.inspirecreativeservices.com

Interior book design by Bob Houston eBook Formatting

First American Paperback Edition

ISBN Paperback: 978-1-942895-00-8
Library of Congress Control Number: 2014954761

Irish Winters can be contacted at:
http://www.irishwinters.com or http://irishwinters.blogspot.com.

In the Company of Snipers

You can find Irish Winters on Facebook:
https://www.facebook.com/author.irishwinters

On Twitter: https://twitter.com/irishwinters1

For news on upcoming releases, sign up for Irish Winters' Newsletter at IrishWinters.com.

For more information about all my books, visit IrishWinters.com.

IN THE COMPANY OF SNIPERS

This series revolves around ex-Marine scout sniper, Alex Stewart, and his covert surveillance company, The TEAM, home-based out of Alexandria, Virginia. An obsessive patriot and workaholic, he created the company to give ex-military snipers like him a chance at returning to civilian life with a decent job.

This is not a serial with each book ending at a cliffhanger. I wouldn't do that to you. *In the Company of Snipers* is a collection of passionate love stories involving women and men who are tough enough to take on the world alone. Each is a stand-alone read, where in the course of an active TEAM operation, one agent comes face to face with his or her demons. The men and women I write about are all patriots and warriors, dealing with what they've lived through or the mistakes they've made

Spoiler alert: Every novel contains adult scenes including sexual situations (some explicit), language, and violence. I don't write sweet romance, so be forewarned.

At the end of each story, it's my hope that you, along with my heroes, will come to realize...

Love changes everything.

Prologue

Eighteen Months Earlier

"Damn it."

USMC Sergeant Isabella Ramos cursed as her ammo clip hit the dirt on the other side of the wall. Sergeant Connor Maher could not help but notice. He didn't write the rules of nature. A real man's always gonna look, and this particular gal's derrière, albeit camouflaged in the uniform of the day and plenty of dust, made for a choice view. What red-blooded, all American male wouldn't?

One minute she was seated all nice and comfortable on that three-foot wall. The next, she was bent over it, damn near ass over teakettles with her boots, legs and butt on display. He glanced away, not wanting to be caught looking—at least not by her.

He and his buddy, Jamie, were part of the United State's military response to the increased violence of the Iraqi insurgency in Fallujah. Both short timers and counting the days, this was their final tour together unless Jamie got another brilliant idea to re-up. With home only a couple months away, Connor was antsy. All he had to do was stay alive. In Iraq. During one of the hottest USMC campaigns of the war. Stolen commercial breaks like this show with Ramos made the grind endurable.

She'd gotten the short end of the stick when their commanding officer decided someone ought to show the two newly arrived non-commissioned officers the lay of the land, and voilà. Just like that, they got a snappy tour of U.S. Camp Baharia and along with it, a floorshow that couldn't be beat.

The good thing about the predominantly USMC camp was the large clear water lake in the center of it. The bad thing was it was still in Iraq. The once-upon-a-time desert resort town was now filled with hard-core military men and women who sometimes forgot how to behave. Like Lance Corporal Jamie Ramos, who by sheer coincidence shared the sergeant's last name, but obviously, not her dedication to the Corps.

Already passed over once for promotion, Jamie was headed for trouble with his CO. He didn't seem to have a problem with his rifle qualification or combat fitness, but his true talents lay in another direction—entertainment. Jamie was a tease to the mathematical power of a gazillion, and that innate need for attention would land him in the brig one of these days.

"You know you want to." He elbowed Connor again, urging him to do the unthinkable. "Just one little smack. It's easy. I've done it a million times. No one else will see you. Just walk over, lay one on her ass and run like hell. She's short. She'll never catch you. Go on. Do it."

"Shut up," Connor muttered out of the corner of his mouth, glancing again at the ass in question and doubting the 'I've done it a million times' line. "You know better than to treat women like that. Knock it off."

"What's she gonna do? You're both the same rank," Jamie persisted. "It'll be fun."

"Cut the crap. She's a lady."

"No, she ain't. She's a jarhead just like us. She's GI. Loosen up, Maher. Walk on the wild side for once in your geeky life."

Connor glanced at the ass in question again. Damn. It was spank-a-licious and hard to keep his eyes off of. This dark-haired and olive-skinned beauty had potential in his book. Lots of potential. He didn't want Jamie's crazy antics to blow his chances before he knew if he had any.

Raised in a house filled with six younger brothers and no sisters, women still perplexed Connor. Sometimes they loved a guy who only two seconds earlier they'd hated. He couldn't keep up. Besides, his mother had taught him early what Jamie's education must have missed. A real man does not disrespect women, even when they cussed like sailors. He'd grown to appreciate Bridgette Maher's wise sayings more now that he was out of her house. *Treat a woman like a lady and she'll never turn into a nag.*

With a twinkle in his eye, Jamie edged closer to the irritated sergeant's backside, a big cheesy smirk on his trouble-making face. She tipped farther over the wall, the toes of her boots nearly off the ground and still cussing a blue streak. No way was Connor getting close to that action. He shook his head and mouthed a definite, *No. Don't do it.*

Jamie's eyes brightened with, *Are you daring me, man?*

Connor didn't know whether to nod or shake his head. Either way spelled trouble.

Jamie's left eyebrow spiked into an incredibly wicked, *Here goes.* His arm lifted higher.

Connor shook his head, disgusted at himself for letting Jamie take a prank this far. He stepped forward to halt the wise guy before things got anymore out of hand. Retrieving the clip in question would solve the Sergeant's problem and torpedo Jamie's stand-up comedy once and for all.

"Excuse me, ma'am—"

Jamie's perfectly white teeth flashed a big shitty grin. His flattened hand lifted over the rump in question.

Apparently, Ramos hadn't heard Connor yet, leaning over the wall like she was. He was nearly behind her. "Ma'am, let me get that for—"

The sergeant tipped one booted foot to the sky and exclaimed, "Finally. Got the damned thing."

SMACK!

Crap. Sergeant Ramos came off that wall so fast she landed in Connor's arms. The deadly scopes of a deadly sniper skewered her one man viewing audience.

Oh, sweet Mother Mary and Joseph.

He gulped and caught a peripheral of his trouble-making buddy. Jamie was on his knees. At the end of wall. Out of sight. Clear out of sight.

Ramos could only see—him.

Those sizzling brown windows to a she-devil's soul were pointed straight up at—him.

Crap. I'll be busted back to private first class.

He should've pushed off. He should've been a gentleman and apologized for the inappropriate contact. He should've done anything, but no. Generations of hopeless romantics from the Emerald Isle had led him to this pivotal moment. His fingers refused to unclench from her biceps. Looking down into two dark pools of what felt like the strongest, bitterest, sweetest coffee, Connor was doing good just to keep breathing.

Hot damn. If I'm dying, it's gonna hurt, but I'm going to heaven.

Equal rank or not, something about this diminutive spitfire had stomped the hell out of his ego from the first moment he'd seen her. With the meanest reputation in the squad, she could teach the drill sergeant's *How to Be an SOB* class all by herself. Ramos was a cherry bomb with a short fuse and right now, he was cannon fodder. Nothing but.

"You want to die right here and now, Boston?" she hissed, her shoulders rolling along with her swagger. How could a gal with such sexy brown eyes be so mean and sound so tough? His eyes refused to move off of her, even though her top lip was curled over a wicked Devil Dog bite.

And here he was holding her. Not just holding her, but chest to breast kind of holding her, and either she didn't mind the contact or he was in for one helluva lesson in smack down, hand-to-hand combat. The woman was pure muscle, her biceps as hard as her eyes. Contempt glittered there, and just maybe something else. Mischief?

"Ahh, no, sir – I mean—no, ma'am—I mean—" He dropped his hands and took a full step back to get out of her personal space, stuttering like an idiot.

Jamie was still crouched with his hand clamped over his big fat mouth he was laughing so hard. Right then and there, Connor should've handed his buddy over, but real men don't do that either.

Ramos stomped right back under Connor's chin, her eyes dark and deadly, full of the promise of nothing but pain.

Maybe death. "You think hitting another soldier's ass is funny, do you?"

"No, ma'am, I do not."

God, she was so damned gorgeous. Yeah, she radiated a certain amount of radioactive hostility, and he was pretty sure he glowed already, but damn. What a package. His nose filled with the lovely whiff of roses and incense. How fitting. The sweetness of flowers mingled with the unmistakable hint of burning ash. He'd been an alter boy. He ought to know.

That drab green T-shirt peeking up from her uniform didn't conceal the rounded landscape beneath from a man of his height, either. Six-foot-three should be the one doing the intimidating instead of peering down a woman's shirt like he was. The thought of peeling her out of those desert cammies tweaked what was left of his common sense. He wanted to touch. Hell, he wanted to fondle, pet, and a whole lot more.

Should I pour on the Maher charm?

Sizzling death glowered up at him, not even blinking once and full on daring him to keep breathing.

Ah, maybe not.

The verbal assault commenced. "I'm gonna make you wish you died during boot camp, you pig-faced, camel-lipped, piece of..."

On and on she went. He took it like a man. Almost. His jaw kept moving, but sound had ceased coming out. Article 128 of the United States Code of Military Justice flashed through his blood-deprived brain. *Question: Is a slap on the butt considered sexual battery?*

Answer: Damn straight. Don't touch. Don't tell. And all that stuff.

Jamie howled, at last overcome by his own hysterics.

Ramos shot a scorching look over her shoulder. "You!"

The instant she looked way, the magic faded. Connor was half-inclined to cup her chin and direct her gaze back to him. Just him. Not Jamie. But he was afraid to touch her. She might be too hot for him to handle.

"Why don't you grow up?" Kicking a boot scrape of sand in Jamie's face, she stalked off, which only made him laugh harder. The dumb ass looked like he was having a heart attack the way his face was all screwed up.

Oddly, Connor felt a chill when Sergeant Ramos left. A chill in Iraq? How'd that work? He watched her walk away, her dark brown ponytail twitching side to side in time with her butt, both sassy as hell. Taking one step forward to follow and apologize, he came to his senses and stopped short. Not now. Let her cool off. Mad women were unpredictable.

"You shoulda... You shoulda...." Still laughing his guts out, tears streamed over Jamie's cheeks. "I mean it. You shoulda seen the look on your face!"

"You could get me court-martialed," Connor ground out, even as his gaze returned to the command tent where Ramos had gone. He wasn't so much scared as interested. Maybe it was all those blond brothers he'd grown up with, but dark-eyed girls always caught his attention. Hers seemed darker than most, full of sparks, promise, and a whopping dose of cayenne. The moment he'd seen her, he knew. They would spend time together.

"Oh, hell." Jamie pulled himself onto the wall, dusting his pants off. "Don't worry. She won't do anything. You're safe."

"Yeah, right." Connor huffed out an aggravated sigh. "You ever heard of friendly fire? She was an MP sniper, jerk-off. Now I gotta watch my back the rest of my rotation."

Jamie guffawed through another laughing attack. Connor had half a mind to kick his friend's ass if it would douse the hysterics, but he doubted it would. Jamie was a fun-loving, risk-taking Hispanic who could charm the socks off most ladies. Didn't seem to have any effect on the sergeant, though.

Finally, he turned semi-serious. "Don't worry. I've got your six. You know that, Bro."

"Bullshit, you do," Connor shot back at him. "You've got nothing."

"No, really. I've seen how you look at her." Jamie almost sounded sincere. "Listen, Connor. Remember how I told you I'd never seen her before in my life, how lots of us Hispanics got the same last names only it don't mean we're related? You know, like Martinez, Gonzales, Sanchez, Moreno, Garcia?"

"So what?" Connor could feel it coming. The joke wasn't over yet.

Jamie winked. "I lied. That's Izza. My sister."

One

"They're coming straight to you," Junior Agent Connor Maher whispered to his Senior Agent Roy Hudson.

"What's your twenty?"

"I'm on the shale ledge above Mossy Creek." Connor stilled to listen to the four men he'd followed instead of the terse voice coming over his Bluetooth earpiece.

He and Roy were on the first day of a two-man operation to observe the Sonoran Cartel activities in one of the canyons along the Wasatch Front in Northern Utah. They'd opted to hike the canyon to get the lay of the land, never suspecting they'd intercept cartel activity so soon. But when an opportunity presented itself, a smart man took advantage.

The Drug Enforcement Agency, the DEA, was already involved, but Utah's Governor Tom Baxter wanted outside help, someone non-federal. He was a worried man with a problem that wouldn't go away. Poor Utah had its share of run-ins with Mexican cartels, first with the Sinaloa Cartel, the world's most powerful drug trafficking and arms running syndicate. After the DEA ran them out, in came the Sonoran Cartel, nicknamed SC by local reporters.

Over the last two years, clashes between the SC and Utah residents had grown more violent. Baxter did what any smart man in a precarious position would do. He called in a favor from an old friend, Alex Stewart, and the best covert surveillance outfit on the East Coast – The TEAM.

And now Connor, trusted agent for The TEAM, was belly to the shale while Roy, his agent in charge, approached from the west, both intent on the obvious cartel activity they'd stumbled across. Connor blamed it on generations of Irish luck and hoped that lucky streak held. Utah scrub oak on a shale outcropping didn't make the best cover. One slip and he could be on his way downhill and into a whole lot of trouble. The SC was not one to toy with.

"Damn it. I'm not seeing you or them."

"You will," Connor breathed as the high-powered rangefinder in his hand brought his quary up close and personal.

"Okay. Got 'em in my sights now," Roy murmured.

Connor rotated his wrist a hair to the right until he located Roy in his lens. Concealed in a stand of quaking aspen, the lead agent had chosen well. The fluttering green leaves and early morning play of light and shadow transformed the motionless black man from prey to predator, not unlike the tactics Connor had employed in the Corps.

A hefty six-foot three Vietnam vet, Roy was also the go-to-guy for anything explosive ordnance related and one of the easiest men to work with. How a sixty-year old guy still looked and acted like one of the younger guys in the office was a testament to his inherent aptitude for his high-risk EOD career. Roy was a hard man to rattle.

"Stay put."

"Copy that," Roy replied. "Got your eyes on?"

"Always."

Roy meant the miniature video camera attached to the stem of Connor's Ray Ban sunglasses. Whatever he saw, it recorded. That Roy even asked was enough to inform Connor that Roy had his ears, the portable parabolic listening dish, already on and transmitting.

Until now, their targets had made good progress toward the cartel camp, which stood west of their current location. So why had they halted directly beneath Connor's position at the edge of the river? Did they know they were being followed? Tension tap-danced across his shoulders.

He recognized all the players from the intel briefing preceding the Sonoran Operation: Jose Ibarra, the slim and trim second in command to Miguel Ramirez, the despicable cartel boss. The two locals with Ibarra were Maka Taufa, boss of a local West Valley Tongan gang, and his buddy, Roger Paxton, a local bad boy.

Both looked none too happy. Had to be because of the gorilla blocking the trail behind them. Nestor Martinez. Known murderer. Cartel muscle. Brutal enforcer. Yeah. Something nasty was in the air. Connor could almost smell it.

"So tell me, Señor Taufa," the impeccably dressed gentleman below inquired of his nervous compadre. "What do you want now?"

Rolling his index finger over the zoom on his mini-cam, Connor brought Taufa's face up close and personal. He pressed the button and took two stills, one of Ibarra, the other of Taufa. Zooming out, he snapped a wide-angle shot of the foursome.

The odd alliance of a Mexican drug lord with a Tongan street gang in the middle of Utah emphasized the awful way of the world. When drugs, money, and greed were involved, anything could happen. Ibarra had enlisted the Tongan's gang as additional muscle to keep the illegals in line. Didn't look like it was working too well.

Straining to hear Taufa's reply, Connor cocked his head, but the man had turned his back to him. Judging by the dark expression on Ibarra's arrogant face, Taufa hadn't provided the right answer. He acted guilty, lowering his head and toeing the gravel path at his feet with his boot.

"Let me get this straight." Ibarra cocked his head, his lip curled and his pencil thin moustache twisted in a sneer. "They told you no? And you let them?"

Taufa nodded quickly, again mumbling too low for Connor to hear.

"Free?" Ibarra rolled his shoulder as if that word annoyed him. "Just because they are in America does not make them free. Remind them where their true loyalty lies. Help them remember how much they have to lose."

Taufa raked his hand over his head as he responded again with what must have been another bad answer.

Ibarra's dark brows angled into a severe V. "They will do as they are told, or they will pay with the blood of the families they left behind. I know every barrio and village in Mexico. Tell them that."

The Tongan's head bobbed. Again he looked over his shoulder at Martinez, his answer drifting up to Connor. "Trust me. I will tell them."

"Go then. Don't bring your troubles to me again. It is not for me to keep your people in line. Next time I will not be so understanding."

Taufa nodded vigorously, one foot already pointed downhill.

Ibarra looked straight up at Connor. Connor held his breath. For a second, he thought he'd been made, but no. Ibarra hadn't seen him. He was only toying with his prey. Distracting him. Without a moment's hesitation, he whipped a pistol out of his denim jacket, turned and fired a single shot. The roar of the shot echoed from canyon wall to canyon wall while the shocked Tongan clutched both hands to his bloody chest.

"Oh, crap," Connor whispered.

"Holy shit!" Paxton jumped back a step, bumping into the business end of Nestor's rifle.

The Tongan boss swayed before he pitched face first to the ground. Martinez pushed Paxton into Ibarra's line of fire. He stumbled to his knees with his arms clenched in prayer. "No. Please. Don't kill me. I'm too young. I got kids. I got—"

"Connor?" Roy's alarmed voice hit Connor's eardrum louder than he expected. "You good?"

Connor tapped his mic once in answer to let Roy know he was still on task. He knew Roy was panicked, but Roy needed to hush. Was Paxton next?

"You will do as you are told." Ibarra's face was now less than an inch from Paxton's.

Taufa's buddy nodded vigorously. "Yes-s-s, I – I c-can. I mean, I w-will."

"Then make an example of this piece of shit for all to see." Ibarra kicked the dead man's booted foot.

Paxton kept nodding. Sweat glistened on his face. If he licked his lips anymore, he could pass for a lizard.

"Let everyone know what will happen to stupid peons who think they are free just because the move out of Mexico. Can you handle that simple order or must I do it for you?"

"No, sir. I got it. I do. I will," Paxton agreed quickly. "I sure as hell can do whatever you want, Boss."

Ibarra sneered. "Good. Martinez will make sure that you do."

"Yes, sir." Paxton kept on sniveling and agreeing. "I'll make it happen. Just you wait and see. The families will remember this. It's gonna be good."

Ibarra tucked his pistol back inside his jacket and walked away. Still sniveling, Paxton lowered his face to the dirt.

"Talk to me, Connor," Roy insisted. "What the hell just happened?"

Connor rolled to his back. The palest blue sky stretched overhead. He swallowed hard. "Paxton just got promoted."

Rain. Again.

Junior Agent Isabella Ramos's flight was weather delayed, and for Seattle in June, that was saying something. Rain was the Northwest's flavor of the month from September clear through May. Year in and year out, it didn't fluctuate unless Mother Nature decided to send... You got it. More rain.

She snagged another magazine from her carry-on: the *Leatherneck's Gazette*, a damned good read and USMC down to its staples. She might not be in the Corps anymore, but that didn't make her less of a Marine. Reading about the previous job she still loved helped pass the time and take her mind off her problem. Sitting in the middle of the bustling SEA-TAC airport concourse without so much as a holster on her hip or under her arm made her feel naked. Travelling commercial air sucked since 9-11.

It had gotten so that a gal couldn't fly anywhere with her nine-inch blade, much less her trusty six-shooter. A smile tugged the corners of her mouth. Six-shooter nothing. She'd be packing two pocket pistols and extra mags if she had her way, but not today. This morning her cargo pants pockets were empty except for a couple cellophane packs of saltine crackers.

Damned Transportation Safety Administration. The TSA's concept of perceived security ruffled every last one of her feathers. Disarming law-abiding citizens did nothing to protect travelers. Not really. It was not her they had to fear. It was that other guy, the one who didn't let rules and regulations get in his way when he had an airliner to take down. But here she sat, neutralized and paralyzed along with everyone else and all because the folks in charge thought compliant people solved the problem.

Her left eyelid twitched in annoyance. The nation's paranoia over possible terrorists in every shadow had now made her one of the dependent ones. Izza hated being helpless. Made her feel like a little girl again. Defenseless. Trapped. Weak.

She flipped another page and stifled the creeping tension in her neck that always accompanied a civilian infested flight. A military hop would have made more sense, but no. Now employed by Alex Stewart, one of the few men on the planet she respected, she had to behave. Follow protocol. Make him proud. That meant flying the friendly skies whether she wanted to or not. Might as well read. There wasn't much else to do.

"Hey, Izza." Mark Houston, her agent in charge, flopped into the seat beside her. Although not an actual Senior Agent, for this op he might as well be. He had her in seniority and experience with The Team, and he was one of Alex's right hand men.

"Hey, Mark," she answered indifferently.

"I brought you another cup." He waved the piping hot beverage under her nose. "You seen Morgan yet? He was supposed to meet us at the gate."

She pointed to the bookstore across the hall, accepting the Starbucks without looking up any longer than she needed to. "Thanks. He's shopping. As usual."

Mark was an excellent example of everything good about working on The TEAM. Calm under fire and levelheaded, he was one of her favorite co-workers. He looked out for everyone, even Alex.

Her nose twitched. Whatever body wash he'd used in the shower this morning smelled pretty fine, too, the perfect combination of manly with a hint of vanilla coffee bean. That was Mark to his toes—tall, dark, and borderline sexy. The feminine streak she usually suppressed sprang to life at the thought of this guy in the shower scrubbing his chest and abs with that body wash. Mark. Naked. Soaking wet. Hmm. If he wasn't married, and if she weren't tied down like she was, oh, the music they could make together.

"Hey. You awake?" He bumped elbows with her, jolting her out of her lust-filled reverie.

"Yeah. Hi," she muttered, hoping her errant thoughts did not reflect in the heat flaming up her neck, but darn. How a big guy like him managed to move as gracefully as he did still caught her attention. Pecs and biceps rippled beneath his black polo as he tucked his carry-on beneath his seat. Mark was built in a big boy, bouncer kind of way, the perfect inverted powerhouse triangle if she ever saw one. Only she wasn't looking.

Thankfully, the latest custom sniper rifle advertisement in the magazine caught her attention. She buried her nose in the article. The less than five K price tag made it affordable in her line of work. Mental note to self: *talk with Alex. The TEAM can stand a weapons upgrade.*

Mark stretched his long legs into the aisle in front of him and pressed his usual large vanilla blend to his lips. The man liked his coffee weak and sweet. Not her. Black, hot, and strong. She didn't care what fancy name they gave it as long as it brought a quick spike of caffeine with it.

Izza took another hit off the hot beverage. Yeah. She needed a new rifle like she needed a hole in her head, but the composite stock and butt pad looked sweet. Mark was a definite no-go. The rifle, however, had possibilities.

Rory Dennison yawned from the chair opposite Izza. The man could literally sleep anywhere. She toed his boot, just to aggravate him, but he didn't rise to take the bait. He was another good-looking agent, taller, athletically slender, and twice as polite as Mark. Even now, instead of rudely sprawling over three or four seats just because he was tired, Rory sat with perfect posture in one seat, his arms folded across his chest and his eyes closed. The irony didn't escape her that she, the only female agent present, was hands-down tougher than any of the guys she was travelling with. Meaner too. She'd have taken as many seats as she needed if she were tired. Why not? There were plenty.

Then there was Morgan Humphries, light brown receding hair, bookworm, and boring as all get out. She brought USMC magazines to occupy her mind when forced to fly. He, on the other hand, ran for the nearest bookstore and bought the latest Wall Street exposé or something equally as dull. She toyed with the concept of designing her own AR. He preferred the world of investments. Go figure. An article on a .338 Lapua caught her eye. Morgan and his big brain were forgotten.

"Not again," Mark grumbled, slapping his thigh with the palm of his hand. "Our flights cancelled again. How do you guys stand to live here? It's always raining."

Izza looked up. The arrivals and departures monitor across the aisle fluttered as all departure flights were cancelled. This was their second weather delay in as many days. Damn it. She didn't want to waste time waiting for a flight she didn't want to be on in the first place. "We're never getting to Utah at this rate," she muttered. "Why don't we drive? We'd get there sooner."

Mark turned halfway in his seat toward her and stretched, cracking his vertebrae with a pop-pop-pop as he flexed that magnificently muscled bod. "I think you're right. All this sitting is hard on a guy." Another stretch in the opposite direction and his spine cracked again.

She had to look away. He might be spoken for, but damned, he was one sexy beast. And he smelled good, too. She took another deep breath of vanilla and *Wild Man Mark* before she shut down her out of control feminine receptors and forced her sex-starved brain back to the business of how to get to Utah.

"You want to see if we can get our luggage back?" she asked, energized at the possibility of leaving modern air travel behind. If they were headed back to their office for a Team vehicle, she could swing by her apartment and be armed like any respectable sniper in no time.

"It's probably already onboard." His dark eyebrow spiked in mischief. "Are you going stir crazy, too?"

"What do you think? We've been sitting on our thumbs for two days now. Come on. Call the game due to rain. Utah is calling my name. Bet it's not raining there."

"You might just be right." Dark brown eyes twinkled. Junior agent or not, Mark Houston was the perfect team lead for this assignment. He always listened, a rare trait among men in her estimation.

Morgan wandered out of the bookstore, his arms full of actual, hardcopy books. "Hey guys. What's up?"

"What'd you do, buy the store out?" Mark pulled his bag from under his seat.

Morgan beamed. "They have a clearance table with lots of good deals if you're interested. I'll go back with you."

"Let me get this straight." Izza didn't even try to suppress her sarcasm. "You carry a butt load of books when you're travelling light."

Morgan shrugged. "I like books. You like guns. Not much difference in the weight ratio if you ask me."

Izza was on her feet by then, taking her cues from Mark. The minute he stood, she was out of there. "Come on, Book Boy. We're moving out."

"We're what?"

"Flight's been cancelled again," Mark explained as he pushed out of his seat and headed toward the airline's information counter. "We're driving instead. I'll see about getting our luggage off the jet. Wait here."

Relief flooded Izza right down to her boots. She took a cleansing breath and stowed her magazine. The day might just turn out after all.

Despite his glasses, Morgan squinted at the departure monitor to his right before his gaze strayed to the bookstore behind him. "When are we leaving?"

"No way." Izza shot him her best drill sergeant stare-down. "I'm not waiting around here just so you can shop."

She jerked her bag off the floor and slung it over her shoulder. There were only two books she needed to get her hands on in the next month or so, both user manuals. One was to argue her case for new hardware with the boss and prove it with cold hard facts. Alex was like that. Hit him with statistics and rock-solid evidence, and he believed. Out came his wallet, and Izza was happy.

The other user manual she needed was written by that guy, that—what was his name?

Oh, yeah. Mr.—no, wait. Dr. Spock. Yeah. Him. The baby doctor.

Two

"I really didn't see that coming," Roy muttered darkly.

Connor walked silently beside him, his empty Camelbak hanging off one shoulder, his full backpack off the other. After calling in the murder they'd witnessed to local authorities and answering a battery of questions at the local precinct in downtown Salt Lake City, they were finally on their way back up the canyon to meet their DEA point of contact. It had already been a helluva day. Thankfully the arresting officer placed a call to Governor Baxter's office as Roy requested, or they'd still be stuck at the station.

Despite the pleasant fragrance of Ponderosa pine and Douglas fir drifting through the dry mountain air, Connor's stomach roiled in protest at Ibarra's cold-blooded execution. The SC was damned nasty, but what had Ibarra meant about making an example of the dead man? Connor knew what it meant in Iraq. Mutilation. Debasement. And other foul things he didn't want to remember. Could the SC be that barbaric? Here in America?

A bitter taste lingered at the back of his throat. The scariest puzzle to the morning came when Taufa's body disappeared from the scene of the crime before the police arrived. All that was left was a bloody splotch on the gravel to confirm Roy and Connor's wild claim. He needed a drink.

Roy stopped him in his tracks with a hand to his chest, jerking him out of his depressing thoughts. "Oh, hell no."

Connor looked up to a thirty-foot long RV. A woman had just climbed out of the brown truck parked alongside it, her hand extended in welcome, and a big smile on her pretty face. "Morning. You guys are late."

Connor's mind switched gears the second his eyeballs scrolled up and down the good-looking woman. Short blond hair, tanned athletic legs that extended from khaki shorts and ended in hiking boots, a good combination in his estimation. This gal moved like she knew who she was and where she was going. Confidence radiated across the short distance between them. His pulse quickened just looking at her.

Setting his gear and the empty Camelbak to the ground, he stepped smartly forward to meet and greet. "Agent Connor Maher, ma'am. This here's Senior Agent Roy Hudson, and you are?"

"DEA Agent Cassidy Dancer at your service." She offered a solid handshake that he swore lingered an extra second longer than necessary. The twinkle in those deep brown eyes of hers seemed to linger also. "Thought you'd be here a couple hours ago. What happened? You run into trouble on the way out of SLC? Traffic heavy?"

"SLC?" he asked.

"Short for Salt Lake City," she explained. "You'll get used to Utah speak soon enough."

"Okay. That's cool, but no, we didn't have any trouble until we ran into your buddy, Ibarra," he answered.

She rolled her eyes. "You didn't kill him, did you?"

"Not yet," Roy muttered by way of a less than enthusiastic introduction. "Nice to meet you, Agent Dancer. What's up with the bed on wheels?"

"Welcome to home sweet home." She grinned as she unlocked the door of the vehicle and tossed him a set of keys. "From now on, you're just a couple guys on vacation. The rig's your cover while you're working with us."

Connor shot Roy a teasing look, totally understanding his senior agent's hesitation. Most undercover vehicles were nondescript. Despite its olive drab color, the RV seemed to shout, *Lookee here.*

"You're kidding, right?" Roy shot Connor a dark look, apparently not much in the mood to be teased.

"It's okay. I like it." Connor smiled, trying to keep one step ahead of Roy's less than enthusiastic welcome before he offended Agent Dancer. "I'm good with living high on the hog while I'm working. Beats sleeping on the sand like we did in Iraq."

Disapproval knit Roy's brows. He stared at the extravagant vehicle, his hands on his hips. "Nothing about this thing says covert."

"Isn't that the point?" Agent Dancer waved them into their new digs. "Who'd think this was a federal rig? You'll be surprised how easy you'll blend in with the other campers. Come on in. Climb up."

Connor followed Roy. While it said luxury on the outside, inside of the RV was a world of utility and high-tech surveillance. Four racks lined the aft wall. Sleeping quarters led forward to the head, which sported a glassed-in shower stall, a nice touch instead of the stark open-wide gym-like accommodations of Navy ships. The galley came next, complete with a full-sized refrigerator already stocked, a range, a built-in table and benches.

And that's where the niceties ended. Where a couch and chair might have been in normal RV's, an ammo storage locker and a worktable loaded with computer equipment declared this was no vacation home on wheels. A big screen television dominated the area over the driver's seat, no doubt where Connor and Roy would be included in TEAM business back East.

Agent Dancer provided a quick tour. "You've also got four outside storage compartments. You'll find canned food supplies out there, an inflatable raft, fishing and hiking gear, plus other things to make your stay look authentic. Use what you need. The river's across the road. Do some fishing while you're working. It might get you inside the cartel's camp if you work it right."

But Roy was already at the computer checking in with the office back in Virginia. Agent Dancer shrugged at his lack of interest and stepped outside. Connor followed.

"So what happened with Ibarra?" she asked.

"Tongans got a new boss this morning," Connor muttered. "Paxton looked a little green the last time I saw him."

"What'd Ibarra do? Kill our island boy?"

Connor rubbed a quick hand over his chin, not sure how much more he should share. "Actually, yes. Shot him point blank. Then he told Paxton to make an example of the body. You wouldn't happen to know what he meant, would you?"

Her nose crinkled into the most adorable scowl. She had tiny brown freckles sprinkled over that cute nose, another point in her favor. "Not sure. Ibarra likes to intimidate the new illegals in town. Poor people are trying to stay under the radar, but he targets them to handle drug distribution for the SC. It's worse if they've entered the country legally and own a business. He uses the Tongan gang to scare the hell out of one of them. The poor illegals end up working for him whether they want to or not."

"He's leveraging the lives of their families back in Mexico to force them to work for him," Connor muttered.

She nodded. "He's a twisted piece of work. How'd you guys happen to run across him so soon?"

"Got lucky. Instead of driving in, we thought we'd pass ourselves off as a couple tourists and hike the trails. Left the car in a parking lot at the mouth of the canyon. Sure wasn't expecting an execution."

"You took the north side?" She nodded toward the canyon wall behind them.

"Yes. You know the loose shale above Mossy Creek? Perfect cover as long as you don't lose your footing."

"Damn. That's close to a lot of campers. Too close."

Roy scrambled out the door with his backpack slung over his shoulder. Tossing the RV keys to Agent Dancer, he said, "Thanks, but no thanks. We'll be in touch."

"Excuse me?" The delicate arch of her brows lifted in surprise as she caught the keys single-handedly. "Where are you guys going to sleep then?"

"In our rental. Won't take long to hike back to it at the end of everyday. It will do," Roy shot back at her. "Come on, Connor. Let's move."

Connor froze, caught between his suddenly unreasonable agent in charge and a pretty gal. He was all about making friends with the DEA, at least this particular agent.

"And here we thought we were doing you guys a favor." She fast-pitched the keys back at Roy. "Sleep in your car then, or use the tent in the basement. Rough it for all I care."

Roy nearly missed the throw.

"The basement?" Connor asked as he followed her.

"The basement is the RV's outside storage compartment," she muttered over her shoulder as she opened her truck door and slammed it behind her. When the engine roared to life, she shoved the gearshift into drive.

"Wait." He gripped the open window, not quite ready for her to leave. "Not so fast."

"Why not?" A teasing smile glimmered on her mouth. She was ticked, but not at him. Good deal. The cutest dimple punctuated her left cheek. Long lashes blinked up at him like maybe she was taking a second look and liked what she saw, too. He sure did.

"It's just that the RV is not what we're used to," he explained. "We like to keep a low profile when we're undercover."

"Listen, Agent Maher. This is Utah. It can get up to one hundred degrees by nine in the morning, sometimes sooner. You'll be damned glad you've got air conditioning on those days. A car turns into a sweatbox pretty damned quick, even in the dead of night. You won't get any sleep in that kind of heat. You'll see."

"So where's your rig?" he asked, needing to diffuse her aggravation with Roy. "Are you working out of an RV, too?" He hoped.

A family with a tent-trailer was camped across the road from what would have been his RV. The sounds of children laughing and squealing rent the air, although none were in sight. The whole place smelled pleasantly of campfire smoke and pine. If he was right, the satellite dish sticking above the trees might be attached to the RV that housed the DEA team. Agent Dancer might be his neighbor. Sweet.

"We're in the next campground two miles east, Agent Maher." Tiny gold slivers glinted in Agent Dancer's coffee brown eyes when she pointed up the canyon. The baseball cap perched on her head added to her sporty look.

"Call me Connor." He offered a truce. His eyes inadvertently drifted down the unbuttoned front of her shirt. Two buttons made a lot of difference. The glimpse of a black bra peeked up at him, along with a tiny black satin ribbon with a white pearl bead tucked between two very lovely breasts.

She squinted up at him, holding her hand to her forehead to block the sun. He jerked his gaze back to her face hoping she hadn't caught his less than gentlemanly infraction. Next door neighbor nothing. He wanted to be friends. Maybe best friends.

"Our post is not as nice as yours, but I doubt you'll have trouble spotting it." She extended her hand again. "My friends call me Cassidy."

"Take care of yourself, Cassidy," he said, her tiny hand snug in his. A guy could get used to his. Her eyes warmed along with her smile. Withdrawing her fingers from his, she stepped on the accelerator and drove away, leaving a cloud of dust behind her. Connor watched until her truck pulled onto the canyon highway and headed east. He would've waved if she'd looked back. Just to be friendly.

"I'm not staying here," Roy murmured grumpily behind him.

By the looks of it, he'd already decided to play the part of a fisherman on vacation. He'd retrieved a fishing vest all decked out with lures and a valid Utah State fishing license pinned to it. The green booney hat on his head sported the usual flies and paraphernalia to make him look the part. He held Connor's now refilled Camelbak at arm's length, the message clear. Roy was moving out. If he'd only stop frowning, he might actually look like a guy on vacation.

"But we just got here. Don't you want to rest for a minute?" Connor stalled. Were a few minutes of downtime too much to ask? "Maybe take a shower?"

"Go ahead." Roy glared at his reluctant junior agent. "I'll be back in a couple days. Join me when you're good and ready."

That's all it took. Connor grabbed the fishing pole Roy had thoughtfully leaned against the side of the rig and hightailed it after his agent in charge. What choice did he have? They crossed the road and headed into the brush on the south side of the canyon.

Connor knew the drill. Walk until you drop. Set Tattle Tales as necessary. Once the minute listening devices were activated, Mother, The TEAM's genius techie back in Virginia, would analyze the video and audio feeds. Standard procedure. Work, work, work.

Roy pointed to a line of stones placed across the river. "How about we cross here?"

With spring run-off from the high mountain peaks done for the year, the current flowed slow, shallow and lazy. Rocks aplenty lined the water's edge as well as the riverbed. Maybe twenty feet at its widest, the only treachery lay in the slippery rocks underfoot. Connor and Roy sloshed across to the south side of the creek without any trouble, still heading east.

Connor had to give it to Alex Stewart. The man didn't follow the federal government's policy of lowest bidder. He only supplied his team with the best gear, boots and socks included. Connor's feet were dry and comfy despite the trek through the river.

"First grow-site is one mile east and up. You ready to do some climbing?" Roy asked, like there was any choice. Connor answered with an abrupt right turn onto a deer trail that meandered up the south wall. Thick with scrub oak and pine, both men traversed the wayward path etched along the canyon wall by centuries of migrating deer and elk herds. They passed several waterfalls, unexpected small pleasures spilling off the arid mountainside where cactus and sagebrush mingled with pine.

Before long, they were looking down into a marijuana garden similar to the one Alex had shown during his briefing. Pulling his rangefinder up and out of his backpack, Connor adjusted the focus until the scenery came into a high-resolution view. Unbelievable.

"The cartel's been busy," Roy said. "It looks like a well kept nursery down there."

Hidden within the trees, Connor spotted carefully cultivated rows of tall, broad-leafed plants, bags of fertilizer, coiled snakes of black plastic tubing between the plants, and a gas-powered water pump. He took deliberate care to scan for any sign of the armed guards who were known to disappear into the scraggly pines as quickly as the wildlife.

"I'm not seeing anyone, but someone's been down there recently. The dirt around the plant roots looks damp."

"They probably irrigate at night to avoid rapid evaporation," Roy murmured.

"I could use some rapid evaporation about now." Connor wiped his brow. Turning the collar up on his shirt helped keep the sun off his neck, but sitting in the shade was still plenty hot.

"They're down there somewhere." Roy's binoculars scanned back and forth.

"Wish me luck." Connor dropped through the dusty oak brush and down to the clandestine garden below. This was what he did best. Penetrate enemy lines. Plant Tattle Tales. And never be seen while he did it.

Always light on his feet, he hadn't realized this particular skill until it came time to complete phase two of USMC scout sniper training. Stalking. He was a natural at it, got closer to the observation post than the regulation two hundred yards it took to qualify, and he did it without detection. Better yet, the walker, another instructor in the training course, damn near stepped on him and never saw him. Connor aced phase two with the highly desirable score of one hundred percent for *shooter never found*.

But dropping into enemy territory was no test. Adrenaline heightened his senses, providing feedback from every sight and sound. It didn't take long for him to place one Tattle Tale in a quakie to the east and another in the most westerly location. As quickly as he went into the grow-site, he was out of there. When the cartel guards returned, they'd never be the wiser. The miniscule listening and video devices were camouflaged and would transmit long after an operation was complete, or until Mother deactivated them.

He rejoined his senior agent on the mountainside in short order.

"Good job," Roy whispered.

Connor took a deep breath and broached what had become a sensitive subject. "You're not going back to the RV tonight, are you?"

"Only to pick up the tent, and it better be a small one." Roy turned, irritation plain on his face. "Don't you get it? They set us up."

"Who? The DEA?"

"Yes, the DEA. Open your eyes. They don't want us interfering with their business, which is exactly what Alex and Governor Baxter sent us here to do. It's called passive resistance. It looks like they're doing us a big ole favor putting us in that RV, but they're not. The only way I'm going back to that monstrosity is under cover of night, and only if I need something. Which I don't plan to."

Connor shrugged. He wasn't going to argue. "Agent Dancer seemed neighborly."

"Neighborly, my ass." Roy got right to the point. "I thought you had a steady girl?"

"Who? Brenda?"

"Heck, I don't remember all their names. Was it Brenda this time?" Roy smirked. "You've only been with The TEAM for a few months, but I can't keep up. Stopped trying a long time ago."

"Brenda likes her girlfriend," Connor muttered, trying to project disinterest as he stood and stretched.

"Really? That cute blond likes other gals? Man, that's just wrong." Roy chuckled. Of course he'd think it was funny. "Bet that was a shock to your ego."

"Yeah, well, did you know you can't get a beer with dinner in this state?" Connor changed the subject. The less said about Brenda the better.

Their breakup had nothing to do with his ego. She'd set him up just to prove a point to her live-in girlfriend; another secret Brenda had kept from him. She'd led him on to prove she could get a guy anytime she wanted. The sad truth was she could. He was a sucker for good-looking women, and he'd fallen for her. Hard. Until he understood what a conniving person she was.

Yeah, she could swing both ways. Point made, only Connor didn't swing. One way was sufficient. He might chase, but only the opposite gender. He was straight, single, and frustrated as all get out. Women these days wanted the security of a steady man friend, but they also wanted latitude to pick and choose. They might expect him to hold the door for them one second, but gripe when he did. They were as much a mystery as that one woman in Iraq who—

He squelched the trip down memory lane before it got off the ground. No way was he going there again.

"What you talking about, no beer with dinner?"

"It's Utah, land of the Mormons, remember? Can't buy liquor in grocery stores like back home."

Roy scowled. "I'm going to have to check into that."

"Check all you want. This state's biggest claim to fame was the 2002 Olympics. It's the perfect state for outdoor enthusiasts, rock climbing and polygamists. Not much else."

"Won't matter. We'll be out of here before you know it." Roy stowed his binoculars and headed east and upward again.

Connor followed suit. Damn it anyway. Why'd Roy have to get all high and mighty over sleeping in comfort instead of on the rocky ground? They tramped for a mile or two before they stopped at another grow-site to plant more bugs. By then, the sun was high and terrifically hot. Roy kept up a stiff pace, but Connor could tell. The dry heat and high altitude was getting to him, too.

After mapping as much of the south canyon wall as they could, Connor was beat, but silent. Soldiers don't complain. They just keep on keeping on. Besides, Roy held the winning hand as agent in charge. It was up to him to decide if they kept working, and also if they camped outdoors tonight. He was right. The RV was over-the-top. It made for a damned big target. Might as well have a bulls-eye painted on the side.

The good news was they'd located quite a few marijuana grow-sites, some guarded, some not. Connor kept a digital record on his tablet, marking GPS coordinates for future need, and assessing collateral damage if push ever came to shove. Because he was often the man out in front of everyone else, he'd often been the eyes on the ground back in Iraq, the guy who recommended armament to fit the target, then sat tight until a Predator Drone or an F-16 completed the air strike.

Connor wiped the sweat out of his eyes, blinking the stinging sensation away. The dry Utah heat had a helluva lot in common with Iraq.

"It's damned hot," Roy muttered as he sank beneath the shade of pinion pine and leaned his back into the tree.

Connor joined him, thankful for the break and the life-saving water supply strapped to his back. Lukewarm, cool, or hot, hydration was the only thing keeping him going. He leaned against the same tree, facing due west in the opposite direction. From his elevation, he could see clear to the Great

Salt Lake. It should make for a picturesque sunset come evening, but it looked sweltering now. Everything did.

His mind pinged to Cassidy. Would she be interested in watching the sunset with him? He had a satellite phone. His mood brightened at the prospect. Tired or not, there was a pretty woman in the neighborhood and that always made him smile.

Pulling out a small bag of trail mix improved with his favorites—M&Ms, jellybeans, and Reese's pieces—he offered it to Roy. "You hungry?"

"No, damn it."

Connor couldn't resist rolling his eyes. What the hell was wrong now?

Roy sighed. "I hate to admit it, but she's right."

Connor's ears perked up, but he kept on minding his business and enjoying his lunch. Or dinner. Whatever meal this handful of trail mix was. More important, who was right? Cassidy?

"Hell, I been awake since zero dark thirty, either on the flight west, talking to the police, or walking these canyon walls. A man can only do so much," Roy grumbled.

Silently, Connor agreed. *That's what I tried to tell you before, you stubborn jackass.*

"Eat some trail mix. Have a sip of water," he offered again.

Roy glanced over his shoulder. "Food is not the problem. And I'm not thirsty."

Connor took a hit off his Camelbak's siphon hose and waited. *Then put up or shut up, you big baby.*

Roy growled again and rolled his shoulder. He'd stretched his legs straight out in front of him. His head was back against the tree, but he seemed agitated.

Connor smiled. The stop was a good call. A sudden uplift from the canyon below brought a welcome breeze. Maybe a night spent sleeping on the mountainside wouldn't be so bad after all. Utah did provide the most amazing vistas. They'd done tougher ops than this before.

"Let's move." Roy pushed slowly up from the ground. Spreading his arms over his head, he stretched a full minute before reaching for his pack.

Connor was ready. His second wind had arrived. He was refreshed and ready to hike another ten or so miles, but Roy headed down hill instead of due east. Down? Did that mean they'd be sleeping in comfort tonight? Was a date with Cassidy in the cards after all?

Sure enough. Downhill was a lot easier. Roy made record time, even had the keys to the rig in his hand before he hit the welcome mat someone had thoughtfully left at the two steps up. They'd no more than opened the door when a cool breath of refrigerated air reached out and welcomed them into their new digs. The first thing Roy did was to darken the windows with sheets of foil so no light would show out and no one could see in.

Connor downloaded to his laptop the surveillance footage from the Tattle Tales he'd planted. All of the listening devices were active and talking, relaying sights and sounds of every illegal garden they'd located. He set up a matrix of windows on his computer desktop to view all video feeds at once.

Satisfaction for a job well done lifted his mood. He and Roy were tired, dirty, and hungry, but they'd mapped every known grow-site on the southern wall of the canyon in one day. He couldn't help but feel a little proud.

When finished, he left the comfort of the RV to set up a web of motion detectors in a circle around the rig. Necessary or not, he needed to know if any neighbors came calling, two-legged or four it didn't matter. He activated a set of Tattle Tales to watch the RV. The more eyes the merrier. Connor doubted the cartel even knew he and Roy were in town. He intended to keep it that way.

After a quick shower, which Connor very courteously allowed grumpy Roy to take first, they ate a dinner of grilled hamburgers, pork and beans, and topped it off with a slice of key-lime pie that same considerate someone had left in the RV's full-sized refrigerator. The twelve-pack of cold Coors Lite didn't hurt Connor's feelings none either.

Roy grinned when he'd spotted it. "You were wrong. They do sell booze in Utah."

"Mom always said we're never too old we can't learn," Connor replied. "Give me one of them bad boys."

After dishes, both men collapsed on their bunks. It was too late to call Cassidy, but no matter. She was a lot closer now. A smile spread slowly across his sunburned face.

"I might have been wrong about the DEA. I really like this RV." Roy muttered before he dozed off in his nice clean bed instead of on the nice hard ground.

"You sure made Agent Dancer mad," Connor reminded him.

"Cassidy's a cute gal."

"Then be extra nice the next time you see her."

Roy snored in response.

Three

Driving through the Columbia River Gorge always made Izza smile. At least it used to. Stifling the icky feeling of motion sickness for the last fifty miles of rain filled curving roads changed everything.

Mark and Morgan were in the front seat, which suited her fine. With slim and trim Rory at her side, she had room to stretch out. Dozing through the nausea took her from Washington though Oregon and into Idaho.

When at last the interstate split south to Utah, it was a day later, the rain had finally stopped, and her back ached all the way to her toes. She was numb-butted and cranky.

They made one more rest stop before they hit the highlights of Tremonton, Ogden, and went southward to Salt Lake City. She blew out a sigh of barely controlled frustration. There was more than one mission needing to take place in the next week, and it was high time she figured out what she needed to say when the moment came. *Oh, hi. Guess what? You're going to be a father.* Or her preferred – *You screwed up. Now you're going to pay.*

Settling her palms over the small mound below her belly button, she felt the now familiar bump-bump of an elbow or knee jabbing her from within. Motherhood. Ugh. Who would have thought she'd get pregnant after just one mistake? She sure as hell didn't plan to, but then, this had been the year for surprises. Or shocks.

Focusing on the bleak desert landscape outside her window took Izza back to a different desert and time. Her CO, Colonel Nesbitt, looked so sad that morning, but what'd he expect? That she'd fall apart when he told her that Jamie, her brother, had been killed in action? Did Nesbitt think she'd cry all over him and need a hug? Hell, no. She'd taken it like the soldier she was, gulped it down like every other piece of bad luck in her miserable excuse for a life.

The only reason she hadn't re-upped for another tour was her pride. In that split second, she'd become the object of pity instead of the bringer of pain. Her tough girl persona was shot to hell. People were talking behind her back, and she floundered. The more she buried the need to scream, the worse it dug into her heart and hurt. Damned if they would see her cry, she left. The Corps could take all their *esprit de corps* bullshit and shove it.

She was alone. Even the apartment she and Jamie shared felt hollow when she'd returned home on that dismal, drizzling Seattle afternoon. No rowdy Seahawks' games blared from the TV room to welcome her. No Rainier beer bottles or half eaten bags of dill pickle flavored potato chips littered the counters or floor. No smelly socks and sweaty running shoes either. Not even dirty dishes. The place felt like a morgue. It smelled too—clean.

God, she used to ride Jamie's ass. Dirty dishes might make it to the kitchen counter, so why not into the dishwasher? And what was so hard about actually turning it on once in a while?

Smelly gym clothes got stacked on top of the hamper. Why not dumped inside? Her own words met her at the door. *Who do you think I am, your slave?* All those annoying habits that used to drive her nuts—suddenly didn't.

And that was when she lost it. By the time her anguish was spent, the apartment was in shambles, the tidiness undone, and her new reality come home to roost. Out of control and as lost as ever, she'd spent the first night in his closet buried beneath every last T-shirt and pair of pants he'd left behind just to breathe him in—one last time. Just to hold onto something that was left of him. Just to friggin' stop crying!

Only she couldn't. All Izza could do was bury the pain left by his death. The morning he fell, she lost everything— her family, her reason to smile, and the one person who loved her no matter how bruised, swollen, or messed up her face was. No matter how hard her father used to hit her.

She'd thought of ending it until she found out she was pregnant. Even though Izza should hate this child, she didn't. It was the ultimate gift from her time in hell come back to save her when she needed it most. For once in all of her twenty-two worthless years on earth, Izza deserved a break and a blessing. Despite its father, this baby was it.

She bit her lip, drawing just enough blood to remind herself that she'd survived worse. An unwelcome tear sparkled in the corner of her eye, catching a ray of the bright Utah sun. She scrubbed it away. Fast. No one needed to see what a stupid girl she was, least of all kind-hearted Mark or gentle Rory. Hell, no. One smidgen of kindness right now, and she'd crumble.

Besides, sunshine always made her cry. It meant nothing. So did the heat. The stifling lack of humidity. It all reminded her of—them. Jamie and Connor. The brother she loved and the man she hated.

Who was she kidding? She hadn't survived anything worse than this.

"Let's go play nice," Roy muttered.

"You're telling me? Seems to me you own that problem."

Roy growled and rolled his shoulders, but Connor could tell. The convenience of the RV was growing on him. They'd gotten up at the crack of dawn, and by noon, had located twenty-two grow-sites in all and possibly the cartel's main camp.

They'd come home to an ice chest on their steps with a note that said, "Enjoy!" written in feminine handwriting. Inside, were two perfectly marbled rib eyes that Roy quickly grilled to perfection. Little by little Agent Dancer was winning him over.

Now Connor and he were dressed in fishing vests and carrying fly poles on their way to visit their friendly DEA neighbors. It had been another successful day, and if Connor had anything to say about it, the night would be just as successful.

"Four agents are headed our way to assist. Two out of the Seattle office," Roy advised as he set a quick pace uphill. He was a lot easier to get along with now that he'd gotten a good night's sleep. That tasty steak hadn't hurt, either. "I'd like the preliminary report filed by the time they get here."

"Already got the video scrubbed and ready to go. Which agents?"

"Morgan Humphries out of Seattle, for one. Mark Houston and Rory Dennison will join us out of Virginia. Not sure who's on fourth. We still need to get inside that camp we found today, though. I'd like to include that in the report. You up for more exploring after our visit with the neighbors?"

"You bet. The sooner the better." Connor knew most of the guys out of the Seattle office. It would be good to see Morgan again and whoever that fourth person was. Maybe Eric Reynolds, the ex-Army medic.

Agent Dancer was correct. Their undercover vehicle was as easy to spot as Roy and Connor's. An older looking rig, it was not as large but appeared to be just as comfortable. She waved from their food-laden picnic table when she spotted them walking up the trail.

"Hey, guys. Good to see you again." She made quick introductions of the three men sitting around the campfire: Randy Burkhouse, Harold Denton, and Brigham Coltrane. Burkhouse was the stuffy senior agent, Coltrane just out of college and as green to federal service as they came. Denton was the proverbial cowboy, complete with handlebar moustache and a plug of chewing tobacco stuck in his cheek.

"You're kidding me. You found twenty-two sites?" Brigham Coltrane couldn't get over the fact that Connor and Roy had located a no-kidding cartel camp along with a couple more grow-sites. A handsome young man with close trimmed brown hair and brown eyes as friendly as a puppy's, Brigham had an easy going air about him as if he'd already seen the world and approved of it.

"Come see," Connor said as he lifted his laptop out of his backpack. Before long, everyone was gathered behind him watching the same video report he'd prepared for his boss. Each framed window on his desktop showed a bird's eye view of every grow-site, including a few shots of their RV.

"Oh, look. There's one we didn't catch." Harold Denton pointed over Connor's shoulder at one of the feeds. Short and squat, Denton was as laid back as any man could get, a definite don't-sweat-the-small-stuff kind of a guy. He clapped Connor's back. "Danged if you didn't find a couple more than us. Good on ya. Look at this, Randy."

"Yeah, I see it." Agent Burkhouse stared at the specific window frame Denton pointed out. Surly and gruff, he hadn't seemed pleased when Roy and Connor showed up unannounced, and he'd grown less so since they'd proven their worth. "It's no wonder we missed it. Look at all the cottonwoods obscuring the view. These guys just got lucky. Anyone can see that."

"Yeah, right. It doesn't hurt they've been hiking the walls of this canyon since they arrived instead of sticking close to camp like we do." Agent Dancer shot Connor a sideways glance, which he easily caught. "Heck, Randy. They're actually looking for the cartel."

"Nah, we just got lucky." Roy leaned back in his camp chair. "'Sides, it don't matter who gets these cartel guys as long as they leave the country, right?"

"Whatever." Burkhouse shuffled away from the conversation and headed inside. "I'm turning in. I'm tired."

No one seemed to care.

"I owe you an apology, Agent Dancer." Roy turned up the charm meter as he faced Cassidy. "You took real good care of us. Almost feel like I'm on vacation. Thank you."

She smirked at his cheesy apology. "Air conditioning is a lifesaver, isn't it?"

"Those steaks you brought weren't too bad, either. And how'd you know I like Key lime pie? A man could get used to being treated this good."

"Don't. Next time it's your turn."

The more she bantered with Roy, the more Connor approved of Cassidy. She could dish it out as fast as Roy could, but he was no slouch when it came to good food. "I was thinking along the lines of baby back ribs, hot homemade cornbread with honey butter, and a big batch of jambalaya with shrimp, sausage, and crawdads. You know, something from down south where folks really know how to cook."

"Where down south?" Brigham asked.

"Birmingham, Alabama." A big toothy smile lit Roy's dark skin. "Used to live there when I was a kid. Best barbecue on the whole damned planet."

"Sounds good." Cassidy turned her attention back to Connor's computer screen. "You mind showing me that video report again?"

She was the only one left standing behind him. Her hand rested light and warm on his back, her thumb rubbing a small circle on his right shoulder blade. That gentle meaningless contact played havoc with his breathing. "You bet," he mumbled as he opened his laptop and prayed his battery had enough juice to keep this woman interested. And close.

"Do you report into your office everyday by video?" She leaned over him to take a better look, making contact with her arm against his bicep. The powdery fragrance she brought with her was a pleasant change from the sweaty hiking boots he was used to.

"Usually. It's no big deal. How do you send your reports?" He glanced up at her, but Cassidy's eyes were fixed on his laptop screen, actually watching the live feeds from the Tattle Tales.

"By phone. Every day. Nine PM," she answered glancing to their RV. "That's probably what Randy's doing now."

Connor took a slow breath in, enjoying everything about this gutsy woman. He'd read her body language when she snapped back at her superior. Randy Burkhouse bugged her.

"I could show you how to set up a simple reporting program. Even without the Tattle Tale feeds, it's easy." He closed the computer. "If you're interested."

"Not me. Show Brigham. He's our token nerd." She gave Connor's shoulder a final pat as she strolled to the rear of the RV. "Sorry, but I don't do computers."

He stowed his laptop in his backpack to follow. "You sound like my boss. Alex doesn't do computers, either."

"I'm a woman of action. Computers are for geeks."

"Guess I'm a geek then." Connor grinned at her not so subtle opinion. He made himself comfortable on an old tree stump while she leaned against the rig, her expression hard to see in the fading light.

"You guys did a good job. Considering," she muttered.

"For a couple of geeks, we don't do half bad, do we?"

"No, I didn't mean that. I meant considering you're ex-military. Randy's ticked because you were more effective in two days then we've been in a month. It's embarrassing when a couple out-of-towners know more than the home team."

"Hey, we've got skills." Connor noticed the earnest tone in her voice. "We're trained in all that marksmanship, observation, and stalking stuff."

"You're taking your chances, though." She turned serious. "The SC will kill you if they catch you in their camps."

"That's not going to happen. They are not going to catch us." That was one thing Connor had no doubt about. He changed the subject. "Thanks for the steaks tonight. The Key lime pie last night, too. That was thoughtful."

She shrugged. "Just taking care of my guys."

He liked the way that sounded on her lips. "Your guys? How many do you have?"

A mischievous smile met his gaze. "Sometimes too many. Right now I've got just enough to get me into trouble, but not enough to cry over when they leave."

"Any of these guys belong to you?" He nodded toward her DEA cohorts still chatting with Roy.

Cassidy grimaced. "Them? Don't make me laugh."

Roy called from the campfire. "Connor? You ready to go yet?"

Connor rolled his eyes at the interruption, but he stood to leave. "Guess duty's calling my name. Thanks for the hospitality."

"We'll have to do this again sometime." She extended her hand, but when he grasped it in a handshake, she pulled herself into him. Suddenly, she was under his chin and looking up with those big brown eyes of hers. A glint of firelight sparkled there. A glint of something else, too. "I restock supplies every Thursday. Anything special you'd like me to bring next time?"

His blood supply fled south. *Duh, yeah. A sexy negligee comes to mind.*

"Connor? You back there?" Roy called again, grating on Connor's last nerve.

"Yeah. Coming," he answered even as he breathed down at Cassidy, his heart thudding loud and clear. This might just be a great op after all. Her lips glistened with the quick slip of her tongue over them. Even in the dark, her eyes beckoned.

"I can think of a few things I might like," he murmured.

"Call me," she commanded.

Words he lived for.

"I'll e-mail you," he countered with a teasing grin.

"I just might be willing to read an e-mail if it's from you," she whispered, her lips so close that he could almost taste her. The cocky smirk on her tanned face was—sexy.

He leaned down to her just as she lifted to her tiptoes. Just a minty fresh breath away and—

"Connor!" His big-mouthed, grumpy, can't give a-guy-a-break senior agent bellowed again.

She stepped back, breathing as hard as he was, her fingers combing over her short hair. "See you around," she said with a suddenly shy, crooked smile.

He nodded. "Count on it."

"Connor!"

Damn it, Roy!

The non-stop drive proved Izza's undoing. Mark had Morgan pull into a hotel in downtown Salt Lake City after he'd noticed how green she was. They were supposed to go straight to the rendezvous point, but that plan had been scrubbed due to Izza.

"You feeling okay?" Mark's brown eyes were bright with kindly concern.

She lied, "Just car sick. I'm good."

He gave her that you're-not-kidding-me spiked eyebrow of his, and before she knew it, they were registered, and she was damned glad. The bed in her hotel room didn't move or vibrate like their SUV. Twenty plus non-stop hours on the road had done her in. She woke up three hours later. The sun had set and her hotel phone blinked with a message. She hadn't even heard it ring.

Cussing to herself, Izza reached for the phone and retrieved Mark's voice message. "Hey, Izza. We're in the lounge downstairs. Come join us if you're up to it. We'll wait for you."

She flopped to her back, too sick and tired to care about meeting the guys for dinner and drinks. Her life was changing awfully fast. She used to be able to drink her fellow soldiers under the table, pull one all-nighter after another, or lead them into battle and back. Once able to set the pace for men to follow, all she wanted now was to sleep. And eat. Not two very desirable traits for a woman of her usual activity level. Even kickboxing, the sport she loved, was difficult when a girl had to run to throw up every time she got her blood pumping.

Another damned tear trickled down the side of her head, completely without permission. Angrily, she dashed it away. Crying was another one of those things she didn't do. Izza rang Mark's cell phone to at least check in with her senior agent. Eat or not, she was a team player.

"Hey," he answered promptly. "What's up? Are you feeling any better?"

"I fell asleep," she confessed. "You guys still hungry?"

"Ah, not anymore. I'm an old guy," he quipped. "I need my sleep."

"But I thought you were waiting for me in the lounge?"

"We were. Two hours ago."

She cringed. Izza hung up before Mark had a chance to pick up on her bitchy mood. She was tired all the time and turning into a bawl baby. And now she was old, too!

Four

Are these guys all dead?

Connor peered closer. Infiltrating the cartel's camp in the dark was easier than he'd expected. After he and Roy left their DEA friends, they returned to their RV, applied a few smears of camouflage face paint, grabbed their gear and headed back up the mountain. A one-man job, Connor dropped from a deer trail just above the camp while Roy entered from the west.

His senses on high alert, Connor crouched at the edge of the camp. Night gear included a trusty pair of NVGs, night vision goggles, and the miniature video camera attached to his headgear. He paused to study the layout. Basically, there was none. But worse, the men sprawled in a half-hazard circle around the place looked dead. He swallowed hard and proceeded to infiltrate. This cartel was brutal. Anything was possible after the murder he'd witnessed.

Wisps of eerie green smoke drifted from the darkened fire pit, adding to the creepy sensation, but no embers glowed. A grate covered the pit with two coffee pots to the side of it and a Dutch oven in the center. Without a sound, he crept around the perimeter, taking a head count.

When one of the bodies grunted, he breathed a quiet sigh of relief. Eleven men, all of them sound asleep or passed out, laid on shabby sleeping bags. He grimaced when it became apparent he was downhill from men who had put in a hard day's work. The pungent odor of beer and body odor wafted through the midnight air. No wonder they looked dead. They were exhausted and on carb and alcoholic overload.

He approached the side of the tent, still keeping an eye on the slumbering compadres. Just as he reached inside the tent flap, another man grunted. Connor froze. The man mumbled something in Mexican and broke into a rumbling snore.

Breathing easy, Connor pressed the audio bug into the seam along the flap where it would transmit sight unseen for months or until detected. Before he left, he planted two video bugs in nearby aspen trees, one to provide a view from the east, one from the west. Standing for a moment at the edge of camp, he watched the men. It seemed surreal for a brutal cartel camp to be so calm and unguarded. This covert penetration was child's play, more like the raids he'd committed as a teenager when he and his numskull friends toilet-papered a neighbor's yard.

Roy met up with him outside of camp.

"Something's not right," Connor whispered. "These guys aren't guards. They're hired hands. Nothing more."

Roy nodded as he looked at the peaceful encampment. "I noticed. Come see what I found."

They headed westward in the direction of their RV to another site. Located on the south bank of the creek, it stretched like a long narrow garden. The two men blended into the shadowy background, their footsteps silent on a well-worn path. Just short of the garden, Connor froze, his arm out to caution Roy not to take another move.

Trouble lay at the tip of his boot. A trip wire. Two fingers to his eyes and then to the ground, he signaled Roy to watch where he stepped. Carefully, they avoided the booby trap. Neither man spoke as they continued deeper into a larger and well-cultivated marijuana patch. Connor's sixth sense shifted into high alert. He signaled Roy to stop again when the hair on his neck prickled with unseen danger. They crouched within the shadows of the tall, leafy plants. Connor pulled his pistol.

Footsteps approached. A single guard appeared with his rifle drawn. Except for the Mets baseball cap on his head, the cut of his clothing looked military. His gun was nothing more than a twenty-two caliber like Connor had grown up with instead of an automatic weapon. The man stopped maybe four yards from where Connor and Roy watched. A carved wooden knife handle protruded from his boot. Looking up into the trees, he spoke into his headset in English but with a heavy Spanish accent. "I heard something. I know I did."

He took another two steps toward their position. "I have not been drinking. That is not true." At last turning his back to Connor and Roy, he paused and listened for another minute. "It must have been another owl. A larger animal would have tripped the alarm for sure. There would have been much more noise." He walked away with his rifle slung easily over his shoulder.

Roy signaled Connor. In single file, they matched the guard's route from five rows away and followed him nearly to the opposite end of the garden. Just as he stopped to light a cigarette, another man stepped into view. And then another. Connor and Roy froze in their tracks. These men were dressed the same, but carried compact assault rifles tucked into their chests.

"You are always hearing things, old man," one of them joked. "Come have a cup of coffee. It is not so good, but maybe it will help your ears work better." Together they bantered back and forth as they headed into the dark of the surrounding trees, their camaraderie obvious.

Connor and Roy backtracked, again avoiding the trip wire at the edge of the garden. When they were a safe distance away, Connor turned to Roy. "We're looking at an army, no two ways about it."

"Agreed," Roy answered thoughtfully. "I'll be glad when Mark gets here in the morning. If all the plots are guarded with this many SC, we're outmanned."

"I left a bug.

Roy smiled. "You did? Where?"

"Smack dab in the middle of all that pot."

"Move it, Book Boy," Izza snapped from the open tailgate of their SUV.

"I'm going in. You want anything for breakfast? They've got bacon and egg burritos," Morgan offered on his way to the convenience store. Book Boy was a shopping machine, but scrambled eggs? Just the thought made her stomach quiver. The last thing she needed.

"No, thanks. Make it quick. We're already a day late and a dollar short."

"And whose fault would that be?" He lifted a teasing brow.

She shot her most evil glare at him. "I said move it. You shop more than a damned woman."

Her temperamental stomach was already on the rampage this morning. The colorless soda she'd been sipping was no help, and Morgan was bringing up the rear. Again. Of course, he had his nose in a book even as he strolled across the parking lot. She dreaded the thought of being stuck on a remote op with a spotter like him at her back. Ewww. So not ever going to happen. Nerds and her? She'd made that mistake once. Never a good mix.

They'd stopped for gas before they headed up the canyon. Daybreak was imminent. Pink brightened the eastern sky while Izza took the opportunity to load up. It was not just saltines in her pockets this morning. No way. She'd already stored her blowout kit, every soldier's handy dandy first-aid supplies for if and when she got hurt or shot. Lessons learned the hard way tended to linger. Extra mags and a couple of preloaded clips for her AR went next. Izza didn't intend to feel naked today. Or defenseless. Her blade was already back where it belonged, tucked into its ankle sheath and hidden under her pants cuffs. Right where she could reach it.

The sun barely lit the eastern horizon. For now, the Wasatch Mountains cast a long stretch of shade across the entire Salt Lake Valley. If she had her way, Mark and his team would do all their work at night or early morning. The baby growing inside of her sapped her energy during the day, and the Utah sun took what was left. Besides, morning sickness didn't live up to its name. It struck at noon. Every damn day.

Casting her gaze upward and east to the magnificent mountain range, her mind wandered to that other nerd in another desert in another time. He was smart, too, but handsome. And strong. His strength had been a revelation she hadn't seen coming. For that one night, she'd almost needed him. The man was uncommonly kind. Sensitive. He knew his way around computers, weapons, and—her.

Lost in the memory, she touched her fingertips to her bottom lip. The guy knew how to kiss, too. She'd give him that much. He had the deepest blue eyes. She'd grown up around Puget Sound. She knew dark gray water, but his were bluer. Deeper. Pacific Ocean kind of blue.

"You're looking good this morning," Mark lied with his usual cheerfulness, his hand on the gas nozzle while Rory cleaned windows and checked the oil.

Izza snapped her eyes off the mountain range and dropped her hand. Who did Mark think he was kidding? She brushed the compliment aside without responding. He'd tell her she looked good even if she looked like something the cat dragged in and left to die in the middle of the floor.

"What's the plan?" she asked, her mind already up that canyon and engaged with the bad guys she'd come to squash with her don't-get-in-my-way Ramos style. Fast. Lethal. No questions asked.

"I'm driving. I want you to ride shotgun."

"No. I'm good."

He raised a brow, with a *What-did-I-just-say?* warning in his eye.

No doubt he thought he was being cavalier putting her in the front seat where chances were she wouldn't get carsick, but still. She hated preferential treatment. Izza bit her tongue instead of arguing. He was right. She just didn't want to admit she'd fallen down on the job like the wuss she was not.

"We rendezvous with Roy and Connor at noon. They're at the halfway point. You sure you don't need anything before we head out?" he asked nodding toward the store.

"Nope. Let's do it," she shot back at him.

Noon, huh? Well, isn't that just damned great?

"So I've been researching the cartel," Connor offered over breakfast.

It was close to 4 a.m. and Roy had once again outdone himself in the kitchen. A platter with eggs, bacon, and French toast covered the small breakfast nook table. The man might be grumpy, but he could cook.

"You and your research," Roy huffed as he restocked his backpack with enough energy bars and frozen bottled water to last the day. "What did you find now?"

Connor spiked an eyebrow in Roy's direction. Very shortly, his senior agent was going to either appreciate him for this particular research or send him to jail. "For one thing, Ramirez lives outside Hermosillo, the capital of Sonora, Mexico. He owns a huge cattle ranch."

"Okay. That's boring. What else?"

"He's married. He's got two kids. Two little girls." Connor focused on the trivia. Might as well deliver the bad news in small doses.

"And?"

"And he's related to Javier Quinones."

Roy stopped restocking to stare at Connor. "The Sinaloa Cartel boss? You sure?"

"Yes. His wife, Alejandra. Javier is her younger brother."

"What else?"

"You might want to sit down for this next part."

Roy dropped to the nearest chair with a scowl skewered on his face.

Connor took a deep breath and let the pieces fall. "The DEA lost three agents last year when they chased the SC out of this same canyon. Two were shot execution style. One was beheaded."

"Say what?" The backpack forgotten, Roy shot to attention.

"The cartel hit them at night. By the time they left, every agent was dead."

"Were they in these stupid RVs?"

"Tents," Connor answered grimly. "Just good old DEA camouflaged tents, like the one you wanted us to use."

Roy was the most genteel member of The TEAM. A charmer with the ladies, laid back and easy going, it took a lot to push this African American ex-Marine over the edge, but he was mad now. "Why the hell am I just hearing about it? How'd the DEA keep that kind of a mess out of the news? And why?" he bellowed.

"I wouldn't have known either," Connor said quietly, "except I kinda hacked into their system when we got in last night."

"Baxter should've told us. He should've at least told Alex." Roy completely ignored Connor's confession.

"The Governor doesn't know. No one does." Connor pushed his plate back and snapped his laptop shut. "I doubt our friends up the road know either. This info was buried inside an encrypted file on the DEA server."

Connor let Roy absorb that other little hand grenade of illegally obtained information. On one hand, hacking made him scary valuable to The TEAM, but the day he got caught dabbling inside what was supposedly a highly secure federal computer system would be the day he went to Leavenworth. Of course, he had to get caught first. That was just plain not going to happen.

"Get your butt packed. We're going to—"

A loud rap at the door startled the men. Roy went cautiously to the window and lifted an edge of foil. "It's Cassidy." He opened the door. "What's wrong?" he barked.

"We've got trouble," she said as she scrambled into the RV, stopping at the desk where Connor sat. Breathlessly, she slapped a picture to the table in front of him. Maka Taufa's decapitated head glowered from a pike at the front entrance to a local Mexican cantina. And right next to it – Roger Paxton's stared blankly from a similar pike.

"Crap. That's what Ibarra meant," he muttered."

Cassidy nodded. "This is hitting local papers as we speak. Who else was with Ibarra the day Taufa was shot? Do you know?"

"Nestor Martinez," Connor admitted.

She ran a hand through her soft curly locks, clearly shaken at the turn of events. "This is Utah, guys. In case you didn't know, everyone owns a gun, at least a deer-hunting rifle. Do you know what this means?"

"The Cartel means to start a war—"

"With everyone," she finished for Connor, her eyes full of an emotion he couldn't pin down. It seemed a mix of defiance and apprehension, as if she had something else to say, but didn't know how to say it.

"That's not the only problem we've got." Roy nodded toward the photo. "We need to talk with your Agent Burkhouse. Now."

"What else is going on?" she asked, her face flushed and a slight sheen of perspiration on her forehead.

"Did you run all the way here?" Connor asked.

She nodded, blowing out a deep breath. "Yes. I couldn't risk Randy hearing the truck start, so I slipped out."

"Why?" He moved in a protective step closer. The idea of her alone in dangerous cartel country irked him.

"Because I thought you guys might actually do something about this. I don't get the feeling he will."

"He will when I'm through with him," Roy declared. "I'll lay odds he knows what went down last year, too."

"What are you talking about?" she asked.

Roy ran an exasperated hand over his head. "Show her what you found."

Connor flipped his laptop open again as he sat down at the work desk. "This," he said somberly as the screen flashed to the copies he'd made of the encrypted DEA files. The label itself raised the hair on the back of his neck—*Operation Scorpion Spider. Eyes Only.*

"What's going on?" Cassidy asked after she'd read the portion he'd pointed out and saw the gruesome pictures from a year ago. "Why wasn't I told?"

"You tell us. It's your agency, not ours."

Her jaw opened, but no words came out.

"What's up with your senior agent?" Roy asked. "Burkhouse didn't seem happy to see us last night."

Cassidy dropped into the chair beside Connor. "I don't know. We've been here for two months, and it's taken us that long to locate less grow-sites than you guys did in two days."

"Something's up," Roy growled. "We need to talk. Let's get this out in the open once and for all. You coming?"

Cassidy retrieved the newspaper article. Connor stowed his laptop. He locked the RV door behind him as the three of them headed east. By the time they walked into the DEA camp, the lights were on inside the RV, but Brigham and Denton were outside.

"Where have you been?" Brigham asked Cassidy. "I've been looking for you."

"Where's Burkhouse?" she asked instead of answering. "Still inside?"

"Where he always is," Harold murmured. "I see you got your East Coast buddies with you. What's going on?"

"Do either of you know anything about a DEA op gone bad last year in this canyon?" Roy intervened. "Would have been with the Sonoran Cartel."

"Sure don't," Harold answered. "Why? You think you know something I don't?"

Cassidy offered the news clipping. "Look at this."

Connor studied the men's reactions. Both registered shock. Brigham looked up at Cassidy. "Our men were killed last year? Are you sure?"

She handed the question off to Connor with a sideways glance.

"Absolutely," he said. "We need your cooperation now more than ever. None of us is safe."

Roy interrupted the amicable discussion with a loud knock on the RV door. "Burkhouse. You in there?"

The door eased open and Randy shuffled down to face Roy at ground level. "You boys are up awful early," he grumbled.

"We get that way when we've been lied to," Roy grumbled back. "And we're not boys, Agent Burkhouse. You need to back that horse up and climb down. We're covert operators the same as you, only we just found out the DEA had some trouble with the SC last year. You guys lost a few agents. Three to be exact."

"Oh?" Randy said without a trace of surprise. He shot a dark glance at Connor. "And how'd you just happen to stumble across that kind of information? Don't imagine it came in the local papers."

"It doesn't matter how we came by it," Roy answered. "What matters is why no one here seems to know about it except maybe you. Do you?"

Connor felt his shoulders square automatically. Roy had just called the DEA's top dog out. Whatever came out of Randy's mouth next would determine the nature of the rest of the op. Harold had already moved to Randy's left. Brigham stood undecided between Cassidy and the agents from The TEAM.

"You see, that's where you're wrong," Randy said still as calm as ever. "Snooping around federal servers is—"

"Is nothing compared to this bullshit!" Roy grabbed the paper from Cassidy's hands and slapped it in the middle of Randy's chest. "Look at this before you pull your high and mighty crap with me."

Randy looked at the news photo and then Cassidy. "Where'd you find this?"

"Wasatch News Online Press," she answered. "It's Ibarra's handiwork. No doubt about it."

"How do you know?" he asked. "What's your proof?"

She rolled her eyes. "Give me a break. I've been working this cartel operation as long as you have. You know damned well—"

"You don't know anything, Agent Dancer. You forget who's in charge. It isn't you, and it isn't these gun-for-hire contractors Baxter had to bring in."

Cassidy pursed her lips and kept silent.

"Oh, I get it now." Roy chuckled in that I'm-not-really-laughing way he had. "Same old story. You feds think we're stepping on your toes. You think we're here to make you look bad while we're stupid enough to think we're here to help." He rolled his shoulder and turned to Connor. "Let's go. We're working for Baxter, not these guys. We'll do our job and let these nice folks do theirs."

"Come with us," Connor offered Cassidy and Brigham before he walked away. Brigham shook his head and followed Randy back into the RV. The same answer shifted through Cassidy's eyes.

"We'll be fine," she said unconvincingly.

"No, you won't. Remember what you told me last night?"

She arched a brow, her eyes unsure and less sparkly than they'd been the night before.

"These guys will kill us if they catch us," he reminded her. "We've seen them, you know."

"You saw who?" She stood at the RV steps, ready to go in.

"Three armed guards, and the empty camp we showed you yesterday was full of a dozen laborers last night. Ready or not, the cartel looks ready to harvest their crop, Cassidy. Between that and the headless gangbangers story hitting the airwaves this morning, what do you think that means?"

"More people are going to die," she whispered.

Connor strode back to her and grabbed her shoulders. "You're not safe here. None of you are. I don't know what's going on with Burkhouse, but you don't have to die just because your boss won't share what he knows. I kind of like you best with your head on your shoulders."

"We're not just a bunch of country hicks, you know," she said quietly.

"I know that. You're smart, but you're not the one running this show. I'll bet the agents who got killed last year were good at their jobs, too." He wanted to say more, but Burkhouse shouted from inside, "Dancer. You coming in or what?"

Connor cringed. Now the gauntlet was thrown down to her. She had to choose. Cassidy did exactly what he might have done on his first job.

"Sorry I disturbed you," she said as she climbed the steps and closed the door behind her.

"You can't help people who think they know everything," Roy said.

Connor didn't answer. One way or the other, he'd be back to help Cassidy. Someone had to.

Five

"What do you think?" Roy asked as they came to a fairly level landing in a grove of quaking aspen. "Is this good enough?"

"It will work," Connor muttered. He and Roy had returned to their RV, but only to secure the tent and other camping supplies. The time had come for them to transform into campers of the week whether they wanted to or not. By the time they'd stopped hiking, the winding road below was more a winding snake than asphalt, and Utah was once again damned hot.

With at least another trip or two to make for water and food, he unleashed the heavy backpack from his shoulders, stretched and looked below. A helpless feeling gnawed at his gut. How could he possibly keep Cassidy safe at this distance?

Roy eased his sat phone out of its hip holster and dialed Alex. And everything went from bad to worse. After Roy shared the ugly news of the day, Connor stared at the trees below, listening to the angry words fly between Alex Stewart and DEA Director Scott Sylvane. Roy had the phone on speaker in case Connor wanted to force a word in edgewise, like that was in any way possible.

"Listen, Mr. Stewart, I know who you are," Director Sylvane said patiently. "You've got a real good reputation around D.C. as the go-to guy for delicate covert ops. I get it. I do, but to be honest, this is none of your business."

"I've got men in the line of fire, and you don't think that makes it my business?" Alex shot back at him.

"There's more at risk here than what you're seeing." Director Sylvane was firm. "Governor Baxter should not have gotten you involved without coming through me first. He knew we had an active operation complete with boots on the ground in his state. His involving you has only complicated the work my people are sworn to do."

"Then bring me up to speed. What are you not telling me, Scott?" Alex snapped, and the gloves came off. "Your own agents didn't have a clue about these murders. How do you send men into the field without telling them straight up what's going on?"

There was a long pause on the other end of the line before Director Sylvane growled back with, "Need to know, Alex. That's all I can tell you. Need to know."

"I need to know, damn it!"

Another long-suffering pause. "You mind telling me how you came by this information on alleged DEA murders? You wouldn't have someone on your staff hacking into my DEA files, would you? You do understand that's a federal offense."

And that was the last straw.

"Need to know, Scott," Alex barked. "Need to know." He hung up on the DEA Director without having gotten the upper hand for the first time in a long time, and still mad as a hornet.

Connor glanced at Roy. At least Alex hadn't hung up on them, a feat for the technically challenged man they worked for.

"You still there?"

"Yes, Boss," Roy answered quickly.

"Something's definitely going on. Scott's a good man. Never known him to freeze me out like this."

"Which makes it impossible to work with his agents."

"What's yours and Connor's take on cartel activities?"

Roy motioned for Connor to answer.

"They're ramping up in the violence department," Connor said. "I'm not up to speed on when pot should be harvested, but it looks like that's what's happening. We've got day laborers in the canyon as of yesterday and two trophies in downtown Salt Lake City this morning. DEA will have their hands full if they're only here to observe. Us too."

"Agreed," Alex said. "Keep track of our DEA friends. I'll contact Tom and find out how he wants to proceed. Where are you guys staying?"

"We're roughing it at about five thousand feet," Roy quipped. "No more lifestyles of the rich and famous for us."

Alex chuckled. "Feel like that op in the Kush back in the nineties?"

"Nothing like it," Roy replied. "Hindu Kush was a lot higher altitude and thinner air. I could barely breathe."

"Stay in touch. Talk to you soon."

Roy stared out over the canyon floor as he stowed the sat phone. "I've got to go back down to meet with Mark and his guys. They should be close to the rendezvous point by now. They can pack the rest of the supplies. You stay put. Get us organized."

"Won't they be surprised they get to mountain climb?" Connor asked. "Where are you meeting?"

"Across from the day park. Be back in a couple hours."

"I'll keep an eye on our muchachos while you're gone." Connor had already arranged some of their supplies into a makeshift table. With his ruggedized laptop linked to all the listening and video devices they'd planted, he was as busy as he would be back at his desk in Alexandria. "Sure going to miss taking a shower every day, though."

"We'll work something out." Roy thumped Connor's arm. "All is not lost, young man. She'll stop by for a visit. Just wait and see."

"Yeah, whatever. Watch your back." Connor was not going to admit anything to Roy, not about his plans for Cassidy. The less he knew, the better.

"Always do."

As Roy walked away, Connor contacted Cassidy. When she didn't answer her cell, he set to work analyzing feedback from the Tattle Tales. The video and audio feeds came in clear and crisp. Bad news came with it. Trouble, with a capital T.

Another camp had been set-up during the night closer to the mouth of the canyon. He listened intently to the scuttlebutt flying between whoever stood beside the unseen Tattle Tale at one of the grow-sites. Ramirez himself would be there later today, his wife and daughters too. The entire crop had to be cut, bundled and ready for transport by the time he arrived. The guard joked. It was a rush job. Ha, ha. Connor didn't get the humor.

He hadn't anticipated another camp, but it made sense. The lack of coverage in what sounded like the most critical place of all concerned him. He needed eyes or ears inside that base camp. Now.

Connor didn't think twice. He pocketed several Tattle Tales, grabbed his baseball cap and headed down to do the job. It took awhile to traverse the mountainside, mostly because he paused at each grow-site along the way to note any increased activity. Two laborers now worked each site with short scythes, cutting and bundling as they moved through the rows. Armed guards watched nearby.

If that wasn't bad enough, a caravan of tour buses pulled into one of the many parks in the canyon, just yards from an un-harvested marijuana patch. Picnickers disembarked and spread through the area. Some of the men and women were instantly busy setting up games while others pulled coolers off the buses. It looked to be a big picnic full of an overabundance of children and activities.

Connor hurried away, his window of opportunity fading fast. Before long, he stood at the edge of the cartel's new camp. Crouched behind a clump of river willows, this was undoubtedly ground zero. The tent was bigger, a perimeter wire clearly visible, and these guys meant business. Three ATVs, the heavy-duty kind with hydraulic bed boxes for moving heavy supplies and equipment, were parked next to the tent along with a portable gasoline tanker truck.

These men moved with purpose. It was more like watching Marines landing from sea. Everyone seemed to know his duty and did it without conversation. Connor estimated his chances of getting into that camp and planting a bug without being seen. Slim to none. So he went in.

One of the most important things a scout sniper learns is infiltration, how to get close to the enemy without being seen. A proper ghillie suit decorated with local foliage, branches, grass stalks, moss went a long way towards helping a man remain invisible. Face paint helped. Connor had nothing, and a blond man from Boston definitely needed to hide the white. He edged closer, careful of the trip wire that could give him away. Nearly ready to break cover, he froze.

Several uniformed men, all of them carrying compact ARs on straps over their shoulders, came from the back of the tent in earnest conversation. The youngest one with the computer tablet in his hand argued with the others while they walked to the center of camp.

With his head down and only a few steps left to go, Connor stepped quickly from the cover of the willows to the back of the tent behind them. No one noticed. Let them argue. A single Tattle Tale could make or break this operation. He activated the bug, stripped off the adhesive backing, and listened intently to the conversation out front while he pressed it into the edge of a seam.

"I am telling you this is different," the youngest man insisted as he stabbed his finger at the tablet. "We must do something before those men cause trouble."

"Maybe they were just hiking like the last guy we caught?" one of his partners asked. "They look harmless enough to me."

"They don't," the third insisted. "Look at the size of them. The black man alone makes two of you. They walk like soldiers, not lazy like campers."

"He does not make two of me," the insulted man argued.

Connor peered around the corner of the tent to watch and learn.

"This is the same problem as last year." The youngest raised his voice. "We cannot take the chance, Carlos. Not with Ramirez due in today."

It seemed Carlos agreed. "Then see what you can find out, Felipe, but don't kill anyone this time. We don't need problems with the Americans when the boss arrives. And whatever you do, don't get caught, understood?"

Felipe grinned as he laid his tablet on the seat of the nearest ATVs. "I was hoping you'd say that. I'll be back in an hour." With that, he jumped in, started the noisy engine and drove east along the creek.

"That boy," Carlos complained as the ATV roared away. "He is too eager to fight."

"He wants Ramirez to notice how brave he is," his friend said. "Besides, he is young."

"And that may get him killed," Ramirez said. The two men moved out of sight.

Bad news seemed to rule the morning. Connor had no doubt they'd been discussing him and Roy, and now Felipe was headed to one of the RVs or maybe even up to their camp in the trees. There was no time to hesitate. Cassidy and the others had to be warned. Connor committed the worst error of any undercover operative. He hurried.

"Hey, you," Carlos called to him, pointing to a stack of cartons at his feet. "Get these boxes inside the tent."

Crap. Connor halted in his tracks alongside the tent. Carlos must've seen his shoulder extending beyond the edge of the tent. How exactly should a blond white boy in the middle of a Mexican army answer a superior office? He tucked the brim of his cap lower and muttered, "*Si.*"

Mission accomplished. Definitely time to go.

But Carlos stood waiting at the front corner of the tent. "Hey, man. Do not ignore me. I am talking to you. Do you have ears or not?"

Connor mumbled nothing in particular, tensed for hand-to-hand combat, and waited for this angry cartel soldier to come to him. *It's now or never, Maher.* The second Carlos rounded the corner Connor cocked his fist back, and decked him with one fast right to the middle of his moustached and very surprised face. Carlos dropped without a sound. Connor caught him before he hit the ground and leaned the unconscious guy against the back of the tent.

"Sorry, *Señor* Carlos," Connor whispered before he hightailed his butt out of Camp Tijuana and disappeared into the safety of the willows. As soon as he was a sufficient distance from the camp, he phoned Cassidy.

Still no answer. *Crap. Where is she?*

"I hate Utah," Izza muttered to herself. The cool humidity of the Northwest was so much more preferable to a pregnant woman's body, which already ran ten degrees hotter, but felt like twenty.

Mark hadn't allowed her to carry supplies like the men. Oh no. She was instructed to climb to camp while he and the rest of the men followed with sleeping bags and other supplies. Being singled out for light duty aggravated her sense of honor and fair play. Since when had she not pulled her weight?

Okay, so maybe she was a little crabby this morning. That didn't equate to the need for preferential treatment, and Mark better get that through his hard head. She had no doubt she could outmarch most of those guys when she was at full term and not be winded when she did it. Being a woman meant nothing to the Corps. It certainly meant nothing to her. She was tougher than most. How many times did she have to prove it?

Her internal argument would have worked if, at that precise moment, the tiny little child residing in her body hadn't decided to do a triple somersault off the high board that Izza was fairly sure now grew inside along with the baby. Wow. How could one little person make one big person's life so miserable?

She paused beneath a fluttering quaking aspen, her palm to the tree trunk as she caught her breath. Noon was not that far away. Ugh. Morning sickness, either.

Squeezing her eyes tightly shut, she willed the creeping sensation of nausea away. Mark couldn't see through her, could he? She'd watched her weight. No one could tell she was over six months along, not with the loose shirt over her wife beaters. So far, so good.

But was that why he'd insisted she go on ahead of the guys? Did he somehow sense she needed to throw up in private? After all, he was a married man. Libby and he had two small children. Had he recognized the signs and been waiting for Izza to spill and tell?

Just the thought was enough to encourage an uneasy sensation at the back of her throat. She gulped and forced it down. *Think of something else. Think of the Hoh Survival training course. Think of that trip to Hawaii you want to take when this op is done. Think of....*

Z-z-z-r-r-i-i-p-p. The sound of a zipper hit her very attentive and overly sensitive eardrums. Izza peered around the tree trunk to see where that out of place sound might have come from. A man stood there with his back to her, but she'd recognize that physique anywhere. What the hell was Connor Maher doing half-naked in the middle of nowhere? She knew she'd have to face him sooner or later, but here? Now? So soon?

She took a step toward him, keeping herself hidden behind the branches of her friendly tree. He'd already stripped his shirt and boots off. His belt was undone. Camouflage printed pants hung loose and low off his hips. God, the man was as crazy as ever. And still as sexy. Ripped shoulder muscles led to a strong back that narrowed to a muscular V that lead to—

She gulped as the sight of that handsome hard body battered down her last line of common sense. Did he ever think about that night? Could he possibly know what it meant to her? Her mouth went dry remembering the intensity of their bodies slamming together. The heat. So much passion.

He was not gentle, but neither was she. It was the most frightening, glorious, feral sex of a lifetime that left her wanting him all the more. And pregnant. And sick at heart. The fool.

Was he thinking of stepping into that ice cold waterfall and—

Izza blushed. Connor stepped out of his jeans and kicked his boxers off next. With a shivering growl, he walked into the thin stream of water sluicing over the gravel ledge from the mountainside above.

"Br-r-r," he declared while his hands raked over his wet head.

The sight of his naked body watered her mouth. Warmth filled her belly and it didn't have a thing to do with the baby within. This warmth was more sizzle and hunger than offspring related. This was desire for Connor all over again. Wanton with a dash of definite need to feel his hands on her body.

Her tongue slid over her bottom lip, remembering how his mouth had tasted. And why the hell was she shaking like a leaf? She didn't want him. Boston was trouble, nothing but pain and suffering, and, *oh, my hell, look at that cute butt.* Her eyes scrolled over his tanned body, taking in the taut and firm ass she remembered digging her fingernails into.

The man was one muscle from his bare feet all the way up to his hairline. He should have been a surfer. Tan, sun-streaked blond hair – what was not to love? Connor radiated the easy-going man she knew he was.

Izza held her post while he proceeded to shower, totally unaware of his audience. He stood there, his back to her and his face tilted upward, his hands busy splashing the thin stream over his shoulders and under his arms. The water skimmed over his hair, off his shoulder blades and down his back. Blond hair darkened to deep gold. *What a picture.*

Izza couldn't breathe. He looked so—hot. Not so much the body builder type as—just damned good. Slim. Athletic. Narrow at the waist, but built. But—wow.

She couldn't stop absorbing every detail, the way he rolled his neck to let the water spill over his chest and then his back; the way he scrubbed his hair with both hands and shook the chilly water away from his face. But when he stepped out from under the waterfall and turned her way....

Izza took another involuntary step in his direction. All of her feminine radar had responded in sync with him. The chilly water hadn't kept him down. Not one bit. Six pack abs dropped down into the perfect trail of water-darkened hair that only grew darker. She licked her lips.

Maybe there was still hope. Maybe she needed to reconsider. Maybe—

"Connor?" A raucous female voice intruded from the trail below.

"Over here," he called as he picked up his boxers and jeans.

Izza stepped back behind her tree before a blond and tanned woman appeared on the scene. *Who the hell is she?*

"Hey, Cassidy," he answered the moment he saw her, pulling his shirt over his head as he finished dressing. At least he'd put his pants on quickly.

Izza rolled an annoying tweak out of her neck. *Cassidy, huh. I hate you already.*

"Sorry about this morning," this Cassidy person said as she walked easily up to Connor. "Randy gets his nose bent out of joint pretty fast these days."

He didn't seem to mind. In fact, he reached for her with a huge boyish grin on his face and pulled her into his still damp shirt and very wide chest. The jerk.

She smoothed her hands over his biceps like this wasn't the first time they'd touched each other. "What were you doing? Taking a shower? Out here?"

Who the hell is Randy?

Connor grinned down at Cassidy, and Izza held her breath. The light in those blue eyes. That smile. He still had irrepressible charm going for him, but he wasn't going to kiss this woman, was he?

"I'm glad you're safe." He smoothed an adoring hand over the side of Cassidy's face, and Izza wanted to puke.

"You need to get word to your boss. The cartel is making a move on the RVs."

Cassidy wrapped her hands around his neck, clutching him like some hooker standing under a street lamp. She had to. She was just as short as Izza. Only—

"I'll tell him what you said, but he won't listen to me." Cassidy lifted up to her tiptoes even in her hiking boots.

Izza's hand fisted. Tiptoes? Really? Connor used to lean down to kiss her.

He eased forward, his mouth definitely poised to plant one on her. Thankfully, a familiar male voice barked from the trail below. "Connor? You around here somewhere?" Roy called.

Izza ducked deeper into the shade of the quakies.

Chagrin shifted across Connor's face as he pulled back from Cassidy's upturned lips. "Damn. He's got the lousiest timing of anyone I know."

Izza turned her face to the shadows and became one with the tree. She gripped the trunk with both hands, trembling so hard. The whole gang was marching by with their backs stacked high with supplies. Rory carried an ice chest in his hands on top of his over-burdened backpack. No way was she going to get caught spying.

"Look who's here?" Morgan teased. "Connor's got a new girlfriend. Why am I not surprised?"

Because you're stupid, Book Boy.

Connor chuckled. Roy chuckled. Hell, even good-natured Mark chuckled. Not Izza.

She waited until everyone passed by before she fell out and followed at a safe distance. Gulping back the bile climbing up her throat, she choked, only this wretched sensation had nothing to do with her biologically scheduled morning sickness.

It felt more like heartbreak. Again.

Six

"How many?" Roy asked.

"Two, maybe as many as three dozen," Connor replied easily.

With Cassidy safe and looking as good as she was, the day that had started out so bleakly had a family campout kind of a feeling to it now. She proved to be the proverbial good sport as she pitched in and passed bottled waters from her own backpack to the thirsty men of The TEAM. It didn't hurt that he'd just proved his worth in aces. His chest swelled with a touch of pride. His head too, but so be it. It never hurt to look good in front of a lady, especially this one.

"Why'd you go down there alone?" Mark asked.

"Because we needed eyes and ears inside the new camp, and I figured the sooner the better," Connor answered as he took a hit off his bottle of water, trying to not sound like the braggart he felt like. "We may have trouble sooner than we thought. Several tour buses pulled into the Beacon Point picnic area. Civilians could pose a problem for the cartel considering what we saw last night."

"What's that?" Mark waited expectantly.

"Enough men to harvest the crop. And armed guards at all the grow-sites I passed." He turned to the pretty lady standing nearby and winked. "You need to call your boss.

There's at least one cartel guard on the prowl. I'm pretty sure Felipe was headed your way."

She nodded, pulled her own sat phone off her belt hook and stepped away to make the call.

"Alex told us to expect trouble," Morgan said.

"You accomplish what you set out to do in that camp?" Rory Dennison asked, his dark blue eyes full of mischief. He and Connor were forever locked in friendly battle with each other, both vying for longest shot, tightest pattern, and quickest draw. Range time might end in a tie, but Connor knew hands down he held the record for longest shot. Only one other person had ever bested him, but that happened a long time ago. She didn't matter anymore.

"What do you think?" Connor couldn't resist bragging to his best competitor. "I not only planted the bug that is at this very moment ratting on Ramirez Central, but I popped a guard named Carlos smack in the chops. He went down like a ton of bricks. You should've seen it. He never knew what hit him."

"Sounds like you took good care of us." Mark clapped him on the back.

Connor turned, feeling pleased with himself. Mark was a bear of a man, as gentle and kind as a guy could be. Rory was much the same. New to The TEAM by five months, he'd been hired shortly after Connor. Only one junior agent was a better marksman, and that would be Connor. The friendly competition between them added to an already great work environment.

Cassidy had returned to his side, still arguing with Randy. She winked coyly up at him from her sat phone. There was nothing better than being surrounded by good buddies and a sexy woman. He grinned. A tough op could not get much sweeter. "Oh, yeah. One more thing—"

Mark stepped aside. Connor came face to face with that other agent from the Seattle office. He stopped dead in his tracks. His ego hit the dirt right between his boots. All that good team-spirit feeling evaporated. When did Alex pick her up? Why?

Crap.

Mentally paralyzed, he couldn't remember what he'd been bragging about. For some unexplainable reason, his feet sidestepped away from Cassidy. "Izza," he rasped, his throat suddenly as dry as grit.

"Nice to see you too, Boston," she snapped, the light in her eyes as dark and deadly as ever.

He groaned, raking a quick hand through his hair while he tried to swallow. *Why did it have to be Izza?*

"What else is going on down there?" Roy asked.

"Ahh, we've got, ahh...." Connor jerked his thumb toward the west, his usual succinct reporting skills gone the way of the wind. "New camp. I... I...."

"You still can't talk worth a damn, can you?" Izza's sweetly sarcastic voice grated over his already tenderized ego. She looked pale, but good in a weird, mean kind of a way. A little on the gaunt side, maybe. Still wearing her hair pulled back into her usual no nonsense ponytail. Still wearing her signature camouflage shirt over the customary two tank tops.

Those once pretty brown eyes seemed a little sunken, or maybe it was all that nasty attitude pouring out of her mouth. "Spit it out, Boston. Your boss asked you a question. What else is going on? Did you forget?"

Connor blinked like a deer caught in the headlights of an eighteen-wheeler rig hauling triples on an icy eight-percent downhill grade. There was no escape, only duck, roll, and pray like hell. Roy's brows lifted. Mark and Rory's did, too. They'd caught onto the not so amusing undercurrent to the confusing, one-sided conversation. He forced his mind back to his report, but his tongue had turned to parchment and his brain to mush. "The cartel's setting up another camp at the mouth of the canyon."

"My, my. Aren't you the efficient one?" Izza needled him as only she knew how to do. "Always gotta be the hero, don't you?"

Connor focused on his senior agent's bemused face, trying hard to remember what he'd told Roy and what he hadn't. Hero, nothing. Right now he didn't know Jack.

"What'd you do, Boston? Draw them a map so they could join us for lunch? Huh?" Izza wouldn't let it go. She dropped her gear bag to the ground at her feet. "What's the matter? Cartel got your tongue?"

Connor took a half step back. Challenge sparked to life in her eyes. Was she calling him out? He wouldn't put it past her.

"I overheard something," he said simply, but for the life of him, he couldn't recall what.

"What else is new?" Izza never had a problem speaking up or being confrontational. She took one step closer. He took one step back. Cassidy was out there on the hillside somewhere watching. Hell, everyone was watching, and he was making a fool of himself for all to see.

"Connor." Roy jerked his head toward the deer path headed downhill. "Sitrep. Now."

Connor put his head down and followed, glad to be doing something besides looking like an idiot. When they were out of earshot, Roy asked again. "What's the matter, son? What kind of problem?"

"I planted a bug." Connor could suddenly speak. The words blurted out of him in a rush. "It's in the rear of their tent, but I was seen. I was in a hurry because of something I overheard. I had to suppress one of their men. A guy named Carlos. I didn't kill him, though. Just knocked him out. He didn't see me. Much."

"You already told me that," Roy said, his hand on Connor's shoulder and peering deeply into his face. "What else did you overhear?"

Connor closed his eyes, forcing his mind to focus on the op, not the female Tasmanian devil in camp. "Three guards arguing. Sounded like they were talking about us." He took a deep breath to clear his head.

Izza. Why did it have to be Izza? Why now? Why here?

"What the hell is going on with you? You're repeating yourself," Roy muttered.

Connor grimaced, his brain still pinging from Izza to Cassidy and overseas to another day seared forever into his memory. Roy and the operation were caught in the middle somewhere.

"You should've waited for back-up, but I'm glad you took care of business. Anything else going on I should know about?"

Crap, yes. I just can't think right now. Connor brushed a hand over his still wet head, aggravated that the sight of Izza rattled him like it had. All his analytical skills were gone. His heart too. *Damn. Why did it have to be her?*

"I found a place where we could grab a shower if we don't mind cold water," he offered weakly, sticking his thumb in the direction of the waterfall. It wasn't important news, but it was something he hadn't said yet.

Dark brown eyes drilled into blue. "Connor. We've worked together the last six months. You can tell me anything."

Connor knew what Roy was probing for. He returned his steady gaze. "Izza and I have a history, that's all. It's nothing I can't handle."

Roy waited, his hand to Connor's shoulder like he had all the time in the world.

"And she hates me." There. It was out in the open, at least as much as he intended to share.

Roy studied him a second longer, but Connor looked away. No way was he answering the unasked why to that confession.

"Guess I just thought you'd be a little more excited to see her since you both served in Fallujah together." Roy nodded back to camp and the woman in question.

Connor bit his lip. What happened in Fallujah was not the problem.

"Okay. Never mind. I get it. I've certainly got enough women who hate me. Let's keep this operation professional. You two work your differences out on your own time, okay?"

"Not a problem." Telling Roy seemed to help. His brain kicked back into gear. "Oh, yeah. Almost forgot. Ramirez is on his way to the main camp. The crop has to be ready to go by the time he arrives tonight."

Roy's eyes widened. "Good to know."

Connor licked his dry lips. Yeah. That last tidbit was damned good to know. Wished he'd thought of it sooner.

He followed Roy back to their slap-hazard camp on the side of the mountain. Mark and Morgan were busy organizing supplies, bedrolls and foodstuffs. Rory had a fire pit built of odd shaped stones. He'd located two boulders, which he'd rolled into place for primitive seats.

Izza had her back to Connor, but worse, Cassidy had left without giving him the chance to explain. He needed to call her. A shudder rolled over his shoulders.

Why, oh, why the hell did it have to be Izza?

"Is Mark there with his team yet?" Alex asked.

"Here, Boss." Mark spoke up. Their ragtag camp seemed an unlikely setting for a teleconference, but that was Alex for you. Connor had his laptop set up so everyone could participate.

"Hey, Alex," Izza piped up with a wave of her hand. He needed to know she was there, ready to rock and roll. A solid team meant team members who weren't afraid to speak up to their boss. Like her.

"I talked with Tom Baxter," Alex said. "He's getting mixed signals from the DEA. They're not happy that you guys are there and they don't want the Utah National Guard involved. Not yet anyway."

Izza grunted. *Feds. Can't work with 'em. Can't work without 'em.*

"That might not be an option," Roy warned. "We've got a canyon full of civilians today. Connor infiltrated the cartel's camp earlier. Sounds like they've pushed the harvest up. Ramirez is due in tonight and the crop is supposed to be ready to go. You should be seeing the intel we've been gathering by now."

"I am," Alex said. "Connor's recon was spot on. UHP pulled Ramirez over on I-15 an hour ago. He's headed north with his wife and daughters. Told the Highway Patrol officer he was on a much-needed vacation. They had no reason to detain him. Assume he's on his way to you."

Izza couldn't take her eyes off Connor. He knew she was watching him, and she meant him to. He ought to feel damned uncomfortable. Thank God that Cassidy woman had gone back down the mountain where she belonged. She should've never left her team like she did. What kind of a DEA agent was she anyway?

"Boss, we have all the makings of a confrontation brewing," Roy advised. "The cartel is suspicious. We'll be lucky if we make the next twelve hours without incident."

"And your question?" Alex got right to the point.

"Do we have your approval to engage?"

"For hell's sake, Roy, I'm not the President of the United States. What do I know? You're the boots on the ground, not me. Bring Mark up to speed then follow your gut. If you need to engage, do it. You don't need my executive approval to do your job."

"Thanks, Boss. We'll be in touch." Roy prepared to sign-off.

"Connor?" Alex delayed the disconnect. "Damned risky move. I'm proud of you."

"Yes, Boss," Connor replied humbly, heat turning his face red.

"Don't do it again," Alex growled. "Next time take someone with you."

"Thanks, Boss," Connor said just as quickly.

Izza smirked. *What a kiss ass.*

The screen no more than went blank than Connor's cell phone vibrated, and he stepped away to take the call. Izza couldn't help herself. She snagged her gear bag and followed, but maintained a somewhat discreet distance. Her bag didn't need to be restocked, but it might need tidying up. A little. She feigned housecleaning and listened.

"You made it down okay?"

Way to go, Maher. A call from your girlfriend while you're on the clock. Of course she made it down okay. She wouldn't be calling you if she'd dropped off a cliff now, would she?

"Have you seen anyone in an ATV snooping around your RV?"

Izza listened to the one-sided conversation. That was the second time he'd warned the bimbo about some guy on an ATV. He really must care about this woman. *The jerk.*

"Be careful." Connor ran a hand through his hair as he stilled and listened. "Right. They must've set it up early this morning near the mouth of the canyon. Looks impressive for a bunch of pot farmers."

The baby bumped against Izza's ribs reminding her of the distasteful chore still ahead. If she were smart, she'd walk away and never look back. He didn't deserve to know. Look at him. He'd moved on faster than greased lightning with a shot of KY jelly.

"I'm sorry you had to see that." He sighed.

Whatever Cassidy was saying, it seemed to relax him. *Damn her.*

"You don't have to tell me." Connor chuckled.

Of all things, another tear dripped off Izza's eyelid. Angrily, she dashed it away. Connor and Cassidy were obviously talking about her. *Hormones. Who the hell needs them!*

"No. I'll be fine," he said softly. His voice had turned to baritone honey. Cassidy cared about him. *Damn her again.*

"Are you guys ready to join us up here in the high country yet?" Connor sounded hopeful. "It's a little rougher than your comfy RV, but it's safer. Besides, it'd be nice to see you again."

Izza cringed. That woman better not be telling him that she was on her way back up.

"That's not roughing it. That's an OJT vacation. Listen, you're welcome to come alone if you'd like. We've got extra gear. I'll keep you company."

Dumb ass.

"You sound tired, but good."

Izza wanted to barf. If this guy said one more sappy thing—

He stepped farther away from camp, his rangefinder lifted to his eyes. "You know if I optimize my rangefinder, I can see the stairs of your rig." He stilled. "Look up. Wave."

She must have waved. The damned idiot waved back.

"You look good."

Oh, my aching ass. You just saw her half an hour ago. How long can you two teenagers keep this bullshit up?

"Next time, you'll see me a lot closer." He ran his hand over his head again. Izza had to give him that, he had nice hair. Gold, the way the noonday sun was hitting it. As big of a liar as he was, he still had that California surfer look going for him.

"Of course I'm coming down. Yes. Tonight. We need to strategize, and we'd like to include the DEA in our plans if we could."

That perked up Izza's ears. *You're going down? Tonight? Who made that dumb decision to work with the DEA?*

"Okay. Talk to you soon." Connor pocketed his phone, a cheerful whistle on his lips until he turned around.

All the reasonable things Izza wanted to say to him flew out the window. All the things she had to tell him seemed too precious to share. The pain in her heart roared back to life. She was caught. "Aww, isn't that just the sweetest thing you ever saw?"

A bright red flush crept over his face. Wordlessly, Connor slanted his shoulder and tried to sidestep her, but she wouldn't let him pass. Not this time. He needed to answer for his crime. She blocked his exit. "What? You gonna avoid me the whole time we're here like you're back in junior high or something?"

"Listen, Izza—" He stopped and faced her.

She stabbed a finger into his broad chest, her voice lowered and threatening. "No, you listen, Boston. I don't need a damn thing from you. Do you hear me? Not from you and sure as hell not from your lady friend."

"Did I say you did?" He stepped back from her jab. *The coward.*

"Well, I don't." He needed to understand that once and for all. She turned to walk away before she fell apart, or worse, before her daily attack of morning sickness struck. "Get over yourself. You're dead to me. A nobody."

"Izza, please...." He tried again.

She whirled on him, her anger barely suppressed and her voice more growl than question. All the pain of the last months roared to be let loose upon the earth. Here he was alive and breathing like nothing had ever happened that day and still so handsome it hurt to look at him. Still playing the field. How many women had he had since? One for every month? Every week? Would that be six, seven, or thirty? Hell, he probably couldn't keep track the way women threw themselves at him. The way she'd thrown herself—

"What. Do. You. Want?" she hissed defiantly.

"I'm sorry," he whispered meekly. The moisture welling in his eyes caught her by surprise. He'd whispered those words too many times before. She had yet to believe them. What did he know about pain? Nothing. He'd moved on and left her and Jamie in the blood and dust of Iraq.

"You don't know the meaning," she ground out. *And there's nothing you can do to change it.* Izza turned her back on him, the baby in her belly kicking up a storm and nausea on the creep up her throat. "I hate you."

"I know." His hands clutched her trembling shoulders. "But I'm still sorry. I always will be."

God, she wanted to lean into him, to feel those bands of steel hold her together again, to rest against the solid support of that all male body. Her nose drew in a full whiff of him, wanting to savor the windblown scent of the man once more, like it would make a difference. Like it could change the past.

A shudder raced through her. Would it hurt to tell him why she'd accepted this particular operation instead of the op in Singapore with Senior Agent Tao? Was there any chance in the universe Connor might want to know the secret she'd carried all the way to Utah to share with him? The secret not even Mark knew? Not even anyone?

The cell phone buzzing in his pocket answered her questions with a slap-down reality check and an unequivocal, *'Hell no.'* She had a baby on the way. He had a woman to screw. Never the twain would meet. The phone buzzed again like she needed to be reminded twice how stupid she was.

"Leave me alone." She shrugged out from the warmth of his hands and stalked away. Tears were weakness. He'd never see them. He'd never know about the baby, either. Connor Maher didn't deserve to know. Not then. Not now. Not ever.

Izza couldn't get out of his sight fast enough. It hit her in one hard, fast wave of rejection. She crumpled behind the first available dusty bush. And threw up.

Seven

Connor couldn't shake the feeling as he walked back into camp. All eyes were on him. He summoned his inner Marine, gritted his teeth, and forced his brain to focus on the op instead of the ornery woman he'd just tangled with. Roy and Mark were heads bent together in a serious discussion by the improvised fire pit. Rory and Morgan had made another trip below for more water and foodstuffs. So why the sensation he was being watched?

Because he was. Not being able to see Izza didn't mean she wasn't there. Those dark brown daggers were digging at him from wherever she had hidden herself. Visibility had nothing to do with safety. She was out there in the trees and laying for him. He wouldn't be surprised if she had him in her crosshairs at this very moment. The fear of friendly fire came to mind, only this was anything but friendly. He glanced to his chest, half-expecting to see a tiny red laser dot. Izza was primed and totally capable. Thankfully, there was none.

Connor checked in with his two team-leads. "I've been thinking. Maybe we ought to intercept Ramirez before he shows tonight. Surprise him for a change."

Roy's eyes lit up. "The whole best defense is a good offense strategy?"

"Sure. Why not? Mother could track him and tell us exactly where he is. We could introduce ourselves to his whole family before he knows what hit him. Get close and personal and surprise the hell out of him when we do. Who knows? It might throw him off balance enough to make him reconsider."

"If it weren't for the civilians, I'd agree," Roy said, "but we've got our hands full. Mark and I are going down to enlist DEA support right now. You staying or coming with?"

Connor went promptly to the orderly stack of sleeping bags and camping gear where he'd left his gear bag. No way was he staying, not with a female wolverine on the prowl and thirsty for Maher blood. He strapped on his tactical gear and loaded up. Roy did the same.

Mark went looking for Izza to tell her they were leaving. She must have been agreeable. He came back alive. They passed Rory and Morgan coming up the beaten trail as they were headed down.

"Izza's on guard." Mark nodded back toward the camp. "Announce yourselves when you get close. She's armed and edgy today."

"Ha," Morgan snorted. "When isn't she?"

"Found some air mattresses back at the RV," Rory interrupted. "Two more pairs of NVGs, too. We ought to be set for a week. Maybe longer."

Connor caught Rory's fast diversion of what could have deteriorated into a bash-Izza moment. Connor had nothing to say on the subject. His thoughts were back at camp on that wolverine with dark brown eyes. Talk about a shock. Not in a million years had he expected Alex would hire Isabella Ramos. Worse, it was Connor's fault that he had. If he'd kept his big mouth shut and not bragged about her outstanding marksmanship, none of this would've happened.

"Drop the supplies and gear up," Mark told Morgan and Rory. "Bring Izza back down with you. Meet us at the Beacon Point picnic area in an hour. Be ready for trouble."

"Will do," Rory answered as he and Morgan continued past.

"You're sure quiet," Mark said to Connor when they hit flat land. "Got a lot on your mind?"

"Planning strategy," he answered, only there was nothing to plan with a woman like Izza. He'd blown that option months ago. The ache in his gut would never go away. Neither would the one in his chest. He rubbed the center of his breastbone where the hollow feeling rested day in and day out.

"Let's see if Burkhouse has his head out of his ass yet," Roy muttered as they drew near the DEA team's RV. "It'd sure be nice to have their assistance tonight."

"If these guys won't play, we need to get over to Beacon Point," Mark added. "It's getting late. We're wasting daylight."

"Agreed," Roy answered as his fist hit the DEA's front door.

Randy Burkhouse opened it and joined them on the ground. Harold and Brigham followed. Cassidy came out from behind the RV with a scrub brush and a grill screen in her gloved hands.

"Hi, guys," she said, and Connor could've kissed her. Just seeing her made the day a little brighter.

"Good afternoon." Roy made quick introductions. "Senior Agent Randy Burkhouse, this is Mark Houston. Mark, Randy Burkhouse, Harold Denton, and Brigham Coltrane. You already know Cassidy."

Handshakes were exchanged, but Roy got right back to business. "We're on our way to Beacon Point. There are a lot of civilians over there, and that puts them directly in the path of the cartel. You coming with us?"

Burkhouse pursed his lips and shook his head. "Not unless I get direct orders from someone besides you."

"You're kidding, right?" Connor asked. "You'd let innocent civilians get hurt while you sit around and wait for permission?"

"No reason to think the cartel will hurt anyone," Burkhouse shot back. "You guys come to me with some cockamamie story about an alleged DEA operation that went bust last year, only it isn't true. I contacted my headquarters. They didn't know what I was talking about, but they were very clear about one thing, which you guys seemed to have forgotten. Our mission is to observe only. Seems to me that's all you're supposed to be doing, too."

"Not when lives are at stake," Connor retorted. "We don't ask for permission to do what's right."

"Lives are not at stake." Burkhouse glowered. The man had gray hairs in his bushy eyebrows, something Connor had not noticed until now. Was he trying to intimidate three ex-Marines by glaring the way he was? It wasn't working.

"How can you think lives are not at stake? You saw Taufa and Paxton's heads on a couple spikes." Connor's fist clenched. What the hell was Burkhouse using for brains?

"Like I said. We're not moving without proper authority to do so. You guys need to back off."

"Listen, we're just sharing everything we know." Roy stood toe-to-toe with the obstinate man. "It would be helpful if you'd do the same."

"I've got a better idea, Senior Agent Hudson." Burkhouse poured plenty of sarcasm into Roy's job title. "Why don't you take care of your business, and we'll take care of ours?"

"Because I get the feeling something else is going on here. You wouldn't want to enlighten me, would you?" Roy leaned forward, his patience clearly gone.

"What exactly are you implying?"

"I'm not implying. I'm telling. You guys don't do proper surveillance, you don't want us in your business, and you don't seem too worried that three of your own men were executed last year. What the hell is going on? Are you running this operation or not?"

Burkhouse didn't flinch, sputter, or argue. His emotionless response was as much an answer as the other. Harold and Brigham hadn't yet spoken up, Cassidy either.

Roy shot an exasperated glance to Connor and Mark. "Move out," he ordered as he pivoted and walked away from the RV. "We're on our own. No problem. We've been short-handed before."

"Wait up." Brigham ran to the already open RV storage compartment and jerked his backpack full of gear out. "I'm going with you—ahh, that is if it's okay with you, Agent Hudson."

Cassidy joined Brigham, her pack as easy to reach. "Me too. I came out here to do a job, not sit on my butt while this cartel runs rough shod over the top of us."

Connor shot a look to Roy. Mutiny was not what he'd expected, but he was not the one to grant permission. Roy shrugged. That was a good enough answer for Connor. Alex could figure out the administrative side of hiring on the spur of the moment when the dust settled.

Burkhouse glared at his treasonous junior agents. "You take one step out of this camp, and you're both fired. You'll never work for federal service again. You hear me, Dancer?"

Cassidy stared right back at him, defiant and ready to fight. "Listen up, Randy. Don't think for one second you can push me around. I've got no problem going straight to Sylvane about the way this operation's been run."

Burkhouse grunted. "Go for it. You think Sylvane cares? Pink slips will be in the mail before you smart-alecs know what hit you."

"Big deal. It's not the first time. It won't be the last." Cassidy pulled her backpack over her shoulders. "I was looking for a job when I found this one. At least we'll be doing something besides sitting around on our fat asses while private contractors do our job for us."

Connor's face should've cracked wide open, his smile was so big. "You just called your boss a fat ass," he said as he and Cassidy walked away.

She shot a hostile glance over her shoulder at her ex-boss. "Well, he is."

Damned Utah.

Izza wiped the sweat out of her eyes. The sun seemed to get hotter even while it dipped lower in the sky. Wasn't that against the laws of nature? Wasn't it supposed to get cooler later in the day? She stumbled on a willow root running across the trail. Rory snagged her elbow before she biffed it face first into the muddy riverbank.

"Thanks," she said. At least the shade trees along the river offered respite from the glaring sun, but she was tired and shaky. The handful of granola she'd stuffed into her mouth back at camp hadn't set well with her queasy stomach, but it was time to man up. The mission was a go, and she was a machine, ready to march into hell and fulfill whatever task was assigned whether her morning sickness allowed it or not.

Morgan had taken lead as they'd drawn closer to Beacon Point. Roy, Mark, and Boston were already in place on the south side of the river. She, Morgan, and Rory Dennison were to take the north side with orders to stay out of sight and not engage unless the cartel engaged with the civilians.

"How are you doing over there, Team Two?" Roy asked everyone over their tactical headsets.

"Good," Morgan responded. "Almost in position."

"Double check your backstop," Roy suggested.

"Always do." Izza could not let that unnecessary suggestion pass without a comment. Any gun owner worth her salt knew to ensure her line of fire was clear behind the target as well as in front. It was lesson one from beginner's gun safety. Who didn't know that?

"Just a friendly reminder, Izza," Roy replied. "Don't take it personally. We're dealing with civilians. Anything that can go wrong will."

"Understood," she replied instead of the standard, 'copy that.' For some reason, all the men on the planet were annoying the hell out of her today, her two senior agents included.

Team Two spread out with Morgan hidden at ground level in a brush-filled stand of pines while she and Rory took the ledge overlooking Beacon Point. She dropped to her belly and extended the bipod to her rifle. Sighting in, she searched for the uniformed cartel guards Connor had described.

Rory grumbled to her left. "A decent countersniper might be able to catch the reflection off our scopes at this angle. It's going to be hot. We're facing the sun. Stay low."

She didn't answer other than to pull a thin sheet of drab green netting from her gear bag and toss it to him. He caught the small bundle mid-air with an appreciative smile. "Good girl. Knew there was a reason I liked you."

That gentle compliment from a guy like Rory eased the aggravation climbing over her shoulders. Izza draped a second piece of the netting over her head and rifle. It didn't take much to blend into the landscape when a person knew how to do it properly. This low cost item distorted line of sight and body angles from anyone who might be peering at her from across the way. It also reduced the glare from sweaty faces, scope lenses and other reflective surfaces, yet it was completely see through at the same time. She and Rory had just made themselves invisible in the blink of an eye.

"Looks like there's lots of happy people down there," he commented quietly.

She grunted in reply, not really caring who was happy or not. A cool breeze lifted up the canyon wall and whispered over them with the sweet fragrance of pine and the river below. For a split second, Izza relaxed. Rory was the perfect companion soldier, never too talkative and never nosing into other people's business. Birds twittered from the shrubbery behind her. The sounds of merriment and happy children drifted along with the breeze. She could almost believe she was not carrying the weight of the world.

Izza stiffened to attention. She'd picked up movement. By the looks of it, Team One had moved closer to the riverbank opposite the picnickers.

"Shit." Izza scrutinized the capable figure in her riflescope. Cassidy Dancer lay secluded beneath the low-lying boughs of a large blue spruce. *What the hell's she doing there?*

"What do you see?" Rory asked. "Cartel?"

"DEA," she growled, her scope busily picking out another DEA agent's sniper hide—Connor's. He'd obviously finagled an op with his girlfriend. Just damned great.

"Good," Rory breathed. "It's about time the DEA joined the party."

Izza bit her lip. Good was not the word she'd have chosen. She hunkered her cheek into her rifle stock. One surprise was bad enough. Where the hell were the cartel guards? She froze. There they were—three men nearly invisible in the shade of a tangled giant willow on the other side of the river. They'd chosen an excellent location as well. The long trailing branches of the tree made them difficult to spot.

Switching to thermal to pierce the deep shade beneath the tree, she adjusted the magnification on her scope. Were they cartel or just men fishing? It was difficult to get a clear picture. No weapon showed, but with all the branches in the way, they looked suspicious. Aggravated, she blew her bangs out of her eyes and looked again. Damn it, anyway. Did pregnancy make everything appear blurry or was it just the blasted heat?

"I see you brought your night vision scope," Rory whispered. "You prepared for an all nighter?"

"Can't intercept what I can't see. Check the willow on the other side of the river. The big one. Do those guys beneath it look like cartel to you or fishermen?"

"Been watching them. I don't see rifles, but they've got gear on the ground. Could be cartel. Let's keep an eye on them."

He turned to silence as the afternoon dragged. It was not until the sun was low on the western horizon that activity kicked into high gear at the day park. The long shadows of evening turned darker. Someone had fireworks, someone else had water balloons, and of course, someone else had brought a garden hose, which was now attached to the campground faucet. Naturally, a wild and noisy water fight ensued with kids and parents alike running through scrub oak and willow.

"I've got three uniformed men by the creek." It was Cassidy's voice, loud and clear. "They're crouched beneath a—"

"I see them," Izza snapped in everyone's headsets. "Been watching them for hours. They're just sitting there in the shade. No big deal."

"Mark?" Connor intervened. "Do you see 'em?"

"Yes," Mark answered. "They're wearing the uniforms you showed us on your video. They're not moving, but they do have pistols. No rifles in sight yet, at least none I can make out."

Izza adjusted her magnification again. Damn. She was not seeing what Mark had just declared. Pistols? NVGs? He must have a better line of sight.

Roy grunted. "That ain't good. You seeing the same thing, Izza?"

She couldn't be sure. Exasperated, she took her eye off the target and turned to Rory. "Can you verify what Mark is seeing? I sure as hell can't."

"Not at this angle," he replied evenly. "Cassidy must have a better scope, or she's got better eyes."

Izza shook the slam off and reported to Roy. "Can't get a clear view from all the way up here. You want me to move in closer?"

"No," he said. "Let Cassidy take the lead. She's already in position."

"Yes, sir," was all Izza could spit out. Cassidy was quickly becoming a pain in the ass. Who the hell was she that Roy would give her the lead?

"Team One, move in," Roy said. "Keep these three guys in sight as well as the civilians. We don't want anyone hurt tonight. Team Two stay put."

It was all Izza could do to not curse. Once again, Team One moved closer to the action while Team Two sat on their thumbs and did nothing but watch. Fireworks shot through the trees along with squeals of delight and the laughter of a lot of partygoers. Water balloons were still flying fast and furious. Squealing children were everywhere, rambunctious young adults too. Two young people in particular wandered closer to the creek with a flashlight. Izza shook the irksome twinge out of her neck along with the pain caused by that other woman.

"I'm seeing a rifle." Again it was Dancer. "The man farthest east. I think he's—"

"It's a branch," Izza cut her off. "Check your scope, Dancer."

She zeroed in on said target to verify her own as yet unverified assessment. Damn it. Dancer might be right after all. The three cartel guards had changed position. They were all standing now. The man farthest east was obscured in the willow branches, and the fading light didn't help. It did look like he had a branch or a fishing pole across his arm, until—

"Correction. Rifle with scope." Connor's voice came steady and sure over the headset. "He's on his feet and aiming toward the two civilians at the edge of the river. Clear shot. I can take him down. Roy, do you copy?"

Izza huffed into her headset. "You would."

"Copy that," Roy muttered softly. "Hang tight, let's—"

"Hold on," Morgan interrupted. "Damn. Those kids are almost on top of the guards. They're walking right up to him like he's not even there. Are you seeing this?"

Izza scanned the scene, her eye tight to her scope. The guard in question stood in full view just as the happy couple arrived at the edge of the riverbank. They hadn't seen him yet, both too engrossed in each other and obviously thinking of skinny-dipping. The young man had his shirt already off, bouncing on one foot as he peeled out of his jeans. The girl stuck her foot into the cold creek water and giggled.

The cartel guard raised his rifle to his shoulder. Standing in the cold creek water in his boxers, the young man beckoned his girlfriend to join him. Izza couldn't hear their voices at the distance. The silly girl splashed him. He laughed and stepped further into the creek, still waving her forward.

"Copy, Morgan. Roy?" Connor asked one final time for the go ahead to shoot.

Roy didn't hesitate. "Do it."

It happened fast. Connor's shot rang out loud and true. The cartel guard fell backwards into the river with a splash. The other two roared from beneath the willow's cover, firing their automatic weapons uphill in Connor's direction. The young man and girl ran screaming back to the park pavilion. And all hell broke loose.

"Team One move," Roy barked. "Get down there. Now!"

At this point, all Izza could offer from her post all the way across the canyon was a status report. "The two guards are in the river dragging their buddy to the south. They're on the south side of the creek. Moving downstream."

"Good job, Connor," Rory added.

She smothered her opinion with a terse, "If you guys don't get your asses in gear, you're gonna lose 'em. Run!"

Connor was nearly at the edge of creek by then. Mark too, but the cartel guards were long gone.

"Way to go, Boston. You lost 'em," Izza reported for all to hear.

He ignored her snarky comment. "Sorry, folks. The SC knows we're here now."

Cassidy's voice came softly into every agent's earpiece. "Way to go, Connor."

Izza bit her lip. *Shut the hell up, Dancer.*

Eight

"You doing any better?" Roy handed her another string of skimpy RV toilet paper, the kind that dissolves on your lips.

"Uh, huh," Izza groaned even as she retched. More vomiting doubled her over. It was bad enough that Cassidy and Connor were best buds and the heroes of the day, but the fast track back to camp and into the closest bushes had done Izza in. Embarrassment flooded her to the core with unbearable warmth she didn't need in this damned hot state. Already on her knees, she sank to her hands and lowered her head for another round of physical torment. Dry heaves would be next.

She needed absolute privacy, but here Roy knelt with her while she puked her guts up. How dumb was he?

"You eat something bad on the drive down?" He sounded concerned right now, but it wouldn't last. He was that nasty drill sergeant at the end of a failed op. All that gentle concern would end in a butt reaming the minute she crawled up off her knees. He was just waiting until she could take it.

"Yeah. Food poisoning. That's all it is." She sat back, shaking and sweating in the pale moonlight. God, she must look like death. Huffing in a shallow breath so as not to upset her traitorous stomach, she wiped her mouth with the back of her hand and hoped it was done.

Retribution lingered on her horizon. Without a doubt, Roy was not happy. Neither was she. He'd probably followed her into the bushes thinking he'd give her a stern talking to, but she'd surprised him by being damned sick. Another round of nausea swept through her entire body. Cold sweats followed. At last, her stomach settled enough that she rolled onto her butt to face the music.

"You gonna be okay?" he asked quietly, his deep dark eyes piercing straight to her soul.

Izza squeezed her eyes tightly shut. *Okay* was not in her dictionary anymore. God, if he only knew. "Sorry." She blew her nose on that flimsy piece of toilet paper and wiped her mouth again. "I hate throwing up."

"We all do. Food poisoning's no fun." He gave her a hand up and steadied her. As luck would have it, Connor and the rest of them were far enough away they couldn't hear anything taking place in the scrub oak. "Are you feeling better?"

Here it comes. The well deserved slap down. For a quick moment she swayed, but then she righted herself and pulled away from his grip. Anger served her well at times like this. "I said I'm okay, didn't I?"

He countered by gripping her arm tighter. Roy peered into her eyes, his own dark with authority she would never submit to. "And I asked you if you're okay, Agent Ramos. Don't give me your bullshit. You've been on Connor's back since you got here. I need to know what's going on between the two of you, right here and now. If you've got something to say, you'd better spit it out and be done with it."

She glared right back, not willing to tell him anything he didn't already know. "What? He come crying to you like the wuss he is?"

Roy cocked his head sideways. "What the hell are you talking about? Connor's no—"

"Listen, Hudson. Next time I throw up, I'll try not to inconvenience you or your op." She jerked out of his hand, her jaw tight, and ready for a fight.

"Junior Agent Ramos!" Roy barked before she made it one step away from him. "Back the hell off! No more, do you hear me? Lay off Conner. Lay off Cassidy. And shut the hell up if you can't contribute to the operation. You damned near cost innocent lives back there. I don't care how sick or pissed off you are, it ends now!"

She kept her mouth shut, her smartest move all day.

"I asked you something," he growled, "and you damned well better have the right answer or I'm firing your ass all the way back to Alexandria. Let Alex deal with you."

She clenched her jaw and lowered her head. *Do it then. Fire me. Maybe Alex will fire me off The TEAM, too. Why'd I ever think working for another Marine was a smart idea anyway?*

Roy took a firm step deep inside her comfort zone, an old drill sergeant tactic. Next he'd be an inch from her eardrum and bellowing, calling names and spitting in her face. She stood her ground, still looking at the dirt.

"Fine," she spat.

"Excuse me?" he growled again.

"Fine, I will shut the hell up when and if I can't contribute," she yelled at him. *There, are you happy now, cuz I sure as hell am not!*

"Dismissed."

She stalked away. *Dismissed, your ass. This isn't the Corps. I quit.*

The sheriff's department quickly overran the day park. Everyone but Izza and Roy stayed below to provide whatever assistance and information the local authorities needed. As the shooter, Connor had no choice.

The blood splatter beneath the willow definitely confirmed a crime scene, but no body was recovered and none of the armed guards were apprehended. One call to the governor's office verified who The TEAM was and their mission in Utah. The police and Mark traded phone numbers. Governor Baxter closed the canyon to all incoming civilian traffic and activities. The war had begun.

"Set up a night watch schedule, Connor," Mark ordered as they hiked back to camp in the wee small hours of the morning. Cassidy and Brigham followed, with Rory and Morgan bringing up the rear. "Two by two. Four hour shifts. Everyone participates."

"Will do," Connor replied. "Guess we gave Ramirez the wake up call we wanted."

"Hope so. It'd be better if we'd been sent to flush these guys out of the canyon and into law enforcement's net, though. Seems to me that's what we should've done instead of all this observation bullshit. We could've had this canyon cleared days ago."

"That's what I don't get," Connor said. "DEA's been here before. They know what's going on. Why are they sitting on their thumbs now?"

"Which is probably why Baxter contacted Alex. He didn't think the DEA was doing enough."

"We aren't, either. It's like our hands are tied. I don't mind hanging around watching and reporting until crap starts flying, but then, by hell, it's time to stand up and do something. Why the hell are we here, anyway?"

"Watch and tell never turns out to be an easy assignment, does it?" Mark replied. "But look at it this way. You were in the right place at the right time tonight. You saved a couple kids' lives. That's worth the time you think you've wasted."

Connor shut up. He wasn't looking for praise. His inner Marine demanded room to stretch, knock off a few hundred rounds, and take care of business. That's what every soldier wanted: the bureaucrats out of their way so a man could clean house once and for all, get the job done and come home proud of a hard day's work. Current rules of engagement made every operation a nightmare. He thought Alex knew better.

Their camp came into view, but only Roy sat near the cold fire pit, his hands locked together in front of him.

"You sure took off like a bat out of hell," Mark said while he peeled out of his tactical gear.

"Had some business to take care of," Roy answered quietly. "Why? Did you need me to stay?"

"No. We handled it. The sheriff wanted to confront the cartel tonight, but we told them to back off. They're more than happy to work with us, especially now that they know what's really going on."

"Let me guess," Roy said darkly. "DEA kept them out of the loop, too."

"From what I gather, the DEA has kept an information blackout on this entire operation. Local PD had strict orders to stay out of the canyon until they got the call tonight."

Connor's eyes shifted to the shadows behind Roy while the senior agents debated whys and hows. No doubt the business Roy had to take care of was Izza. Silvery moonlight glinted through the pines. She was close and listening to every word. Connor could sense her hatred from wherever she lay. What possessed her to argue with a judgment call like she had?

He changed the subject. "Cassidy and I will take first watch. Then Rory and Morgan if needed. Not sure we'll need to keep watch once the sun comes up."

"Sounds good." Morgan yawned. "Where's my bunk? I'm out of here."

Rory pointed into the trees. "Mine's over there if you want to set up nearby."

"Will do." Morgan lifted his sleeping bag and shuffled away.

"You ready?" Connor asked Cassidy.

"Sure. Let me grab a couple waters."

They sat in the sagebrush downhill from camp, listening and watching for cartel activity. The smells of the canyon swirled around them—fragrant sage, pine, and too many other pleasant scents to distinguish one from the other. Connor took a deep breath, and, as inconspicuously as possible, shifted his hand closer on the ground to hers. "Man, this place smells good tonight. You live in a beautiful state."

"It's Utah. You gotta love it." Cassidy took the hint, covering his hand with hers. "I meant what I said before. Good shooting."

"Someone had to take the shot. Good intel on your part, too. You didn't back down one bit."

"What is her problem anyway?" Cassidy nodded back to their camp. "Agent Ramos acts like she hates me. I've never met her until today. What'd I ever do to her?"

"Don't know. Don't care." The last person he wanted to discuss with Cassidy was Izza. He moved a little closer. "You have the brownest eyes."

She turned shy. "They came with the package. You know, two eyes, one nose, two lips—"

"Good deal." He leaned in with a whispered breath. "Too bad we're not closer to the waterfall."

"Why's that?" she whispered in the same conspiratorial tone as she scooted closer into his side. "What's on your mind? Showering together under the moonlight?"

His eyes twinkled down at hers. "Well, now that you mention—"

"For hell's sake!" A nasty screech rent the quiet night. "Will you two shut your pie holes so the rest of us can get to sleep?"

Cassidy's eyes widened. She covered her mouth with all eight fingertips and giggled like a little girl. "Oops. She's closer than I thought."

And despite the wild woman in the trees behind them, Connor stole his first kiss. He would've settled for two, but some madman who worked twenty-four-seven on the East Coast decided he needed a sitrep in the middle of the night.

Connor scrambled to get the sat phone before it woke everyone, but he was too late. Roy and Mark were still at the fire pit where a small blaze burned. The expressions on their faces made him look twice. They looked too serious for a couple old geezers.

"I've got it," Roy said quietly as he answered the call and set it to speaker.

"Join us," Mark ordered Connor. "Your girlfriend will be fine by herself for a couple minutes."

Ouch. Connor nodded, chagrined at the term Mark had used.

"Just got off the phone with Tom Baxter," Alex said. "He wants us to take the cartel down first thing tomorrow with DEA support or not. His Narcotics Task Force and the Utah National Guard will meet you at first light tomorrow. You're to take the lead, Roy."

Roy's answer was sure and quick. "The sooner the better."

"Boss, we've already decided the best plan is to sweep the workers and guards toward the mouth of the canyon," Mark said. "We'll divide the force Baxter sends to get it done. It sounds like we'll finally have the right manpower to be effective against the cartel."

"Good answer. Look for them at 8 a.m. at your old location. Is that doable, given the increased activity you engaged in tonight?" Alex asked.

"Not a problem. We'll be at the RV by eight," Roy replied. "Tell 'em to sit tight if we're late. It's a bit of a hike."

"Hey, Boss, we picked up a couple new hires," Mark advised. "I thought you ought to know. DEA Agents Cassidy

Dancer and Brigham Coltrane offered to assist at Beacon Point. They stand to lose their jobs because of it."

"They know how to shoot?"

"Yes. They're two sharp agents, extremely qualified by what I saw tonight, and they're not afraid to step out when the going gets tough."

"I'll talk with Scott," Alex said. "He and I will work something out to keep them employed.

You do know if we handle this right, you may be home by the weekend."

"Sounds good," Roy answered solemnly.

"Be safe. Talk with you soon." Alex hung up.

Roy didn't break eye contact with Connor. "Mark and I have reorganized. Team One is me, you, Morgan, and Izza. Team Two is Mark, Rory, Cassidy, and Brigham. Any questions?"

"Nope," Connor replied quickly. "Totally your call."

"First order of business tomorrow will be what you just heard. Team Two will proceed to the mouth of the canyon and maintain eyes on cartel activity. If Ramirez shows, they will apprehend. Team One will meet the Governor's Task Force at the RV. Once we divide up our additional manpower, Team One will hit the brush to move the cartel westward and out of the canyon. Team Two will take whatever means necessary to apprehend. You will command Team One; Mark, Team Two, while I oversee both maneuvers and keep the Governor apprised. Any questions?"

"No." Connor relaxed. Finally. Direct contact with the cartel that meant something. "It's about time."

"It's also time you stopped to think about what you're doing, son," Roy said softly. The man did not blink, but

Connor got the hint. He'd been caught walking a fine line called fraternization.

"You're right," he admitted, ready to get back downhill to Cassidy. "Anything else?"

"Yes." Mark stood to leave. "Hit the sack, junior agent. I'm taking this watch with your girlfriend."

Izza lay wide-awake and listening. Seemed like everyone was getting their butts reamed tonight, not just her. Connor took his chastisement much easier than she had, but why not? He'd be in charge tomorrow. She'd be just another one of the guys. At least Cassidy was on Mark's team instead of Connor's. That helped.

Her mind drifted to her brother. Before Jamie died, he had a way of looking at life like it was one big game. Nothing got him down, not the abuse he and she had suffered at the hands of their father, or any USMC drill sergeant. He made everything fun, even in the worst of times, and Izza missed him now more than ever. He'd never get to hold the baby in her belly. Uncle Jamie would never get to be proud of his big sister anymore, either.

She sniffed back her ragged emotions. She'd placed her sleeping bag at the farthest point from Connor's. She didn't need to see him now or first thing in the morning, Cassidy either. The stars blinked through the pine branches overhead. With the night came a chill she'd not expected. This damn state was hot as an oven one minute and cold the next. She couldn't keep up.

Connor's soft deep voice drifted across the clearing. "Goodnight, Izza."

She rolled to her side and blocked the unexpected kindness with her palm to her ear. *Go to hell, Boston.*

Nine

"I got you in trouble, huh?" Cassidy asked the minute she saw him.

Connor couldn't help but grin. "It was worth it."

They'd both rolled out of their bedrolls at the same time everyone else did after a few hours of not enough sleep. Mark and Roy had prepared a quick breakfast of the last of the eggs and the slab of bacon from the RV. From now on, food would be dehydrated or meals-ready-to-eat. Living high on the canyon wall made everything simple. Tough and chewy maybe, but simple.

"What a bunch of bullshit," Izza murmured under her breath.

Connor shot her a quick glance, not sure if she was talking about the breakfast or him. She looked tired, but something else was going on with her. He could see it in her eyes as they stood nearly side-by-side strapping into their tactical gear. She looked—off. Pale. Fragile.

"Today's the day," he offered just to keep things friendly. "We finally get to do something right."

She grunted and turned away. Poor Izza It had to be Jamie's death. Her brother had been her only family. Connor couldn't imagine being alone in the world. He'd always had more brothers than he knew what to do with.

By the time Roy said, "Head out," Connor was armed, geared up and ready. He'd double-checked the Tattle Tales he'd planted at the RV. The coast was clear. All systems go. Every team member held a loaded AR to their chest with the barrel down. Working team ops was as close to military as he wanted to get anymore. He nodded to Cassidy when she left with Team Two. There would be time later for the two of them. No doubt about it.

Team Two headed west while Team One dropped quickly to the canyon floor. Before long, they'd crossed the river and next the road. Connor checked his cell phone for the time. Right on schedule. The new order from Alex energized him. Today was the day he would get to do what he was trained for. Fight back. About damned time.

"Comm check," Roy's voice came through Connor's headset loud and clear.

"Copy," Connor replied, followed quickly by Morgan and Izza.

"Take it slow," Roy cautioned as they approached the campground where the RV was parked. The police had cleared out all the other campers, making the grounds eerily quiet.

"Watch for trip wires," Connor advised. The hair on the back of his neck lifted. He glanced over his shoulder at Morgan. "You good?"

Morgan's eyes widened. He must've felt it too, but he'd no more than nodded when—

WHOOSH!

As soon as Connor heard it he knew. They'd been ambushed. The RPG blast kicked all four agents to the ground. One second he was standing, the next minute he was flat on his back and watching the smoking roof of the RV fall lazily back to earth. Bat wings. The dammed thing looked like bat wings.

Another whoosh and the ground trembled. He rolled to his side and pushed to his knees, crouching while he caught his breath. Holy crap. The entire RV had exploded outward and up. Shrapnel still whistled in flight through the surrounding shrubbery. Smoke made it impossible to see clearly.

His heart pounded. It hadn't been too long since he'd survived a very similar explosion in Washington D.C. and lived to talk about it. Morgan had already recovered his footing but Roy and Izza were slow coming around. Morgan knelt, his pistol gripped between both hands, aiming at the rear of the RV.

Connor started toward the same direction when he saw the hit out of the corner of his eye. One minute focused and aiming, the next, Morgan's face disappeared into foamy pink spray.

"Morgan! No!" Connor bellowed.

The bowels of the RV carcass exploded, forcing another riptide of shooting embers and sparking debris outward, covering everyone with the stench of burning diesel. A fragment of what had once been a propane tank thudded to earth with a tremendous thud.

"Connor?" Roy yelled from within the cloud of smoke.

"Here," Connor replied. Gunfire erupted from where he couldn't tell. Bullets zinged all around. He dropped to the ground, unable to get to his friend, Morgan. Crossfire. They were dead center of an ambush. The veil of smoke lifted in one gigantic sheet from the ground. Roy came into view.

Already bleeding from his upper thigh, he pushed to one knee. Another shot to his chest bulldozed him backward and down.

"Roy!" Connor screamed, his boots propelling him forward. The sonic boom of another explosion reverberated in the air around him, sucking what little oxygen was left out of his lungs.

"Connor! Where's Morgan? Izza?" Roy bellowed.

Connor never got the chance to answer. Hell slammed into his tactical vest, knocking the life out of him. Another dug into his gut just above his belt. The world pitched him into blackness.

And he fell.

"No! No! No!" Mark bellowed as he knelt over Roy's prone body, his hand pressed hard into his friend's chest to slow the bleeding.

Cassidy had already wrapped her belt around Roy's leg, a quick tourniquet to slow the blood flow. Team Two had raced to the scene within minutes of the explosion, but the damage was done. Roy was down with two gunshots. Morgan was dead. Connor and Izza had yet to be located, but worse, the Narcotics Task Force was nowhere in sight. The whole damned thing was a set up!

"They missed his femoral," Cassidy muttered as she pushed harder on the bloody leg wound. "Keep him flat to the ground, Mark. Don't let him get up."

As much as Roy moaned from the pain and pressure, Mark didn't back off with his first-aid measures. Roy would not die on his watch.

He peered up at Mark with shock and disbelief etched on his face. Blood trickled from his mouth to his neck in a steady drip. "Where's my... my kids? Where's Connor? Morgan? Izza?"

"Not here, buddy. Where'd they go?" Mark needed to know everything. Roy was fading fast.

"Exploded...." Roy tried to point to what was left of the RV, but his arm flopped uselessly to the ground.

"Right. The RV exploded. The cartel has RPGs. I get that," Mark said. "Help is on its way, but where's Connor? Where'd he and Izza go? Were they inside when it blew?"

Roy shook his head. It took longer for him to reply, his eyelids blinking heavily as he tried to focus. He only repeated Mark's question. "Where... are... they?"

"Come on, man. Stay with me. Talk to me. Where are Izza and Connor?"

"M-m-mark?" Roy's voice slurred as a stream of blood gushed over his teeth.

"What, man?"

"Where's my boy... Where's Morgan?"

Mark shook his head. He didn't want to say the words. All of the junior agents were Roy's boys and girls. Morgan Humphries, a kid of twenty-six and a junior agent of less than a year, lay twenty feet away, his head blown apart by what Mark suspected was a large caliber round.

Rory and Brigham still searched the area for any sign of Connor and Izza. The two disgruntled DEA agents, Randy Burkhouse and his sidekick, Harold Denton, had finally shown up to offer assistance, but all they could do was establish a perimeter to ensure the cartel didn't strike again. Even that was futile. The cartel had vanished, their dirty deed done.

Roy clutched Mark's hand, his breathing labored and weak, his eyes half-closed. "Mark. Tell my kid... tell Stevie... I'm proud as hell."

"Knock it off, Hudson. Tell him yourself, you hear me?"

"And tell Colette... I never stopped loving—" Roy's head slumped to his shoulder, the fight knocked right out of him. He'd survived hell in Vietnam and numerous operations the world over, only to die at the hand of a two-bit drug lord in the state Mormons called Zion. Land of milk and honey? Heaven?

Mark gulped his fears back as he tried to save his mentor and senior agent, his friend. It felt more like the land of hell. "Where's the sonofabitchin medic?" he bellowed at Rory.

Rory pointed straight up with a bloody index finger. The whirring chop of a helicopter blade sounded through the trees. Mark hollered into Roy's unconscious face even as tears drenched his own. "You hang in there, damn you! You hear me? Help is here. You've got a grandson. Jacob Roy, you remember? And you got Stevie. You got everything to live for!"

Roy no longer responded. The blue and white life-flight helicopter hovered overhead, then landed on the road. Mark watched as the medics moved in what seemed like torturously slow motion. They'd done this before, but Mark couldn't wait. They walked too slow.

"Get the hell over here!" he yelled, waving frantically.

And then everything fast-forwarded when the medics lifted Roy onto a gurney and whisked him away. The helicopter took off with them hard at work on Roy, the body bag that carried Morgan Humphries stowed onboard as well. All Mark had left was the blood of his friend all over his hands and shirt, and a ragged hole in his chest where his heart used to be.

A caravan of ten black SUVs roared into the campground. The Utah Narcotics Task Force had finally arrived, a conspicuous one hour late.

Mark looked back at the rubble of the RV. Smoke billowed off the still burning remains while the cottonwoods around it burned a crackling symphony. Other emergency vehicles could be heard screaming their way up the canyon, but for nothing. They were too late.

"Mark," Rory said gently, his hand to Mark's bicep. "We're still here."

Cassidy, Rory, and Brigham stood waiting on him, expectation clear in their eyes. For what? He wasn't the team lead. Roy was. These people weren't his to command, but they were ready and waiting. He saw it in their eyes. All he had to do was bark an order, and they'd obey.

He stared at them, his gut churning with indecision. In a flash, his trusted friend was dead and another at death's door. Mark didn't know what to feel or think anymore, and he didn't know where Connor and Izza were, either. The cartel could have them or they might be in the RV, dead for sure.

The odds seemed extremely stack against The TEAM. He took a deep breath. Leadership kicked in. His brain remembered what needed to happen next, even if his heart didn't want to.

"Team," he ground out. "We can't help Roy or Morgan."

His voice sounded like it belonged to someone else, someone strong and confident. It sure wasn't him. He looked from agent to agent. Rory nodded back at him, ready and willing as always to follow and obey. Cassidy's jaw was set in hard determination. Brigham still looked shocked and concerned as if he wanted to cry.

Mark knew the feeling. He pulled the only rule he had left out of his mental playbook. *When you can't do what you want to do, do what the hell you can.*

"I don't know where Connor and Izza are, but it's time we kick some cartel ass and find out. Who's with me?"

"Oo-rah!" Rory's deep baritone declared with typical jarhead emphasis. Tears streamed down Cassidy's cheek, but her's and Brigham's hands were fisted and raised high over their heads in some kind of a silent battle cry. Another roar went up around them. Mark finally saw beyond his shattered team. Thirty members of the Utah Narcotics Task Force had circled them, their fists lifted in the same somber tribute.

One man stepped forward. "Special Officer Justin Viera at your service, sir. How can we help?"

Mark blinked his momentary weakness away. He had a job to do and finally the men to do it with. This was the day the Sonoran Cartel would finally crawl back to hell.

Shot. Bumpy road. Dust in his mouth and eyes. Connor winced.

Crap. Crap. Crap. Through and through he hoped. Shot nonetheless. The stabbing pain radiated hot waves of fire through his gut all the way to his backbone. *Not gut shot. Please not gut shot. Mom will be so sad if I—God, please not gut shot. I'll die for sure. It'll kill her.*

A jarring bump. More breath-robbing pain. More bumpy roads. Then smooth sound of singing tires on pavement. Another bump. Potholes. Jarring wrenching potholes. Something smelled funny in his nose. Somehow sweet. Kinda like—blood. His. Not what a man wants to smell. Ever.

He sucked in a gasp of wretchedly hot air, but breathing hurt. Too much grit and dust. Not enough oxygen. He was in a dark place. Too dark to see. Face down on what felt like heated metal. A truck bed, maybe? Another wrench of pain clenched his side and stomach. Not good. The awful smell in this small dark place didn't help. He gagged. Fresh air would sure be nice.

The truck stopped with a jerk. He'd have played dead if he wasn't already so close to it. Someone grabbed his boots and dragged his body off the truck bed, only now he wasn't sure that's what it was. Chopper maybe? Connor couldn't tell. He had no strength to contest the rough treatment, either.

His face scraped over the floor of the vehicle. It didn't matter that he was no longer strong enough to shield himself from what came next. Dropping face first to the ground broke his nose anyway. Blinding pain followed the crunch in the middle of his face. Before that pain really got underway, some jackass kicked his side. Once. Twice.

He rolled away or at least, he tried to. A third kick landed in the middle of his back. And a fourth. He couldn't even scream. Just groan, take it, and gasp for enough air to endure. Skewering pain lanced through him with each attempt to breathe and he was suffocating. Cruel Mexican taunts rained down. Crushing patterns of black against flashes of blinding light pinged around in his brain, a psychedelic light show that hurt.

He squinted, trying real hard to see something real. How does a body absorb so much pain and live through it? With one last kick, they were done with him. By then, an odd crackle sounded from his throat. A death rattle? No matter. Dead would still be dead. Maybe welcome too. It sure couldn't hurt any worse.

Something crashed on top of him. Hard. Like a rock. Or a body. It groaned. Maybe Roy? Morgan? But his abductors didn't kick whoever it was. Good thing. Those hard boots might have missed their target and hit him. One good thing about that last body drop—the force of impact knocked something loose inside. Connor pushed it out of his mouth. A rag. He'd been choking on a rag stuck in his mouth. Hot dusty air filled the void, but at last he could breathe.

Forcing the pain aside, he struggled to see. Not going to happen. Too much trouble even to turn his head. He spit the blood and dirt of out his mouth before it choked him. His eyes burned like hellfire when he tried to crack them open. The grit all over his face didn't help, but at last he could see. Barely. A shadow. Something. Someone.

God, just kill me now.

It was Izza.

Ten

"And you must be Agent Mark Houston."

Of all things, Tom Baxter, the Governor of Utah, had arrived on site, already dressed in appropriate tactical gear befitting the ex-Army Ranger he was. The rifle in his hand made it official. He knew what he was doing, and he was intent on assisting The TEAM. By then, the last two DEA agents had joined with the Narcotics Task Force to drive the cartel west and out of the canyon while Mark and his team joined with the Utah National Guard. Push had come to shove.

"Yes, sir," Mark said somberly. "Good to meet you, Governor."

"You've had a tough day," Tom said as he clasped Mark's hand. "I'm sure sorry about your agent, Morgan Humphries. How is your Agent Hudson doing?"

"He's in surgery. Critical, but hanging in there."

"Saint Mark's is one of the best. They'll take good care of him. There must be something about the name."

Mark ignored the gentle compliment and changed the subject.

"You get your deer with that every year, sir?" He took stock of the Governor's choice of weaponry—a stainless Browning A-Bolt, complete with a high-powered scope that offered laser sighting.

"And a couple moose as long as you're asking." Tom Baxter had transformed from a western state governor into another skilled sniper. His own dark eyes glittered when he caught Mark's assessing glance skim over his weapon of choice. "I keep five in the magazine, one in the chamber. You think I'll need more?"

Mark cracked a tired smile. "Not if we do this right, sir."

Tom slung the weapon over his back with a determined glint in his eye. "I happen to know a guy if you're interested. I'm all yours. Where are your men?"

Mark pointed to the utility road that ran along the upper edge of the canyon wall.

"Let's go. We've got work to do." Tom Baxter was no slouch. Silver-haired and pushing sixty, he was still agile and full of energy. Before long, he was at Mark's side, keeping up and barely panting at the vertical climb.

Rory gave the men a sideways glance when they cleared the path. "You brought another shooter. Good."

"Rory Dennison, meet Governor Tom Baxter. My other two agents, Cassidy Dancer and Brigham Coltrane," Mark gestured toward his beleaguered team. *Damn it. Where the hell are Connor and Izza?*

"Good to meet you folks," Tom said. "Don't get excited. I'm just one of the guys as far as you're concerned. Now let's get these bastards the hell out of my state."

"Status," Mark requested of his team.

"We've got them pinned down," Rory said, "at least the twelve guards left in base camp. We're up too high for them to reach us, and we're damned good at taking potshots, excuse the pun. There could be more cartel up farther in the canyon, but UNG seems to be intercepting them before they make it this far. Your Task Force, Governor, has already cleared the north canyon wall. They're working our way while they clear the south. We've been hearing gunshots all morning."

Tom took it all in stride as Rory continued. "As you can see, the cartel is using the trucks north of the only remaining cartel tent for cover. Three cartel ATV's are not accounted for. Assume they're east of our location. The only problem is what's in that tent."

"Enough C4 to bring these canyon walls down," Mark muttered. "Brigham spotted it earlier. We were debating how to use it to our advantage when you showed up, sir. There is another problem." Mark looked to Brigham to explain.

The young man rolled to his side to face his governor. He nodded respectfully. "Yes, sir. From what we've been able to determine there are eleven migrant workers still unaccounted for. Connor and Roy spotted them a couple days ago, only neither the UNG nor the Task Force has located them. It's a slim possibility, but they may be inside."

"You're thinking hostages?"

Brigham shrugged. "We're not sure, but we won't blow the tent until we are."

"Can't blow C4 by shooting at it anyway, son," Tom replied.

"True," Mark agreed. "Which is where Rory comes in. He can get inside."

"At which point, I'll wire the C4 with blasting caps or free hostages," Rory said.

"What about you, young lady?" Tom looked to Cassidy. "You're awfully quiet. What's your take on all this?"

Cassidy had been silent all morning. After sitting on watch with her the night before, Mark knew her heart was with Connor. She was hurting. Hell, they all were. "I'll do whatever Mark tells me to do, sir," she answered quietly. "He's my boss now."

Mark looked out over the Salt Lake Valley to the west and bit his lip. Becoming boss by attrition was never a good thing, but he had work to do. He assigned Cassidy to, "Keep close watch on Rory. Cover him."

With one curt nod, Rory slipped off the path they were lying on and slid feet-first down the canyon wall.

"He's good," Tom whispered as he tracked Rory's progress through his scope.

No one else spoke, and Mark was glad. Whatever success they achieved today could not outweigh the hit The TEAM had taken earlier. Alex would be on his way west at the soonest flight out. Mark didn't relish the arrival of his over-the-top boss.

When Rory's boots hit the edge of the winding riverbank, he crouched low in the willows that offered cover for miles in either direction. Once known for nothing more dangerous than the occasional moose taking cover in those willows, now beautiful Utah sported snipers and armed guards instead. Mark pushed the thought away and focused, willing Rory to return with honor.

"He needs five minutes of distraction, Governor." Mark tossed his tactical headset for the governor to use. "You've got men in place who can assist. Need you to place a call."

"You bet." The Governor clamped the earpiece to his ear. In a minute, he had Officer Viera's attention. "We've got a man headed into their supply tent. Can you give him five minutes of hellfire?"

He handed the headset back to Mark as automatic fire lit up the camp below. Cartel guards promptly returned fire.

"One. Two." Mark counted as the cartel guards fell to Special Agent Viera's assault. "Three."

"He's almost there, Boss." Brigham reported what Mark already knew. Within seconds, the tent flap barely moved when Rory slid inside.

"He's in," Brigham announced quietly.

Mark wiped the sweat off the back of his neck. Rory was inside all right. One man against eight was nothing to feel good about. The clock was ticking.

"Four." Mark's eyes glued to the scene below. *Hurry it up, Rory. Don't get caught. Don't get dead. Not you, too.*

The roar of an ATV pulled his attention from the tent. Four more cartel men scrambled off and ran to take position with their cohorts behind the trucks. One of them immediately dropped dead, a victim of Agent Cassidy Dancer.

"Five," Mark muttered as he turned to her and said soberly, "Good work."

She responded by chambering another round and preparing to take another shot.

"I've got two men at the rear of the tent. Coming around this side, south," Tom reported as he took careful aim. "I'm ready if you are."

"No, sir. Wait." Mark studied the scene, hoping Rory would exit the tent and get his butt back undercover. "Give him time."

Another guard fell. The world stopped revolving. The sound of incoming ATV echoed up the canyon wall. Rory needed to get the hell out of there.

Tom was worried. "Your man's in trouble. Maybe we should—"

"No." Mark peered intently at the exact spot of the tent flap where Rory's face would show. "He's not."

Rory could take care of himself in a tight spot. The ex-Marine was as steady as they came. More guards scrambled off the newly arrived ATV and joined forces behind the barricade. That tight spot just got tighter. *Come on, Rory. Get the hell out of there.*

"These guys are loading a grenade launcher," Brigham reported. "Yep. That's exactly what they're doing."

"Possibly. Seven." Mark continued the tally as another guard went down. "Keep your eyes on them, team. On my signal."

Cassidy hadn't said a word, but Mark knew without having to look that all three of his agent's weapons were trained on the two cartel guards skulking around the tent. If any of them made a move for entry, Cassidy, Brigham, or Tom would drop them.

Mark clenched his jaw. *Time's up, Rory. Get out. Now.*

As if in answer, the tent flap barely moved.

"He's out, Boss." Brigham exhaled loud enough for all to hear.

"Light 'em up," Mark ordered.

Instantly, his team provided cover for Rory's return up the canyon wall. Tom Baxter squeezed the chrome-plated trigger on his pride and joy. Once. Twice. Cassidy kept up a steady stream of lead. A momentary shiver of pride offered Mark respite in the middle of a damned hard day.

As soon as the cartel knew they were taking fire from the south side of the canyon, several scrambled to return fire with an enemy they couldn't see. Rory was suddenly at Mark's side, panting from the quick climb, his hands on his knees as he drew in deep breaths to restore his oxygen. He lifted his hand to reveal the remote detonator. "Just C4. No hostages. Whatever doesn't explode from this charge will cook off. Ready when you are."

That same shiver hit Mark's shoulders. "Your call, Governor. We can take prisoners if you'd prefer."

Tom looked up from his scope with a half smile. "Not if I know the Sonoran Cartel, you won't. These guys will kill you with their last breath."

"Advise your men to fall back then. It will be a hell of an explosion." Mark tossed his headset back to Tom.

"Officer Viera. We're ready to blow the tent. Pull back to a safe distance. How many down?" Silence. "That many?" He relayed the body count. "Five of mine; two dead, three injured. Plus four of yours from the earlier incident."

"And the three DEA agents the cartel murdered last year." Mark watched Tom Baxter's face when he dropped that bombshell. It was obvious the governor didn't know what Mark referred to.

Gunfire diminished. The Task Force pulled back. Mark watched the scene below for another second. Ordering death was not in his skill set. This would be a first.

One of the cartel guards must have misinterpreted the temporary lull for retreat and cartel success. He'd slinked back to the ATV and began pulling several rocket propelled grenade launchers from the bed.

"Boss. You seeing this?" Brigham asked in disbelief. "Is this guy a moron, or what?"

The foolish man hurried back to their barricade with his arms full of ordnance.

Mark turned to Rory. "We don't owe these guys shit. Finish it."

"Cover your ears, guys." Rory adjusted his own protective headset, and with one last nod to Mark, pressed his thumb to the detonator switch.

The pyrotechnic display of all that C4 reverberated up the canyon walls. Rocks and gravel slides tumbled around Mark's team while they hunkered low. A brilliant ball of orange and black fire spewed heavenward like a fiery dragon unleashed from its lair. Cottonwoods in its wake ignited. Smaller explosions rocked the canyon floor as the cloud of dust and white smoke billowed upward, engulfing everything and everyone in its wake.

No gunfire from below announced the absence of armed survivors, but Mark waved the smoke out of his eyes and waited.

"Agent Houston," Special Agent Justin Viera's voice sounded in his headset. "The enemy has been neutralized. Good work, sir."

The Utah Task Force moved in with deliberate caution. Officer Viera stood in the middle of the campground parking lot. He gave the Governor and Mark the thumbs up sign. Tom Baxter returned the wave, but there was no sense of satisfaction in the victory for Mark. The Sonora Cartel was officially out of business in Utah, but his team had suffered an unforgiveable loss.

"Good work," he told them. They looked as unimpressed with that statement as he felt.

"What's next?" Cassidy asked, her eyes red-rimmed from more than the thick fog of dust in the air.

Mark shot her the only hope he had to offer. "Ramirez."

With a concentrated, herculean effort that cost every last ounce of his strength, Connor flopped onto his stomach. It hurt when he bumped his nose against solid ground, but he had to shield his eyes against the harsh sunlight. Besides, everything else hurt. What was one more pain?

He lay there and panted from the effort. Squinting into the laser light of that blasted fiery orb in the sky had already baked his lips and eye sockets dry. He needed the shade of his hard head to survive. Sunburn stretched its blistering fingers over the parched skin that now rested against coarse-grit desert. There was no relief, only less burn to this side of his body for now.

An object moved in his blurry line of sight, but nothing as large as the vultures he'd half-expected. The object evolved into a curious horned toad. The goofy thing sat an inch from Connor's bloodied nose, licking its eyeballs so fast he couldn't see its tongue move. But then, he couldn't see much as dry as his eyes were anyway.

"Hey," he croaked at his new neighbor. "Get outta the way. I'm gonna... move. Soon."

Two beady eyes winked. First one, then the other. Either the toad was not impressed, or Connor was out of his ever-loving mind and seeing things. A man who talked to toads just might be crazy after all. He groaned at the stabbing fire in his side. Every rib hurt. Every breath. And he was thirsty, his tongue as dry as the baby dust devil swirling around him and his new buddy.

Crap. Am I still in Utah? Must be. It's hot. Dry. Feels a lot like hell on steroids.

He decided to move. Baking felt too much like burning to death. Struggling against his own weight, he elbowed his way to his hands and from there pushed to his knees. His face lingered in the dirt, but getting most of his body off the floor of this hellish oven was something all by itself. It dawned on him who had fallen on him yesterday – if it really happened yesterday. Might have been an hour ago. Felt like forever. Time had become an abstract commodity he no longer needed. Only this very second counted. This moment. This breath.

But where was Izza? She'd been real, hadn't she?

Rippling heat waves rose up from the vast desert floor. Sagebrush and rocks came into perspective, but Izza was nowhere in sight. Was he delirious? Had he dreamed her into this nightmare? Licking his parched tongue over gritty lips, he struggled to clear his mind. No, he was positive he'd seen her. She was here somewhere. Maybe she'd walked off and saved herself? Good. It would sure make dying a lot easier. Quieter, too.

Sinking back to the sand, he tried to spit. Honest, he gave it his best shot, but a man cannot spit when dust and sand coat every taste bud, every tooth, his gums, the inside of his lips and all the way back to his tonsils. Not one hint of saliva obliged. He was stuck with a mouthful of Utah desert. Felt like sandpaper. Did not taste like chicken. The grit moved into his windpipe, making breathing a suicidal chore.

Blinking didn't help much either, other than to scratch the hell out of his eyeballs He rested for an eternity before he made another effort. It took a lot, but finally he balanced on shaky knees and shakier arms.

Scrape marks on the hardscrabble ground indicated someone else might have been there. Even that clue failed in the optimism department. Dinosaurs could've made those marks a million years ago for all Connor knew.

His mother's sweet smile came to mind. Every good Catholic boy knows how to pray, and Bridgett Maher had taught her sons well. Now seemed as good a time as any. His forehead hit the ground in supplication. "God. I gotta find her."

He lay there a moment longer as the dust devil lifted out of sight. He knew it. The prayer was already answered. And he was the answer. Connor groaned. God must have a helluva sense of humor to have sent him to find Izza. Funny guy.

He started out slowly, moving in inches to keep the pain in his gut at bay. Determination drove him. Squinting into the glare of bleached white sand, at last he saw her facedown ahead of him, just beyond a raft of dried, twisted shrubs. With one hand and knee stretched forward, it looked as if she'd collapsed in the middle of a crawl.

Connor moved to her on hands and knees with the speed of an octogenarian. "Izza," he croaked when finally at her side.

She blinked against the glare, her half-open eyes as full of dirt and dust as his.

He tried again. "Izza? You with me?"

"Huh?" Her one scratchy syllable sounded as desiccated as his.

Balancing on one trembling hand and two weak knees, Connor reached for the edge of her shirt and gave it a quick tug while he still had strength. "Come here. Gotta... go."

"Let go... me," she growled.

He nudged her arm, hoping to piss her off if nothing else. Anger would get her moving, but all this chatter came with a high price. A drop of blood trickled over his lip, splattering like a black bug on the hot sand below him. It turned solid the moment it landed, already baked to a crisp.

"I said—"

"Shut up," he muttered hoarsely.

She blew a puff of dust where she lay. "You... shut up."

"Move... your ass... soldier."

It worked. Izza peeled her body off the dirt, groaning all the way. "Hate... you."

"Keep... moving," he rasped. Hate was acceptable if it got her moving enough to save her life. Connor edged his knees forward. The blistered palms of his hands scraped along the scorching trail he was blazing. Inch by desperate inch, he moved.

Like an elderly woman, she shuffled on hands and knees beside him. "Hate... you."

"Shut up."

"You first."

It had to be the stupidest dialogue on the planet, but it served its purpose. Izza moved ahead, first by inches, then by feet. When a stiletto of pain robbed his air, Connor ground to a shuddering halt to let it pass. Breathing shouldn't hurt so badly, but it did. By the time he recovered and could suck in a decent breath again, she was several feet ahead, still cussing, still telling him to shut up, but still creeping forward.

Going was slow when a man's been shot. He ground to a halt, his forehead to the dirt again as he struggled to keep up with her. Just one deep breath would sure feel good.

Another "I hate you" drifted back on the still desert air. That's the one thing he knew for sure about Izza. She was always trying to get away from him. Always mad. Always mean. And she would always hate him. Well, now she'd get what she wanted. He'd be dead soon and out of her life for good.

His arms and legs gave out. With a soft sigh, he sank back to the floor of this unforgiving oven of granite and sand. Chagrin for the tiniest shred of a silver lining offered a measure of comfort. The Lord had answered his prayer. Connor now knew where Izza was.

He weighed the poetic justice to his death. His mother would be sad, but she had six other sons to comfort her. Izza had no one.

"Keep her safe," he whispered to the sky and sand. And then—he let her go.

Eleven

Izza crawled until she could crawl no more. Her strength gave out just as her fingers relayed the change in texture of the desert floor to her sun-stroked brain. Gritty sand had turned to splintered wood. Good enough.

The problem with crawling with your eyes closed is you don't know where you end up once you get there. She didn't care. The welcome of a cool draft pulled her into the dark recesses of wherever she was. Collapsing to the first surface that didn't burn the skin off her face when she touched it, she sucked in a deep breath.

Her nose twitched. Could it be possible? Summoning one last spurt of energy, she climbed back to her hands and knees and followed that smell. Funny how dying of thirst enhanced her sense of survival, and all because of her baby. This child would live if she had anything to say about it.

The instinct to survive pulled Izza into darker shadows and earthier smells, places she wouldn't ordinarily have gone alone. She went there now. What could possibly be worse than what she'd already survived? Not a damn thing. Besides, this new smell promised hope and tomorrow. It promised life.

Pushing rocks and tumbleweeds aside, she found the source. Haste made her careless, but what did she have to lose? With a heartfelt groan of gratitude, Izza lowered her face into a shallow stone pool of water. Her nose grated against the rough edge while she slurped a noisy mouthful and then another. The water tasted metallic but sweet. Felt cool. Refreshing comfort slid over her poor dried tongue and filled the parched recesses of her—

Connor.

His name shot through her mind with startling urgency. He'd been right behind her. Where was he now?

She pushed to her hip and looked around. The place she'd crawled into was half-building, half-cave. People had been here recently. Beer cans and plastic soda bottles littered the floor. Fast food wrappers, tumbleweeds and other garbage, too. Tattered plastic bags of various colors, pieces of paper and cardboard, even what looked like a plastic garbage can lid lay along the edge of the cavern as if the wind had swept them inside. Graffiti she didn't care to decipher scrawled across the walls.

But where was he?

Izza took one last swallow from the tiny pool before she climbed to her unsteady feet. Brushing a hand over her forehead, she encountered an egg-sized bump beneath a layer of dried blood. Someone had gotten a lucky punch in. She'd never seen it coming.

The ceiling was high enough she could stand, but its rounded walls sloped to the floor. This was just what she needed. Her child would survive. With one last glance at the water that had fortified her, she faced the bright door of endless sunshine at the end of the dark tunnel.

Lined with vertical wooden supports stuck into a ceiling of horizontal beams, this cave-like room made no sense, being stuck out here in the middle of a desert like it was. Splinters from the rough timbers pricked her palms as she moved from one vertical support to the next, gathering strength with every step.

Halting at the entrance to this odd habitation, a blistering wave of arid desert air hit her like a wall. Going back out there to find Connor meant death. Her baby deserved to live. Staying here in this odd shelter meant life. Izza took another step and then another. Her baby also deserved a father. The question in her heart remained. Was he good enough? Did he deserve this child?

She took another step. He might.

Walking back was easier. She found him face down in the sand and unconscious. Dropping to her knees, her eyes swept over him hungrily in one long motherly assessment. Her warrior nature still battled her heart. Izza flattened two fingers to his neck. His pulse fluttered at her touch. She hooked her arm through his to wrangle him onto his back.

"Oh, crap." His favorite cuss word sprang off her lips when she saw the damage to that elegant straight nose he used to have. "You poor baby."

For some reason, it was easier to be nice to him now. Izza traced the edge of his cheek. The blood bath his broken nose had produced crackled over his cheek and mouth in one messy black stain. An open gash still glistened raw and bloody across the bridge of his nose, but it was nothing compared to the dark red hole in the side of his abdomen.

"You're shot. Damn it, Connor. You're hurt real bad."

The anguish in her voice surprised Izza. Why should she care? Now was her chance. Walk away. Leave his sorry ass. Let him die, that will teach him. No one would ever know, no one but her.

All the hatred she'd bottled up inside for this man came back for closer scrutiny. Love and hate warred within. Could she do it? Damn straight if it meant her baby's survival. But would she? For one brief moment, she honestly didn't know what to do.

She took his dirty hand and rested her hand inside of his palm. The natural curl of his fingers enfolded hers. And there she was once more remembering the curl of his hard body around her in the middle of the worst place on earth. He'd made her feel safe that night when she needed it most.

"I can't carry you," she told him in no uncertain terms, smoothing those long straight fingers of his over hers again. "You'll have to walk."

He didn't so much as grunt, but she did. She dropped his hand. The decision was made.

"Wake up, soldier. Let's get moving."

No response.

"Connor." She patted his cheek, adding bite to her tone. "Get moving. I found water. If you want some, you'd better wake up, buck up and get up."

Even verbal abuse made no difference. He didn't move, not even a twitch of an eyelid. Determination flashed to life. Izza Ramos was not just any woman, and she sure wouldn't take no for an answer, not now that she'd made up her mind. He was coming with her if he liked it or not.

"Then lay there," she mocked him as she pushed to her feet and latched onto the yoke of his shirt. Fisting the fabric, she created handholds for the long chore ahead of her. "You just lay there, while I pull you all the way home"

Leaning backwards, Izza strained until at last he budged. Connor's body only slid twelve inches or so, but every twelve inches was a foot, and every foot meant they were that much closer to living. Unfortunately, every twelve inches also threatened to put her on her butt.

"You weigh a ton," she snarled at thirty-six inches. Three damn feet and it had taken all of her strength. She growled down to the depths of her soul and found more.

At one hundred and forty-four inches, they were still baking in the sun and her backside was covered in dust. The rest of her, too. Twelve feet felt like a mile. Her hands shook from clenching the fabric of his shirt, and her shoulders ached. His head tilted backwards like some fall down drunk. Connor looked like hell, but she'd checked again. He still had a pulse. As long as he breathed, they were in this together.

"Home," she declared as the process began all over again. And again. And again. Twice her fingers slipped and she fell to her butt, only to scramble to her knees and begin again. "I'm taking your... sorry ass... home… if you like it or not."

At last the scabby rock ledge where she'd found comfort came back into view. Her lip curled at the sight of the squalor it offered. Damn, not even a blade of grass broke the bleak desert front yard. No matter. She hunkered down, dug the heels of her boots into the sand and dragged him inside.

With Connor finally out of the sun, she dropped beside him. "Shit, you're a big guy."

By then, her energy was depleted. She crawled to the only thing worth crawling to, that tiny reservoir in the darkest recesses of the cave. Dropping face first into the cool two-inch depths, she sucked a long draught of the water until she could swallow no more. Again, it coursed over her throat and down to her toes with hope and promise. She might die out here in the desert, but not from lack of water. That single thought buoyed her spirits.

But how to get some of it back to Connor?

Izza improvised. She pulled her shirt off and over her head. It was only then she noticed that each pocket on her pants had been sliced and its contents gone. That meant she had no pocketknife, no blowout kit, no matches, no nothing. She shook the pessimism of that rude revelation away. She was alive, and if she had anything to say about it, Connor would live if only so she could kill him later.

Izza folded her shirt into a hasty square bundle and dunked it into the water. Back at his side, she squeezed it over his face and dribbled water into his half-open mouth. He choked and turned away from the dribbling stream, but she made him endure the torture until at last he swallowed. Cupping his chin, she let the water work the same miracle on him that it had on her.

That simple act of service worked another miracle. A totally involuntary smile tugged the corner of her lips. She felt the damned thing crinkle her cheeks before she put a stop to it, but the good feeling lingered.

Tenderly, she smoothed the wet shirt over his face and wiped the blood off his cheeks. Kneeling at his head, she cleaned his poor nose the best she could. Her gaze shifted to his waist. How had he taken a bullet while wearing a vest? For that matter, where was his vest? Where was hers? His cargo pants pockets were sliced like hers. She could barely recall the shootout, much less what happened afterward. Her hand wandered to the crease on her forehead. It might have been a bullet that had laid her low. There was no way to know.

A low rumbling moan sounded from deep within Connor.

"I'm not a doctor," she told him wisely. "I don't know how to remove bullets. I'm no medic. I'm the gal who puts 'em in guys remember? I don't take 'em out."

Izza weighed her options. Something had to be done. She couldn't let him lie there and bleed to death. "This is probably gonna hurt," she advised as she unbuttoned his shirt. Damn, this was not how she'd prefer to undress this man, not with him half-dead and his life in her hands.

Spreading the shirt opened, she found what she was looking for. Sure enough, he'd been hit just above his right hipbone. She sniffed at the wound for any odor that might indicate a compromised bowel or intestine. Detecting nothing disgustingly rank other than the metallic odor of blood, Izza prodded gently around what she was pretty sure was an entry wound.

"Hang on. I've got to look at your back," she advised while she folded his arm over his chest and pushed against his shoulder to roll him onto his side.

"Looks like that stupid Irish luck is still with you, Boston," she murmured when she detected the corresponding exit wound. "There's no bullet to dig out of you."

She eased him back to the ground. "The good news is I'm here. I know how to take care of a hole like this one." She patted his limp arm as if he were awake and listening. "The bad news is—I'm here and all you've got. I've got no blowout kit, no sterile gauze, and no antibiotics. Neither do you unless you're keeping 'em in your back pocket cuz that's all you got left. They cut everything else. Left us nothing. You're in for a rough haul."

Just then, the baby in her belly decided to practice its kickboxing routine. A tiny knee or elbow tracked across her abdomen. Izza lifted her shirt, latched onto Connor's big hand and placed his palm against her bare stomach where his child lived.

"But you want to know the really, really good news?" she asked with a twinge of make-me, I-dare-you. "Even if you die right here and now, you've already given me the best part of you."

She dropped his hand to the dirt.

"Shall we get started, tough guy?"

Connor peeled his eyelids open. Stars twinkled overhead. It had to be night. Oh, wait. No. It was still too hot. Dark or not, it couldn't be night. Those weren't stars. They were holes in a—what? Wood ceiling? Rock ceiling? The sky?

Hell. He didn't know, and he didn't care. He wiggled his toes. His boots and socks were missing. Even that didn't worry him. He was too tired to care and thirsty, a dying kind of thirsty.

"I still hate you," a familiar voice declared from the shadows.

Oh, great. She was here, wherever here was.

"How—"

"Cuz I dragged your sorry dead ass, that's how," Izza hissed from close by. "We're in some kind of a mine. Now shut up."

Connor wanted to sit. He willed himself to do it. Not one muscle responded.

"Where—?"

Again she cut him off, her voice as nasty and mean as always. "How the hell do I know where we are? We're in the middle of the freaking desert, that's where." She gave him a shove that didn't move either of them. Izza was as weak as he was. That was kind of good to know. At least they were on semi-equal ground. One more thought filtered through the dust storm in his brain. "Water?"

This time she didn't cut him off. For some unknown reason, Izza dripped the sweetest moisture he'd ever tasted between his parchment dry lips. He let it trickle over his tongue until it welled up at the back of his stuck dry throat. Only when he had enough for one decent swallow did he let it slip down into his stomach. He guessed right. It was water. He was sure of it. She wouldn't poison him, would she? Another squishing sound and she dripped more of it over his lips and into his mouth. Not enough to gulp. Just enough to live. Maybe.

Her cool hand rested for a split second against his cheek and forehead. It felt good, but it was really odd. She dripped another steady trickle of water into his open mouth. Ahh. Heaven. Who knew a few drops of water could feel so good?

"You've been shot," she murmured kindly in a strange personality shift. "But if you're strong enough, you'll pull through."

Gentle fingers traced the line of his jaw. Izza wiped a wet cloth over his face, pausing at his eyes to clear the grit and sand gently away. Connor lay very still lest he open his big mouth or do anything else that might make her stop. She dabbed the cloth around his nose. When the gentle administration ended, he heard water sloshing and what sounded like a rag being rung out. Then more sloshing. Izza had found water. They were going to live.

"Open," she said softly.

He obeyed, parting his lips as another lukewarm stream coursed over his tongue. Connor swallowed, not wanting the moment to end but hoping she hadn't just given him a drink off the same rag she'd washed his bloody face with. The dumb things a dying man thinks of.

"You're still bleeding, but I've packed both wounds. Are you strong enough, Boston?"

That word, her nickname for him from a tender moment overcome by tragedy, almost sounded sweet again. But God, he hoped he was strong enough to live. Maybe strong enough to survive Izza.

"I'm—"

She stopped his answer with a fingertip to his lips. "Shhhhh. Rest now. Talk later."

He had no choice but to obey. A swirl of blackness reached up from the treacherous floor and swallowed him alive. Connor went willingly, just another leaf caught up in a very dark and dry wind.

Twelve

What Alex Stewart didn't know wouldn't hurt him.

He owned The TEAM. His covert consultant business included two offices, one in Alexandria, Virginia, and one in Seattle, Washington. He employed forty agents in all, twenty at each location. But Mark was the lead agent in charge of a miserable operation in Utah, and Alex was still in the air. Besides, he trusted Mark, didn't he?

Mark was about to find out. He phoned The TEAM's over-qualified woman in charge of everything—Mother.

"I need you to track Miguel Ramirez for me," he ordered.

"Already doing that. Alex has Ember and me following Ramirez and his wife's GPS signals. The downside of owning cell phones, huh?"

"Where are they?"

"Alejandra is going south through Arizona at the moment, but Miguel Ramirez is still in Salt Lake City. Hold on a second. I can tell you exactly where he is."

Mark listened patiently as Mother worked her usual miracle from the East Coast.

"He is at a bar on the west side of town, the Rio Palms."

"Address?"

Mother provided the address, but by then, Mark had another idea. There was a better way to deal with the man who thought he could come to Utah and kill as he pleased.

Ramirez had spread nothing but death and mayhem since he'd created the Sonoran Cartel. It was time to return the favor. Let him stay in Utah and think he was untouchable. Mark planned to show him otherwise.

"Thanks, Mother," he said as he prepared to hang up.

"There's something else."

"What?" Mark held his breath.

"I found the missing migrant workers you were worried about." Her tone held no hint of good news. "Remember when Governor Baxter closed the canyon after Connor shot the cartel guard? Well, something happened just before the Utah National Guard was in place. Three big rigs with horse trailers pulled out of the canyon, all three headed south on I-15. I contacted the Utah Highway Patrol to intercept, but by then, the rigs were long gone. When UHP caught up, one had already turned east at Fillmore."

Mark cringed, dreading what might come out of Mother's mouth next. "What's in Fillmore?"

"Eleven bodies," she said somberly. "He murdered the men who harvested the crop, Mark. Ramirez had his own men killed."

"Not Connor or Izza though," he reaffirmed, letting out the breath he'd been holding. They couldn't have been in that trailer. No way. But odd things happened when psychotic killers ran loose. He needed to hear the words.

"Course not," Mother said. "I'd have told you if we'd found them by now."

"How about the other two trailers?" he asked.

"They were full of marijuana, a couple cases of small arms, and ammunition. UHP did a great job locating them. No one was hurt."

"Still no sign of Connor or Izza?" he asked just to confirm what he already knew.

"Not yet. We're not going to find them though, are we?" Her usual perky voice was subdued. "Look how many people get kidnapped every year. Do you know how many of them are recovered alive? It was nine months before they found Elizabeth Smart, and by then—"

"Knock it off, Mother. We will find them."

"Man, I hope you're right."

"I am right. Thanks. Talk with you soon." Mark ended the cell phone call, but then he turned to the team members in his hotel room. They'd gone to their rooms earlier to clean up and shower, but now Rory, Cassidy and Brigham waited on his orders like he was still in charge. Like he knew what he was doing. Like they'd follow him into hell and back.

Covert operations were all about taking risks. He paused on the verge of an exceptionally large one. The dividends could go either way. Payoff would mean saving Connor and Izza's lives, but failure could mean certain death. Mark refused to draw anyone into the next step of his plan unless they made the decision for themselves.

"I'm going to Mexico," he said quietly.

Rory bolted to his feet. "Not without me, you're not."

Cassidy stood. Brigham, too.

"When?" she asked.

"As soon as I can get a flight out of here," Mark answered truthfully. "We can't take any weapons with us, but they're easy to find once we're there. I know a couple guys."

"Count me in," she said.

Monsters visited Connor as he slept. Hot fiery monsters with sharp licking tongues that ripped the skin off his body wherever they slithered against his skin. They lapped at the hole in his stomach when they got close, sucking at his intestines and the blood that still ran out of him like a red hot river. But it was his to keep, not theirs to take. They had to go.

He kept his feet positioned between them and him, kicking their heads off when they got too close. Protecting his gut became more important than water, but it took every last shred of strength.

Eventually, there were too many monsters to fight off. He fell backwards, down into a wall of flaming rock that hurt worse than the monsters' tongues. Just when all hope dried up, just when he knew for sure he couldn't hold on another second, a glance of cool, refreshing snow flitted across his face like a teasing kiss. And then another.

The prettiest angel lifted his head onto her lap and bathed his face and neck in snow. The cooling splash of frosty cold soothed him down to his core. Heaven. He was finally dead and gone to heaven. He hoped. But too quickly the cold turned into shivers that rattled him. The lovely angel curled around him with his head cradled into her warm body.

The monsters faded. So did Connor.

When he lifted out of the fog again, someone had washed his face. It couldn't have been Izza. Still, the grit and dirt were gone from his eyes, nose, and mouth. He flexed his fingers. Both hands were intact. His shirt was missing and his belt was gone. No matter. He could live without those things. With an effort, he pulled himself into a semi-sitting position until a searing pain in his side laid him flat. He groaned on his way to the ground.

"What are you bellyaching about?" Izza's sharp voice jolted him, but he couldn't speak. Not yet. The ground still moved.

She came closer and sat cross-legged next to him. Connor didn't open his eyes, too busy concentrating on the plans his stomach had for him. It didn't matter. She was going to say what she was going to say, and it would all be mean. She leaned closer until he could feel her breath on his shoulder. Any closer and he could have kissed her if he had a death wish. He turned his face away.

Breathe in. Breathe out. Hold it together. It will pass.

"So, I went through your wallet."

Good. Fine. Whatever. Until now he didn't know he still had a wallet.

"Why do you have this?"

"What?" Bile crept up the back of his throat with the effort of just that one word. He swallowed it back down. *Why is she bugging me?*

"This. Look at it."

He could feel something close to his face. He squinted into the dark. She held something round just inches above his eyes, something that looked like—

Crap. She'd found the Iraqi coin he'd kept in his wallet all these months. Now he was really sick. Damn sick.

"So why do you have it?"

"I... I...."

"Knock off the poor me routine. You're a man, for hell's sake. Get up and start acting like one instead of some worthless piece of...." For once, Izza couldn't finish her insult. She was too mad.

He didn't say a word. She didn't move away. She really should.

"I just want to know why you kept it. You do know what it is, don't you?"

"Yeah."

"Then say it. What is it?" She spit on him with her angry words.

"A dinar." There. He said it. The thing she held was an Iraqi coin called a dinar, but she didn't leave. That creeping sensation tickled again at the back of his mouth. He cringed. She really should move farther—

"Yeah, it's a dinar all right, but it's not just any dinar, is it, Maher? Say it. Go on. Say it. Tell me what it is."

"You need to move."

"Yeah, sure. Figures you'd wimp out. You're nothing but chicken shit, that's what you are. You can't even face me like a man and—"

That did it. He rolled away from her and threw up. Darkness swelled in the stifling cave that was already trying to suffocate him, and now he'd made it worse. He heaved, but not much came up from his gut. Izza shrieked. It didn't get much better than this, a nut job screaming in his ear while he was sick as a dog. *Crap.*

At last the spasms ceased. By then, he was spent and couldn't spit the vile taste out of his mouth. A drink of water would have been nice, but he knew better than to ask.

And still she shrieked. "You think I've got nothing better to do than clean up after you? I'm sick of it. Sick to death. Do you hear me?"

His stomach felt better, but his ears sure hurt. She was spitting nails kind of mad, and when she got this mad, her normally all American, mean girl voice picked up a decidedly Hispanic accent. "This is bullshit, Boston. I drag you all the way in here, I save your life, and you do this to me? Bullshit. That's all you're good for."

Izza scraped up the mess beside him, and then she was gone. It was quiet until he heard her coughing just beyond the entrance to the cave. Hmm. Maybe she was as sick as he was? He knew better than to ask that, too. He felt bad for her. Throwing up was not fun for anyone involved. But then she came back.

"Here." She knelt beside him and squeezed a trickle of water between his lips. Even her one word command sounded impatient, like she didn't want to help him anymore than she had to. It seemed a fair trade. He didn't want to be beholding to her either.

"Sorry."

"Shut up. You're nothing but a pig."

Yep. Still mad. Connor tried to at least lean up on one elbow so he could see her. Lying flat on his back felt too much like he was in the middle of the Spanish Inquisition.

"It's your challenge coin. From Iraq." He waited. More accusations would surely follow.

"Yeah." Her voice went down a couple decibels. "It's my challenge coin all right. I recognized it because of the hole dead center in the palm trees on that dinar."

"You smoked the palms that day. Two coins. Remember?"

"Yeah. I did."

He detected a note of pride in her answer. That was short lived.

"So why do you have this one?"

A groan escaped from the back of Connor's throat. He was not up to true confessions.

"What made you think you could walk off with something that belonged to me?" Man, she just wouldn't let it go. "Where's the other one?"

"I don't know. You left them both behind." He eased his weary body flat to the ground again, already losing the battle.

"Did not. You stole this one. That's what happened."

"Night raid. We had to leave quickly, but I—"

"You what?" Even without name-calling, every word out of her mouth was razor sharp.

"I was going to give it back to you. Honest. I was."

"Then why didn't you? You've had it for what, six months now?"

He hesitated. Nothing he could say would ever make it better. Not if he begged or pleaded, cried or repented for a million years could he change what had happened in Iraq over six months ago. And it had nothing to do with the coin.

"You know why," he whispered finally.

Atonement never came easy, and apparently, forgiveness either. Her lip quivered. All this foolish banter had only dredged up more of what neither of them could change.

"I hate you," she said sadly.

At so many levels, he longed to hold this tough-as-nails woman, to feel her in his arms just one more time. Maybe if he could hug her, all this bitter hostility would fade away, and he could make things right. His gut hurt and his heart hurt worse. The grief in her voice wrenched him like never before.

For the gazillionth time he said the same old words, "I'm sorry, Izza. Honest. I am."

He wasn't surprised when she launched herself at him, pummeling his chest and arms with hard punches and jabs. At least she didn't hit his stomach or his broken nose. That was small consolation.

He didn't resist, not even one iota, just lay there like the corpse he wished he was and took it. She could never hurt him as much as he'd hurt her. Besides. She was crying, a rare event for Izza.

But then, so was he.

Thirteen

I hate him so much!

Sitting at the door to their decrepit shelter, Izza fingered the silver dinar and let the tears fall. In caring for Connor's wounds, she'd come across his wallet in his back pocket, the only one not slashed and emptied. Of course, she snooped. That would teach her. Expecting to find flavored condoms and two-by-threes of porn stars, instead, she'd found Jamie. And she'd been crying ever since.

How damned stupid was she to rescue a man like Connor? Life had never been fair. It seemed excruciatingly unfair now. A life for a life? She brushed the stream of tears off her cheeks, mad at herself more than anyone else. Once again, she'd drawn the short straw and ended up the loser, lost the brother she adored and for who? A spineless man from Boston? Worst trade ever.

She rubbed the end of her very sore nose and stared in anger at the world. Her world. And his. Sunset stretched across the beautiful desert, tinted pink with rosy hues of the evening. It would have been pretty if the gnawing feeling in her stomach would go away. She'd walked near and far in search of anything edible. Nothing showed.

In the process, she'd collected useful trash because her baby needed to live no matter what, damn it. The bottom of an old-fashioned, broken glass soda bottle turned into her fire-starter, which would work really good if she ever came across an animal that would hold still long enough for her to kill it. She built a small campfire just to prove she could do it, but her stomach growled. She'd never hunted animals before. Never needed to. Izza didn't even know how to start, not without some kind of gun or knife.

So she kept on walking and collecting. How an old battered tin coffee pot ended up in the desert she didn't know, but she kept it. Her daily wanderings took her back to the place where she and Connor had been dumped. She hadn't seen them before, but lying there in the dirt were two canteens, both full of water. Had the cartel meant for her and Connor to survive? It seemed a ridiculous notion. She kept them anyway.

But why kidnap two enemy combatants in the middle of an ambush in the first place? Why not kill everyone? That was the whole concept behind surprise attacks. What did that bastard, Ramirez, have up his sleeve that he needed hostages to barter with?

If she'd still been in Iraq, she'd have been tortured or murdered by now, her body mutilated and displayed off some bridge to prove the decadence of Western society. The surety of that truth shivered up her spine despite the desert heat. She brushed her hands up and down her biceps to ward it off. One thing seemed sure: the cartel would be back. She needed to be better prepared. To fight. To kill.

And where on earth was she? Could be Utah or Nevada. Izza honestly didn't know. Hell, this god-forsaken desert could be the middle of Mexico, but she suspected it wasn't. If the cartel wanted them alive for whatever reason, they'd keep them close to the action, wouldn't they? That's what she'd have done with hostages – if they'd lived.

Connor coughed quietly from the mineshaft. The irony poked at her. Only a couple days earlier, she'd been the one sick to her stomach while Roy stood faithfully by her side to wipe her nose and mouth. Yes, she'd been mad, but she'd also been pretty disgusting, too. Yet he'd stayed. So why couldn't she cut Connor any slack for the same misfortune? Simple. Everything wrong with her life started that day six months ago. With him.

Izza rubbed the Iraqi dinar between her index finger and thumb. Jamie was there the day she'd made her record breaking shot. He and Connor were jaw jacking over who was the better long shot until she showed up. Jamie never could resist a dare. His face lit up when he saw her. Connor's too, only his handsome face glowed like he was more than just happy to see her.

Man, she had to give it to him. The guy did have some seriously blue eyes. Pacific blue, as if he'd come from an underwater world instead of Boston, Mass. His dark blond hair had lightened in the sun. The sight of him always took her breath and just as easily warmed her from the inside out. They had a connection from the get go, like he was made to command and she was made to follow.

Yeah, right. Izza growled at that insane notion her mind just came up with. She'd fought her feminine nature for years. Being a woman in a man's world only bought trouble. She'd go where she damned well pleased.

But that day....

She shook the memory off. Everything ended abruptly. There was a firefight. They had to gear up and leave in a hurry. Like most firefights, it started fast but didn't last long, only long enough to change her life forever. She glanced over her shoulder to the injured man in the shadows behind her. Why was Connor the one who got to live?

"You want to tell me why I'm in Utah and you're not?" Alex barked.

"Surveillance," Mark barked back. By the time Alex's flight landed at SLC International, Mark and his team were deep in the heart of Sonora. Damn all cell phones with their GPS locators.

"Why?"

"Because it's time Ramirez got a taste of his own medicine. Are you calling to assist me or not?" Mark cranked up his own obnoxious meter in response. "How's Roy?"

"In Intensive Care."

"But he's doing good?" Mark needed to hear the words. When he and his team flew out of Salt Lake City, Roy was barely out of surgery and still in critical condition. He'd been shot twice, once in his upper thigh, once in his chest.

"He'll live," Alex muttered. "Might need a cane. We'll see."

"Which is why we're here. Ramirez has Izza and Connor, maybe not in Mexico, but he knows where they are. I'm going after him, Boss. I'm getting our people back if it's the last thing I do."

"No shit." Sarcasm. One of Alex's ready tools. "Not only are you out of line, Junior Agent, but you're way past the scope of my contract with Tom."

Mark ignored the warning implied when Alex reverted to using titles instead of his agent's names. "Need you to brush Ramirez to me, Boss. Stir the water. Bait him with the intel me and my team intend to send you. Light him up. Make him need to come home."

"And I need you to get your ass Stateside where it belongs." The gloves were off. Alex didn't brook mutiny.

"And I need to finish the mission you gave Roy, Connor, and Izza once and for all!" Mark shot back. "Ramirez is running this show, Boss. Not Baxter. Not you. And sure as hell not the DEA. Let's bring the point home to the damned boss of the SC for a change. We're in his country now. His hometown. And later today, I'll be inside his damned quiet hacienda planting Tattle Tales. Let him understand we can hurt him too. That we can. That I will."

A moment of silence stretched between Salt Lake City and Hermosillo, Sonora. At last Alex grumbled, "Anything else?"

Mark took the snide hit from his OCD boss on the chin. Alex hadn't continued to berate him for outright disobeying a direct order. That alone felt a lot like winning. He pushed the limit. "I'm not walking away from this. Neither is my team. It's the only way I can get Connor and Izza back and you know it. I'd like to think you'll fly cover when I decide to do something stupid and stick my neck out."

Alex didn't miss a beat. "When haven't I?"

Instant relief eased over Mark's shoulder. He went for broke. "While you're at it, I need you to up the balance in my expense account. I'm gonna need cash to operate while I'm here. Black marketeers don't take credit."

"Already done."

"And I need you to put Cassidy Dancer and Brigham Coltrane on your payroll. They're busting their ass down here."

"Tell me something I don't know, Mark. That's what I'm paying you for."

"I will get Connor and Izza back," Mark promised.

Alex sighed. "Like I said, tell me something I don't know."

Cool air flooded the place where Connor lay. He'd lost track of time. It was pleasantly quiet. Izza hadn't been around for what seemed like hours now. For all he knew, she'd walked away and left him. He wouldn't blame her. In a way, it would make things a lot easier. That way he could die in peace.

But not yet. He elbowed himself off the ground. This time his stomach and head allowed him to stay upright. The holes in his side hurt plenty, but at least now they were clean. But there was no Izza in sight. That was good and that was bad.

Izza Ramos. The eternal paradox in his life. One minute she'd do something kind. The next minute she'd half beat him to death. He never knew which side of her would show up.

Thankfully, Cassidy hadn't been with him and Roy when they were ambushed. Had he really seen Morgan die? Without a doubt, Mark would've raced to their rescue. Was he and the others caught in the crossfire as well? Was Cassidy okay? What happened to Roy?

Connor closed his eyes at the awful scenes that emerged from his mind, not knowing which were real or not. The somber thought lingered. He was pretty sure Morgan had been killed. Maybe Roy, too.

The worst part of war was always the not knowing. A soldier could read reports of battles and catch up on all the news afterwards, but the not knowing what was going down while it happened was every soldier's worst nightmare. Connor hated suspense. Even home in America, so much could happen in the blink of an eye. And the next time you saw someone might be the last time. He hoped Roy and the others were safe. Especially Cassidy.

Her brown eyes came to mind, teasing him. Her short blond hair said as much about her personality as the rest of her. Cassidy had potential. He figured her for an athlete who either biked or hiked, maybe skied. Mentally he calculated the logistics and cost of a Christmas vacation to one of the ski resorts in Utah or Colorado. Maybe Cassidy would join him. Who knows? She'd be a lot of fun if he got the opportunity. And Connor was all about opportunity.

His stomach growled. With a few grunts and groans, he managed to get to his knees. And then to his bare feet. He braced one hand against the wall for balance and looked around for his shirt. Finding it hung up on a piece of wood stuck between two upright timbers, he reached a hand up to pull it down. Examining the garment proved what he already knew. It had two bullet holes in it. So did he. But it didn't look as bloody as he remembered. Had Izza washed it? She must have. There was hardly any blood left on the fabric.

He pulled it over his shoulders and prepared to greet the world. Stepping into the bright sun for the first time in days, he immediately covered his eyes with the back of one hand. It was blinding hot, and nothing but sagebrush and sand as far as he could see. A water bottle rested next to a squared off chunk of granite.

So this is where she goes when she runs away from me. Hmmm.

Izza was one tough gal, especially if she'd dragged him all the way in here like she said. He vaguely recalled her taunting him, but it could've been another dream.

Too weak to stand on the hot ground, he shuffled back inside where it was cooler. He'd actually been laying on a combination of old shirts, torn jeans, and a ratty vinyl jacket. It was an awful mattress, but it had kept him off the dirt while he was unconscious. That much was good.

Three old glass soda bottles lined the wall beside a dented tin coffee pot. He looked closer. The bottles were filled with—water? Hmmm. That was odd. So Izza had found water out here in the middle of nowhere? Leave it to her. She did have a knack for survival.

Connor sat on a lump of granite beside the slanted wall. Bumpy and hard, it made a sufficient chair. *A sufficient sufficiency to suffice the insufficiency,* as his mother would say. He smiled. Bridgette Maher, the widowed mother of seven sons who idolized her, thought she walked on water, and would do anything humanly possible to make her happy. Thinking of his mom brought a bright spot to this very dark place.

"You're up." Izza stood at the mouth of the cave, her hands on her hips. Hostility radiated off her like the heat waves off the desert behind her. She could glow in the dark with all that stored up negative energy she possessed.

"Yeah, I'm actually feeling—"

"It's going to rain," she declared. Her weather prediction cut him short. Okay, so she didn't care how he felt. No big deal. He should be used to that by now.

"Okay. It's going to rain."

"That means it's going to get cold, dumb ass. When it rains in the desert, it gets cold. You ever think about that? How the hell are we supposed to keep warm with nothing but rocks around us?"

He shrugged, not going to offer what naturally came to his mind. She'd shoot down the suggestion of snuggling with him pretty damned fast. "Not much I can do about the weather."

She glared at him, still more shadow than not, the bright light behind her providing only a dark silhouette of a woman with a nasty attitude. Even with that limited view he saw the sharp jut of her stubborn chin. Was there ever a day she was NOT mad at the world?

"Thanks for taking care of me."

"What was I supposed to do, let you die?" The girl just could not say anything without filling it with venom.

"Yeah. You could've walked away and saved yourself. You could've left me."

"I guess that proves I'm not anything like you, doesn't it?"

He sighed. Talking with Izza was the same as playing with a baby alligator. It might look cute, but it always got a man hurt.

"Thanks for the water." He kept trying. Whether she had wanted to or not, she'd been kind to him. She turned away, still at the mouth of the cave and mostly silhouette.

He saw it then. *What? No way. It can't be.*

"Izza?"

She faced him again. "Spit it out. What do you want now?"

"Are you...?"

Even with the sun behind her, her razor sharp glare dared him to speak one more word. She already knew what he was going to ask. He almost didn't, but he had to know. "Are you… Are you pregnant?"

She whirled on her heel and left. This time he followed, slowly making his way back to the mouth of the cave. The minute she saw him, she faced the opposite direction. Connor braced himself against the timber at the doorway and studied her. There were so many facets to this woman, all of them sharp and pointy.

"Well? Are you?"

"Butt out, Boston. It's none of your business."

Ah. So I'm right.

"How far along?" He probed for details.

"I'm not going to tell you again. Butt the hell out of my business." She continued with her blank stare routine, but he was getting to her. He could tell. There was so much rage in that tiny body and most of it close to the surface. It was just a matter of knowing which buttons to push.

"Six and a half months," he said softly.

She bit her lip, nothing more to say, her eyes staring off into the bleached blue sky and pretending he was invisible.

"I think about that night, you know."

That did it. In a split second, she was off her stone chair and in his face with blood in her eye. If looks could kill, he'd be dead, embalmed, and buried. Or on-the-spot cremated.

"Will you shut the hell up? Why don't you go back into your damned cave and puke your guts up like before? That's all you're good for." She returned to her rock, her knees pulled tight to her chest and her arms wrapped around them like a human fortress of solitude.

He couldn't help but smile. Izza was so sure she didn't need anybody. That's why she was tough. And mean. Because deep down—she wasn't. And despite all the nasty anger directed at him, there was more to the story.

Connor leaned against the cave opening, still watching and hoping. "They were lobbing RPGs at us all night long, remember? I thought they'd never stop."

She stared, nothing to say.

"It was a tough day. We lost Huffaker and Carter. The medics were out of their minds with all the evacs and injured. Choppers kept setting down and lifting off. I'm surprised none of them got shot down."

Her chin jutted a little too far. Want to or not, she was thinking. Most of that day he didn't want to remember, but some of it—he did.

"They thought we'd already caught a chopper out and were back at camp. They left us." His voice low and steady, he watched the reaction shift over her face. Mean girl Izza looked very small and fragile. Her fingers clenched her arms. She breathed hard. A tear dripped off her nose. One tear. There wouldn't be another. That was one of her rules, part of her code. Never cry. It was a stupid rule, and when she broke it, she turned on everyone as if it was their fault she'd shown weakness. That's why she'd hit him before. He'd made her cry.

"There was only the two of us when the thunder started. I was scared," Connor admitted honestly.

"You would be." She wiped her face with one quick stroke of her palm, the tear already ancient history. "Wuss."

"Yeah," he agreed. Denial didn't make fear go away. It only compressed it until something as tiny as a single teardrop blew the concealed ammo dump of pain and anger skyward. "Guess I'm the kind of guy who would be scared. We had no way to call for help, air support or backup. Cut off from our squad all night long. Insurgents were camped not a stone's throw away and dying to torture any American soldier they could get their hands on. Yeah. I'm not ashamed. I was damned scared."

She wouldn't respond, but she didn't need to. Connor knew for a fact she'd been scared that night too, scared enough to seek him out in a way he'd never expected. Only dreamed of.

"Do you ever think about that night?"

"No!" Her answer came too fast and too definite. Of course she did, especially if....

"Is it a boy or a girl? Do you know yet?"

She didn't answer.

"It's mine, isn't it?" The words unspoken were just words, but the minute he heard his question out loud, his heart gave a funny little lurch. *It's yours, Connor. Izza's pregnant with your baby. Your son or daughter. You're going to be a father.*

He got it now. She'd never meant for him to know about the baby. He gulped. As quickly as he was surprised by this unexpected news, he was sad. They should be celebrating the prospect of a new life that they'd created together, not hating each other.

"Why did you keep it if you hate me so much?" One thing Connor knew to his soul. Life began at conception. His mother drilled that truth into all of her boys. *If you want to dance,* she declared, *you better know up front that you're going to pay for the music.* And he agreed. So did Izza, which is why he'd baited her with such a mean question.

It worked. Like an angry mother bear, she charged him with murder in her eye and stuck her finger so deep into his chest that he had to catch his balance not to fall over.

"What the hell kind of question is that, Maher? Are you asking me why I didn't get rid of this baby? Why I kept her? Is that what you're asking, dumb ass?"

He smiled again. So much information in just a few seconds of angry ranting. He was the father of a baby girl, and Izza planned to keep her. She wanted the baby, but she'd also planned on raising it all by herself. She loved his daughter enough to protect her from the man Izza thought might hurt the baby. Him. Connor. That wrongful assessment hurt his heart. How could Izza ever think such an ugly thought of him? She of all people should know him better.

"Izza—" He should've known she'd turn on him. Ramming him with the point of her shoulder, she knocked him off balance. Already unsteady on his feet, it didn't take much.

"You're a jerk, you know that, Maher? Did you think I'd get an abortion? Is that what you want? Would that make your life easier? Then you could just walk away like you did last time! Isn't that what the whole damned world should do, make your life easier?"

"I didn't walk—"

She shoved him. Hard. With a thud, the back of his head met the stone outcropping just inside the cave entrance. Stars swirled, and down he went, a veritable ton of free-falling bricks. He grabbed for anything to stop his descent, but ended with an armful of Izza. They toppled over together, his back to the floor, her chest to his chest.

For a fraction of a second, they were locked in each other's arms with the breath knocked out of them. Like the stupidly hopeful man he was, he cupped the back of her hard head, wanting to cradle instead of fight her. Her heart pounded against his the way it had that night in Iraq. Tears filled his eyes, but not from the pain in his head or gut.

"Izza. Please," he whispered.

She pulled away, but he held on tight, hoping for God knew what. If only she would hear him out... If only she would give him a chance to explain....

Izza hesitated.

God, please. Give me the words to get through to her.

Connor no more than thought the prayer when she pushed away. "God, I hate you," she muttered as she rolled to her feet and left.

He closed his eyes and stayed where he'd fallen. One of them definitely had to learn to pray better.

Fourteen

"Ramirez has been busy." Alex stepped onto his veranda to answer the phone call from the governor. The television reporter had just announced that Governor Baxter had declared a state of emergency in Utah due to the wildfires burning from Weber Canyon, just north of Salt Lake City, all the way to Mount Nebo in the south. More flames glowered on Ensign Peak to the east of Salt Lake City. It seemed all Utah was on fire tonight.

"Which is why I'm calling you," Tom Baxter said.

"Do you know where he is?"

"DEA and FBI have him under surveillance, but he's not the one setting these fires."

"Of course not. He has hired help for that."

"Can you find the men who are?"

Alex didn't hesitate. "Yes. I'm on my way to meet him right now."

"Who? Ramirez?" Tom asked in disbelief.

Alex fingered the photos Mark had provided. "He doesn't know it yet, but yes. We have things to discuss. He needs to understand the rules have changed."

"Do you need assistance? I'd be glad to send a couple of Utah's finest for backup."

"I'd prefer them to DEA or FBI," Alex remarked drily, "but not now. You'll know when I'm ready. I'll have Mother contact you."

Tom chuckled. "She is a pistol, isn't she?"

Alex didn't respond to that question. Pistol was not one of the words he'd use to describe his nosey techie. At the moment, he and she were on amicable terms, but only because he'd learned to exercise restraint instead of biting her head off when she overstepped her authority. Still, the woman could make the Pope swear.

"I'll be in touch." Alex slipped his SIG Sauer P290 inside his underarm holster as he ended the call. Less than six inches in length, the pistol carried six .9mm rounds in the magazine, plenty enough for the conversation he had in mind. Two extra magazines in his pocket might come in handy if the discussion lagged, but he preferred to rely on the laser sight. It was funny how a little speck of neon red dancing across a man's chest could change a belligerent mind. Lifting his backpack to one shoulder, he phoned Mother on his way to ground level.

"You're still tracking Ramirez for me, aren't you?"

"Yes, Boss. He's dining at a little joint called the Pink Iguana not far from your hotel."

"Anyone with him?"

"Some dude dressed up like a biker."

"Send me coordinates?" he asked instead of ordering. Somehow, that little change in his approach worked wonders with his employees. Alex smirked to himself. Old dogs could learn new tricks.

"On their way to you now," she answered.

"One more thing. Are you and Ember tracking the fires here in Utah?"

"Yes. Ember's down loading the latest satellite imagery right now. She'll have that info for you shortly."

"Thanks, Mother," he replied sincerely. Gratitude was another skill set he'd recently acquired. Sometimes it worked.

By the time Alex stepped out into the street, he was surprised how close the Pink Iguana was to his hotel. Two blocks south, one east. Either Ramirez wanted to enjoy the view of the flaming mayhem he'd created, or he was keeping track of someone himself.

Hmmm. That possibility gave Alex pause. Could Ramirez be watching the owner and CEO of the very team called in to put the drug lord out of business? Were two watchers watching each other? How bizarre.

He knew he had a tail the minute he set foot on the pavement. Easy to spot, the man stood out like a sore thumb, an unmistakable wolf among the flock. Mother called it right. Another bruiser type, leather vest over a muscle shirt and tattoos. The man was all biker, but definitely not trained at undercover surveillance.

Lowering his head, Alex walked west. Biker Boy followed. Storefronts lined the sidewalk. Alex was close to the light rail transfer station. With all the people coming and going, it was as good a place as any to play ditch the dummy.

A group of excited, young people raced around Alex on their way to board the just arrived train. One young man bumped him hard, knocking his backpack strap off his shoulder.

"Hey. I'm sorry, Mister. Did I hurt you?"

"Nah. I'm fine," Alex replied. "No troubles."

"Here. Let me get that for you." The young man grabbed his pack up from the ground and handed it to Alex with a big smile. Off he ran to catch up with his friends.

Alex followed the youngsters onto the train, turned left at the door and walked to the opposite end of the car. He intended for Biker Boy to see him board, so Alex went upstairs to the second level, doubled back and came down the stairs right behind the guy. He'd barely boarded and was still looking for him, just headed in the opposite direction.

Alex pulled his tweed jacket and Irish flat cap from his bag, put them on and exited the still boarding train, this time joining ranks with a young mother, a doublewide stroller, and her two little boys. She had too much gear and one too many little ones to move quickly.

"Hey, look, Mama. That man's going to the zoo with us!" Her precocious, oldest son pointed at Alex. She smiled, her arms full of her other wiggling son.

"Can I help you with that stroller, ma'am?" Alex offered.

"Thank you," she said. "I'm afraid hauling two boys means hauling twice as much stuff."

He helped her stow a diaper bag on the bottom of the stroller, along with a couple kid-sized blankets and another bag full of treats and water bottles. Before long, the curly-haired adventurer in her arms was safely belted into the stroller. As Alex secured the second little guy into the seat behind his baby brother, he noticed Biker Boy had hurried off the train right behind him. The man was so close Alex could've reached out and smacked his back in friendship if he'd been so inclined. He wasn't. Biker Boy looked worried and mad, a good combination.

The young woman didn't look old enough to have two children already. "That was very kind of you to stop and help us. Thank you again."

"No trouble at all, ma'am. Have fun at the zoo." He dipped the brim of his cap to her in a friendly salute.

"Oh, no. We're not going to the zoo." She beamed. "We're just visiting my mother up in the Avenues. I hope we get there before the rain hits."

"Have a good night." Alex winked at the boys and walked away, while Biker Boy headed safely in the opposite direction. No more tail. Alex proceeded to the Pink Iguana. He called Mother again. "I'm late. Is Ramirez still there?"

"They just ordered after dinner cocktails."

"I got side-tracked."

"I saw that."

"You've got eyes on me, too?"

"Sure. Traffic cams are wonderful. I didn't know why you were taking the train 'til I saw you had a tail."

"Yeah. Lost him."

"It's too bad I can't just highlight creeps like that with my mouse and hit control-alt-delete, huh?" Mother was feeling a little better tonight. "Then I could really help you."

"You help me plenty, Mother," he praised her again, wondering what the hell control-alt-delete meant. Acronyms he understood. Techie talk? Never.

Food. He had to have food. Connor awakened where he'd fallen, close to the cave entrance and not sure how long he'd lain there. Hunger overrode any need for trivial information.

"Ouch!" He touched the newest knot on the back of his head. Damn. Something had to change soon or he wouldn't survive rescue by Izza. He wasn't up to any more battery, and she was too fired up all the time. Food would help them both. Of course, Izza wasn't inside the cave. She was probably sitting out on her boulder again, planning ways to make him suffer.

Easing into a sitting position, he looked for his socks and boots. If Izza really hated him like she claimed, would she have set his dusty boots side by side with the socks folded neatly over the tops? Heck, even the laces were tucked inside where they belonged.

He retrieved his boots and sank to the granite rock to put them on. Another paradox revealed itself. He was pretty sure his socks had been washed or at least rinsed. Lifting one to his nose, he sniffed. Right again. His eyes didn't even water. Not even a little bit. Will miracles never cease?

The paradox that was Izza Ramos made him smile. There were still feelings there; she just didn't want to admit it. Heck, she might not even realize it. His heart swelled. Despite his thoughts for Cassidy, that prior moment spent with Izza still meant something especially now that there was a baby involved.

Wow. I'm going to be a father. He couldn't restrain the surge of pride at the knowledge that it was his seed inside that fierce woman's belly. At least they'd loved each other once. His baby was all the proof he needed.

Connor shuffled around the cave, looking for something to make a trap with. Anything. At last, he found a long piece of rusty wire half-buried in the dirt floor. He dug it out and within minutes, he'd fashioned a couple of loops for a rabbit snare. His father had taught him how to trap the little varmints. Now. Where to place it?

Exiting the cave, Connor spotted Izza sitting on her granite throne and looking just as miserable. She looked away the minute he stepped into the light.

"Hey," he offered amicably despite her chilly reception.

She didn't acknowledge that he still breathed the same air. Dizzy from the short walk, he gripped the wall so he wouldn't fall on his butt again.

"It's kinda bright out here," he said as he took a solid step forward without support, just him and his two jelly-legs. The earth wavered. He halted dead in his tracks until it held still. The horizon rocked back and forth. Connor gulped. Maybe this was not a good idea. The gurgle in his stomach offered a different argument. They needed food. With sheer determination, he flattened his two big feet to the hard-packed sand beneath him. As quick as it had come, the vertigo ceased. He took a deep breath and counted himself successful. *I can do this. Go me.*

"Where do you think you're going?" Sarcasm dripped off her lips.

"Hunting." He staggered a few more steps, careful to keep his feet close to the ground. It wasn't walking as much as it was shuffling like a very old man with a very bad back. "And yes, my head is fine. No thanks to you."

"In case you haven't noticed, there's nothing out there but sand and dirt, dumb ass." She huffed her annoyance. "Besides, you're not smart enough to catch a cold, let alone something we can actually eat."

He winked over his shoulder at her. "We'll see."

"Whatever." Her eyes were extra mean until she turned away.

Yep. Still mad.

Connor made it a few steps before he fell. Holding one hand to his abdomen to hold everything in, he shuddered. Every damned movement hurt like hell. Very slowly, he pushed himself back to his knees and then to his feet. Izza didn't offer to assist. No matter. This was not about her. This was about doing what a man had to do.

Finally flat-footed and halfway steady again, Connor shuffled along, knowing she might be right. He was probably making a bigger fool of himself than he already had. He might not catch anything with this piece of rusty wire.

Connor smirked. Now he sounded just like her. Not going to happen. When he got far enough away from the cave, he turned to take in the view. Man, it was ugly—nothing more than boring, gray granite. He'd expected something a little grander, maybe snow-covered peaks. Mountains rimmed the valley they seemed to be stuck in the middle of, but those peaks were a long ways off and there was no snow capping them. Looked like the desert. Now he knew why the mine was abandoned. It was butt ugly.

Huge thunderheads rose black and high in the sky behind it. Rain would probably be cold even in Utah, wouldn't it? Izza said it would. That was good enough for him. He stumbled on. At last he came to a cluster of sagebrush. As careful as if he were setting blasting caps in C4, he set the simple rabbit snares with shaky fingers. Not too small of loops and not too big. The smaller loop within the larger loop. Anchor them. Good. And pray like hell there's a stupid rabbit in the vicinity.

His mother came to mind again. She always offered a prayer over her vegetable garden at the first of summer. She'd plant her tomatoes and cucumbers, stick her onion sets into the dirt and stand back with her head bowed. Why not? It was worth a try.

Heavenly Father. Please send me a dumb rabbit. Or better yet, send me two dumb rabbits. Amen.

Connor smiled. His mother would have smacked him a good one for that kind of a disrespectful prayer. He sat by the snares for a while, exhausted with the small effort he'd just made. It was a long walk back. Izza was nowhere in sight, her disinterest in whether he lived or died forever obvious. Taking a deep breath, Connor forced himself to his feet. The cave suddenly seemed farther away. He pressed onward.

No sooner did he step inside its entrance than the first raindrops fell. Lightning flashed. Connor ducked at the loud crack of booming thunder. Wow. The weather had gotten real nasty real fast. It sounded a helluva lot like artillery. The ground shook. Tiny showers of gravel and dust fell down from the rafters overhead.

Turning from Mother Nature's magnificent outdoor light display, he spied Izza curled up in the opposite corner of the cave, her arms around her knees again. She looked pale. Scared.

He had to ask. "You feeling okay?"

"What's it to you?" she snapped and looked away.

"Just asking." Connor proceeded to his side of the cave. What was he thinking? Of course she was okay. That USMC sergeant was too damned mean to be anything else. Let her sit there.

Very slowly, he lowered his butt to the makeshift mattress and lay down. Every muscle shook, and he was spent. The dirty clothes on the hard ground beneath him actually felt good.

He closed his eyes, thinking about his next problem—how to cook a rabbit if he caught one. He couldn't eat it raw. There was some rule about eating rabbit meat in months with an R in them, but he couldn't recall which months were safe and which were not. Dehydration as an alternative to roasting the meat came to mind. This was Utah after all. Dried rabbit jerky might work. As hot as the sun was, it ought to take about a minute. But how was he going to gut the rabbit and clean it in the first place? He needed a knife.

Another whip crack of lighting ripped the sky. Thunder followed. The hair on his arms stood up. Damn. Mother Nature was putting on a helluva air show in the desert tonight. He'd love to be outdoors watching, but the walk had done him in. He settled for lying still and enjoying the simple act of breathing instead.

A chilling breeze blew through the entrance. Connor closed his eyes and left the cool draft float over him. Another streak of lightning lit the world outside. Booming thunder followed on its heels. Again the earth trembled, while he prepared to bask in the glory of it and let it put him to sleep.

Connor shot one last glance toward the opposite corner, meaning to say good night to his very grumpy companion. His heart melted. Scrunched into a tight ball with her face pressed into her kneecaps, Izza jumped at every burst of lightning and crash of thunder. She would never ask for help. Not in a million years.

The folks who know everything in the world call it Post-Traumatic Stress Disorder. They even gave it a cool four-letter acronym: PTSD. But soldiers who had to live with it called it hell. And they all came home with it in one way or another.

He shook his head in bewilderment at the puzzle before him.

Izza. It had to be Izza.

Fifteen

"Good evening, Ember," Alex acknowledged the call from Ember Davis, Mother's assistant techie and the more agreeable of the two. Tall, buxom, and a little on the ditsy side, the day he'd hired her he'd also learned that appearance could be damned deceiving. Despite her current blue hair color, she was as smart as they came and one hundred percent reliable, discreet, and intelligent. He could not have asked for a better team member. And better yet, she was not prone to gossip like Mother.

"Hi, Alex. Wow. Lots of fires out there in Utah, huh?" she asked brightly. And that was another thing. Ember was struggling with the death of a team member tight now, but you'd never know it to talk to her. She kept her personal life and troubles to herself. Another plus.

"Yes," he agreed. "What can you tell me about them?"

Standing across the street from the Pink Iguana, his nose filled with the delightfully spicy odors of the Mexican cuisine wafting through the open doors of the establishment. An arbor of brilliant red and yellow roses offered outside dining, but it also offered a plate glass view of the lighted interior as well. Just inside sat Miguel Ramirez, boss of the despicable Sonoran Cartel.

Another bruiser type sat with him, stuffing his face with chips and salsa even though the meal appeared to be over.

Apparently Biker Boy had a twin brother. They looked to be identical.

Seated at Ramirez's right hand was the murderer, Jose Ibarra. Alex glanced over his shoulders. Where the hell was the brutal enforcer, Nestor Martinez? He wouldn't have gone far.

"From what I'm seeing on satellite recon, the cartel started setting fires two days ago. They drive twenty miles or so, stop and throw something out of the back of their truck. They go another twenty miles and do the same thing. Looks like Molotov cocktails maybe, I don't know, but whatever they're throwing, it's a ball of fire by the time it hits the ground."

"Where are they now?"

"Interstate Eighty, west of you, headed toward Nevada. They just passed the airport. There's a line of fire behind them and it's spreading fast. And Alex, there are a lot of industrial type complexes west of the airport. Just thought you'd like to know."

"Any residential areas?"

"Not until they get to Grantsville. The lakes will be to the north of them pretty soon, the mountains to the south."

"Call Baxter. Ask him to intercept. In the meantime, I'll see what I can do to stop any more fires from being started."

"I've seen the weather report. Aren't you supposed to get rain?"

He glanced at the dark clouds moving in. "So?"

"Why not let the weather take care of the fires?"

"The cartel will just start them again. Call Baxter. Let's get these bastards before they run."

"Will do."

Alex hung up and stared at the meeting across the street. The notion that the DEA knew where Ramirez was, but had taken no steps to take him down, galled Alex. Mark was right. Ramirez deserved a taste of his own medicine.

The cartel boss nearly jumped out of his chair when Alex sat down at his table. Body language speaks loudly to a trained observer. Ramirez's screamed, *'How dare you?'*

Wearing a linen sports jacket over a casual yellow polo, he looked the part of a true Mexican aristocrat. His short black hair was combed with a distinct part on the right. A neatly trimmed mustache graced his upper lip. Most women might think him handsome, but to Alex, he was just another immaculately groomed sepulcher concealing a rotted corpse.

Dropping his cap to the table, Alex leaned his backpack against the leg of his chair and removed his cell phone from his pocket. He placed it face up on his cap, and smiled at the startled man directly across the table.

Ramirez had yet to speak. Alex could wait. Glancing at the brightly displayed antiquities and boldly painted pottery displayed on the walls and tabletops, he absorbed the layout of the quaint Mexican restaurant. One rear exit emptied into the courtyard and arbor. No other bodyguards beside Biker Boy came into view. Only Ibarra. A sniper hates anyone at his back, but Alex stilled. Now that he knew what and who was behind him, there was no reason for alarm. Good to know.

"Alex Stewart," Ramirez hissed. "Owner of assassins and liars." He pushed away from the table, his arms across his chest and his black eyes hooded.

That statement alone was excellent news. So. Ramirez had heard of Alex Stewart and no doubt, his company of ex-military snipers. Alex rolled his shoulder, his senses on high alert and every nerve engaged. Let the showdown commence.

"Miguel Ramirez. Owner of drug dealers. Arsonists. Murderers." He leaned his elbows, interlocked his fingers and stared back. "I know we've never met before, but I believe we know each other well. I also thought you might like to see some pictures."

When Ramirez didn't answer, Alex reached down into his bag. Immediately, Biker Boy pulled his weapon, a pearl-handled Colt revolver.

"You're scaring the locals," Alex murmured as he revealed the thick envelope of photos in his hand. "You might want to put that toy away before someone calls the police."

Alex tossed the envelope to Ramirez, but Ibarra was quick. He intercepted the envelope in mid-air and opened it. The second he saw the pictures he glanced at his boss, his nostrils flared. He handed the photos off to Ramirez, but Alex caught the glint in his eye. Ibarra was pissed now, too. Good deal.

Instant contempt flashed across the table when Ramirez glanced at the first photo. His breath hitched. He fingered through the stack without taking them out of the envelope.

Alex allowed him time to understand the new rules of the game. Every single picture in that envelope depicted someone near and dear to the cartel boss's heart. In one photograph, his beautiful wife Alejandra stood in her rose garden, tending to her pink and yellow flowers with a smile on her sweet face in the gold of early morning light.

In another shot, his dark-haired three-year-old daughter, Sophia, played with her dolls on the red brink veranda. Her little dog, Pepper, was dressed in a doll dress with a china tea set on the blanket beside him. Pepper didn't look happy, but Sophia's smile was radiant and as motherly as a three-year-old could be. Another photo showed five-year-old Christina sound sleep in her bed with her arms wrapped around a floppy stuffed teddy bear. At night.

And finally, the very arrogant Sonoran Cartel boss looked at a photo of his own bedroom suite, complete with lace-shrouded windows, vases of freshly cut pink roses everywhere, and Alejandra's champagne-colored peignoir laid across the foot of the huge brass bed. His bed.

One brow spiked high with anger. The longer Ramirez looked, the more his refined appearance changed. His right eyelid developed a tick. His upper lip lifted into a deadly sneer. By the last picture, he was the epitome of an angry rattlesnake, full of poison and coiled to strike.

"You have been in my home," he ground out between clenched teeth.

"Have I?" Alex asked nonchalantly.

"Do you have any idea who you're playing with?" Red-hot hatred flashed across the cheery red-and-white checkered tablecloth.

"Stop the bullshit, Ramirez. You can't touch me, and you know it." Alex kept his voice calculating and steady. "I'm not the guy in Mexico taking these shots now, am I? Besides, you know damned well I'm not playing."

Ramirez kicked the table leg beside him. "I ask you one more time, Stewart. *WHAT DO YOU WANT?*"

His roar caught the attention of every diner in the place. Eyebrows raised. A server ducked nervously into the kitchen.

"Calm down," Alex replied, his voice still friendly. "These are just a couple of snapshots."

"They are of my children. My wife!" Ramirez spit venom.

"Yeah. You're right. They are. Pretty good photos if I do say so myself. You have a lovely family in *Herm-o-sill-o.*"

Ramirez trembled with suppressed rage. "What. Do. You. Want?"

Ibarra hadn't moved since he'd looked at the first pictures, but Biker Boy tensed for action. Alex had no doubt he'd take the first shot if he were dumb enough to try.

Alex leaned over the table conspiratorially toward Ramirez and whispered, "Well, I'll tell you, old buddy—"

"I am not your buddy, *cabeza de mierda*!" Ramirez cursed him. "*Pendejo!*"

"What you really want to know is how I got these pictures. Right?" Alex asked casually, ignoring the slur.

Ramirez's eyes seethed, but he didn't answer.

"Maybe another time." Alex picked up his cap and phone and stood to leave.

"Sit!" Ramirez hissed.

Alex sat at the edge of his chair. Almost obediently.

"I will play your game, Mr. Alexander Stewart," Ramirez muttered with restrained politeness. "What can I do for you?"

"The thing is that I like Utah. I like it a lot. It's the kind of place where a man can step away from the city, breathe in fresh mountain air every morning, and feel like he's living in paradise." Alex crossed his arms as he leaned forward again. "But then someone like you shows up and decides he's going to make a big name for himself."

Ramirez's upper lip twitched.

"He starts leaving trash around the state. He dumps a few bodies. He floods the street with meth, coke, horse, and every other brand of his kind of dirt. And then he trots his ass back to Mexico to spend quality time with his pretty little wife and beloved daughters, like what he did in America was all in a day's work."

Ramirez stared, his eyes black and cold.

"He thinks he's untouchable, doesn't he, Miguel?" Alex's voice turned deadly when he finally used Ramirez's first name.

The powerful man glared across the table. "I will not ask you again. What is it you want?"

"For starters, you've got two trucks out on I-80. Call your boys off. Make 'em stop. Right now." Alex didn't blink. "No more fires."

Ramirez pulled his cell phone from his inner suit pocket without breaking eye contact with Alex. He spoke only a few words before he hung up and laid the phone on the table in front of him. Biker Boy made a move for his gun, but Alex was quicker. All Biker Boy felt was the barrel of the SIG suddenly pressed against the bottom of his jean's zipper. Awareness glinted across his face. He looked knowingly at Alex.

Alex winked. "Be damned sure you're a faster gun than me," he said quietly. "You won't even be able to sing soprano with the equipment you'll be missing."

Biker Boy lowered his weapon beneath the tablecloth.

"That's better," Alex whispered. "Good boy."

"What else?" Ramirez snapped. "Why did you really come here? What do you want?"

"Me? If it were up to me," Alex was ready to play, "I'd just want you to die. You killed eleven Mexican citizens like they were nothing—"

"They were nothing! They were stupid farmers, that's all. Mexico is full of them!"

"And beheading people?"

"You cut the head off the snake, you solve the problem!"

"And what else? You burn the state of Utah down and take over? Is that what's going on? Is that why you're here? You moving on up or something?"

Ramirez snarled. "Why are you here? Just to threaten my family? Me? My children?"

"Where are my agents?" Alex demanded.

"What agents?"

"The man and woman your guys grabbed when they attacked my team in the canyon. Where are my people?"

"I don't know what you're talking about!"

"You do, too. You kidnapped them. Where are they?" Alex's fist hit the table, his anger uncontrolled for a scant second.

The game changed. Ramirez's eyes went blank. Expressionless. Like a snake's. He stared back at Alex, his voice devoid of his previous disgust. "I don't know what you are talking about, Mr. Stewart. I took no agents. What use could I possibly have for your people?"

"Cut the crap!" This time it was Alex who raised his voice.

Ramirez dabbed his lips with his napkin and folded it before he stood to leave. Ibarra and Biker Boy followed suit. Like a slick cat with a mouse, the cartel boss smiled as if he suddenly knew a secret. "I think I am ready to leave now. You are not the kind of man who would hurt women and children. We have nothing more to discuss."

"Fine. Go. If that's a risk you're willing to take, have a nice day, but if they were my family...."

Ramirez walked away.

"Would you like to talk with them?" Alex asked.

The arrogant cartel boss kept walking until Alejandra Ramirez's voice called out to her husband from the speaker of Alex's cell phone.

Ramirez spun on his heel. "You have my wife?"

Now it was Alex who played the part of a snake, his lip lifted in a sneer.

Ramirez came swiftly back to the table and snatched the phone out of his hand. "Alejandra! Is this you? Are you safe? Where are the girls? How? They... What?" He listened for a moment. He choked, his eyes full of fear. Frantically, he spoke with his beloved wife. "No, you are not making sense. Speak slowly. Please. I will be right—"

The call disconnected. Ramirez stared at the phone, visibly deflated. Tossing it back to Alex, he sat again. Ibarra and Biker Boy stood behind him.

"Please tell me what else you want," Ramirez said. "I will do anything."

Alex leaned forward, his voice low and menacing against the soft ambience of the affluent restaurant. "I want you to go back to hell where you came from, Ramirez. Leave Utah. Leave Arizona. Leave this country. Never come back. Never set so much as a toe across the border again."

The cartel boss nodded, no longer willing to look his adversary in the eye.

Alex leaned closer. "You and your familia are not safe, my friend. I can reach out and touch you anywhere. Anytime. If I find that you lied to me, I will do every single thing you're afraid I'll do. To your wife. To your children. To you. Every single bloody thing."

Ramirez stood to leave. "Come. We go," he said to his henchmen.

But he didn't make it to his lovely estate in Sonora, Mexico, with its finely decorated walls and lavish gardens. He'd barely stepped out the door of the fine eatery when the Utah Task Force apprehended him and his two armed cohorts. It was pouring rain by then. He looked good with his face to the sidewalk, his hands cuffed behind his back and rain reducing him to the thug he truly was. Damned good.

Governor Baxter met Alex outside the restaurant with a grin and a big handshake. "Well done. You had him going. I think Ramirez really thinks you're holding his wife and daughters."

"Modern technology is amazing. At least, that's what my techies tell me." Alex shouldered his bag, his weapon again safely stowed from sight, and the cell phone with the recording his techies had spliced together from Mark's audio feeds tucked into his jacket pocket.

"Well, they're right. With everything he told you in there, Ramirez will die in prison. Smart thinking, by the way, to call my number and leave the line open before you went in. It worked."

"It did until I needed him to think I had his wife on the phone," Alex groused, wishing he'd been better prepared. A Tattle Tale would've made all the difference. Or two phones. Or an umbrella. "Did your men apprehend the guys setting the fires?"

"They did. They've arrested the four arsonists involved, all Ramirez's men. You've got good people working for you, Alex."

"I do."

"Of course, I've still got a state on fire."

"And I've still got two missing agents."

"I need a drink. Come over to the house for a nightcap?"

Alex declined. "Not until my people are safe. Goodnight, Governor."

Walking back to his hotel, he called Mother and Ember. Thunder boomed overhead, but what the hell. The rain felt good. "Ramirez fell for it," he told his East Coast office.

Both techies were on speakerphone. "Great!" they replied in unison.

"Do me a favor. Call Mark. Tell him thanks for the work his team did collecting those audio feeds and pictures. And thanks for patching together a seamless conversation. Each of you did a good job. Damn good."

"We'll call him right away. Anything else?" Mother asked.

Alex scrubbed a hand over his tired wet head, his cap drenched through. "Tell me you found Izza and Connor."

"We will find them," Ember answered softly. "You know that, don't you?"

"I do," he added quickly.

That's what she needed to hear, so that's what he said.

Sixteen

Izza cringed. Every blinding stab of lightning and crash of thunder drove it home. Jamie was gone. His bright brown eyes forever closed. He'd never tease or tickle her again. He'd never take a beating for her either. He'd never come home.

It hit her like a ton of bricks that day at Mountain View Memorial Gardens, the day she had to walk away and leave him behind. From that moment forward, she was alone in a bitchin' cruel world.

Closing her eyes against the storm and praying it would end as quickly as it had sprung up didn't help. Neither did burying her head against her arms to block the thunder.

BOOM! There was no place to hide. No escape for bad girls who lied to their fathers.

CRASH! No salvation for those who stole out of the refrigerator because they were hungry.

Bang. Bang. BANG! And Jamie's body kept falling no matter how tightly she squeezed her eyes or shut her heart.

"Hey." Connor's gentle mellow voice reached across the barren cave.

"What? Did you throw up again?" she snapped. He didn't know how close she stood to the edge of not wanting to live. He'd never know.

"I just thought you'd like some company. It's getting kind of cold in here." He reached his arm toward her from where he lay. Was he freaking serious? He wanted to snuggle? Now? Dumb ass.

She turned away, shaking like a leaf in the wind, but damned sure he'd never see it. "Leave me alone."

Another explosion of light and noise pillaged the world outside. It was an assault by nature against nature, the elements of earth and sky at war with each other. Any minute now some part of the desert landscape would be blown to bits. Soldiers would fall. Men would die. Jamie would—

That was the problem with loud noises, car backfires and thunder. One minute she was perfectly fine, adapted into civilization like normal people. But the next, she was on the floor having a heart attack and trying to hide. The littlest thing jerked her back to Iraq and its twenty-four-seven nightmare. Some kind of a switch automatically flipped in her mind, and when it did, it sent her into full-blown panic mode. It made her look like she was crazy. Maybe she was. Every crack of lightning meant Jamie kept falling. Kept dying. Kept leaving....

The cave lit with a bright white flash that illuminated every timber and dusty corner. Lightning stabbed the ground while thunder followed with fierce detonations like hellfire bombs dropping from high overhead. Panic sucked the air out of her lungs. Fear made it impossible to swallow. A whine escaped, but thunder masked it just in time not that anyone could've heard it with all the noise going on outside. Izza steeled every muscle and nerve to not allow another show of weakness. Connor could not know.

"Come here, Izza," he said kindly. "You know I won't hurt you. Just for tonight. Please?"

"I said no already. Stop asking! Damn! You're so stinking stupid!" She jerked herself around until he could only see her back, but it didn't change anything. The storm raged and she was afraid. Her resolve trembled as much as her fingers digging into her arms.

A tumbleweed burst through the curtain of rain at the cave's entrance. She startled. Ambush! But no, she steeled her mind to stop lying to her. It was just a plant, but the damned weed's attack was followed by a blinding laser show of horrific snaps, crackles and booms. Thunderous blasting caps shook the walls of the cave. A yelp escaped her lips. An image of cannons and RPGs flashed through her mind. The battle couldn't have sounded closer or more frightening. She had no weapon and she was outmanned! How many damned enemy soldiers were out there?

The nightmare persisted. Jamie fell. And fell. Over and over again. She ground her fists to her temples to block the hysteria creeping into her soul. If only—

"Come on, honey. I'll keep you warm. Let me help you, just for tonight." The calm in Connor's voice reached across the cold space between them. His open arm invited her to safety again. Just like last time.

"No." She shook her head in denial. Every storm had to end. It had to. It was just a matter of holding herself together until—

CRACK! Thunder shook the earth with a loud negatory at her lie. She shot a quick glance over her shoulder. Damn, Connor looked like hell. That dried bloody gash in the middle of his face gave him more of a troll appearance. Two blackened eyes didn't help. Surfer boy was gone. Some scary looking Halloween freak had arrived, but the tenderness in his blue eyes hadn't changed. The kind and gentle man was still there. He never did know when to let go. Not once that other night, either. Just held her. Saved her. Loved her.

No! I can't! I won't! I—

Mother Nature interrupted with another thunderous volley that reverberated as loudly as the cannons in the clouds, only it was not really cannons, only—it was. Another whine swelled up from her soul.

I'm so damned tired of being scared. Alone....

She scurried over to Connor, still angry and her chest heaving in panic. Izza stopped. How could she admit to—?

BOOM! Connor didn't even flinch at the terrible noise, but she did. The tenderest emotion shifted across his face, and she had to put a stop to it right then and there.

"I hate you," she said, but even she noticed her usually harsh declaration sounded more breathy and scared than angry.

"I know. It's okay. You can hate me and still be warm at the same time." He reached for her hand like he was asking her to dance, the dummy.

"And I'm not your honey," she declared. He needed to understand. Just because she might be having a weak moment didn't mean anything. Nothing. Not a single thing! She glanced toward the entrance where a curtain of rain glistened. The howling wind scoured the bomb-cratered earth clean. Lightning lived and Jamie—

"I stand corrected. You're not my honey," Connor assured her, but he was hers. The deep baritone honey of his voice vanquished the ghosts of war. "It's okay, Izza. Really. It's just a thunderstorm. Everything's going to be okay."

"It's not." Her lip trembled. *Jamie's gone. It will never be okay again.*

She debated changing her mind. As if on cue, another deafening rumble shook every nook and cranny of their hole in the wall, and Izza lost the war. She threw herself at Connor and burrowed into his side.

He groaned when she hit him, but held her with one arm while his hand smoothed up and down her bicep. Warmth trailed in the wake of that gentle touch. He was so calm. She was so scared. Closing her eyes, she found that safe place under his chin. Lightning cracked another whip of thunder. Every muscle ached. She pushed in closer and squeezed her eyes shut to block the storm. The little girl inside of her cried, *Make it go away, Connor. Make it stop. Make everything be okay again.*

"Pretend my arm is just a big ole ugly blanket," he whispered into her hair. "You can push it off anytime you want."

Of course she didn't reply. Right now she could barely breathe, she was shaking so hard. He seemed to need to make small talk. "I don't know how to cook our first dinner in the desert. I'm leaning toward dehydration. Rabbit jerky should be fairly simple to make, don't you think?"

I don't care. Just hold me and shut up! She buried her face against his chest, wanting nothing more than a safe place to hide. The smell of this damned man instantly soothed her ragged nerves. Inhaling deeply, she pulled the comfort she needed from him. *Save our baby, Connor. Save Jamie. Save me. Please.*

"You're cold." He rubbed warmth into her bare arms. She couldn't understand how he could be so warm and she so cold. Trembling, she conformed her body to absorb his heat.

Another crack from Thor's hammer shook the tiny cave. Izza yipped and all but bulldozed into his ribs. He grunted in pain, but not for one second did he let her go.

"I'm sorry," she whispered. When his breath hitched, it dawned on her that she'd just said what he'd said to her so many times before. She felt the need to explain. "I meant, I'm just sorry because I hurt you. I mean... I'm sorry because I didn't mean to bump your side. I mean... I mean...." Izza stopped trying as tears filled her eyes. She didn't know what she was sorry for, hurting his abdomen, or hurting—his heart.

Without a word of admonition, he gathered her like a little girl inside the circle of his two very strong and capable arms. She didn't want it, and she surely didn't expect it when he kissed her forehead and sighed. But the moment he did, she knew she'd craved it since the day she'd lost it.

And then Izza was really sorry.

Connor held her with the greatest of care. The storm lasted throughout the night so she stayed put. He knew the exact moment she dozed off by the way her body relaxed against his. He felt it all. Once asleep, she'd placed her hand lightly on his chest and under her cheek. It rested there still, a more than friendly touch he tried to ignore the same as her warm breath in the hollow of his neck.

Odd. As much as she hated him, she'd fallen asleep in his arms even while all that heavenly artillery still hammered away at their earthly position. For most of the night, the ground had shaken. The thunder rolled, echoing off the mountains in a roar that seemed to go on forever. But once in his arms, she'd fallen asleep as if there was nothing to fear. Odd.

Yeah. He knew he had a reputation. He was always hopping from one woman to another, but it's not like he'd loved them and left them. No. He wasn't really like that at all. None of them had actually made it into his bed. That was the funny part about having a bad boy reputation. Just the slightest hint of misconduct spread like wildfire until the lie was a hundredfold more interesting than the facts. The truth was he hadn't found any woman who could hold a stick to that one night with—

Oh, hell, no.

Even as the thought came into his head, he rejected it. Emphatically and absolutely, *No way!*

Izza snuggled under his arm just then, sound asleep and still as mean as a mother Javalina pig with a litter of piglets. He gazed down at her olive skin, her dark hair pulled back tight into her usual ponytail. He'd only seen her hair down once, the night that he and she—

Come on. No way.

She pressed against him again, somehow in tune with his rambling heart and so peaceful in his arms. His breath caught. It had been months since she'd been this close or so sweet. Long eyelashes swept against her cheeks, pleasantly flushed in the cool of the cave instead of the anger he'd come to know her by. The peacefulness of the moment spoke to him of another night and another feeling they'd shared. *That night.*

He knew little of Isabella Ramos other than her mother died when she was a little girl and her father was an abusive alcoholic who didn't know what to do with his own children. No wonder Izza grew up tough. Neglected as a teenager, she and her brother joined the Marines out of high school. She had no other family.

Connor made a mental note to check into that once they were rescued. For some reason, he felt compelled to make sure. Family was everything. He couldn't imagine dealing with the ugliness of Iraq without phone calls home. Those talks had saved him, but whom had Izza called? Who was the bright light at the end of the tunnel for her? It wasn't her brother, that's for sure. The answer niggled at the back of his heart. *Y. O. U.*

No way.

It had happened so fast. One minute they were both crouched inside a bombed-out concrete building while the pompous Iraqi insurgents crept around outside. Both he and she were decked out in full combat gear with armored tactical vests, the latest weaponry, and you name it. She was so scared she was hyperventilating. It surprised him that this tough gal had suddenly become a scared girl, but hell. He was pretty scared, too.

He fully believed he and she were the walking dead, that before dawn they'd be overrun, dragged from their hiding place, their dead bodies mutilated and never found. Yeah, he was afraid. Damn straight. But the next minute—silence. Not a sound. It seemed the Iraqis had just walked away.

"It's awful quiet out there," he'd said.

Her dark eyes blinked back with terror. They both knew what could happen to a female soldier. They'd seen the pictures on the infamous Al Jazeera network. He'd reached for her wrist to reassure her. "They won't come in here. Don't worry."

"How can you be sure?" she'd asked, her voice tight and breathy.

She trembled beneath his hand. In a gallant bluff, he'd shrugged her question off like it was a no-brainer. "Because two of the meanest Marines in the Corps are still here, what do you think?"

That false bravado must have been the comfort she needed. The next moment she'd grabbed his neck and kissed him. It was no peck on the lips first kiss, either. No. She'd planted her mouth full on his like she'd finally found food. With that hungry kiss, one thing led to another, and the next thing he knew, they were plastered together in the heat of— what? Insanity?

It was bizarre that he couldn't restrain his need for her that night. He didn't even try. And she certainly didn't, either. Not the way she peeled out of her pants like she did. They'd made love so hot and passionately, he thought for sure they'd left scorch marks on the concrete floor by the time they were done with each other. He didn't remember asking or refusing, only complying until she was spent in his arms.

And then they'd just hung onto each other until morning light when their squad returned. It seemed so natural. They'd dressed and chatted in muted whispers about where they went to school, what sports they liked, why they joined the Corps. He'd learned all about her penchant for physical confrontation, which explained a lot now that he had time to put two and two together. For whatever reason, Izza was born mad at the world.

But now? She was spent again. The feel of her in his arms unleashed a warming flood that filled his body to the hilt. Izza was fine silk. She was molten umber, sleek, and strong, her dark eyes pulling him in with the most powerful magnet he'd ever known. Part of him was still back in that bombed-out concrete building, locked in the embrace of his own fierce warrior goddess. Maybe that night hadn't ended up being a one-nighter after all. Maybe there was still time for them. Somehow.

She stretched. He ceased his foolish thoughts at the feel of her arched body against his. She'd wake up any minute now, push away, tell him she hated him and life would be back to normal. But then he felt it. The baby inside her belly kicked against his rib. And then it, no – *she* kicked him again. That nudge from another tiny person, so vulnerable and one hundred percent dependent on him took his breath. A girl. Izza was carrying a tiny, baby girl inside her belly. A daughter.

My daughter. My baby girl. What was I thinking that night? I never thought of using protection.

She murmured in her sleep and turned her head into his shoulder. His every muscle was suddenly attuned to the shape and feel of her body. Her knee rested across his thigh, the other leg pressed firm along the length of his leg. Soft warm breasts pushed against his side and chest, but her shoulder felt way too bony. Her arm, too.

He hoped he'd caught a dumb rabbit. Izza needed to eat. That baby growing inside of her needed nourishment. His foolish prayer over the snares came back to him. *Okay, so now I'm serious, God. Please send us a rabbit. Izza's hungry. I'm the only one here who can take care of her. Amen.*

He fought the wave of tenderness sweeping away what little common sense he had left. Suddenly he wanted to roll away from her. She was too close and his head too full of feelings he wasn't ready to own. Truth was mingled in there, too. A startling image flashed to his mind. Bridgette Maher. Smiling. So damned proud.

Not you too, Mom.

Seventeen

Tom Baxter called bright and early. "You're not going to believe this. Your friend wants to talk."

"Who? Ramirez?" Alex asked.

"One and the same. Says he's got information to share, but he'll only talk to you and me together."

"When?"

"I cleared my calendar for the next two hours. I'll be at the front door of your hotel in twenty."

"I'll be ready."

Before long, both men sat opposite Ramirez in one of the Salt Lake County jail's interrogation rooms. Shackled and cuffed, the notorious Sonoran Cartel boss didn't look nearly so impressive or powerful anymore. Alex cut to the chase. "What do you want?"

Ramirez's eyes flitted to Tom Baxter and back to Alex before he spoke. "I want to know what you can do for me."

"What *we* can do for *you?*" Alex glared across the table. "Like I said last time, all I want is you dead. That's what we can do for you. A needle in the arm sounds damned fair consid—"

"Is this how you let your lackeys talk to me?" Ramirez turned to the Governor, his voice angry and low. "I am a Mexican citizen! I am an important man in my country!"

Tom didn't blink. "This man is not my lackey. Alex is more like a pest exterminator, and I agree with him. I don't care what country you're from or how important you think you are. You're nothing but a terrorist in my country, and I intend to treat you as such. Nothing more. Nothing less."

Ramirez seethed.

"So what will it be? Why'd you call this meeting? I've got better things to do," Alex asked. Impatience showed in every word.

He was adept at reading body language and other minuscule tells an opponent might inadvertently give away. The flare of a nostril, the blink of an eye, or tilt of a chin – all these seemingly inconsequential bodily actions told their own stories during an interrogation. They were lies and truths just waiting for the astute man to decipher and use to his advantage. Ramirez showed all the signs of a man with his back against the wall, but not necessarily ready to crack. Not yet. He needed a shove.

He faced Tom Baxter. "I have information that concerns a new cartel in my country, but I will not divulge it to you without the promise of two things."

"For hell's sake, what now?" Alex pushed himself away from the table. His next step would be to get on his feet and head out the door. Tom followed his lead, a clear signal chances were slim the imprisoned drug lord had any leverage in this negotiation.

A glint of panic registered in the man's eyes before he controlled it. Ramirez didn't fidget, lick his lips, or hyperventilate the way many prisoners did, but the panic was there nonetheless. And Alex had seen it.

He waited for an answer to his question. Ramirez seemed stalled, maybe too arrogant to ask or too powerful to beg. Whatever. It was all the same. Alex pushed his hands to his knees and stood to leave. "Come on, Governor. We've got better things to do. This is a waste of—"

"Sit!" Ramirez uttered the one word command like he had authority to do so.

Alex sat with a smirk. "I'm only going to give you that one time, Ramirez. You're not in charge here. Now what the hell do you want?"

"Your solemn oath as a man and a gentleman. Is that too much to ask?" Ramirez shouted, enraged and loud. "You come to me in the middle of my dinner. You threaten my family. My wife. My children! But I saw something in your eyes that night, Mr. Stewart. I know you would never hurt my baby girls. Am I right?"

Alex stared. That was the problem with body language. It worked both ways. The pretty smile of his deceased daughter danced through his mind. Of course Ramirez saw it. A man can only hide so much.

"There it is. I see the truth in your eyes even now." Ramirez breathed a sigh of relief as he too stared into the soul of his adversary. "You would never hurt my Christina or Sophia. I knew you were a good man."

"I'm only asking one more time," Alex muttered. "What do you want?"

"I want your solemn oath you will not hurt my daughters. On your life, Mr. Stewart. That you will save them if you can."

Alex slouched back in his chair, feigning disinterest but deeply touched. "Why the hell would I care to save your daughters?"

"Because...." Ramirez caught himself. He studied Alex as Alex had studied him, both men locked in nonverbal communication that Tom Baxter could only observe. Alex noticed how intense the dark eyes were that stared back at him. And desperate.

"You saw something in those pictures, didn't you?" he asked as he leaned forward with interest. "Something besides the danger to your wife and daughters from my men?"

The question was no sooner asked than Ramirez dropped his gaze for less than a second. Some might have said that he blinked, but Alex saw the truth. Whatever Ramirez had seen in those photos at the Pink Iguana concerned him.

"Why should I promise to save your daughters after what you've done in my country?" he asked drily.

The conversation turned from interrogating a prisoner to one father speaking with another. Ramirez's tone transformed from arrogant to naked honesty. "Because I saw how close your people came to my children. Your men were inside my home. They didn't harm my family, and yet they could have."

He looked deep into Alex's eyes, his voice soft and pleading. "Please. Your word as a gentleman that you will save Christina and Sophia is all I ask. If not for me, save them because you are a better man than me, Mr. Stewart. Save them just because they are two sweet little girls who deserve to live, to grow up and to have their own babies."

"Why do they need to be saved?"

"Because...." He faltered, his eyes staring off into the distance. Ramirez was thinking too hard. Too many angles, too many chess moves must have clouded his senses, obscured his deepest desire. A proud man does not fall easily.

"Listen, Ramirez. You've given me no reason to promise anything. In fact, why should I lift a finger to help you? You've abducted two of my agents. God help you if they're hurt in anyway. I'll tell you what. I'll save your daughters, and you give my agents back." Alex cut to the truth, but then he saw another signal from the cartel boss, a scant twitch of his lip. A twitch that exaggerated could become a snarl. And a snarl meant hatred. And hatred meant—something else was going on here. Ramirez hated somebody worse than he hated Alex Stewart. Interesting.

And still the proud man couldn't bring himself to breach his own ruthless code. Despite the initial plea for his children, the mask of a cartel boss shifted back into place once more. Absolute control. Absolute power. No need of help from anyone.

"Never mind. I see I was mistaken." Ramirez pushed away from the table as far as his chains and manacles would allow and signaled the guard to release him. "I am done here. Take me back to my cell."

Alex leaned across the table to offer one last incentive. "You know I'm the only one who can help. You tell me. What's going on in Hermosillo?"

Ramirez blinked. Yes. He had recognized the truth of Alex's words. But no. He was done playing the unfamiliar role of beggar. He stared, unspeaking and unwilling, the moment of cooperation past. The guard closed the interrogation room door as he led the proud man away.

"Well what do you make of that?" Tom asked as he and Alex walked out of the building.

"He doesn't know who to trust." Alex lowered himself into the passenger seat of the governor's car.

"What do we do now?"

Alex sighed. "First of all, I'll have my techies in Virginia take a second look at those pictures. I know Ramirez saw something I didn't. And I've got a man in Mexico. Maybe he knows what's going on by now. In the meantime, let this bastard stew."

Izza was right. It had gotten cold overnight. Connor was thankful she'd given in and decided to join him on his ratty bed or he'd have been doing his own share of shivering. As it was, he awakened with her in a warm embrace, his hand firmly cupping the swell of her very feminine backside. She didn't seem to mind, and he sure didn't. Of course, she was sound asleep and didn't know where his hand had wandered.

Very slowly, he flexed his fingers until they encompassed most of that luscious part of her anatomy. As small as she was, Izza was like his own private toaster. The tips of his fingers descended to the seam of her pants. If she'd have been naked, they'd have descended to more, but that day was gone. Still, a man could dream.

She stretched against him, and he stilled. She yawned. Just before she opened her eyes, he closed his. Feigning sleep, he fully expected she'd push off the minute she awoke. She didn't. Unborn feet fluttered against his ribs again. Izza felt it too. She rubbed her stomach, her hand between him and the baby, her head still resting in the crook of his arm. She wouldn't stay any longer than she had to, so he shallowed his breathing and relaxed.

Easy does it, Maher. Steady.

She didn't move, but she was staring at him. He could feel the pinpoint laser burn of her gaze drilling into the side of his face. The feeling in the air had changed the moment she'd awakened. Izza was no longer relaxed, but neither was she ready to leave. Yet. He'd felt her head turn as she noticed where his hand was. Oddly, she didn't move his hand like he'd half expected. She seemed to be studying him, looking without getting caught looking. In a million years, he'd never be able to figure out how her mind worked. He didn't care. In this one perfect moment, he hoped she'd stay.

But that was not to be. With a grunt she rolled to her side and got to her feet. And straight out the door she went. Of course, she probably had to find a bush or a tree this early in the morning. So did he, for that matter, but the place under his arm where she'd just been felt empty.

He stretched, his hands high over his head. Just as he rolled to his stomach and pressed his dead weight off the ground, she burst back into the cave. Man, she could pee fast.

"You did it." Her eyes were wide with excitement. "I never thought you could, but you did. It worked."

Okay, so he wasn't his brightest early in the day. Connor cringed. "What'd I do now?"

"You caught a rabbit!" Izza was smiling. Now that was something to get up in the morning for.

"Cool," he muttered as he crawled to his feet, but moving was difficult. His stomach wound felt hot and wet beneath the bandage. That wasn't good. As stiff as taffy in the dead cold of winter, he staggered out of the cave.

Wow. The view. There were actually puddles on the desert ground. All that dusty sagebrush was the most vivid shade of dark mint green this morning. The sand had transformed from bleached out tan to shades that ranged from deep browns to oranges and reds. He stood wavering on his feet as he breathed in a lungful of cool, moist air. And then another. His poor broken nose actually felt better.

A flock of noisy birds tumbled through the sky overhead, chirping a melody that sounded happy. Brilliant pink hues stretched toward him for the most perfect sunrise he'd ever seen in his life. He sucked in another fragrant breath until his ribs expanded enough to make his gut hurt. Okay. Enough fresh air for now.

"Damn it, you're slower than dirt," Izza grumbled while pointing toward the snares he'd set. "Look. See 'em? What'd I tell you?"

Connor turned from the heavenly scenery to Izza. She was so excited she hopped up and down. He cast his gaze to the snares. Sure enough. He'd caught not one but two rabbits. Now the hard part began.

"I'll go get them." He meant to sound confident, but his words came out breathy like he'd just run a mile. "See if you can find something sharp and pointed to help skin them. Maybe a piece of rock." Just that fast, he dropped to his hands and knees, dizzy from moving too fast. *Crap.* There was no easy way to look like a man while in that position. Once again, he dragged himself upright and headed out. The two snares seemed a lot farther away this morning.

And then I have to walk all the way back? He groaned at the prospect. His feet moved like lead. His head buzzed, and his insides felt like they were falling out. *Keep it together, Maher. You can do this. You'll feel better after you eat.*

He stumbled on. By the time he got to the rabbits, all he could do was sit and stare behind him at the cave. It looked like it was a mile away. His energy was spent and the bright Utah sun was back on the job. The rain created waves of humidity, steaming up from the rapidly heating desert. The air felt more like a damned blanket of stifling sweat. There was no way to win.

He untangled the snares. For two scrawny jackrabbits, they were awfully heavy. Just the smell of them brought on a wave of nausea that laid him flat to the steaming desert floor. Black birds with enormous wingspans circled in the acid-washed sky above. Vultures. Buzzards. Eyeball eating ravens.

That's not funny, Lord.

He lay still for another minute, hoping the world would stop spinning. It didn't. As hard as it was, he forced himself to sit again. Izza needed to eat. Their baby would die without him. He had to do this. There was no other choice. Grabbing the two rabbits by their ears, he lurched to his feet and headed back, lucky to be moving at all. Step after step on a drunken path, he kept going. The damn cave got farther away instead of closer.

Izza stood with her eyes shielded, searching for him, probably cussing too. Yep. She'd be mad by now. His legs collapsed. He bowed his head for a one on one pep talk. *I can do this. Marines don't quit. We keep going until we die. We do.*

Gritting his teeth, he shoved off one more time. This was it. If he dropped again, there would be no more getting up. The dead rabbits flopped against his leg. Each step became a do or die mantra. *For Jamie. For Izza. For our baby. Gotta keep moving.*

Suddenly, she was at his side, her hand to his chest like she was holding him up. Too busy watching his feet he hadn't seen her approach. He looked down into her pretty face. She didn't scream or growl. What was wrong with her now?

"I... got two rabbits." He turned into an idiot who just had to say something. Yeah, she already knew he got two rabbits. She wasn't blind. "I can do this."

"I know you can," she answered confidently, but those deep brown eyes looked worried when they scrolled over him and stopped at his gut. It had to look pretty bad for her to be so kind.

"For Jamie," he said weakly. "For Uncle Jamie."

Silently, she hooked her arm through his, and let him lean on her as they stumbled along. He tried not to lean much, but there was no way he could make it back to the cave without help.

"Did you find something sharp?"

"Yes." She held him upright, her palm flat to his chest. Finally, they were at the cave. She guided him to the rock where she usually sat. The rabbits flopped to the ground. He didn't care. He needed to breathe. Izza brought him a bottle of tepid cave water. That was nice of her. He gulped it down, panting his lungs out from the short walk.

Izza was watching him too closely. *What did she want now?*

"Where's the sharp... thingee?" He could barely catch his breath to talk.

"Here." She handed him a long rock, semi-sharp on one edge like a knife. It would have to do.

Picking one jack up from the dirt, he dropped to his knees and forced himself to the gruesome task at hand. Bunnies were never his first choice for a menu item. He didn't like the sounds they made when they were caught. They screamed and his heart always hurt for the scared little creatures. But that was then, and this was now.

He dropped to the ground and laid the bunny flat on its back. The hardest part was the first cut in their soft and fluffy gut. He sawed at the rabbit's belly for a long time. Once the stone blade broke through the tough hide, everything went easier. Finally, the first carcass was skinned and cleaned, and he could not bear the smell anymore.

"I found this." Izza showed him an old dented pan. Once upon a time, it had been covered in white enamel with blue specks. Today it was mostly rust. Connor grunted. By the looks of it, she'd scrubbed most of the rust away. Damn, she was good in a tight spot.

"Maybe we could boil them?" she asked. "What do you think?" She looked so damned excited that they had something to eat.

"You got matches?" he asked.

"No, but I've got this." She handed him the bottom of an old soda bottle.

"What's that supposed to be?" His vision blurred as the last of his energy faded.

"It's my fire starter. It works. I've already used it. Want to see me start a fire?"

"Yeah. Okay. Good then, I guess." He turned to the cave. "I'm going to lie down for a minute."

With one hand on the wall and the other clutching his gut, Connor staggered into the dark cave. He was sure of it now.

He was bleeding. And oozing. *Crap.* He collapsed onto the pile of junk clothing. Being horizontal and finally out of the sun felt great. And it was easier to breathe in a prone position.

Izza stayed away. Good. A man should die alone.

By the time she did join him, he'd lost track of time. She didn't say a word. Instead, she'd brought that old coffee pot to where he lay dying. Without asking, she lifted his shirt and pushed it all the way up to his chin. Very gently, she pulled the bandage away.

He tried not to groan, but even that gentle touch felt like a razor slicing away at his insides. The minute he saw the soggy bandage in her hand, he knew what it was made out of. She always wore two tank tops, one over the other. Wife beaters. What a stupid name for a woman's shirt. So she'd used one of them to dress his wound? Hmm. He watched her eyes, still too serious as she examined the bullet hole in his side.

"I have to take your shirt all the way off." She didn't look at him, just the hole in his side. Reaching her arm under his neck, she pulled him forward until the shirt was out of her way.

Out of breath again, he stared at the ceiling and let her do whatever she wanted. He didn't speak, afraid she'd bite his head off, and he just didn't feel good enough to fight with her.

Silently she poured cool water over the burning hole in his abdomen. It stung, but it felt cold which probably meant he had a raging infection. She tugged at his wound a little. He grimaced, growled, and endured. Somewhere along the line, she'd placed a cool cloth on his forehead. He hadn't even noticed.

"I need to see your back," she said before she rolled him to his other side and cleaned the exit hole. By now, he knew he was not gut shot. A small caliber through and through was the safest way to get hit, no bullet to dig around after and less tissue damage. But it still hurt like hell. And he needed real, no kidding medical treatment. Creeping tendrils of fever invaded every muscle and nerve. His teeth hurt. His eyes. Every last damned part of him.

Finally, staring at the ceiling again, he panted like a dog. The pleasant morning had changed into an endurance test, and all he did was go for a walk and pick up two little bunnies.

"You know I... I really thought... umm...." He forgot what he wanted to say. "Never mind."

She finally met his gaze, looking down on him like she knew what she was doing. Like she was a nurse or something. "You thought you were some kind of cowboy, didn't you? You thought you'd be able to jump up after you've been shot and ride off into the sunset on your trusty horse, huh?"

For some reason she was getting prettier as he got sicker. And her brown eyes were so dreamy. She did remind him of an angel. Kind. Thoughtful. Sweet. Okay, so maybe she wasn't as mean as he thought.

"Well, yeah. Kind of. I guess," he admitted. Isn't that what every Marine thought? They could take a licking and keep on ticking?

"The cartel took everything I had when they dumped us." Again, she sounded friendly and competent. "They slashed all my pockets."

"Huh?" He didn't have a clue why that bit of trivia was noteworthy.

"You know what I'm talking about—my knife, my blowout kit, matches, extra ammo and MREs. They took all of it. Stripped 'em bare. Heck, they even took my clean pair of underwear and socks. Sure could use them now."

Hmmm. Izza. Stripped bare. Underwear and socks....

"I found something when I was exploring. I think it's time I used it. Your wound is infected. You're sick." She left but came right back with a brown flask in her hand. Izza knelt at his side again, her cool hand to his forehead.

He shivered at her gentle touch. What now?

"How much of a cowboy are you, Boston?" she asked. "Are you really tough, or do you just talk tough?"

Man, he was too exhausted to play mind games. "Why?"

"You can scream if you want." Without a single word of warning, she poured scalding, gut-wrenching, piece of shit, brown liquid from hell out of that bottle and into the hole in his gut!

"Sweet Mary and Jesus!" He jerked away from her as fast as he could go, which was not fast at all. She'd just burned the living hell out of him. He smelled singed flesh. His!

As soon as he rolled over, she poured that same damn crap onto the hole in his back. By then, he was belly against the wall with no way to get away from her. Tremors lit him up from the inside out. "God! Stop it already! Izza! Stop it! Don't kill me!"

"It's going to be okay," she soothed while she eased him to his back again, but why should he believe her? She danced in and out of focus. Forget the angel of mercy. Izza was a three-eyed troll from Hell.

Connor placed both hands flat to the ground, intending to sit up and get far, far away from the beast he shared the cave with. He couldn't. The cave spun in a fantastically awful terror ride with him caught dead center like a stupid fly in a mean spider's trap. Fragments of the bright Utah sun darted through the cave's entrance with tongues of liquid flame until—

He passed out. Again.

Eighteen

Poor Connor.

With a dented old hubcap full of water, Izza rinsed the rag and smoothed it over his fevered brow again. Everything she'd come across in her wanderings had been repurposed. The hubcap made an excellent, albeit shallow washbasin. Her own clothing had become bandages or washcloths. Connor's breathing had at last settled into a normal rhythm, but the look on his face when she'd disinfected his wounds with that old bottle of whiskey she'd found? Priceless.

She actually felt bad dosing him unexpectedly the way she had, but she didn't have a choice. The second she'd touched his hand out there on the desert she knew he was sick. High fevers demanded drastic measures. Poor Connor. Already hurting so much, she hated hurting him more.

All night long, she battled his fever with cool water baths that evaporated as quickly as she'd smoothed them over his burning chest, shoulders, face, and arms. Nursing him became her number one mission; preparing the food he'd caught, secondary.

Sunrise the next morning funneled the blast furnace of dry desert heat straight into the east facing entrance. As the cave grew warmer, his fever ramped up. So did Izza's efforts. She lost herself in service to the man she thought she hated. Connor would not die, not if she had anything to say about it.

At last he opened his bleary, bloodshot eyes. Yeah, he was still sick. She could tell. His breathing quickened when he caught sight of her. Easing to her feet, she went to the pool of water in the back of the cave and filled a fresh bottle. Back at his side again, she lifted his head and pressed the bottle to his lips. His brows knitted together in the cutest V, but he would not drink. The tables had flipped. Now she was the sorry one and he the angry one. She couldn't hold back the small smile that tugged at her lips.

"It's just water," she coaxed. "Come on, Boston. I wouldn't hurt you. Have a sip."

He scowled, but accepted the offer. His hands were shaking so she held the bottle with him. Watching his Adam's apple bob while he gulped half the bottle down brought an unexpected measure of satisfaction.

Encouraged, she left his side and returned with a cup of the broth she'd made from the rabbit meat. She had to smile. He still looked suspiciously at her, and she didn't blame him. Once again he tried to pull back when she urged him to try it.

"Connor, open up. You have to eat," she scolded. Honestly, this full-grown man acted like a little boy. He took the tiniest sip from the cup, just enough to wet his lips while those dark blues pierced her with suspicion. The broth must've hit the spot, though. After one taste, he relented and eagerly slurped it down. She wiped his mouth and face with another cool cloth when the meal was gone.

"Do you want more?"

Izza was by far the meanest, nastiest woman he'd ever met. And what was that stuff she'd poured on his gut before? The damned crap burned the hell out of him! He was pretty sure he had blisters. As soon as he was strong enough to take her on, he wanted answers even if he had to torture them out of her.

But not now. Connor was too tired to think so he lay quiet and watched the she-devil he was unlucky enough to share this stinking hole in the wall with. She was in and out of the cave, busy with something – hopefully nothing painful. Eventually, she brought another cup of broth and held it so he could drink it without slopping it all over his neck. Her gentle deceit made him wary. *What's next? A poke in the eye with a sharp stick when I'm not looking?* He drained the cup anyway, but he kept an eye on her.

She placed a cold compress to his forehead. *Damn.* He must be really sick for her to be so nice. He'd let her do anything she wanted as long as she didn't hurt him again. Theirs was the relationship from hell. When he felt good, she treated him like crap. When he felt like crap, she treated him good.

Izza peered kindly into his face. "Did you like it?"

"What?" He couldn't believe she was being nice to him. That alone made him want to push her away so he could get a better look.

"It's rabbit stew," she said. "It's thin. Maybe I should call it rabbit soup. How does it taste?"

"Good." He offered his standard answer. That seemed to make her happy. At least she didn't attack him with the stuff in that brown bottle again.

Izza jumped up and was back in a minute with another cup. And she was chatty. "I cut the rabbit meat into pieces. Some of it's drying on a flat rock, but I have to keep a close eye out. There's a coyote sneaking around our cave. I don't want him to steal our food, but he keeps coming back. I named him Boomerang."

She held Connor's head up so he could take another sip of the warm broth. "The skins are drying. Maybe you can find a use for them when you're feeling better."

He looked at her smiling face. Izza was the most beautiful woman in the world when she was kind. He felt like a fool, ready to forgive her the first minute she was decent. What a sucker. "The soup is very good. Thank you."

She wiped his mouth again. "You need to rest. You've had a couple of very hard days."

Connor closed his eyes and faced reality. *I've got to be dreaming. This can't be real.*

The next days blurred together. One moment Connor wanted Izza to come lay with him, but then she'd pour more of that satanic poison over his wound, and he'd wish she'd fall into the deepest darkest hole and never be seen again.

He slept, only to wake to the gentle sound of Izza humming outside the cave. It was a lovely sound to a dying man's ears. Holding very still because he had no energy to move, he closed his eyes, content to listen to his heart beat in time to the melody rising out of her throat. The evening breeze through the cave soothed his weary body.

He opened his eyes to four Indian maidens. Fire grated up his throat only to drip over him until it became more shroud than breath. And still they filled the inner sanctum of his deathbed, hovering over him like vapor. And mingled amongst their ghostly shapes was Izza. More smoke than woman, she entered the cave, humming softly as she brought a light and a basin.

Connor had no strength to turn away, so he watched through eyes too weary to decipher shadow from truth. She knelt with her back to him. The lovely maidens circled her, chanting softly when she pulled her tank top off, folded it and set it aside. Izza had lovely olive-colored skin, her back so wonderfully strong and supple. Her slender waist tucked at her beltline, and he very much wanted to see the rest of her. Her hips. Her belly. Her baby bump.

Connor reached for her, but she didn't see him. Instead, Izza proceeded to wash her body. The maidens fussed in the quiet murmurings of women and girls at work while Izza hummed along with them. Her skin glistened with the soft light of the candle she'd brought with her. When she smoothed the damp cloth down her neck and over her breasts, she sighed. But when she reached her belly, she began to sway and the maidens swayed with her. The tenderest lullaby filled the cave.

The words made no sense, but the time for logic was gone. Connor recognized the truth. These women were spirits come to bless his daughter, not him. They'd come to take his life, a fair trade in exchange for hers, the tiny child in Izza's belly. That she might live. That Izza and she might live.

And that was enough. Izza's tiny light cast shadows across the walls of the cave. His eyelids grew heavy. He'd done all he could. Killed that Izza might survive, his daughter, too. A man cannot want for more. Life for his woman and child was the best gift to leave behind. The best legacy. His heartbeat slowed. He breathed his last breath.

The maidens raised their hands over their heads in a sign language only he seemed to understand.

Rest easy, Connor. The Great Spirit is in everything.

A light breeze brought refreshing air from the dark night beyond the cave. A man knows when it's his time to go. The lovely apparitions signed along with the lullaby of Izza's heart to her child.

Listen wisely, Connor. Mother Earth has named us all. Wind. Fire. Earth. Sky. We are the same and one.

Their arms lifted in heavenward supplication. He smiled. They were beautiful, their soft feminine curves and sensual contours inviting. They swayed around and over him. Through him.

Know, Connor. Life flows in one continual round. Partake. Breathe deep. Let go.

He did. Just stopped holding on. Just stopped believing in the ways of mortal man. A wave of celestial calm lifted him from the floor of the dingy cave. The grime and sweat from too many days of misery slipped from his battered, naked body. Like a well-used garment, it fell softly back to earth, an unnecessary impediment for the journey ahead. With gentle hands and welcoming arms, the maidens enveloped him in divine synchronicity until he too was part of their dance toward home. Toward—

"Connor." An angel had just spoken, shattering the dream.

The dance jolted to an end. All of the lovely maidens vanished into desert dust and smoking sage. He crashed to earth, back into the husk of his damaged body once more. For some ungodly reason, he wanted to cry, suddenly bereft of their sweet promise to be free from the agony of living. Pain sprang awake inside his body once more. He didn't want to stay. He didn't want to live.

"Connor," the angel's voice called to him, only it was Izza, not an angel, leaning over him and calling him back to earth. The saddest black eyes rained the sweetest shower onto his parched lips. Burning sage filled his nose with a profound sense of peace while her soft whisper breathed an ancient blessing called truth in his ear. "Don't die, Connor. I lied. I don't want to live without you. Jamie's gone. I can't lose you, too. Please don't go. Please stay."

Cool hands rested on his brow, weighting him solidly to dirt. To life. To—Izza.

He decided to stay. And he slept peacefully.

"You up for another visit to the county jail?"

"He's ready to talk?" Alex pulled his suit jacket on even as he closed his hotel door and juggled his cell phone against his shoulder. It had been a couple days since the failed attempt to negotiate with Ramirez. Leave it to the arrogant man to demand an evening visit with the Utah State Governor. He really did think he was important.

"Should be waiting for us in interrogation by now. Pick you up in five," Tom said.

The governor's car met Alex at the curb. He climbed in to see Tom in the driver's seat again.

"A man could get used to this," Alex chided.

"What? Curbside service?"

"No. Having a state governor for a chauffeur." Alex smirked right back at Tom. "How'd Ramirez sound?"

"The last time we spoke, he acted like some high and mighty king granting us an audience. Tonight he sounded tense. Pressed for time. Kind of rushed."

"I hope we get something useful out of him tonight."

"Yes, it's not often a man asks the guy who destroyed his drug business to save his family. What do you think is really going on?" Tom steered his car into the evening traffic.

"Two things. First, Ramirez saw something in the photos Mark sent. Second, he didn't know my agents were abducted until I told him. That was news to him. I'm sure of it."

"You don't think he planned to make an example of them like he did the DEA agents?"

"No, he doesn't know where Connor and Izza are anymore than I do."

"Then who has them?"

"Not Ramirez."

"I sure didn't expect him to ask you to save his children," Tom muttered. "Didn't see that coming."

Alex watched the city scenery go by, the haze of smoke from the wildfires still heavy in the air. He had two agents caught somewhere between the DEA's need-to-know embargo on truth and the cartel's outright deceit. Nothing was what it seemed. "I'll tell you something else I didn't see coming."

"What's that?" Tom Baxter asked as he pulled up and parked in front of the county jail.

"He never asked me to save his wife."

Connor did feel better in the morning. In fact he felt so much better that he was awake before Izza. It took him a few minutes to get moving, but sitting outside the cave and watching the sunrise spread across the eastern horizon helped. It was a beautiful world.

And he had his bearings for the first time since they'd been abducted. Their cave faced east. The rabbit snares were set to the north, down the incline from their cave where the sagebrush grew extra thick and tall.

Izza had been busy. Six rabbit skins lay across the rocks around the cave entrance. She'd become quite the provider during his illness. A supply of hand-sized stones was stacked near the granite chair. Plus she'd built a fire pit. The battered old coffee pot sat on the center rocks of the pit, waiting for water and heat. A supply of all sizes of branches was bundled against the outcropping of granite they called home. It was the barest bones kind of camp, but it had saved his life. And hers, too. And she'd done it alone, plus took care of him in the process.

Who'd have thought? Izza Ramos: hunter, gatherer, nurse, warrior, and expectant mother all rolled into one. Hmm. But where was she getting the water? And it was good, too, not full of mud, silt or one shred of string algae. That's one question she'd have to answer. He stood, testing his legs as well as the wound at his side. Much better.

But that was enough activity for the frail old man he felt like. Making his way slowly back to his corner of the world, Connor settled onto his back and folded his arms behind his head. The cave was enough for now. Drawing in a long slow breath, he was content just to hear himself breathe. Glancing across the cave floor, he caught sight of Izza. He knew it then.

Somehow they would manage. They'd survive. Together.

The scene that met Alex and Tom inside the jail was another surprise altogether. Normally an orderly place of business, it was in turmoil when they opened the entrance door. Paramedics rushing headlong to the interrogation room with a gurney pushed them to the side. Alex and Tom followed on their heels. It was a sorry sight. Ramirez lay on the floor in the throes of a seizure. A sheriff knelt next to him performing chest compressions while the paramedics scrambled to save the life of the man in crisis.

What the hell happened?" Alex barked.

The sheriff looked up, acknowledging the Governor with a nod before he responded to Alex's question. "Don't know, sir. I brought him down for interrogation and had just secured the prisoner's shackles when he started choking. At least I thought he was just choking, but then he started foaming at the mouth. He seized and blacked out. When he stopped breathing, I started compressions."

Frothy white foam oozed from Ramirez's open mouth, his skin chalky, and his eyes wide-open and unseeing. The paramedics hoisted him onto their gurney. Just as they wheeled him past Governor Baxter and Alex, Ramirez lurched under the restraints that held him. One hand snaked out wildly. He clutched Alex's sleeve, his eyes roaming around the room. "Stewart! Stewart!"

The medics halted when Alex grasped Ramirez's twitching hand. "I'm here, Miguel. What do you need?"

Ramirez coughed bloody foam. "Stewart!"

"I'm right here. What do you want from me?" Alex asked again.

Tears of blood ran from the man's swollen eyelids. His voice more snarl and spasm than voice, he wrenched Alex closer. His final words hissed out of him. "She... she lies-s-z-z-z."

Nineteen

Connor spent the next two days sleeping. Izza visited often, and every time she did, he was more amazed. Their world had changed. Everything she did seemed kinder, friendlier. But on the third day he was sick of being sick. Rising early, he felt full of energy, shaky maybe, but energy nonetheless. The fever was gone and he needed to get out of the cave.

Connor walked the short distance to the snares without any trouble. One rabbit lay strangled and dead. He unwrapped the wire and plucked the snares from what had proven to be a very productive hunting ground. He was glad for that moment of clarity when he'd remembered snaring rabbits as a teenager with his dad. This one thing might just have saved their lives.

Still, it was time for another location. After another short walk he'd moved the two snares further south and set them farther apart. The sun was warm. By the time he made his way back to the cave, a fire crackled under the coffee pot full of water, but Izza was nowhere in sight.

He wished for a cup of coffee. That would be a very nice way to start the day. Instead he set to work cleaning the meal. In no time at all, the rabbit was ready for roasting. He skewered the bunny with an old iron rod Izza had found, and before long, breakfast sizzled on the spit.

"You're feeling better." She observed as she rounded the corner of their cave. With her dark hair pulled back in a fresh ponytail, there was no other word for it. She looked great.

"Thought I'd fix breakfast. For a change" He studied her stance, not sure how she'd feel about him being mobile again. It hadn't made her too happy a few days ago.

"How's your side?" she asked.

"Better." He nodded toward the pile of rabbit skins. "You've become quite the hunter."

That made her smile. "You're better at it than me. I've only caught one rabbit a day. We might need to try another location."

Connor pointed to where he'd re-posted the snares. "Already did. See that flat rock over there?" Izza leaned toward him to follow the direction of his arm, her hand at his elbow. A jolt of tingling warmth radiated up from the casual contact. For some really stupid reason, his heart skipped a beat. "If we can find more wire, I'll set more snares."

She wrinkled her nose. "Wouldn't you like to eat something different for a change?"

"Sure. You found a grocery store nearby that I don't know about?"

"Come on. I'll show you." Izza took his hand. Again that same jolt sizzled up his arm. His breath caught, but it was her excitement that made him smile. She pulled him around the backside of their rock pile home. She'd found a desert tortoise, a big old lumbering fellow that stared up at him with black beady eyes.

"Aw, I can't kill that." He petted the crusty reptile's round head. "Let's give him a name. How about Homer?"

"Name or not, I can kill it." Izza had the sharpened stone in her hand, ready to do the deed. Hunger had brought a whole new reality to their lives.

"Okay then." Connor stepped back and folded his arms over his chest. "Turtle soup it is."

She clutched the tortoise's head in her hand. She pulled its neck all the way up. Homer protested, pulling his head into his shell, but Izza had anticipated that move. She dug her nails into his wrinkly neck skin and pulled his head back out. The contest was on. Tortoise hide had to be tough. Izza was tougher, but the real outcome depended on that knife-like stone in her hand. Could it inflict enough damage to bring this old fellow down?

Connor rolled the knot out of his shoulder. The tortoise struggled to pull its head into its shell, but the more amusing scene was playing out on Izza's face. All that determination was gone. She probably could've killed the old guy before she'd thought about it, but now that she'd looked into its eyes, she wasn't nearly as cocky. At last, she huffed out a big breath. And then another. Finally she tossed the makeshift knife to the ground and let the tortoise go.

Homer ducked his head into his shell where he was safe from Izza.

"Damn it. I can't kill it either. Give it a name." She plopped down on the ground beside Homer and whined, "I'm hungry, Connor. I'm hungry all the time."

He crouched beside her and patted her knee without thinking what the intimate gesture might mean to her. "Me, too. Maybe with two hunters in the family, we'll do better now. You think?" She was comfortable to be around this morning. It was easy to forget how prickly a cactus she could be.

Izza sniffed at the sizzling meat on the spit. "I see you found my rotisserie skewer?"

"Yeah, but where are you getting all the water we've been drinking? We're in a desert, for Pete's sake."

Her eyes lit up. "I'll show you." She waved him back into the cave and the dark tunnel beyond the little area where they'd been sleeping. When they'd gone maybe twenty feet past the end of the light, she stopped. "Listen. Do you hear it now?"

Connor cocked his head. The smallest dripping sound reached his ears.

"Smell," she ordered in her very drill-sergeant way.

He inhaled. His tender nose picked up the scent of moisture and wet stone.

"If I had a flashlight, I'd show you, but I've felt it. The water runs down the wall back here and into a hollowed out rock. It's not very big, and it's only an inch or so deep, but it tastes pretty good." She sounded pleased with herself.

"Hmm. Survival. Evasion. Resistance. Escape." Connor cited the four elements of their S.E.R.E. training on his fingers. "I think we've aced the survival part." He took a chance and hugged her against his side in the dark. "You did good."

She didn't pull away. "I found the water the very first day. You were lying out there in the sagebrush, and I was checking around this cave, and... and.... I was going to leave you and save myself."

"Oh. Okay." That confession surprised him, but it was missing the usual inflection of radioactive hostility.

"I mean I was going to save myself and the baby," she clarified. He didn't say anything as she rattled on. "I didn't think I'd live the first day anyway. I mean, I was dying of thirst, and it was so hot. You were shot, and I was hurt and...."

Connor waited. She was a lot more talkative in the dark.

"And then I found this cave and smelled the water."

He felt her sigh.

"And then I knew I couldn't leave you," she whispered.

"I do remember that first drink," he said quietly. "I thought I was dreaming."

"I didn't have any bottles then," she said. "I used my shirt. It's all I had, so I soaked it and carried it back and forth to give you a drink until I knew for sure you were going to live."

He didn't know what to say. Wow. He'd come damned close to dying. He gave her shoulder another small squeeze before he turned back to the mouth of the cave. She followed.

"Yeah. You were a mess, blood all over your face and pouring out of your side. And you didn't want to move. I had to kick your butt to get you inside the cave in the first place." Again she chatted like they were old buddies, filling him in on all the events he'd missed.

Connor stopped at the cave entrance on purpose. He wanted Izza to have to squeeze around him to get out. When she did, he stopped her, his arm around her shoulder again. This squeeze was intentional, and he wanted her to know it.

Looking down into her eyes, there was no anger there. If anything, she looked shy, maybe a little embarrassed, unlikely characteristics for Izza. Maybe it was just the fact that she'd had something to eat? He doubted it. She'd changed. Heck. So had he.

"You saved my life. Thank you," he said earnestly. "I'm glad you changed your mind that day."

"Yeah, well." She patted his chest like it was no big deal. "Let's go eat. I'm starved."

After their usual breakfast, Connor rigged up a torch with strands of dried rabbit hide wound around the thickest sagebrush branches he could find. A splash of Izza's deadly brown liquid provided the fuel. Her nifty fire-starter provided the spark, and together he and she went spelunking. All the junk she'd found had played a huge role in their survival. He wanted to know what else they could get their hands on.

"Look at this," he said.

The pool she'd told him about drained into a second pool, another flat rock just below the first but further back in the cave. The shallow basins with their concave surfaces proved the water had been dripping in the cave for ages. The bottom of both basins sparkled with a hint of turquoise and gold flecks.

"Too bad it's not the size of a bathtub." Izza was good company for a change. "I would so love a bubble bath, wouldn't you?"

He nudged her hip with his. "I'm not really a bubble bath kinda guy. Course, I could be persuaded."

She nudged him back playfully. "Bet me. Anyone who screams like a girl is a bubble bath kinda guy."

With that beautiful smile on her face, his heart stalled. The glow from the torch highlighted her dark eyes. They sparkled. And something sparked to life within him as well. He wanted to pull her close in the worst way; the best way wouldn't be so bad either. But he shook his head, remembering whom he was dealing with. Izza, the mean and powerful.

They went deeper into the cave. The rocky path descended into a tunnel. Almost like a stone staircase, it was too narrow to stand, but still maneuverable if they crouched low and held the ceiling for support. In twenty more feet or so, the tunnel expanded into a sizeable intersection of tunnels.

By this time, they were deeper underground. The air was cooler, which also explained the draft they'd both been feeling. There was no flat floor, just enough room to stand. An old pick lay across a rubble of rocks to the left, a reminder of another time in the state's history. Part of the tunnel branched off to the right, the other straight ahead into another rocky descent.

"Shall we?" Connor asked before he continued the tour.

Izza giggled like a little girl. "Geez. Let me check my calendar."

"Straight then? Or would you prefer to tour the hallway on the right, ma'am?" He arched his brows in his best evil imitation.

When she pointed straight ahead, they kept going. Their next stop was another small cavern where someone had definitely done some excavating in the past. Gouges and tool marks declared a treasure seeker's prior intentions on the low ceiling and walls. A rusted metal hammer and chisel lay off to the side on a small wooden chest while a dusty kerosene lantern hung from a hook wedged in the stone ceiling.

"Hold this a minute, would you?" Connor handed Izza the torch. He set the hammer and chisel off to the side, then opened the chest. Inside the dust-covered box lay a leather pouch and another brown bottle of Izza's miracle cure for gunshot wounds. He grinned as he handed it to her. "Here, Dr. Ramos. More poison to torture your patients with."

"You did scream like a girl." She examined the dusty brown flask with a smile. Izza was proud of her tough reputation.

Connor chuckled. "Wait until you get hurt, young lady. I get to play doctor then."

Suddenly coy, she had no smart-alec comeback.

"What do you think? Had enough exploring for one day?" he asked.

"Yeah. It's kind of spooky down here." Izza peered up the long tunnel behind them. "It's giving me the creeps. I keep hearing something move."

"Rats-s-s," he hissed, "or spid-erz-z-z-z."

She laid a clenched fist into his bicep. "Knock it off. I'm not afraid of those things, but something's been bothering me. The cartel left two full canteens of water the day they dumped us. I thought they were just being cruel because they took everything else, but," she shrugged, "it just makes me wonder."

"Sounds like they intended one of us to survive," Connor said thoughtfully. "That would have been you since they'd already shot me. I wondered why they didn't just kill us on the spot."

"Me, too." Izza rubbed the back of her neck. "I mean, why stick us out in the middle of nowhere? Do you think they already knew there was water in this cave? Do you think this was all part of their plan?"

"I don't know," he answered. "That depends on what their plan is. Or was. Have you figured out where we are yet?"

"Not sure. Might be Mexico. It's hot enough. Heck, it might be hell. It's hot there too."

He wiped a bead of sweat from his brow. "Yeah, but we're still breathing. I don't think we'd be doing that we'd died and gone to hell. You're right, though. This place is creepy. Let's get out of here."

He put the flask back in the chest. Between the two of them, they carried the hammer, chisel, lantern, and chest back to the surface. Tools always came in handy.

Before long they were topside at their smoking campfire. The lantern was empty of kerosene, an unfortunate fact of time wasted. Izza sat on her stone chair and opened the leather pouch. "Check this out." Several nuggets of gold rested in her hand, along with a tarnished gold locket. "What do you think they're worth?"

"Probably not as much as we'd like. So what's in the locket?"

Izza opened it. She squinted, holding the locket closer to see it better. With a gasp, she stiffened, dropped the locket to the sand and stalked away.

Puzzled, he retrieved it from the ground. Inside was a black and white portrait of a woman with a baby in her arms. Both the woman and baby had serious faces; both dressed in the fashion of the 1800s. There was nothing he could say. The inside of the locket was inscribed with: *Love Forever, Jamie.*

Connor called to her as she disappeared into the cave. "Izza. Come back. The chances of that happening are—"

"Shut up," she shot over her shoulder as she vanished inside.

Damn. Just when things were going good the most bizarre coincidence in the whole universe dropped out of the sky. If Connor didn't know better, he'd say this was a sure sign from the great beyond.

He studied the portrait. The woman sat with the baby in her arms facing the camera. Life back in the 1800s must have been damn tough judging by the lack of smiles on either face. Her dark hair was swept back with waves and crimped curls, a typical style back then. The baby was dressed in a long white gown and matching cap with dark curls around its face. There was no way to determine gender. Boy or girl, it was as somber as its mother. The woman wore the locket he now held in his hand. It rested over the buttoned-up high collar of the dress she'd worn.

He set the locket on Izza's granite chair. The sun was high in the sky. Time for a nap. Connor peered toward the empty rabbit snares before he ducked inside the cave. Still cool from the night, it was a welcome relief. Right on cue, Izza jumped to her feet and left the moment he entered.

Here we go again.

"Of all the stupid damn… Sonofabitch! Damn him!"

All that swearing outside the cave entrance meant she'd found the locket. He cringed. Let her deal with it. And she did. Mad as hell, Izza stormed back into the cave. "You think that's funny, Maher?"

So now I'm Maher again. Not Connor. Not Boston. The world according to Izza is a very confusing place for a dumb guy from Boston.

He shrugged. "Didn't mean to make you mad, Izza, not like that's hard to do."

She glared from the doorway, her hands on her hips, ready to pick a fight.

"You know what?" he asked. "I'm taking a nap. Do what you want with the locket. Keep it. Throw it. I don't care."

"I threw it!" she screeched. "I threw it and you'll never find it!"

With his hands clasped behind his head, Connor closed his eyes, hoping that would end the conversation. It didn't.

"I never should have saved your life. I should have let you—"

She never got the words out. Connor was up off the ground and in her face in a quick minute. "You should have what?"

This time her words were too mean. He wasn't going to take it anymore. He never should have in the first place. All he'd done was allow her to bully him and it had to end. As soon as he grabbed her arm, the discussion went south in a hurry.

"You want to lose that hand, buster?" The look in her eye was deadly.

He couldn't help but smirk at her tough girl comment. That was a mistake.

"What? You think I can't take you?" Temper flashed in her lovely brown eyes and he was even more enamored. It was hard being mad at this woman. Damn, he wanted her. He'd throw her to the ground right now if he thought she'd let him. So much passion in those fiery eyes. Nose to nose, pissed off as usual, and all he could see was the real Izza beneath the bluff.

"None of this is about that locket and you know it." Connor kept his voice low and steady. He didn't want to fight, but neither did he release her arm. "It's about your brother and what you think happened out there."

"I know what happened. I read the citation!" She jerked away, but he held her fast. She couldn't break free; she couldn't run away. Not this time. He'd never get through this very important argument if he had to keep chasing her ornery butt all over the desert.

"Come on, Izza. You and I both know what a stinking citation is worth in a war."

"Liar! You got the Navy Cross out of it! You got a commendation!" Her chin jutted out strong, forever leading her hard head into battles she didn't have to fight.

"Do you honestly think any medal is worth what went down over there?"

"They called you a hero," she spat.

"And we both know better, don't we? The heroes are the ones who didn't come home. Not us. Sure as hell not me."

Her silence declared her agreement, but there was more he needed to say. She glared at him, pulling away from his grip, but he held tight. It was time she knew his side of the story. Connor was not one to yell and bully. He leveled his voice. Calm and steady. Always go smoothly into a fight.

"War sucks," he said. "We go. We try to do something decent. Sometimes we make a difference. Sometimes we don't. Your brother was a damned good soldier when he wanted to be. It's not like Jamie had to be there. He wanted to be there, Izza. He volunteered because he wanted to help. You know that as well as I do."

She bit her lip; her jaw clenched so tightly that the chords in her neck stood out. Every piece of her soul was pulling away from him. He held on tight. He didn't want to lose her. Not again.

"You can believe it or not. Yes, I saved those guys in the MRAP, but what's not in the report is a woman named Amirah. She was caught in the crossfire with the rest of us, only she was standing there with a little girl hanging onto her skirt and a screaming baby in her arms. Jamie and I met her family when we were out on patrol. They were good people, only that day she was in the wrong place at the wrong time. She was scared. Her babies were going to die. You tell me. What was I supposed to do?"

The smell of battle drifted up from the depths of memories he'd never be able to forget. The noise. Men's fierce bellowing. And wailing. Always women and children wailing. Connor pointed to his right as the ghost Amirah's frightened face appeared right in front of him. "I should've put her in the report. I should've saved Jamie. I should've...."

Suddenly back in the land of his worst failures, he choked. The day came back in all too vivid Technicolor, complete with surround sound and the uniquely vivid smells of battle. Body odors. Gunfire. Sulphur. Cordite. Blood.

And down Jamie went, first to his knees, then to his face. He never felt a thing, just fell, his body riddled with armor piercing rounds designed to rip a man to shreds.

Connor pointed to his left, positive the images were real. The pain sure was. "It happened right there. Jamie was a few feet away from me. I saw him. Yeah, I should've knocked him down. Yeah, I should've protected him, but… I didn't. It was either Jamie, a gun-toting, armor-plated Marine with an M16 assault rifle, or… or… her."

And in his mind he remembered screaming at Jamie to lay low, like the smart ass ever listened to what he was told. He should have. God, he should have. By the time Connor got to him, the light had left his eyes and Amirah had run to safety with her babies. And Connor bawled like a baby, hunched into the dirt with Jamie in his arms like a brother.

Amirah and Jamie faded into the Utah sun. Once again, Connor was left with the oddest mix of regret and forgiveness in his gut, that empty, hollowed-out feeling he'd never be able to fill or forget. "God, Izza," he said tiredly. "Don't you think I'd save them all if I could go back and do it over again?" He didn't feel his own tears until they dripped off his chin. Then he let her go.

She jerked away, her hands braced on the outside wall of their piece of crap cave, her whole body heaving and her back to him as usual.

"Do you think a day goes by that I don't see Jamie's face? And every night I see Amirah. I get to see the terror in her babies' eyes, again and again." He was making a fool of himself now, but he couldn't stop. The memory stormed over him like a tank. Izza was right. He was an ass for making all the wrong decisions. And now he was a blubbering fool on top of it.

With an angry hand Connor scrubbed the tears off his face. He'd thought he'd put all this behind him months ago, but standing here in a desert again it felt like Jamie had just died. Maybe this wasn't such a good idea after all. He looked at Izza's back. She hadn't left, but she wasn't facing him either. Still running away. Still mad as hell. Still blaming him as much as he blamed himself.

Connor blew out a huge sigh. He'd done all he could. At least now she'd hate him for the right reason. Already high overhead and hot, the sun had turned their little stone oasis into a pizza oven, and he was melted crap. "I couldn't sleep for weeks," he whispered to himself, only half aware Izza was still there. "Every time I closed my eyes, all I could see was Jamie's face. But it doesn't haunt me like it used to."

Her shoulders heaved and her head was down. She was crying. He wanted to pull her back into his arms and give her a friendly squeeze like he'd done earlier. But he didn't.

"Don't you want to know why, Izza?" He was calmer now as he wiped his face, knowing he'd just destroyed the only good thing in his life. She'd never forgive him, no matter what. All of this true confession crap was in vain. It hadn't changed a thing. The bottom line was that Jamie had died. A strange woman in a far off land was alive. And it was all Connor's fault.

"Please. I need you to at least *want* to know why."

She didn't answer. He told her anyway, his whispered voice as weary as that day in Iraq. "I don't have nightmares anymore because Jamie would've done the same thing. I saw it in his eyes. He wanted me to save them instead of him. He knew what he was doing. It was like he gave me the nod, like he said, "*Go ahead, Connor. Save them, not me. Just do it.*"

"No," she bit out, her one syllable denial more razor than word.

Connor sank to the solitude of Izza's granite chair, tired to death of explaining, only to always end up the sinner. A man can only lose so much.

"Yes, Izza. Jamie knew what he was doing. I'm only going to say this one more time. God, I'm sorry."

And she came unraveled.

"No, you're not! You killed him, you sonofabitch. You could've saved him, but you didn't. He was your best friend, but you had to be some damned hero, didn't you? God, I hate you, Connor Maher!"

With that she launched herself at him, ready to kick, punch, slap or whatever. He saw it coming. She would have let him have it, too, but Connor didn't take it this time. Instead, he intercepted her wrists, twisted her backward into his chest, and wrapped his arms around her so she couldn't hurt him anymore. Or herself.

"Stop hitting me, damn it!" he bellowed, interlocking his fingers. His abdomen clenched from the hard impact, but he held on. "Jesus Christ, Izza! Stop hitting me!"

The damn broke. "I hate you so much!" she sobbed, writhing against him.

"No, Izza," he whispered against her ear, fighting as much to hold her as she was fighting him to get away. "You don't. Sweetheart, stop fighting me. I know better. You don't really hate me at all."

Twenty

"I miss him!" Izza hurled her grief to the sky. She stomped the ground, slamming her back into Connor's chest again and again. He groaned and took the hits. "God! I want my baby brother back. You don't need Jamie. I do. Do you hear me? Do you even care?"

"He cares," Connor whispered. "Believe me, he cares, Izza. He knows."

"N-no he doesn't!" She choked. "He doesn't even know I'm down here. I'm, I'm – nothing." The pain and heartache of years strangled out of her.

"Trust me. I miss him, too." Connor pressed his face against her cheek. "You were right. Jamie was my best friend."

Izza thrashed. She bucked. She tried everything to make him move, but Connor only held on tighter. Not tight enough to hurt, just enough she couldn't get away. This damned man wouldn't let her go. He just kept hanging on for no good reason. To her.

All of her training told her she could still make him pay. She hadn't used her hard head as a battering ram into his already broken nose. She hadn't bitten him yet.

"Let me go," she pleaded.

"Never," he murmured deep and low.

The need to hurt him subsided with that single word. The surety of it reverberated deep and low into the deepest black of her soul. Izza heard Connor. His strength encased her. Even his breathing sounded strong and sure. Lifting her easily off her feet, he settled onto their granite bolder with her on his lap. She twisted sideways in his arms, half facing him, half wanting to bolt away. The bitter memory came back with a vengeance.

"I just want to see him again," she sobbed, her arms twisted in front of her. "I want him to laugh at me. Just once more. He… he was all I had. We used to hide in the basement. Dad never came down those stairs when he was drunk. He thought he'd fall and break his neck. It was the only place we were safe."

"You had a damned hard childhood, Izza," Connor said, gently massaging the tight knot between her shoulder blades.

"No, I didn't." Anguish poured out of her. "I had Jamie. He was always there for me, but now he's gone. Aww, Connor, I just want him back."

"I know it's tough." He smoothed a strand of hair off her sweaty face as the outburst waned.

Izza sobbed. "No one's left. They're all gone."

"No," he said softly, his hands still wrapped around her shoulders. "Not everyone."

She turned to face him. Connor blinked to hide his emotions, but she saw the tears—and the love. Her world had turned upside down. She cupped his chin in her palms. "Please don't cry. I've been so mean to you. God, I'm so sorry. I don't hate you. I never did."

He wiped his face and swallowed hard. "I know that, Izza, but you've got to stop hitting me. You pack a helluva wallop for a little gal."

"Connor. I...." She smoothed her thumbs over his whiskered cheeks. "I don't even know why I do it. I just get so mad."

He leaned his forehead to hers. "You hit me because you need someone to hurt as bad as you do. I get it, but believe me, Izza. I do hurt as bad as you. Maybe worse. Jamie was my best friend. You lost your brother that day, but I lost both of you."

She burrowed into his chest. "But you've never stopped loving me."

"You're the meanest woman I know, but you're right. I do love you." He tipped her face up to his again.

Her response came with tears and sobs, "And I love you."

"Izza?" he asked hoarsely. "May I please kiss my baby girl's mother?

Her heart leapt into her throat. Connor could not have asked a more perfect question. A different kind of warmth flooded her heart, and she knew she had a lifetime of penance ahead of her. It had to begin today. Now.

"I meant what I said. I do love you." With that soft pronouncement she pulled her tank top up and over her head, and wriggled out of her cargo pants, her eyes fastened to his.

Connor about dropped his teeth, he looked so flustered and surprised. He shook his head. "No, Izza. Not here. You don't want to—"

"Yes. I do." Wearing nothing but her underwear, she straddled his thighs and prepared to prove herself, big belly and all. "I'm tired of fighting with you. I loved you then. I love you now. I need you to know. Please forgive me. Let me show you."

"I already know." His breath hitched as he took in the sight of her. Amidst the desire, sadness shadowed his expression. "My God. You're so thin."

She shrugged, needing him to not look so stricken. "It's all them bunnies you keep catching."

"We need a break," he muttered even as his hands smoothed over her shoulders and headed lower. The deep rumble in his voice struck a chord in her belly.

She leaned in for a kiss. "I want you, Connor."

He didn't have to be asked twice. The only problem was his gunshot wound. And his nose. And, oh yeah, she was definitely with child. But the more Connor kissed Izza, the less he worried. Izza's mouth was a taste of heaven. He deepened the kiss, savoring every stroke of her tongue, every nibble and sigh. That same ferocious hunger he'd only known once before leapt to life. Now he knew why and how that night of passion had happened. There was no choice. He had to have her in his life, all of her, then as much as now.

With a grunt, he clutched two handfuls of her backside and stood. His gut didn't complain as much as he expected, maybe because another body part spoke up loud and clear. He meant to comply.

A hint of worry deepened her brown eyes. "Are you sure you can carry me?"

"Yes, ma'am," he said with conviction. The best mission of his life lay ahead. He would deliver.

Placing her center on the makeshift mattress of other people's cast off clothing, she never looked more stunning. The moment jelled. There she sat with her knees to her chest and her arms circling her knees, half-naked and beguiling as hell. No hotshot celebrity or model could compare. Rags or not, she was the rarest pearl, the treasure he'd been looking for.

"I'll try to go slow," he said, "but it's been over six months and I—"

"Wait. What? You haven't been with anyone since me? Really? Not even—her?"

He had to grin. She looked so happily shocked.

"No, ma'am," he declared with honor. "I won't say I haven't been looking. I just have a knack for picking the wrong women."

"But you and that Dancer woman looked so—together."

"But we're not," he said. "I might need to explain things to her one of these days. Maybe not, but Izza. You were my first, and you're going to be my last."

"But what about—? You mean you never—?" Suddenly shy, she'd loosened her ponytail and tossed her head. "But you're so handsome. I've heard about your reputation in the East Coast office. All the ladies think you're a stud. I find it really hard to believe women aren't falling all over you."

"Ha," he said with a cheesy grin. "People like to talk. What about you, gorgeous? How many guys am I going to have to fight off back in Seattle?"

She snorted. "I'm too mean. Guys are scared of me." Scintillating curls rolled off her shoulders. He forgot to breathe. She held her hand up for him to accept her offer. He doffed his clothes and joined her. And very gently, she pressed him to his back.

"Besides, you're my only, too," she murmured.

And the rest of the world slipped away.

The tenderest assault began the second her hands and lips roamed over his battered body. He closed his eyes and soaked it all in. She knew which areas to avoid and which to encourage, and it took so little encouragement. Unlike the last time, they had all the time in the world now. He explored her curves with his fingers and tongue. But each touch and taste brought a need for more. Exploring and fondling transformed into ardor that couldn't wait. Izza groaned against him when he clenched her backside again.

"Come here," he breathed, and that's all she needed to hear. She gave him everything. Passion. Energy. And the gentlest love.

With her still panting above him, he took charge. Rolling Izza to her back, he stared down into the dreamiest eyes. An aura of pure contentment glowed around her. This wasn't just the physical act they were doing. They were pouring love into each other, joining energy and lives, etching memories and bonds that would stand a lifetime. And beyond.

He sank into her with their eyes locked on each other. There was no world beyond the one they'd just created, only deep browns that drew him into their eternal depths.

"I've always loved you, Isabella Ramos," he said reverently as he acknowledged what he'd been searching for in all those other dalliances.

The heat in her eyes reached all the way through him. In a flash, Connor was on fire. It swept up from the backs of his legs and into his groin. Her lovely body clenched and he poured all that he was into her. Again. And again.

He collapsed into her arms with one prayer on his lips. "Izza. My love."

What the hell else could go wrong?

Alex was in his rental car on his way to the Utah State Capitol. On top of everything else, Tom wanted him to add his two cents worth to a meeting with the press, not Alex's favorite people on a good day. Mother and Ember were in the process of running all of Mark's video intel through their facial recognition program. That was the only thing that made sense. Ramirez had seen something in those pictures from his own hacienda that panicked him. Apparently, it panicked someone else too, enough to murder him. The County jail was in lockdown, no one in and no one out until Governor Baxter knew exactly who'd done it and how.

Turning left on State Street, Alex had to admit the view of the state's capital was breathtaking with the Wasatch Mountains for a backdrop. The smell of smoke still tinged the air, but all the fires had made for outstanding sunrises and sunsets over the past couple of days.

His cell phone vibrated. Alex answered it expecting Mother or Ember. He got Mark.

"Boss, got a few developments you need to know."

"Hope it's good news," Alex growled.

"Are you still in Utah?"

"Yes. Ramirez is dead. Poisoned at the jail." Alex was pissed.

"Shit," Mark cussed. "Then it's not him. I was going to tell you to grill that bastard for more information, but now—"

"Why? What's going on?" Alex pulled into the closest vacant parking stall and killed his engine.

"A convoy of trucks showed up yesterday at the Ramirez hacienda. Looked like an army. At first, we thought it was a peaceful takeover, but when one of the trucks left in the middle of the night, we followed. Ramirez also owned a gravel pit, Boss. The truck was carrying bodies."

"Who's dead?"

Mark huffed over the phone. "That's the thing. Most of the bodies are buried under a ton of gravel. Only one was close enough to the surface. I just sent at picture of it to Mother for positive identification, but we think it was Ramirez's housekeeper. And we found the little girl's dog, too."

Alex checked his watch. Mark and his team must have been digging for bodies during the night to have this kind of information so early in the morning. He gulped at the unsettling thought before he asked, "What dog?"

"His daughter, Sophia's," Mark answered somberly. "Fuzzy little mutt. It looks like whoever's taken over the cartel is executing everyone and everything loyal to Miguel Ramirez."

"Stop digging, Mark," Alex said somberly. "You may be right. This whole thing just keeps getting better and better." A stab of fear jolted him. "Where are his daughters? Have you seen them yet today?"

"Yes. They're still inside the hacienda. You don't think they're in danger do you? Ramirez's wife seems to come and go as she pleases."

Alex shoved his hand through his hair, frustrated at what he was about to order. "You need to secure those two girls."

The dead silence on the other end of the phone was not unexpected.

"Did you hear me?"

"I heard you," Mark said quietly. "Guess I don't understand what you're telling me to do, though. You want me to kidnap two little girls?"

"Yes." Even as he gave the order, Alex knew what he was asking was over and above his four man team's capability.

"And do what with them?" Mark's tone was incredulous.

"Not sure, but if I'm right, they're in mortal danger."

"Why? What do you think is going on?" Mark's question belied his disbelief. "I mean we didn't come down here to save the world, Boss. This takeover stinks of cartel business to me and as long as it's in Mexico—"

"As long as it's happening in Mexico, it will keep happening up here. Someone from that hacienda just ordered a hit on a very powerful cartel boss locked inside a secure United States jail. Whoever that person is, they may also know where Connor and Izza are. They're very much in control of what's happening here in Utah. We need to take this cartel down once and for all."

Weariness pegged Mark's voice. "Boss, I've got one trained sniper with me, and two DEA agents. I only came here to bust Ramirez. Now you're telling me to steal not one, but two little girls?"

"Not steal. Rescue. Ramirez was about to turn state's evidence when they got to him. He knew he was going to die. The only thing he asked was for me to save his daughters.

Can you do it or not?" Alex waited through the silence on the other end. He knew what his junior agent was going through. Want to or not, Mark was mentally working a strategy, weighing risks, scenarios, and back up plans against the talents and skill of his team. Two small little girls would be difficult to handle. They'd have to be removed from the hacienda at the same time and without a sound. That alone would prove daunting.

Alex went through the same mental exercise. Mark and his team were on the ground and capable, but this was Mexico they were talking about executing a covert operation. The most proper course of action would be to go through the State Department. Maybe the DEA too, since they were already somewhat involved.

But Alex knew better. All those very proper channels spent more time covering their asses than getting the job done. By the time they stepped up to the plate, two little fatherless girls would be in that same gravel pit with their dog.

"I'm coming down," he decided. "I can be there by—"

"No, Boss," Mark ground out. "You're too late. If we're right, those girls won't live the day."

"Exactly," Alex muttered. "What are you thinking?"

That Mark didn't respond quickly verified the serious nature of this additional effort. At last, he said, "I'm thinking if we get caught, we stand to create one helluva firestorm for U.S. and Mexican relations."

"True." Alex let his agent work it out. Covert ops always carried the risk of offending friend or foe alike, but when it came to intentionally putting his team's lives on the line, Mark had to be the one to make the call.

"I've got Rory and the others watching the Ramirez estate right now," he muttered. "He and I have both been inside. God, it's huge. Two little girls. Might need to dope them to keep them quiet. Military-type guards all over the place. No dogs. The housekeeper's dead. Damn. Two little girls."

Alex listened while Mark went through a mental list. He did notice Mark's focus, though. *Two little girls.*

"Shit, Boss. We can do it. I'll tell my team."

Alex blew out the breath he hadn't realized he'd been holding. "How are they?"

"They're good troops," Mark answered. "Damned glad they're down here with me."

"You mentioned Ramirez's wife came and went as she pleased. Does she take the girls with her when she goes out?"

"Not that I've seen, but she's got servants. At least, she used to. I'm not sure who's left inside. Why?"

"Watch her," Alex said. "She may be the key we're looking for."

"Will do, Boss." Mark sighed as he hung up.

Alex did as well. He had the nuisance of a press conference to endure while his men were putting their lives on the line on foreign soil. The familiar throb of his daily migraine ramped up. There were days when he wondered why the hell he did what he did, but not this day. Mark had said it well. It all came down to those *two little girls.*

Twenty-One

"So where do you think we are?" Connor peered into the east, still thinking that might be their best direction to start hiking. Now that he was feeling better, he wanted to get back to civilization. Izza needed proper care and so did the baby. He could stand a little medical attention himself.

"I think we're in, umm, Utah?" she teased, crouched busily at the campfire turning the latest rabbit on its spit.

They'd worked out a trade. He'd catch and skin the rabbits or maybe a rattlesnake if he could find one, and she'd grill them. She'd become quite the domestic little woman lately, filled with the compulsion to clean and organize their very rustic hole in the wall camp. It seemed she couldn't gather enough sagebrush for the fire or enough rocks to keep the pesky Boomerang at bay. She called it the nesting syndrome. He called it good.

Connor pulled Izza to her feet, his arms around her again and his hands forever on her wonderfully rounded belly. "You might be right, smart ass," he muttered playfully.

She pushed her butt into him. They didn't fight anymore. The passion they felt for each other was finally focused in the right direction. She'd even retrieved the locket and wore it around her neck, another sign of her acceptance that Jamie was gone.

With his arms full of Izza, Connor stared to the east, calculating everything he could remember from his computer searches on Utah, if that's where they were. While he'd checked on the peculiar liquor laws and religion of the state, he'd also studied the enormous areas owned by the Bureau of Land Management. More than fifty percent of the state belonged to BLM, a lot of it closed to mining and oil exploration. Most was still open to grazing, sheep or cattle, but it was dry, arid, and unforgiving as all get out. Like Nevada. Arizona. Texas for that matter. And, oh yes, Mexico. Bingo. In other words, he and Izza could be just about anywhere.

"I've been to Arizona before, and Moab, too." Izza pulled his arms tighter around her. "There's a lot of good rock climbing and red sandstone in that part of the state, so I'm pretty sure we're not there."

"That's helpful. At least we know where we're not. Like we're not in Alexandria. We're not in Seattle. And now we know we're not in Moab, Utah, either."

She gave him a sharp nudge with her elbow. "Where do you think we are if you're so smart?"

"I don't know, but I don't think the cartel would have driven too far just to dump a couple half-dead bodies in the desert to die. They could've killed us at the RV in that case. No, they wanted us isolated for a reason, but close-by. Utah makes the most sense. Just the fact that they left two canteens scares the hell out of me. They meant for us to survive. We can't stay here much longer. They're going to come back. East looks like our best shot."

"What if there's no water when we get there?"

"You're right, but smoke means fire. Fire might mean firefighters. And yeah, the water thing is a big deal, but we have to do something. I'll hike over there tomorrow and see if there's any kind of help to be had. If not, I'll come right back, okay?"

Leaving a pregnant woman alone in the desert was not his idea of a good scenario, but not doing anything put her and the baby in more danger. At least this way they might have a chance.

She scanned the distant mountain. "How far do you think it is?"

"A good day's walk. Twenty miles maybe."

"Do you think anyone's even looking for us?"

He sighed. "This is a big state with lots of desert and nothing much in between. Only the cartel knows where we are. That's the best reason to get the hell out of here."

"Every time I hear a plane fly over I throw more sagebrush on the fire, but they're all too high. I don't think they can see the smoke."

"Airliners fly over thirty-thousand feet high, Izza. They'd never see us."

"Hey, I have an idea." The excited look in her eyes made him smile. Connor was the first to admit it. He was a sucker for this woman through and through.

"Mother and Ember are always studying satellite images, aren't they?" she asked. "Why don't we give them something to look at?"

Connor didn't have any idea what Izza meant, but after packing rocks for a couple hours in the summer sun, he found out. By then, they'd constructed a huge SOS sign on the desert floor just beyond the cave's entrance. Hopefully visible by air and satellite, they amended their call for help by adding another acronym that only someone from The TEAM would understand. C.M.I.R. – their initials. By late afternoon, they were both tired, but pleased with their handiwork.

Their little pile of granite cast just enough of a shadow to shade them from the sun. He took advantage of it, a bottle of water in one hand and Izza comfortable in the other while he sat on the ground at the cave entrance. The sign was extra large. That meant big rocks, and big rocks meant two sore backs. Connor and Izza were dirty, tired, and thirsty as usual.

"You like our new acronym?" he asked.

She breathed out a tired sigh. "It's just another acronym, but if you like it, whatever."

"You've got to say it right. Go on. Say it." As usual, Connor saw joy where Izza did not.

She enunciated each letter patiently. "C. M. I. R. There. Are you happy now?"

"You're not doing it right. Don't spell it out. Say it like you mean it. It really says 'Come here.'" He grinned down at her, all tired and sweaty in the crook of his arm. "It's what I always say to you when we're making love. Come here, Izza. Come here. And you always do what you're told."

She pushed him away with a half-hearted shove, blushing. "I'm not in the mood. Should have spelled, 'Go on.'"

"No, Izza, come here. Come here," he teased, pulling her onto his lap, his hand already under her tank top. His fingers worked their way over her stomach to the soft swell of her breasts. Her nipples sprang to attention.

"You're nuts." She giggled under his fun-loving attention, his hands all over her by now. "I thought you were tired."

"I am, but you're irresistible," he breathed hit hot against her neck. "Come here, Izza. Come to me."

She propped her bottle of water against the granite chair before she gave in to him for some 'Come here' time together. Connor made love with Izza under the wide desert sky.

Boomerang watched from his safe distance at the crest of the granite cave. Homer stared unblinking from his rock corral. And somewhere miles above the earth, a Defense military satellite snapped photo after photo after photo....

"You don't understand," DEA Director Scott Sylvane said evenly. Out of the blue, he'd flown to Utah and gone directly to Tom Baxter to request a meeting with Alex. Sitting across the Governor's conference table from two very polished politicians only irked Alex all the more.

"Then enlighten me," growled Alex. "Your last words were 'need to know,' Scott. Well, I sonofabitchin' need to know."

The only encouraging part of the afternoon was that he'd been required to leave his cell phone with Tom's secretary, which meant the Governor's office was SCIF enabled, a Sensitive Compartment Information Facility. SCIF rooms were safe rooms, specifically designed to protect top secret intel against electronic surveillance from corporate spies or foreign operatives. That was the first hint of possible DEA cooperation. Scott might actually have come to Utah to share some of his top-secret intelligence for a change.

He removed a thick gray business file from his briefcase and slid it across the table to Alex. "This won't help much, but it's yours. You've got smart people working for you, Alex. They should be able to extract what you need to know out of this report."

Alex flipped through the report. Just as he'd suspected. The file contained page after page of redacted, blacked-out intelligence. He slapped it shut and tossed the file back to Scott. "You're as much help as you were last time. I don't have time to decode this, and you know it." He deliberated for all of one second before he went for broke. "I've got boots on the ground outside Hermosillo right now. Tell me what's really going on inside that hacienda."

Scott straightened in his seat. "You do? Since when? How many?"

"Four. Since my op was compromised. Now speak."

"I didn't know the State Department approved—"

"They're sightseeing," Alex lied. "The State Department doesn't even know they're there. My team came across a moral dilemma they could not ignore while they were... hiking."

Scott Sylvane was a tall, silver-haired man with the self-control of a saint. Never once did he raise his voice or pull rank like many other federal directors of important agencies who Alex had dealt with in the past. Those good traits rankled Alex all the more, but especially now that he'd confessed to an unauthorized operation inside a foreign country, and an ally at that. Civilian contractors just didn't do those kinds of things. Usually.

"That moral dilemma your agents are up against wouldn't have anything to do the Sonoran Cartel, would it?" Scott asked, his long fingers sedately interlocked on the table in front of him and the corners of his mouth crinkled with sarcasm.

"Yes," Alex admitted point blank.

"Before we go any further, Director Sylvane, there is something else you need to be aware of," Tom Baxter interrupted. "Miguel Ramirez is dead."

"He is?" Scott turned on Tom, his eyes widened with shock. "When did that happen? How?"

Tom nodded. "It doesn't matter. We believe the cartel got to him inside the secure portion of our county jail."

"Why am I just hearing about this now?"

"Probably for the same reason I only recently found out three DEA agents were murdered in one of my canyons last year," Tom shot back. "I placed a temporary gag order on my people to keep this out of the news so we could get one step ahead of the SC for a change, something I don't seem to be able to do with DEA in my backyard. You want to explain that?"

"How can you be sure it was someone from the cartel?"

"Because I don't know many Americans who know how to poison a man with the venom from bark scorpions, do you?"

Scott blew out a deep sigh as he glanced from Tom back to Alex. "Okay. Okay. It's time we put all of our cards on the table, gentlemen. Me first." He turned to Tom. "You're right. The SC likes a gruesome death. Scorpion venom would work. They've used it before. It's one of their trademarks. And yes, I squelched the press reports about the DEA murders last year. They were barbaric and cruel. The citizens of Utah didn't need to know. Besides, I couldn't allow the SC to believe for one second they had the upper hand in your state."

"Did they?" Alex asked.

"Momentarily," Scott admitted. "Not anymore."

"What happened?"

Scott hesitated. "Let's just say that we had an unfortunate confrontation that led to an awful mistake. That's all I can say."

"But those agent's families deserve to know the truth," Tom insisted.

"No." The DEA Director shook his head bleakly. "They don't. Right now, they think their sons and husbands are on an extended undercover operation that required a complete information blackout. When the time is right, I will tell them their men died honorably for their country in the line of duty, but I will not reveal the brutal nature of their deaths. No family deserves that final memory."

"That's a damn low way to treat their families," Tom muttered.

Scott Sylvane offered a shrug and a tired smile. "Believe me. I sold my soul long ago to protect my country. If I have to sell another piece of it to shield these families from atrocities committed, you can bet I will."

"The truth will out," Alex warned. "You're sitting on a ticking bomb with the kind of press we have today."

Scott nodded, his eyes to the table. "And I hope the American people will understand when the day comes that I'm explaining to Congress and other so called important people who've never once stood in the line of fire. My intentions are pure. I've done what I've done to save more than just one state, Tom. In case you haven't noticed, we're in a war. The SC smoked through Arizona like it was nothing. Fast forward ten years. Hell, fast forward just two years. Our borders are already breached. I don't want to burst your bubble, gentlemen, but cartels far worse than the SC are headed north." He lifted his head and his eyes went straight to Alex. "You're a Marine. You know the drill. Men like you and me who actually believe in our country are just in the way."

"Then why the slow roll this year?" Alex asked, his appreciation for the DEA Director at an all time high. "You've got a team up the canyon right now sitting on their thumbs."

"Actually, I don't. Special Agents Burkhouse and Denton are two of my finest. Randy had strict orders to infiltrate the cartel. He's accomplished more—"

"You've got a man inside," Alex hissed. Instantly, he understood the perceived lack of DEA cooperation. They'd slow-rolled his team because they couldn't risk endangering their undercover operative.

Scott nodded. "I do. Carlos Santiago has been deep undercover for the last three years. I believe one of your men met him during a close encounter in the canyon. Broke his nose. Left Carlos with some explaining to do, but also made him look more authentic. One of your men wouldn't be a surfer out of California, would he? Tan, blond, moves like a cat?"

"Connor Maher. From Boston," Alex answered, pleased that Connor had made an impression on the DEA's face. "Was Santiago involved in the ambush of my men?"

"No," Scott declared quickly. "He was on his way back to Mexico with Ramirez's wife when it happened."

"So what now?" Tom asked, his fingers tapping impatiently on the heavy wooden table.

Alex revealed his last card. "Ramirez begged me to rescue his daughters. Do you know why?"

"Yes," Scott said. "For the last seven months, Carlos has been working with operatives of CISEN, the Mexican Center for Research and National Security. They've suspected Alejandra of running her own game behind Miguel's back for a while now. She's used his influence to build her own very considerable power base. Carlos suspected she might have her eye on taking over the cartel her husband built. Not until he and the agents from CISEN were able to put two and two together did they realize how truly devious she is. You see Alejandra has another child, one whom she's kept secret from Ramirez for fifteen years. Ricardo Quinones."

"Javier's kid?" Tom asked. "She's got a son with her brother?"

Scott nodded. "At first Carlos thought Ricardo was just a nephew or something. Javier's got enough brothers and sisters. But then one of the CISEN informants embedded inside the Quinones hacienda discovered the truth. The kid's no nephew. He's next in line to be run the cartel."

Alex pressed two fingers to his throbbing temple at the lengths people went to for power and greed. "Sonofabitch. Then Quinones must be grooming his bastard son to take over the cartel. The purge is to eliminate any other heirs or opposition to the Ramirez throne. That's why the—"

"What purge?" Scott asked in alarm.

"The one taking place right now in Sonora," Alex said. "Javier's army showed up yesterday. My team believes they're killing anyone in the Ramirez hacienda loyal to Miguel."

Scott breathed in a huge breath as this new intelligence registered. Alex could almost see the wheels spinning in his head. "Then Operation Cristero must conclude tonight," he muttered to himself.

"Operation Cristero?" Alex asked.

Suddenly, Scott looked very tired. "Yes. You know how the people of Mexico think. Everything has to do with saints and honor. In the late 1920s, Elías Calles was the fortieth President of Mexico. He waged a bloody war in Sonora against all Christian clerics because, as he saw it, organized religion had grown too powerful and threatened his country. It was nothing more than a lie to further his own power play, but many priests and monks were executed for their faith. The people fought back in a counter-revolution they named Cristeros in honor of—"

"Christ the King," Alex said. "Understood, but why? This cartel is not attacking religious freedom."

"No, but Javier and Alejandra Quinones are heirs of Elías Calles. Why else the name of their hacienda?"

Alex paused. Why did he not know that piece of information if it was so important?

Scott offered a bemused smile. "The people of Hermosillo call it Hacienda de Jefe Máximo, the title Elías Calles bestowed upon himself when he was in power. The man was a flaming ego maniac."

Alex got the connection. The current residents of the hacienda were as ruthless as Calles, but that only explained the name of the operation. He didn't really care. "What the hell is Operation Cristero about?"

"It is the Mexican government's complete takedown of all drug cartels throughout their country. The people are tired of living in fear. Their Presidente had finally heard their cries for justice. He has vowed to send his army."

All Alex heard was his men were in the middle of a hornet's nest about to get hit with a big stick. "When can you get hold of your man inside?" he asked bluntly.

"Immediately. Where are your men?"

"They're keeping watch outside the Ramirez estate. I told them to retrieve the girls. They planned to go in tonight."

"They're going in alone?" Scott asked in dismay. "You sent four men against an army of hundreds?"

"No," Alex barked. "I sent two damned good ex-Marines and the agents your superstar Burkhouse canned."

Scott didn't bat an eye. He turned to Tom. "I need my damned phone."

For hours they slept, wrapped up in each other's arms and oblivious to the scorching sun that rolled across the sky. Izza lay with her back to Connor, his arm a pillow for her head. Their bedroom was nothing more than a cave full of rocks, dirt, a few old soda pop bottles and a banged up coffee pot. And she couldn't have felt happier.

"Remember the fireworks the first time we made love?" Connor murmured.

She squirmed around in his arms to face him. "I'm pretty sure those were RPGs. Not fireworks."

"Nope. They were big, beautiful red fireworks that spelled I. Z. Z. A. They were way up high in the sky. You couldn't miss them." He lifted his palm to the ceiling as if he could make her see what he'd seen that first time. Watching the glow in his eyes never ceased to amaze her. Connor could make the sun shine on a dark day.

"Nope. Sorry. RPGs," she teased just to see the light in those Pacific blues again.

"It was you." He kissed her forehead. "When we get back to civilization, I want a do-over. I want the chance to do this right."

"Are you telling me we didn't do it right this time?" she asked, lifting one eyebrow in mischief.

He rubbed her baby bump. "Not exactly. We've both done good, but I want to make love to you on something besides dirt. I want to feed you chocolate-covered strawberries and champagne. I want to spoil you rotten like the brat you are."

Tears sprang to her eyes. The day she never imagined would come had finally arrived. She was finally willing to be loved, and here lay the man who actually did.

"Do you ever wonder why things happen the way they do? Like those words in the locket?" she asked pensively.

He pulled her under his chin. "What do you think?"

"I think it was a message from Jamie. I know it sounds weird, but he'd do something like that. Like when Dad would come home drunk, Jamie and me would hide. Sometimes Dad caught me anyway, but Jamie always made me laugh after it was over. You know? He always found a way to show me that he loved me even when I felt like no one else did."

"Your dad was real hard on you, wasn't he?"

"Yeah," she admitted. Connor might as a well know the truth. "He was a mean drunk. Didn't care which one of us he got hold of. He'd used anything within reach—belt, the phone cord, a chair. It didn't matter. He just kept hitting, like somehow that would bring her back."

Connor squeezed her tightly. "Your mother?"

She nodded. "Yes, my Mama. When she died of cancer, everything good in Dad died, too. At first, he spent days sitting in their bedroom drinking and crying. I don't think he really saw Jamie and me after that. We were just in his way. We got to be good at hiding or just not being home when he was. One time, we even planned to make him fall down the stairs. It didn't work."

"Where is he? You want me to look him up?"

"No, I don't care where he is. I've got you." Izza eased herself on top of Connor's hips as carefully as she could. The last thing she wanted right now was to talk anymore about the monster her father had become. "Enough about me. Tell me all of your brothers' names again."

He rolled his eyes. "Again? Okay. There's Matt, Tim, Keenan, Sean, Patrick, and the baby, Brendan, only he's not much of a baby anymore."

"And Matt, Tim and Keenan are already in the Corps?"

Connor sighed. "Yes. Matt's in Afghanistan. Tim's shipping out to places unknown in a week, and Keenan's graduating from boot camp soon. My poor mother. She'll be all alone before she knows it."

"She raised you boys all by herself?" Izza asked.

Another long sigh. Connor curled a tendril of her hair around his index finger. "For the last nine years. Dad was a detective on the Boston police force. I was fifteen when it happened. He and his partner went after Paddy O'Donnell, the Irish arms dealer. Things went bad. Mom never told us boys the whole story. The mayor shut down the city for the funeral. It was like one long sad procession. Even when I go home today, people I've never met before come up to me on the street and tell me a story about him. It's like he's still there."

She studied Connor's somber countenance. His eyes drifted to the curl on his finger and she knew he was reliving the loss of his father.

"Tell me his name," she said.

"Connor James Maher. Just like mine." A tender smile brightened his face. Connor loved his father. He missed him. Regret poked a pointed fingernail into Izza's heart. Yet there were many times she'd wished hers had never come home.

"Where do you live now?"

"Silver Springs, but you know that, too. I've told you before." He tapped the end of her nose, breaking the somber moment. "And Mom still lives in the same clapboard house in Boston. You're going to meet her."

"I know. I just like to hear you talk about your family. It sounds so—normal."

"Ha. There's nothing normal about us Maher boys. Just ask my Mom. Oh, the stories she could tell you."

"I intend to. Your gunshot wound must be feeling a lot better today, huh?"

He smirked. "I think all of me feels a lot better."

"I'm sorry that I—"

"Shush." He stopped her with a finger to her lips. "Stop saying you're sorry. What's past is past. Let's concentrate on our future."

Warmth filled her body. "I'd rather concentrate on the present."

Blue eyes darkened to smoldering and sexy. "They do say the present is a gift. Was there something you, umm, wanted to give me?"

Oh, yeah....

Twenty-Two

Mark Houston was not a happy man. He and his team had been on surveillance in the hot Sonoran desert for days now. They were tired, dirty, and deserved a three-day pass instead of an additional mission that was guaranteed to turn the already troubled hacienda upside down.

What the hell was Alex thinking?

The answer was obvious. *Two little girls.* That much Mark knew for sure because he'd storm heaven and hell if anything ever happened to his daughter, JayJay.

He headed back to those good troops he'd left in the Sonoran desert. All dressed in similar desert cammies, guilt rattled him as they gathered around him, sunburned and half-baked. They should be lounging around a brightly tiled swimming pool, sipping margaritas and stuffing their faces with shrimp, chips and guacamole instead of planning a kidnapping. He didn't want to stick it to them one more time, but he did. Orders were orders. And Alex was right.

"Change of mission," he declared. "We're going into the Ramirez estate to remove his daughters."

Cassidy's eyebrows arched. Brigham nearly choked on his gum. Only Rory had the nerve to ask, "Why?"

Mark laid it on the line. "Because of what we saw at the gravel pit, and because Ramirez was poisoned in his Salt Lake City jail cell."

"Some one killed the cartel boss?" Cassidy exclaimed. "Damn. I wanted to do that."

"I know how you feel, but the hit came from within the Ramirez hacienda," Mark said. "There is a coup taking place. We can't take the chance the girls won't be next."

"Any word on Connor yet?" she asked.

Mark shook his head. It was hard to miss the hopeful tone to her question, but he also noticed she hadn't asked about Izza. They'd better be found alive, or God help whoever the new cartel boss was.

"You've got to be kidding." Rory scanned the two recently hired junior agents at his side. "It's an armed camp, Mark. One peep from those kids and we're dead. That means you and I are going in."

"Not necessarily. I can do it," Brigham spoke up.

"So can I," Cassidy said. "Just because we weren't military doesn't mean we're slouches."

"That's not what I meant," Rory muttered. "You two are damned good shots, but this is a ghost op. You've seen the influx of armed guards into the hacienda the last couple of days. We'll be outmanned twelve to one the minute we pass go."

"Ghost op?" Brigham asked.

"Like Ninjas," Cassidy muttered out of the side of her mouth.

"No," Mark interrupted firmly. "It's not like anything on television. Military ghosts are specialty operators trained to go into the worst circumstances. They know how to avoid security cameras, how to spot infrared detection systems, and how to kill with their bare hands while they remain unseen and undetected. A ghost operator will lie in the mud for days to acquire his target even if it's a suicide mission and he'll end up dead. Will you?"

Cassidy shook her head. "Sorry, Mark. I didn't mean anything."

Rory stared his agent in charge down. Instead of arguing, he said, "Brigham and Cassidy will have to cover us. That's the only way we stand a prayer. But what happens if something goes sideways while we're inside. What if we get those little girls killed?"

"Don't think I haven't asked myself the same questions," Mark replied evenly. "Trust me. I know you don't have any kids yet, but I keep thinking of JayJay. The problem is that if we don't do anything, those girls will be dead by morning."

"Are we sure about that?" Rory asked, an odd shadow shifting over through his eyes.

"Yes," Mark answered. "And speaking as a father, if that was my daughter in there, suicide would be an option. I would die for my family."

"Shit, Mark. What are Libby and JayJay going to do if you—" Rory didn't finish. He didn't have to. Mark stopped short of answering. His wife and daughter's lives were on the same line as his. The day he fell in the line of duty would destroy them.

Cassidy and Brigham had grown silent.

"Listen team," Mark said quietly. "I don't have all the answers, guys, but if those were my girls in there, I'd pray to God someone was brave enough to try to save them."

Rory nodded one short affirmative and the debate was over. "When?" he asked.

"Zero dark thirty," Mark answered. "Tonight."

"Until then?"

"We prepare for hell."

And so they did. Undercover work in a country where only drug lords and criminals were armed was not as difficult as the honest citizen might think. Black market resources provided all Mark's team needed, definitely at a higher cost than usual, but available nonetheless. Tactical gear, American made military weapons, computer systems, you name it. As well as items they'd never thought of buying, from weapons grade plutonium to eleven-year old virgins. Operating out of the dilapidated van they'd all but lived in since arriving in the country made keeping track of their ill-gotten gains a lot easier. A thief couldn't steal what he couldn't get his hands on.

By late afternoon, they were ready to go and finalizing strategy. They hadn't strapped on yet due to the heat. Rory and Brigham were sitting cross-legged on the ground while Cassidy sat in the open side door of their van.

Mark stood before them to explain the mission as he saw it. "Getting inside the walls should be fairly straightforward. Cassidy, you will follow at left flank and walk us in. Sit tight at point A and wait for our exit signals. Three clicks on your walkie-talkie means I'm coming out. Two, it will be Rory."

"By then, both packages will be secure," Rory added. "We'll be moving fast, so stay alert. I'll have Christina. Mark will have Sophia. Be ready for anything."

"Brigham, you're Mother for the night," Mark continued. "Remain undercover with Cassidy but keep us informed. We've planted enough Tattle Tales in that hacienda for you to be eyes and ears once we're inside. Talk us through any hots spots. Keep us safe. Can you handle that?"

"Absolutely," Brigham replied. "You call all your communication guys Mother, do you?"

"Nope," Rory answered without really explaining. "Just the genius types. Again, three clicks on the walkie-talkie for Mark. Two, it's me."

"How many clicks if something goes wrong?" Cassidy asked

Mark grunted. "I'm afraid you'll hear a lot more than clicks then."

"How will you keep the girls quiet once you get them?"

Mark held up two palm-sized aerosol cans. "Mild sedative. They won't feel a thing. Are we good with this plan?"

"How will we get the girls out of the country once we've got them?" Brigham asked.

"Don't worry about that," Mark said firmly. "Both Rory and I have done this before on domestic abductions operations. I have a point of contact back East who can put a boat in the Gulf of California by the time we hit shore."

"Unless we head straight north to Nogales," Rory offered. "I know a guy—"

"No, Guaymas is closer," Mark said. "I'd prefer we go south anyway. It's a diversionary tactic. They'll be expecting us to go north or due west."

Brigham raked a hand over his head, his eyes definitely wide open now. "Man. You guys are good."

Mark caught the look of deep down concern in Rory's sharp blues. He only hoped he and Rory were as good as they sounded. A lot of lives depended on it.

"There is one last thing." Mark lowered his voice. "We go in. We come out. From now on, everything we do is to cover each other. There is no United States Army or cavalry coming to our rescue. It's only us four. We make this happen. We save these girls. We go home tonight."

Rory reached across the space between them to fist bump. Mark met him halfway. Cassidy and Brigham did the same. Funny how that simple caveman-type contact felt like a whole lot more.

"Let's get into position." Mark nodded toward the stately Ramirez hacienda. "Until go time, we keep eyes on the funny farm."

"Good enough." Rory stretched his back as he stood. "Operation Funny Farm it is."

Returning to their posts in the grass and sagebrush outside the estate proved just as hot as the previous days. Their grid consisted of four-points of observation, one at each direction. Since their van was parked out of sight to the east, Mark took the farthest post and hoofed a wide circle to the western most point.

"Comm check," he muttered into his walkie-talkie. A Bluetooth headset would have been nice, but the black marketeers had fallen short in the communication department for some reason.

"Copy that," Rory responded.

"Loud and clear, Agent Houston," Cassidy added quietly.

"Copy," Brigham said.

"Watch and pray, guys," Mark muttered before he hunkered to the ground to see what he could see. The compact ARs he'd midnight-requisitioned for his team came with Leupold riflescopes that offered 18.00 maximum magnification and state of the art digital cameras on a side-mounted rack. He'd have some explaining to do once this op was over for the horrific cash outlays to his expense account, but he wasn't worried. Alex always maintained that if he could fix a problem with money, it wasn't really a problem.

Mark positioned the rifle's bipod and made himself comfortable. The sun hit him from behind, but the slight swell of land and the Leupold put him over the wall and right inside Alejandra's rose garden. The classic red-tiled roof on the one level, ranch-style mansion made it almost romantically southwestern, but the green and black camouflaged cargo trucks parked on the brick courtyard quickly corrected that notion.

He scanned the courtyard for activity. The odd thing about these newly arrived guards was their lack of military demeanor. They dressed the part and seemed to have no problem killing, but they acted more like lazy teenagers otherwise. The two in his scope at the moment were lounging beneath the wide porch that encompassed the entire estate. One appeared to be scrolling through his cell phone. The other had a beer. Both of their rifles were leaned against the wall and out of reach.

Mark's cell vibrated in his shirt pocket.

"What's up, Ember," he answered quietly.

"Hey. How's the vacation in sunny Mexico?"

"Hot," he said while he flicked a tiny scorpion that had gotten too close to his elbow into the wild blue yonder. "Hope you're calling with good news for a change."

"I wish I were. You're not going to like this."

"Haven't liked anything for a week or two now. What's up?"

The lovely Alejandra had just stepped out of one of the many French doors of the estate. She was a beauty. No doubt about that. Her raven hair was pulled back in a cascade of curls that fell down her back to her butt. A full-figured woman with a tiny waist, she was bombshell material. Mark could feel the sizzle all the way from where she stood in the courtyard.

A man walked with her. Mark zeroed in on the man's face. Who was this guy? The new boss? He had the same dark hair, but short-cropped. He didn't radiate the same confidence, not the way he followed her as if he worked for her.

"It took me awhile to find it, but listen to this," Ember continued excitedly. "Remember the pictures you took inside the hacienda?"

"I do," Mark replied as he watched the scene below.

Alejandra and her male friend were making their way into the rose garden. They appeared to be in earnest conversation. Alejandra was definitely more animated. She used her hands a lot when she spoke and kept glancing over her shoulder at the man behind her.

"You took a picture of a picture. I almost missed it. In Alejandra's bedroom, there was a picture on the table beside her bed. Remember?"

"Sure don't," Mark replied. He'd been in a hurry that day and just took the shots he thought would spike Ramirez's ire the most.

Alejandra and her escort were now inside the low brick wall surrounding the rose garden. She'd leaned over to smell one of her prized flowers, cupping it gently in the palm of her hand while she lowered her nose into its petals.

"You want to know who else was in that picture with Mrs. Ramirez?"

Mark could hear it all the way from Alexandria, Virginia. Ember was gloating. She'd just emphasized Alejandra's married title.

Just then the man with the lady in question stepped in close behind her. Real close. He circled her waist with one arm and spun her around to face him. She laughed, her head thrown back in what seemed like pleasure. Mark looked closer. It made no sense that she would be so happy with her home and family overrun by—

"It's Javier Quinones," Ember announced proudly. "That's who's in the picture with her.

Alejandra had just wrapped her arms around the man's whole head while he buried his face in her neck. Mark's throat went dry.

"He about five feet eight? Dark hair? Mustache and scrawny goatee?"

"Yes. Oh, good. You do remember."

"I'm looking right at him," Mark muttered. A cringe reverberated up his spine at the spectacle of a brother lavishing kisses all over his sister's neck and bosom. Mark rolled to his back, staring at the faded-blue overhead in disbelief.

"Shit," he growled, not wanting to believe what his eyes had seen. "It's Javier Quinones."

"Mark?" Ember asked quietly in his headset. "I just told you that. What's going on?"

"He's the new cartel boss," Mark answered, the disgusting sight burned into his memory. Alejandra and Javier's lip-lock had just given the genre of torrid romance a nasty cold shower.

"Shit," he muttered again as he put two and two together. "Ember. My hell. Alejandra and Javier are lovers. They're the ones killing off everyone loyal to her husband."

Mark's stomach pitched. He rolled back to take another look to confirm. Alejandra and Javier were still at it. He had his hands all over her right there, out in the open for all to see. She didn't seem to mind because she was just as grabby. Her hands were inside his now open shirt.

"Wow," Ember said. "That's just plain sick."

"You have no idea." Mark's mind flew to the little girls hidden somewhere inside the hacienda. JayJay's sweet innocent face flashed to mind. He and his team had to move. Now. "I'm going to send you more video. Need you to work the same magic. Shit. No. Wait."

The guards lounging on the porch suddenly snapped to attention. The front door to the hacienda had just burst open. Four guards marched out, and in the middle of them were the two Ramirez daughters with an older woman.

Mark zeroed in closer. Little Sophia's sad face came into crystal clear view. Tears ran down her reddened cheeks. Her lips stuck out. Christina gripped her little sister's chubby hand as a guard rudely shoved them forward. The older woman attempted to comfort them, but one of the guards struck her in the back with the butt of his rifle. She fell to her hands and knees on the brick courtyard. The girls shrieked and ran to her side.

Rory's alarmed voice growled through the headset. "Mark? Are you seeing what I'm seeing?"

"Copy that," Mark replied.

"What's going on?" Ember asked. "Are you guys okay?"

"What do you want me to do?" Cassidy's disembodied voice chimed into the fray. "I have a clear shot. Tell me who to shoot."

Mark bit his tongue at this new development. There was no way to save the girls now. They were obviously on their way to execution.

"I can't watch this," Rory declared. "Come on, Boss. Let me take these bastards out."

With his heart pounding in his ears, Mark made the hardest call of his life. "Do not fire," he ground out. "Stand down. Hold your positions."

"But I—"

"Hold fire," Mark growled at Rory. The girls were already dead. Just because it hadn't happened yet didn't mean Mark would endanger his team for something he could no longer prevent. The daring rescue was a no go. They'd missed their only window of opportunity.

"I have to do something," Rory bit out, and Mark totally agreed, but one shot would sign all four agent's death certificates.

"Stand down, Dennison," Mark ordered firmly. "We've already lost this battle."

"Shit," Rory hissed, and once again wholeheartedly Mark agreed.

He scanned back to the disgusting couple still in the rose garden. Alejandra's daughters were noisily upset and being woefully mistreated, yet she seemed unaffected. One of the guards ran to her and her pig of a brother. The guard stood smartly at attention and relayed a message. She waved him off dismissively.

Acid poured into Mark's gut. He was looking at two dogs in heat who could care less about the suffering babies less than ten yards away from them. His finger twitched to finish Alejandra and Javier off right there and then.

"Mark?" Ember asked timidly.

He didn't answer. Mark tracked his scope back to Christina and Sophia instead. Damned, they reminded him of his own dark-haired JayJay. His stomach lurched as the little ones were escorted by four brutish bastards away from the rose garden. Sweet Christina turned around and called something to her mother. Alejandra didn't give any indication she heard, much less cared.

A sudden calm enveloped Mark. His talent. His God-given gift beckoned. The universe had automatically offered a damned good plan. The first shot would go through Alejandra's pretty black hair. The next, straight into Javier's left eyeball. All hell would break loose. By then, Rory would know exactly what to do. Body shots for all four guards. The girls would scream, run and—

The cold hard truth of reality intervened. Mark gulped past the anger in his heart and came back to his senses. The girls would still be out of reach and dead within seconds. All his heroic act would do was get his team killed and the girls killed. His heart pounded at his powerless position.

"I don't think they're going to execute them, Mark," Cassidy spoke up. "Check out the concrete bunker inside the front gate. Closest to me. North side. Bars on windows. See it?"

He did as directed. Sure enough. The guards appeared to be taking the older woman and girls to the bunker. Concrete blocks and bars? He rolled the stabbing knot out of his right shoulder. It took four tough guys to contain two tiny children and an old woman. What the hell kind of people were these?

They came to a halt at the door to the bunker. One guard pulled the door open. The older woman seemed intent on shielding the girls from the men. She turned on one of them after he shoved sweet little Christina through the doorway. The guard's response was an instant and cruel pistol-whipping to the poor woman's face. When she fell, he kicked her back. Alejandra never turned once to see what all the crying was about.

Mark ground his teeth and planned that fiendish guard's early death. The older woman crawled to her feet and ushered the wailing Sophia inside. Two guards took post outside the bunker while the others walked away.

"We got recon inside that bunker?" Mark bit out. He knew he hadn't thought to secrete a Tattle Tale inside the building. He'd been focused on finding a way to taunt Ramirez, not outbuildings.

"No," Rory answered. "There are no electrical lines running to it either. That means no air-conditioning for those babies trapped inside. They're in a sweat box."

Mark heard the tenderness in Rory's very astute observation. His right shoulder just plain hurt like hell, Mark's muscles were clenched so tightly from not being able to execute any plan of defense for the defenseless. He scanned the rose garden for the girls' devious mother. Alejandra and Javier had moved their disgusting antics to the shaded porch where she and he sat dining. Laughing. Enjoying each other's company.

"Are you going to talk to me or not?" Ember asked, and Mark had to admit. He'd forgotten she was on the line.

"Sorry, Ember. I need you to get hold of Alex. Tell him what we now know. Assume we're looking at a power merger, not a hostile takeover. Looks like the Sonoran and Sinaloa cartels are one. Also assume the grieving widow is conducting a purge of all things and everyone related to her husband."

"Wow," Ember breathed. "These cartels were scary before. Consolidation will make them more powerful than any of the ones in South American."

"If Governor Baxter thought he had problems before...." Rory left the warning unfinished.

"Change of plans," Mark continued. "Come sundown, we go in as two teams. We go over the wall together. Team One will be Rory and me. We will take out the two guards at the bunker. It has to be clean and silent. Once that part of the courtyard is secure, Team Two will enter the bunker, grab the girls and retreat to safety. We leapfrog out of there, two by two, covering each other on the way back to our van. Our only object is to protect those girls. And their nanny."

"Now we're abducting three people?" Rory asked quietly.

"Rescuing." Mark emphasized his choice of words. "We don't have the means to take care of two children. The nanny does."

"How will we keep them quiet?" Brigham asked.

"I'm thinking once we explain that we're there to rescue them, that won't be a problem. She'll take care of the girls. Talk, people. If you've got something to say, now's the time. Spit it out."

"I'm with you," Rory answered as Mark knew he would.

"Count me in," Cassidy said.

"And me," Brigham concluded.

"Me too," Ember said quietly all the way from Alexandria.

"Team," Mark said as calmly as he could. "When we go in tonight, we go silent. Remove the batteries from your cell phones now. Don't carry anything that might make a noise, not even a plastic bottle of water."

Obedient silence answered. Mark rolled to his back with a deep sigh. He knew it. His team knew it. Despite the fact that they were the absolute best, their quest for payback had turned into a suicide mission.

Twenty-Three

"I'll be back before you know it," Connor whispered into her hair.

Despite the SOS sign, he and Izza knew there was no choice. They were stalling. So they prepared for him to walk to the closest mountain in search of help. If he walked during the cool of night, he was certain to make it by sunrise. Once there, he hoped to find something that would help their predicament, maybe a camper, a cabin, or a hunter.

Water would be an added dividend, but they both knew that was a long shot. Izza loaded him up with as many water bottles as he could carry, keeping just one for herself. She had the spring inside the cave. He'd used a discarded shirt they'd found to improvise a backpack. He didn't plan to stay more than the time it took to get there, spend the day exploring and walk back the next night. The only thing she had to worry about was a thieving coyote. He hoped.

In the slim possibility that someone from the cartel returned, she was to hide in the deepest recesses of the cave. He'd made two torches for her. One to get her to safety, and the other to bring her back to the surface once all was clear.

But leaving Izza was hard. They stood wrapped in each other's arms as the last rays of sunlight faded. Their logical plan seemed full of more risk than certainty. Neither of them was in prime condition for the undertaking. And Izza had transformed from a hardcore drill sergeant to a moody, emotional, and prone to tears pregnant woman.

"I should get walking, you know." His chin rested on the top of her head as she burrowed into him, clinging for all she was worth. Despite his words, he made no attempt to untangle himself from her arms. Evening turned to night. Boomerang barked in the desert somewhere, no doubt on the hunt for a midnight snack. The crescent moon hung high in the western sky casting just enough light for the long walk.

With eyes brimming, she looked up at him. "I know you'll be back, and I know you're strong enough to do this. I know this is what we need to do, but I don't want you to go. What if something happens? What if I lose you, too?"

That made him smile. Izza had changed so much since he'd stood up to her. Holding her on the verge of their first separation, he felt like he was holding his whole world.

"Everything will be okay. Remember us? We're two of the meanest Marines in the Corps."

She didn't even smile at his reminder of what he'd said seven months ago.

"You take care of that little girl of ours," Connor whispered as he kissed her forehead and nose until he finally made it to her lips. She was an easy armful, her feet off the ground as he kissed her hard enough to take her breath away. There was no doubt in his mind that he'd be back, if only for another kiss. He set her feet back on the ground. "I love you, Isabella Ramos."

"I love you, Connor." She looked so sad.

He blinked hard. "I'll be home before you know it."

"Ha." She choked on her tears. "This isn't our home. It's a piece-of-shit hole in the rocks."

Connor gave her another hug and patted her belly. "You're right, but I meant this home, as in us. You, me, and this little rascal in your belly are the home I'm coming back to." He kissed her again and stepped away before he changed his mind. Damn. Leaving her was hard. Every step away from her stabbed a hole in his heart.

The cool night air filled the void between them. He headed east. When he got far enough away that he knew he couldn't change his mind or reach her, he turned around once to wave. Izza sat on the ground where he'd left her, her hand raised in a quick wave back. And that made him sad to see her sitting there alone in the dark. She was crying. He choked back his own tears as he faced east again and kept walking.

Damn. I hope I'm right.

Connor knew he wasn't in shape for the endurance test ahead, but walking during the cool of night made a huge difference. He figured he was going at least three miles an hour. He could do it. At what he thought was the halfway point, he turned and faced west again. Like an idiot in love, he waved just in case. Izza couldn't see him anymore. It was too dark, but she was there and maybe looking in the same direction.

Damn. I hope I'm right.

He trudged onward, dodging cactus and stones, pitfalls and the occasional shadow that looked like a rock in his path. The going was smooth and easy until he heard the distinctive whump-whump blade slap of a helicopter in the distance. It wouldn't have caught his attention if it hadn't sounded like it was drawing closer. Soon, the damned thing zipped right over the top of him, hugging the ground like it was looking for something. Someone.

He turned to the west again. The helicopter circled in a wide arc around his and Izza's cave. Sweet Mother Mary and Joseph, was it possible? Was that a search and rescue chopper? Were he and Izza found? Relief flared for the first time in weeks. God, yes! Izza's brilliant SOS signal must've worked. They should have thought of it sooner.

Connor started to run. She'd be thrilled. No more rotisserie bunny. No more sleeping on the dirt. He ran faster. *Crap. My side. I can't run like this.*

He slowed to catch his breath, keeping his eyes on the chopper. Black as night, all he could make out was its running lights while it skimmed low back and forth almost directly over their camp. Suddenly, a spotlight from the underside of it turned the desert below to daylight. Did Izza not see or hear it? He was too far away to see her.

Connor gulped a deep breath and willed his body to comply. *Rest later. Run now.* He set a steady pace back to camp. At last the chopper touched down, but he was still too far away. He waved his arms and yelled as he ran, but no one heard or saw. Several men with bright spotlights jumped out of the aircraft door. Dogs barked.

Oh, thank God. They've brought search and rescue dogs. Connor could only imagine the joy on Izza's face when she was rescued. He willed his legs to pump faster. This was without a doubt the best time to celeb—

A gunshot split the air. Connor froze in his tracks. S&R teams didn't shoot the victims they rescued—not unless they weren't S&R to begin with. He dug the toes of his boots into the sand and took off with a burst of speed. It was the cartel, not S&R. Izza was alone. The need to protect her and his unborn child flared hard and heavy. His legs pumped as he put everything into making it back to her in time.

Another gunshot, and he ran faster still. *God, save her!*

Almost there. He couldn't make out any figures in the dark anymore. They'd doused their searchlights. Either Izza was safely hiding in the lowest tunnels of that cave, or—

They had dogs. His heart sank. Connor couldn't force any more speed out of his screaming muscles. He was still too far away. The chopper lifted up into the dark silence of this remote desert. He couldn't hear the blade slap over the roar in his heart. A rescue chopper wouldn't have left without him. Izza wouldn't have let them. Anguish at what he'd done flooded his soul.

CRAP!

The black aircraft zipped over his head again, headed southeast. He stopped to suck in a burning lungful of air. No searchlights scanned the desert below any longer because they weren't looking for anyone else. They had what they wanted, and it was not him. It was her. Izza. Connor watched it veer to the east and fade into the night.

His heart pitched. She might still be safe. Izza was smart. Mean. Nasty. All those good qualities for a Marine. Maybe she'd gotten the upper hand. Maybe they'd left because they couldn't find her. Maybe she'd killed one of them and they had to go for medical help. Izza could surely give them more trouble than they'd expect. His brain kept tossing out pieces of hope to hang onto. At last he burst into camp, out of breath and out of his mind.

"Izza!" He stumbled up to the cave entrance. "Izza!"

Connor panicked. He ran to the back tunnel of the cave. "Izza! Izza! Are you down there?"

But all he heard was his own voice echoing back. Connor flew out of the cave, searching their meager campsite for the torches he'd made. Both lay burnt in the campfire. She'd lit them, no doubt thinking, as he had, that she was welcoming rescuers. How could she have known the cartel would return in a helicopter?

He relit one of the torches from the dying embers in the fire-pit. There was still hope. She might have gotten away. Entering the cave, he made his way to the tunnel and headed down. "Izza? Answer me, baby. God, please answer me if you're down here. They're gone now. It's just me. You're safe."

The only thing he could hear was his own heavy breathing and an out of control heart rate thrumming though his entire body. Finally convinced she was not there, he turned back again.

As Connor made the last sweep of their camp, a glint from the sand caught his eye. There lay the bottom of the old soda bottle that Izza used for lighting campfires, only it was broken into smaller fragments. He dropped to his knees. This was Izza's pride and joy, proof that she could beat the odds and survive. Blood smudged the glass. He saw the tracks in the weak firelight. Connor jumped to his feet to follow them. Men's boot prints along with an irregular pattern of smaller boot prints intermingled with long slashes in between.

The evidence was clear. They'd dragged her to the helicopter. She'd resisted and tried to cut one of them. A stab of fear sliced through him. Had she been successful? Had they retaliated? Did they hurt her? Were they hurting her now?

Jose Ibarra's ugly words came back to him. *Your first order is to make an example of this piece of shit.* The grotesque memory of Maka Taufa and Roger Paxton's decapitated heads knocked the breath out of Connor. A shiver ripped his soul apart.

The cartel had Izza.

"The bitch stabbed me. Look at my hand. I'm bleeding."

Damned right I stabbed you, you creep! Blindfolded and mad as hell, Izza struck out with a booted foot toward that whiny voice. Reprisal came swiftly when the coward at her left punched her stomach.

She gasped in pain, lurching forward protectively over her unborn daughter, but he shoved her backward into the seat. An arm clamped across her neck while a heavy hand slid over her breasts to stop at her stomach. "Now I have your attention. It is time you understand that you are not in charge anymore, not even of your own body. I will do whatever I want to you."

She turned away from his stinking breath. His fingers drummed one by one on her belly. "I see you have something to live for. Is it a boy or a little girl like you?" The man leaned into her cheek and sniffed. "I like them both, you know."

That did it. Izza turned her hard head into a battering ram, and then he was bleeding, too, the bastard. A string of Mexican profanities exploded from his big mouth. One of the other men in the back of the helicopter chuckled. "I told you.

She's a mean bitch. We may have to tame her before we hand her over."

She heard it coming. The man she'd head-butted struck her across the chest with his open palm. The blow left her reeling. At least he hadn't punched her stomach again. He growled and she guessed he was wiping his nose or mouth. This time when he spoke, he kept his distance. "You have no idea who you are dealing with, *Chica*."

An involuntary shiver rippled over her shoulders and up her neck.

Her father used to call her *Chica*.

"Where the hell are you?" Alex muttered to himself while he stalked the hallway outside the Governor's office. Mark's cell phone kept transferring instantly to voice mail. An incoming call from the Alexandria office interrupted.

"This better be good," he growled.

"Alex!" Ember's excited voice hit his eardrum with more enthusiasm than he needed or wanted. "Guess what?"

"Just tell me," he answered. He'd had enough drama.

"Alejandra Ramirez and Javier Quinones are lovers," she all but squealed. "But that's not all."

"They have an illegitimate son," he shot back at her. "I already know. Have you talked with Mark? Do you know where he is?"

"Yes. Just got off the phone with him, Boss. It's getting scary dangerous down there. He and his team have already gone dark. You won't be able to reach them until—"

"Sonofabitch," Alex hissed. The toughest part of any op was being out of radio contact with his operatives. "Where is he? Do you have pinpoint coordinates?"

"I do," she answered promptly. "Sending them to you now."

His migraine ratcheted tighter inside his skull. Patience was never his strong suite. All this pent up stress would vanish if he could just let it out of his system and swear a blue streak at everything and everyone. The coordinates pinged in his inbox. Immediately, he forwarded them to Scot Sylvane. "What else?"

"Boss." Ember's excitement had dropped to zero. "Are you okay?"

He forced the cramp out of his neck with one deep shoulder roll and ignored her question. His health didn't factor into an operation of this magnitude. "Why did you call?" he asked as patiently as he could. The last thing Ember deserved was his profanity in her ear.

"Mother thinks she found Connor and Izza," Ember answered quietly. "Actually, one of her friends at SATGEO-TECH spotted it first. There is a SOS signal in the west desert. Possibly two people. They found it this morning when they were—"

"Are they alive?"

"Movement was detected. We think. The images were a little grainy. Kinda hard to tell. It looked like they were on top of—"

"Coordinates."

"On their way."

"Alex," Ember cut off his intended disconnect. His techies knew him too well.

"Yes?"

"I'm worried about you," she said firmly, almost *Motherly*. "Should I send Murphy to assist?"

"No. Schedule an early flight to Salt Lake City."

"For who, Boss?"

Alex sighed all the way to his weary soul. "Mark's wife. Get Libby Houston in the air. One way or the other, he's going to need her."

Connor sat in the dirt outside the cave entrance in brain-numbing agony. Pain radiated across his abdomen. He'd overdone it running back to save Izza, but he didn't care. Rest was hard medicine right now and the last thing he wanted. His heart screamed, *Run to her. Help her. Save her!*

But there was nowhere to run. Helpless frustration galled him. They'd come so far together, but now she was gone, and it was ALL HIS FAULT!

"Give me a freaking break!" he screamed at the dark night sky. "Was she right? Do you have any idea we're even down here? That we need you?"

Nothing answered. Not even the hint of a breeze whispered through the still desert air. He couldn't even kick at the dirt, his gut hurt too much to move. Just the simple act of breathing pained those damned two holes in his body that were once more alive and screaming.

Connor doubted himself to his core. Sitting alone with no hope left to hang onto, he second-guessed everything he'd ever done. Was he also to blame for Jamie's death? No doubt. Tactical gear or not, he would have made an entirely different decision if it had been Izza in the line of fire that day. Did he have some sick creeping inner need to be a hero all the time? Maybe. It came with the eagle, globe and anchor, and yet he'd failed the woman he would die for. He'd let Izza down in every sense of the word. First Jamie. Now her. Possibly their daughter—

"No! Hell, no!" He struggled to his feet. A coyote howled in the darkness. The eerie sound only emphasized the hollow feeling within Connor. Heartache hurts so much worse than gunshot. Profanity and despair clouded his vision. Tears came next, and then he was really angry. Kicking at everything in sight despite the pain in his hut, he caught his second wind.

"Bullshit," he bellowed to the sky again. "If you won't do something, I will!"

He wasn't going to stay here and wait for someone to come find him. Hell, no. Connor proved it to himself by running to find that stupid backpack he'd dropped, the one filled with bottles of water and rabbit jerky. He proved it again by taking the rest of the tough-as-nails rabbit jerky in the camp and stuffing it into the bag. The broken pieces of Izza's fire starter went next.

Pulling the ratty makeshift pack over his shoulder, he started walking due east. It might take a week. It might take a month. But make no doubt about it. Connor Maher was getting Izza and his daughter back. The SC better get the hell out of his way.

Twenty-Four

"Am I even close?"

Searching in the dark desert for a single person was as bad as looking for that proverbial needle in a haystack. All Alex's SUV's headlights had found so far was plenty of sagebrush and the glitter of a startled animal's eyes that disappeared in a wink.

"Yes. You're close," Ember muttered through his Bluetooth earpiece. "Those are the coordinates SATGEO-TECH gave me. Do you see anyone?"

"I don't." Alex slammed his SUV into park and reached for his gear bag in the back seat. Pulling out his pair of NVGs, night vision goggles, he pulled them over his face and lit the desert up with the warm glow of lime green. All that showed was sagebrush and rocks. He stepped out of the off-road vehicle and began searching on foot for his lost agents. The only thing visible was a damned desert tortoise the size of a flattened basketball. Alex stepped around it and kept going.

"You're right on top on them. Look around."

"I am."

It sure didn't look like he was on top of anything, much less his lost agents. The problem with night vision is the limited peripheral that comes with looking through any binocular-type device. In order to see, Alex had to physically rotate his neck to look directly toward his target. He knelt to examine the sand. It looked like the place had been used for a fireplace. Felt warm too. Rising to his feet, he heard the body hurtling toward him before he saw it. They went down together in a flurry of fists and defensive arm holds.

"You bastard," a very familiar voice spat into his face. "Where'd you guys take her?"

Alex pulled the goggles off. "Connor?"

"Boss?" Connor pushed to his knees. "Alex? Is that you?"

"It's me," Alex said as they both scrambled to their feet. "Where's Izza?"

"They took her. Come on. We've got to go. Where's your helicopter?"

"I'm in a Land Rover." Alex grabbed Connor's arm to lead him to the SUV. "But you're hurt."

"No, I'm fine." Connor's feet were pointed in two different directions. "Come on. We've got to save them. Let's go. Now. Move it."

"You're not fine. You're shot and your nose is broken. You look like hell. Who is them? Who's got Izza?"

"Are you coming or not?" Connor barked instead of answering.

"Connor!" The sharp tone in Alex's voice snapped his agent's head back around. "Settle down. Who took Izza?"

"The SC."

"When?"

"Maybe an hour or two ago."

"What were they driving?"

"A chopper like I said." Connor pointed due east. "That's where I was going. They flew that way."

"Alex?" Ember finally spoke up. "Tell me you found both of them."

"Just Connor," Alex reported. "Hang on. Sounds like the cartel still has Izza."

It was obvious Connor was anything but fine. Alex wasn't real sure his agent wasn't partially delirious the way he rambled, but if he was right, Alex had just missed the cartel.

"Over here." Alex pointed toward where he'd parked. "I'm surprised you didn't see me drive up."

"I forgot something so I had to come back." Instead of walking in the direction Alex indicated, Connor ran to a group of small rocks and proceeded to kick at them. Another tortoise crawled between two of the rocks. "Beat it, Homer. You're off the menu. Go have a good life."

"You ate turtles?" Alex asked when Connor headed back toward him.

"Jack rabbits. Where did you park?"

When Alex pointed to the Land Rover again, Connor nearly beat him back to it, muttering, "Couldn't kill 'im after we named 'im. Come on Boss. Let's get out of here. We need to save them."

By now Alex was confused. Kill who? Save who?

"Where are we going?" He strapped in and hit the ignition button.

"Hell. I don't know," Connor said. "Don't you?"

Alex flipped the dome light on to get a better look at his junior agent. Connor was pinging, and not making much sense while he did it. The bright light revealed an anxious, frightened man. Connor must have spent most of the last two weeks looking like a raccoon from that broken nose. The yellowed skin around his eyes was evidence enough. The full beard he sported might have filled out his face, but it didn't hide the broken nose or the gaunt look of a hungry man. The poor guy was shaking and breathing heavy. Sweat glistened on his forehead.

Alex throttled down into calm and steady. He lowered his voice. "Tell me again. The cartel took Izza, right?"

Connor's head bobbed. "Yeah. I already told you that."

"You said they came for her in a chopper? Why didn't they take you?"

"Because I wasn't here. I was trying to save us all, but they came back and dragged her away. I should've stayed. They need me."

"Did you get that, Ember?" Alex spoke to Ember, still not sure exactly who Connor was talking about with all of his mixed up pronouns.

"I did," she replied. "So I'm looking for a flight plan filed with FAA within the last couple of hours."

He gripped Connor's shoulder while he waited on Ember. "You thirsty?"

Not waiting for an answer, Alex reached behind the passenger seat and pulled a couple chilled bottles of water out of his personal-sized cooler. The younger man latched onto both and popped the caps off.

"Thanks," he mumbled before he downed the first bottle in two seconds flat. By the time Alex handed him several protein bars and an apple, both bottles were empty. Connor grabbed the bars, but stripping the wrapper off the first brought tears to his eyes instead.

"I'm eating," he cried, but he wasn't. The food hadn't even touched his mouth yet. "I'm eating, but... they might already be dead." He burst into tears.

Alex gunned the engine and shifted the SUV into four-wheel drive. "Talk to me, Connor. What kind of condition is Izza in? Was she hurt in the ambush at the RV?"

"No, but the baby's—"

"What are you talking about? What baby?"

"I shouldn't have left them. I should have stayed!" Connor lifted both wrists to his cheeks, growling in torment.

"Connor." Alex steadied the young man's shoulder as he weaved over and around the desert terrain. "Settle down and talk to me. What baby, son?"

"A baby?" Ember whispered in his ear. "Izza's pregnant? Wow."

Alex ignored Ember's amazement. Suddenly, Connor's rambling made better sense. He leaned heavily against the passenger door with a thud, exhaustion finally claiming him. "My baby. Izza's pregnant with my baby girl, and I... and they.... God! What have I don't?"

"Wow," Ember muttered quietly again.

Alex focused on Connor. "You only left her because you went looking for help."

"I should have stayed. I shouldn't have left them."

"You did what you had to do. Eat up. I've got more water. Ember is going to tell me at any moment now where that flight went," Alex hinted to his very capable and eavesdropping techie. He had to admit. At times like this, having Ember or Mother in his ear was as good as having an annoying guardian angel on his shoulder.

"Alex," Ember whispered as if Connor could overhear. "I can't find anything. No flight plan was filed."

He'd suspected as much. Why would drug runners do anything legal?

"But Mother's on the phone with her friend at SATGEO-TECH. They're pulling down images from the last five hours."

"Call me when you have something," Alex said. "In an hour," he added. "Or sooner."

"Copy that. Boss, would you do something for me?"

"Sure." Alex kept an eye on the young man at his side. Connor had devoured three of the five bars. Number four was on its way to a quick demise.

"Would you give Connor a big hug for me?" Alex heard her tears all the way across country. "Tell him I love him." She hung up before Alex could argue or agree.

Aw, shit. What was he to do? He withheld the news that Mark and his team were in serious danger as well as the fact no flight plan had been filed. Right now, there was nothing good to share. Alex gripped Connor's shoulder.

The younger weary man's gaze shifted from the bar in his hand. "Yeah, Boss?"

"Ember says hi."

As emotionally exhausted as he was, Connor couldn't sit still to save his life. Alex turned up the SUV's air-conditioning and handed him another bottle of water.

"How'd you break your nose?" Alex asked once they got on asphalt and headed east.

"They dropped me off the truck. Course, then they dropped Izza on top of me. She's something else, Boss. She's a damn good survivalist. Honest, I didn't know about the baby until we got here. Not sure she'd ever have told me now that I think about it. Maybe it's a good thing we got stuck out here. Maybe—"

"No." Alex put a stop to Connor's rambling. "Being shot and left to die in the desert is never a good thing. How far along is she? Seven? Eight months?"

"Seven."

"Fraternization, huh?" Alex kept his eyes on the freeway.

"It happens. But what happened after the RV blew? Is everyone okay?"

Alex was slow to answer. "Roy took a couple hits. You guys were abducted."

"Roy got shot? Damn it. I thought I saw him go down. How bad is he?"

"Took one in his upper leg and another in his chest. He's still in the hospital, but he's doing better. You'll have to visit him when you get there."

"But Morgan's okay? And Mark's team? How about Mark?"

Alex didn't answer fast enough.

"Boss? Is Mark okay? What the hell happened?" Anxiety rippled up Connor's spine.

"Mark's fine, but we lost Morgan," Alex finally answered. "His funeral was last week."

Connor stared out the window, a sudden catch in his voice. "That's why you're here."

"No, I'm here because you guys did a good job. The cartel is dismantled. Their business is in shambles and—"

"Bullshit," Connor growled. "They got Izza." Finally safe and on his way to civilization again, he broke down.

"Tell me about the baby," Alex urged gently.

Connor turned with more accusation in his voice than he intended. "Why was she even here? Didn't you know she was pregnant? God! What were you thinking sending her to Utah?"

"I'm thinking she must have left that out of her personnel file," Alex said calmly.

Connor closed his eyes. "You're right. Sorry. That sounds just like Izza. It's a girl. She's carrying my daughter."

Alex gave his arm a hard squeeze. "We're going to find her. Mother and Ember are the best. They haven't slept since you two went missing. They're the ones who spotted your SOS and your telltale signature. C.M.I.R. was a good idea."

"Yeah. It was her idea. It was...." Connor couldn't finish. He stared out the window, his heart set on a mean-tempered Hispanic woman who thought she was alone in the world. And she was fighting it again. Without him.

"I'm taking you to the emergency room until we hear from Ember," Alex stated.

"No. Not until Izza is safe. I'm not going—"

"Yes, you are. You'll be better able to fight once you're stitched and—"

"No!" Connor bellowed, his fists clenched and ready to fight again. "I said no. I can't be doped up. I need to be ready to run the minute Ember calls and tells me where to go."

"Us," Alex corrected. "You are not in this alone, Connor."

Whatever. Alex might be in charge and he might be right, but there was no damned way Connor would submit to medical treatment before he had Izza back.

"My hotel room then," Alex muttered. "At least you can shower while we wait. I'll order room service and get you some clean clothes."

Connor nodded. That would work. He couldn't control his shaking. The food and water he'd consumed only enhanced what might be happening to Izza at this very moment instead of nourishing him. He turned on his boss, shaking like a man possessed. "Can't you drive this piece of shit any faster?"

Alex obliged. The miles flew by.

Twenty-Five

That same night fell dark across the Ramirez hacienda, with only a pale moon to expose intruders. Just the way Mark liked it. Discussing the plan to rescue the Ramirez children was simple. Implementation was a different animal all together. Murphy's Law never failed to change perfectly good theories into nightmares.

They geared up outside their rental van in the dark. Each agent wore desert cammie pants with black shirts and face paint. Except for the whites of their eyes, they were a close match for sand, rock, and shadow.

Mark carried his sniper rifle as well as a SIG SAUER .9mm pistol holstered on his right hip. The silencers on their weapons would only provide a brief window of opportunity. Misnamed and misunderstood by most, silencers still made enough noise, especially in the dead of night.

He stuck four magazines, eight rounds each, into his left pants pocket for the pistol. All agents wore two bandoliers of extra ammo across their chests with extra magazines, thirty rounds per mag for their rifles. There was no way to tell how this operation would go down, and Mark needed them prepared for a fierce gun battle.

Strapped to his boot was a seven-inch knife if push came to shove. Mark hated close combat battles, but things happened.

Everyone had to be able to carry two small children, so they took no water. The only other items he would've preferred for his team were body armor and helmets. Yes, it would've added weight but the security was undeniable. Bottom line, they didn't have any. It didn't matter.

Time to go.

Their plan was simple. Slow and steady. Gain entry to the grounds, neutralize the guards at the front gate and then the bunker, rescue the girls and their nanny, and evaporate into thin air. Their contingency plan was another story. They'd left a cache at two checkpoints. Checkpoint A contained grenade launchers and extra weapons with enough extra ammo to buy more time. Additional bandoliers waited for each agent, something quick and easily acquired if they were pursued.

Checkpoint B was the getaway vehicle with yet another supply of weapons and ammo clips at the ready along with water and first-aid. Extra gasoline was stored in the back. Mark didn't intend to stop once they were on their way.

It was an all or nothing kind of night. If the worst happened, if they weren't successful at taking out a sufficient number of the armed guards by the time they reached the van, the water and first-aid wouldn't matter. But Mark planned for a positive outcome. They would ALL be alive when this was through. The girls would BOTH be rescued. And they would ALL go home tomorrow and leave this stinking desert far behind.

Time to go.

The initial problem was proximity and invisibility. Just after midnight, they'd started edging closer to the estate. They moved as one, Mark and Rory a few steps ahead, Cassidy and

Brigham following close on their heels. Unseen. Noiseless. As silent as arrows, Mark and Rory easily dispatched the two guards at the hacienda gate and just as quietly dragged their bodies from view.

They entered the gate and pressed toward the target building. Just short of the cinder block structure, Mark and Rory crept into prone positions beneath a huge flowering bush and prepared to take down the two guards. Cassidy and Brigham took position around the corner of the gate. They gave Mark the thumbs up sign. So far so good.

Sitting casually on the wall, one guard puffed on a cigarette while the other cleaned his fingernails with a pocketknife. Neither appeared concerned. They chuckled at each other's jokes and talked like two old friends with nothing better to do. Mark suspected both men would soon be asleep at their post. Takedown would go a lot smoother then, but he didn't have that kind of time.

The clock was ticking.

With silencers in place, Mark hand signaled Rory to take the guard on the left while he dispatched the one on the right. But just as they laser-sighted their targets, a man and woman's laughter could be heard. It was the lady of the house herself, Alejandra Ramirez, and her incestuous cohort, Javier Quinones. Brother and sister had come to take care of the final family business of the day. The guards snapped to attention.

Alejandra was dressed in riding breeches and tall riding boots. Her tight equestrian jacket made her look as if she'd actually dressed up for the despicable occasion.

Javier stood five inches or so taller than his sister. A pencil thin moustache lined his mouth and disappeared into the neatly trimmed beard at his chin. Except for the rakish look of lust in his eye as he followed his sister's sensual movements, there was nothing to distinguish him from the other guards. No insignia, badge, or ornamentation marked the gray uniform he wore. By all appearances, he was just another man at her disposal.

Disgust watered the back of Mark's throat at their continual petting. They laughed at some private joke, their heads together as they strolled toward the cinderblock bunker. Mark wanted to spit. They acted like cold-blooded teenagers in heat. Javier held his hand to her neck as he pulled her to him, kissing her full on her mouth, his hands in her hair. She laughed a throaty laugh, her head back as her brother kissed his way to the unbuttoned swell of her cleavage. Even their own guards looked away rather than witness the spectacle of a brother and sister pawing each other.

"This won't take long, my love." She smoothed a slender hand down his cheek, dismissing the guards with a curt nod. Javier stayed at the door while she entered the bunker alone. He chatted quietly with the guards who by now were seated on the wall with him.

Within minutes, Alejandra returned, pulling her wide-eyed daughters along by their elbows. The nanny followed close behind. As soon as the poor woman stepped through the doorway, Javier was off the wall. He stuck his pistol into her back. "One wrong move and both these brats die, Juanita. Will you do as you are told now?"

She nodded, her head bowed as she focused on the frightened girls. Christina and Sophia cried. Javier pushed Juanita away from the girls and toward the two guards. The nanny and girls looked weak from the heat. Even in the dark, it was easy for Mark to see the girls' bright red cheeks. Their hair hung in sweaty ringlets around their faces. Both appeared dizzy. His heart went to them. They needed water. Not their mother.

"I told you both to be quiet, now didn't I?" Alejandra knelt with the little girls, almost motherly as she turned them to face her. While her voice was soft and sweet, her eyes were deadly and cold. She pinched Sophia's chubby cheeks in her fingers. "There now. Be a good girl. Don't cry because if you cry, Mommy will make you be quiet." She twisted Christina's arm up behind her back to get her point across.

"Mama!" the little girl yelped in pain.

"See what you made me do to your sister?" Alejandra still spoke to Sophia who cried at her sister's tears. "Do you want me to hurt Christina again? I will, you know."

Alejandra wrenched Christina's arm one more time. When she screeched, Sophia wailed harder still. Javier stood watching his dead brother-in-law's family drama with an amused smirk on his face.

"Girls. Girls. Listen to me. You must be quiet. Shut up!" Alejandra's sharp command cut the air. "Mommy wants you to be quiet!"

Both little girls silenced their sobs. Alejandra shoved Christina away from her. As quick as she did, Christina pulled little Sophia into her arms and hushed her whimpers even though she'd been the one who was hurt. No words were spoken as the trembling baby sister relied on her older sister for comfort.

"There. That's better. Mommy can finally hear herself think." Alejandra stroked her temples as her daughters gazed up at her. "You will be good girls one last time, won't you?"

"*Si, Mama*," Christina's small voice could barely be heard where Mark lay watching. Both Christina and Sophia nodded like the two obedient children they were, their faces shining with tears. "*Te amo*," Christina said just as softly.

He cringed at the love in her voice. His own childhood had been wasted in much the same way as these little urchins—by wanting the love of a parent. At least his father had only verbally abused him. Not that it excused John Houston, but Christina and Sophia's parents were a thousand times worse.

Little Sophia wiggled from Christina's grasp and stretched her arms to her mother. Alejandra ignored the child, her eyes only for Javier. "See? Like lambs to the slaughter. It will be easy. And I am going to do it with the silver knife you gave me. Just think. It will be like an ancient sacrifice. Maybe I should have waited for the full moon."

Mark heard the weird excitement in Alejandra's voice at that disgusting declaration. Her next words chilled him to the bone. "Do you want to watch?"

She walked slowly back to where Javier stood, her behavior bizarrely seductive. She whispered something in his ear that Mark couldn't make out. Javier pulled her to his mouth in a vulgar kiss, but when she pulled away and laughed, Mark saw the dribble of blood on her chin. Javier's leer told him plenty. He'd bitten her. And the growling excitement in her voice was unmistakable. These two enjoyed cold-blooded murder and rough play.

Alejandra's attention was focused on her lover, but Sophia still stood with her chubby arms raised. Her lip stuck out in a pout, tears ran down her cheeks. With typical childish drama, she stamped her foot and squealed, "I want Mama!"

Alejandra spun on the child and jerked Sophia off her feet by one arm. Alejandra raised the little girl to eye level, her hand clenched at the child's throat, screaming, "You sniveling slut! I wish I'd never had you. Your father was a pig and you're nothing better. Shut up!"

Mark winced at the shocked expression on that little girl's face. With a sneer, Alejandra dropped the baby back to the ground. Sophia had no time to catch herself. She landed with a thump and fell back. Her head struck the brick. Instantly, Christina grabbed her little sister, soothing her before Sophia could cry.

But Javier was bored. "Come on, Alejandra. All of this must be done by the time Ricardo arrives tomorrow. You don't have time for a full moon. He knows nothing of these two. Just get it done."

At the mention of Ricardo, a bright smile illuminated Alejandra's face. "As you wish, my love. Come girls." She snapped her fingers. Obediently, Christina and Sophia followed their mother to a nearby pickup truck. She placed them in the front seat beside her and started the engine, throwing a backward glance and a kiss to Javier. "I won't be long, my darling. Will you wait for me?" she asked coyly.

Like a lovesick playboy, he blew her a kiss. "You know I will."

With deliberate slowness, Alejandra pulled the truck away from the building, her eyes still locked on her brother as she drove away.

It was now or never. Mark hand-signaled his team—Rory to take out the two guards with Javier, and Cassidy and Brigham to take out Javier. Mark intended to stop the truck and apprehend Alejandra. A quick nod came from everyone.

They were ready. Mark held up three fingers. Two fingers. One. Go.

Simultaneous shots burst from their silenced weapons. Down went both guards to the dust. Juanita screamed when Javier fell alongside the guards. The truck jerked to a rumbling stop.

"No!" Alejandra exploded from the driver's side. With one swift movement, she pulled her daughters out with her, pushing them between her and the advancing team of snipers. "You've killed him! No! No!"

And then she howled one ear-piercing, pain-filled cry to the dark like an animal with its leg in a trap. Dangerous eyes flashed from Mark to Juanita. "You murdered the man I love!"

Christina and Sophia screamed, their pitiful voices adding to the bedlam. Alejandra flattened herself against the side of the truck, her daughters still clutched in front of her. She held them tight, her fingers digging into their necks to keep them in position.

Juanita called to the girls. "I am here, *mi corazon*. I am here. I will never leave you. I am here."

An ugly spite-filled laugh rent the night air. "Juanita. You pig! You talk of heart, but you have killed mine! *Mi corazon*! My brother! Ahh!"

Mark advanced, his voice strong and calm. "Let the girls go, Alejandra."

"You!" she yelled. "Who are you to come into my home and kill my family?"

He stopped. Again he gave her the firm command. "Let the girls go. They don't need to die anymore than you do."

"Never! They are from my body! Not yours! They are mine to do with as I please." Her eyes flashed from Mark and back to Juanita, before they settled on the prostrate figure of Javier. "You've killed him! My lover! My life! Ahh!"

Rory and Cassidy approached while Brigham held Juanita back. She was still focused on the girls, her arms extended to hug them the minute they broke free. Both girls' eyes were locked on her. "Please, Alejandra," Juanita pleaded. "I will take them far away from here. Ricardo never needs to know. Please. Let me take them."

"No!" Alejandra dragged her daughters to the tailgate of the truck. "That is not good enough and you know it." Tossing the truck keys into the dark, she reached inside the truck bed and pulled out a pistol. Now the gun dug into Christina's neck. The little girl sobbed, still clutching her baby sister tightly to her chest. "I will end it right here and now, Juanita. You and your friends are too late. Tonight we die together."

"No!" Juanita made a move toward the girls, but Brigham stopped her.

"Alejandra. Give me your daughters. Now. I will let you live. You have my word." Mark took another step forward. By now he stood less than six feet from Alejandra and the frightened girls. Little Christina sobbed while she clutched a crying Sophia. Their dark eyes glistened up at Mark and Juanita. Rory stood on one side, Cassidy at his other. Three guns drilled down on Alejandra.

"Ha!" She shook her head, her glossy black hair billowing across her shoulders, her eyes dark and deadly. "You would have me believe that lie? Why would I want to live now?" She licked the blood of her brother's last kiss off her lip. "You've killed my love! My life!"

"She will kill them," Juanita pleaded with Mark. "Please, sir. Save my babies."

With that righteous plea from a good woman's heart, training took over. The sniper's many calculations rolled automatically through Mark's mind as he studied Alejandra's defensive position for one last second. She shrieked in defiance and hysteria, still shielding herself behind her daughters. He heard the trigger click at her finger. He saw the wild insanity in her eyes. And his own sweet baby daughter's smile, safe and sound in her loving mother's arms, flashed into his heart.

No conscious decision relayed between brain synapses; no spotter at his side whispered calculations to assist. The round leapt from the chamber of his SIG seemingly of its own accord. Alejandra pitched face first onto her daughters. Both girls screamed. Mark shoved the dead body off the girls and knelt to gather the frightened little girls into his arms. Their insane mother was dead, but they were alive. His heart filled with intense appreciation for his talent. His God-given gift.

Sophia and Christina clung to his neck, wide-eyed and sobbing, their little bodies shaking as he held them tightly. "It's okay, you're safe," he whispered. They clung to him, their little fingers dug into his shirt in pure hysteria. "I promise. You'll be okay now," he murmured, needing to soothe them the same as if they were JayJay.

Juanita joined him in comforting the frightened girls. Mark looked toward the hacienda. Despite all the noise, no other guards had arrived yet to investigate. But he knew better.

Time was running out.

"We have to go, Juanita." Again his strong voice was calm and assuring.

She gathered the girls from his arms into hers. Sophia still whimpered, but Christina seemed to understand that silence was necessary. Over and over again, she soothed her frightened little sister. Rory, Cassidy, and Brigham stood ready, still maintaining vigilant cover, their rifles aimed toward the hacienda.

"Let's move," Mark ordered calmly.

They were almost clear of the gate when the first shots rang out. Rory staggered a step and then righted himself, a grunt of annoyance in his usually calm voice. "Damn it. I think I'm hit."

But he kept moving, his rifle spitting fire on the now advancing army of guards that seemed to have come out of nowhere. Mark took out two, then three as they engaged in rapid fire. He shouted to his team what they already knew. "Cover the girls! At all costs we cover the girls and Juanita!"

"Understood," Rory yelled back, his body already positioned between the girls and the advancing army. He fired sure and steady, another guard down, then another. And still the army kept coming. Mark and his team finally took cover against the wall outside the gate.

Time was gone.

Twenty-Six

Thwack. Thwack. Thwack. The helicopter's blades changed itch as it descended. At last it bumped earth, bounced slightly and touched down. Steeled for assault and already on the defensive, Izza still jumped when the cruel man at her left slapped the side of her head with his open palm. "Move it," he ordered, his hard hand jerking her to her feet.

The gun barrel in her back prodded her to walk. Her guards didn't speak. They already knew what was going to happen next. Fear climbed up her throat. Blindfolded and with no way to run, all she could do was wait and find out. Not sure how many men walked alongside, she strategized the simple dynamics of a roundhouse kick. *Hunker low. Keep your balance. Make every contact count like hell.*

The baby in her belly bumped her ribs. The roundhouse kick would have to wait. Izza walked where she was directed, but the men were cruel. Not one of them warned her about the single concrete step into the building. She fell, hitting the floor hard and face first. A sharp kick to her backside and the men laughed. Another kick struck her belly. She curled inward to protect her child.

"Stop!" The guy who'd struck her in the helicopter hissed at his partners in crime. "She wants her alive."

Izza cringed. *She who?*

Connor was in the shower. They'd stopped at a twenty-four hour department store on the way into Salt Lake City. Alex ran in and purchased new clothing for his agent, complete with a shaving kit and a few medical supplies. Connor would've gone into the store by himself, but Alex didn't want him to scare the hell out of any late night shoppers.

The room service tray with a steaming hot meal was at his hotel room door by the time they arrived, but now the waiting game began in earnest. Alex had faith. Ember and Mother were good. They'd find something if only because they had to. That was the way Alex disciplined his mind to think. He aimed for a specific outcome. His techies and the universe obliged often enough that he employed the same approach to most problems. Mother and Ember would locate Izza, and they would do it tonight. God willing.

The shower slammed open. He glanced at the half-closed bathroom door. Connor was close to collapse. He'd devoured the hot roast beef and potatoes before he'd even sat down. The extra big slice of cheesecake disappeared in one mouthful. After he'd showered, Alex intended to take a good look at the gunshot wound. How that young man was still on his feet was a testament to the kid's sheer willpower. Connor was gaunt from his all-protein diet, badly sunburned, and seriously dehydrated. That meant Izza was in the same condition, only she was also with child.

What the hell was keeping Ember?

As if she'd read his mind, his phone cell vibrated. "Alex?"

It's incredibly eerie how one angst filled word two thousand miles away can kick-start the acid pouring into a man's gut.

"Yes?" he answered quietly so Connor couldn't overhear whatever came out of Ember's mouth next.

"We just received a video from the guys who are holding Izza. Sending it now."

He scrolled through his text messages and tapped the file to open it the second it arrived in his in-basket. Dark and grainy, the film revealed concrete floor and walls of corrugated steel. His heart stalled. In the middle of all that darkness, a blindfolded person sat tied to a wooden chair. An overhead spotlight flashed on—Izza.

Sonofabitch! His hackles rose. The camera zoomed in closer. She still wore her cargo pants and tank top, her hair pulled back in its usual ponytail. From the sideward camera angle, it was easy to tell she was pregnant and in the same depleted physical condition as Connor. Her arms and legs were secured to the chair with plastic zip-ties. Her face was wet and sweaty. Blood trickled down her chin. The back of a man came into view, his arm already raised.

"Don't do it," Alex growled a warning to no avail as the man struck her with his open hand. Alex jumped to his feet, vowing agonizing pain the minute he got hold of that bastard's neck.

The slap knocked her head back, but tough girl Izza pulled her face off her shoulder with a sneer of contempt. "That all you got, you piece of—"

He hit her again. Her head snapped backwards and Alex planned outright cold-blooded murder for the animal striking her. He stepped into the hallway, carefully closing the door behind him with one thought on his mind. *Connor must not see this.*

For a couple minutes, Izza didn't move. Her chest heaved beneath the tank top. Alex swore hell for the man beating her. Torture. Limb from limb suffering. God awful pain.

"Stay down," he whispered to Izza.

She should have. Hell, the woman should have pretended she was out cold, but no. Painfully slow, Izza rolled her neck until she faced the man again. Through swollen lips and with her nose gushing blood, she belittled him yet one more time. "You hit like a girl."

Three times the sonofabitch hit her! Alex raked a hand through his hair, groaning at the spectacle he could do nothing about. She could barely hold her head up. Blood poured down her neck. He cocked his head to hear her barely audible voice. "Connor's coming," she murmured. "Just you wait." Her chin dropped to her chest. She'd finally passed out.

The man stepped away from view. Scuffling and Mexican voices sounded in the background. A hand-written paper that read *Ramirez for Ramos* was held up to the camera lens. The back of the man who'd struck Izza returned to view. The video ended with him striking her again and again until the screen went blank.

"They don't know Ramirez is dead," Alex hissed to Ember. "What else did they send?"

"Nothing. Mother is back tracking their IP address and—"

"Sonofabitch!" Alex cursed in every language he knew, pacing up and down the hall with the need to kill unleashed and out of control. "What about satellite feeds?" he barked.

"We're trying, Alex. We've expanded our search of the same coordinates where you found Connor. A black helicopter landed there earlier. Three men with two dogs tracked Izza into a cave. She put up a good fight until they knocked her out. I've tracked the helicopter to a private airstrip outside of town, but then they pulled a fast one. I would have called you sooner, but—"

"But what?" Lightning cracked all the way to Alexandria.

"They transferred her from the chopper to the trunk of a black sedan. I watched them do it, but then they drove into the hanger, and twenty cars just like it drove out the other side. They know we're tracking them. We're running each vehicle down. Murphy's helping us, Harley's helping. I've even asked—"

"Stop!" Alex had no patience for banter. Not now. "You said this came through e-mail?"

"Yes, Boss," Ember replied meekly.

He calmed enough to be civil, trying real hard not to kill the messenger. "Can you send a reply?"

"You bet."

"Tell those bastards anytime. Anywhere. You hear me? I'll meet them anywhere!"

"I'm doing it. Right now." She hung up.

Alex raised his arm in a fast pitch, but Connor was suddenly behind him. He caught his boss's arm just before Alex would've blasted his cell phone into the wall. By then, Connor had heard enough of the one-sided conversation. In a fit of rage, Alex blasted the younger man beside him instead of his phone. "What the hell are you doing out here?"

"No, Boss. What the hell are you doing out here?" Connor demanded, his eyes bright with fear.

Alex had no choice but to spit it out. "The cartel has Izza."

"I already know that." Connor said, one hand pressed hard against the bloody dressing at his side and the other gripping Alex's forearm. "What's really going on? Tell me!"

"Mother and Ember received a video of Izza. They're tracking—"

Connor went ballistic "Let me see it. Give it to me. Where is she?"

"I don't know. Right now, I don't know any more than you. Get back into the room and let me bandage that—"

"Where's the sonofabitchin' video!" Connor all but climbed over Alex to get at the cell phone in his hand.

Alex tapped the screen to replay the video and handed it over.

"God, no." Connor choked, his knuckles clenched to his lips as he watched. "I'm leaving. I have to find her."

"We don't know where she is." Alex grabbed his agent's arm in a steely grip. "Let me dress your wound first. Ember and Mother will locate her; I promise you that. Do you hear me? Then you and I will go get her, okay?"

Connor stared at his boss, the stark terror in his eyes proof he no longer comprehended logic. He shook his head even as Alex forced him back into the hotel room. "I shouldn't have left her. She didn't want me to go. You don't understand. I can't stay. I have to find her."

"We will." Alex closed the door behind them. "Trust me."

Connor broke down on the edge of the bed. "Don't let me fall asleep. I can't help her if—"

"No way." Alex leaned into his agent's still bearded face. "As soon as Mother gets back to me, we're going to get Izza. Everyone back in Alexandria is looking for her."

Connor gripped Alex's wrist. "But they're not here. Don't lie to me, Boss."

"Every man's got the right to take care of his family." Alex pushed Connor onto his back. "Trust me. I want them as badly as you do."

Connor leaned back, his fists clenched and his belly tight with the need to run. "I need a gun."

Wordlessly, Alex went to his gear bag and pulled out two loaded pistols. He handed them grip first to Connor. Trembling with more rage than weakness, Connor clutched the weapons across his chest. "I'm going to kill them all."

Alex didn't even nod as he peeled the bloody bandage from Connor's side. First things first. The wound had to be stabilized. Connor needed one less thing to worry about tonight. And then they were going to war.

Izza groaned just to hear her own voice. Every breath seemed so damned hard to draw in. Exhaling was easier, but at least the ragged noise in her throat meant she was still alive. That was good. She could turn this nightmare around.

Somehow.

The jerk who'd hit her was going to pay. She didn't know how she'd get out of these ties yet, but when she did, the sucker had a helluva beatdown coming. Left jab, upper cut, both followed by lightning combos of cross hooks and crotch kicks. He better start running cuz he was gonna cry like a baby when she caught up with him. And then she was going to kill him.

She clung to the promise of dropping his sorry ass to the ground. He'd be the one to bleed, not her. He'd never know what hit him. Not until she stood with her boot on his throat. Not until she crushed his larynx. Then he'd know. By hell, he'd know.

Her fingers flexed to reach her tender stomach and the infant within. She groaned again to let that tiny little girl nestled inside of her know her Mama was still there. Beaten maybe, but Izza had been beaten plenty before and lived to fight another day. It was that other pain that worried her, that one in her lower back. As weary as she was, righteous rage ignited in her soul. If these men hurt her baby, they were all going to die. Every last one of them.

Somehow.

Darkness rolled around her like waves on the ocean. Blue waves reached up with tender comfort. Deep Pacific blue....

"Connor," she whimpered. "Come here. Hurry. Come save me."

Somehow....

"Take the girls and Juanita. Run for the van," Mark yelled to Cassidy and Brigham over the gunfire. "Get them out of here. Rory and I will cover you. Move it!"

Cassidy stared at Mark, knowing full well what that order really meant. Her eyes were dark. Determined. Fierce. She didn't argue. With one last piercing look, she pushed Juanita, the girls and Brigham away from the battle. The five of them disappeared into the dark.

"This sure as hell sucks," Rory said in his customary understated manner.

Mark gave him a quick nod as he slapped another magazine home. "Yeah. I saw this going down a little differently. How many do you think?"

Rory ripped a portion of his shirt and wound it around his bloody elbow. "Looks like a hundred. Probably less. Sixty maybe."

"Agreed. We stop them here," Mark muttered calmly. "They have to look for us once they clear the gate. That's our only chance. Mow 'em down the second they show their faces. Don't leave a single man standing."

Rory nodded, silently accepting his last order. Mark drew a deep breath. They lay a foot apart and belly to the ground, perpendicular to the gate opening and in a perfect defensive position. For a while, they'd have the upper hand. While exiting the hacienda, the cartel guards would initially be exposed. They'd have to have to turn left and locate the two snipers before they could make a killing shot. Mark would have felt better with a few more men at his side, but there was no time for what-ifs now. The wait for battle was too short and the advancing army too many.

He laid out his extra magazines on the ground to his right for quick and easy access. Less than a split second passed before the assault unleashed upon them again. The guards crowded out the gate, firing steadily. They quickly located the two snipers left behind. A triumphant roar went up in their ranks. Only two intruders!

Mark and Rory were more difficult to hit, but not impossible. A bullet grazed Rory's shoulder as another dug itself deep into his thigh. Mark heard him grunt, but amazingly Rory continued firing, his aim more deadly as the battle raged. He took out guard after guard until the gray uniformed bodies began to pile up near the gate.

Mark felt the sting of steel in his shoulder and wondered why his gun quit working. Only visual examination revealed his bloodied hand, shattered bones exposed, his index finger and thumb useless. He moved his weapon to fire left-handed, not his strong hand, but still usable. Oddly, neither his shoulder nor hand hurt.

Another bullet lanced the side of his head, just above his left ear. Blood drenched his neck. That one didn't hurt either. Yet. Adrenaline worked wonders. He kept firing.

His last thought was simple. The beautiful, sweet face of his darling wife, Libby, flashed to his mind. She smiled up at him from their bed, her curly blond hair framing her perfect face, her bright blue eyes full of nothing but love for him. Him – a simple farmer's son, a man so unworthy of such devotion.

And here he was dying too far away and not in her arms like he'd dreamed. She would be sad. She would cry. His own little JayJay would grow up never remembering her daddy; she'd never know how much he loved her tiny pink toes and happy baby giggles.

Mark fired faster, the thought of his family a sudden burst of energy in a losing battle. If he had to die, let it be for the innocence of children, the laughter of three little dark-eyed girls in the world.

Libby. JayJay. God, I love you both so much. Please. Don't cry too long.

Twenty-Seven

"You ready to go?" Alex was no more than finished repacking and taping the wound when he offered Connor an arm up.

Connor stood in answer. He hefted the solid weight of the spare SIGs. Covert operators never carried one when two or three would do. His body ached, but his mind grew harder and more focused with every passing minute. The time had come to kill. Men were going to die tonight.

Alex grabbed his gear bag. "Let UHP and Ember handle the wild goose chase. I'm not following any damned cars. You saw the video. Izza's in a hangar, not the trunk of some sedan."

Connor bolted for the door. Alex followed, locking his hotel room behind him. By the time they hit ground level, Connor was weak-kneed and shaky again. The most important covert op of his life lay ahead and he was falling apart. He stiffened his spine and hid the truth. But Alex saw through him when he fumbled the seat belt in the Land Cruiser. Wordlessly, Alex pulled the strap across Connor's chest and fastened the belt for him.

"You good?" he asked without looking into Connor's eyes like he normally would have. The man's blue eyes could pierce walls of concrete when he wanted the truth.

Connor nodded, already exhausted and panting for air. Good had nothing to do with how he felt. He didn't care if he lived or not. Tonight was all about Izza. He leaned into the supple leather seat, drawing down the calm of the universe to help him accomplish what lay ahead. Killing was never his first choice, but tonight all that changed. Whoever was in that hangar with Izza, if that's where she still was, had better be ready to die hard. There would be no head shots to take these guys out instantly, only lingering, bloody, screaming pain until they begged to be put out of their misery.

He shot a sideways glance to his boss. The man's jaw was hard-set and squared off, his eyes sharp and deadly. The same darkness clung to him that Connor felt. War waited in the very near future. As Connor prepared himself mentally, so did Alex. They were back in battle-mode and going in hot. Izza damned well better be alive when he found her because Connor knew exactly how many fingers and limbs a man could live without until he prayed to die.

Pulling onto the interstate, Alex swung south. He'd locked in the coordinates of the hangar on the vehicle's GPS. The disembodied voice of Bitching Betty directed them for less than thirty miles of freeway before Alex exited and headed due west. Ten more minutes of travel time brought them to what appeared to be an abandoned airfield. Only the lighted windows along the eaves revealed the truth. Someone was home.

"I see three points of egress," Alex said calmly as he killed the headlights and rolled to a stop beyond the circle of mercury vapor lighting. "Hangar doors at the rear and front open upward. Side door opens out."

"One window at ground level," Connor reported, his brain instantly offering strategy and reconnaissance.

"One chopper. Look familiar?"

"That's it," Connor hissed, never so sure about anything in his life. The chopper sitting in front of the hangar was the one he'd seen in the desert. One click and the seat belt slipped out of his way. Adrenaline kicked in. His nerves steeled. The mission was go.

"Let's make sure," Alex said grimly as he set one booted foot to the gravel. "Window first."

Connor followed a half step behind his boss. The window looked too dark. Maybe they were wrong. Maybe Izza wasn't here. Flattening himself against the corrugated hanger wall, he peered in one side of the window while Alex took the other.

There she was, all the way at the back of the hangar, in the dark and still bound to the chair. The lights were dimmed. Connor's heart jumped to his throat. He honestly could not tell if she was still alive from where he stood. Anger flared up from his soul at the four men seated on a nearby, dilapidated couch watching television while she suffered. He took one step toward the side door before Alex stopped him.

"Not yet. Stick to the element of surprise. Let them invite us in."

Connor nodded once. He and his boss were linked through years of military experience and combat ops. They might not have worked alongside each other in the Corps, but they knew how the other's mind worked and what each lifted brow and innuendo meant.

"You packing tracers?" he asked curtly.

"Always," Alex answered, his knee already to the ground, his hands cupping his SIG and aimed at the helicopter. "The second they open up, we go in. I don't care if they're packing nothing but a cup of coffee, mow the bastards down."

Connor wiped his sweaty face and nodded. Alex squeezed the trigger to start the war. One single incendiary round hit the fuel tank. With a tremendous roar, the helicopter jumped up off the concrete pad in a fiery whoosh of orange flames and flying wreckage. Black smoke spewed skyward. Metal and glass flew. Sure enough, the hangar door burst open.

"On your knees! Now!" Alex roared, his pistol aimed at the surprised cartel guards despite his order to mow them down. Three of the cowards opened fire, while the fourth ran back into the hangar, his gun drawn.

Connor didn't duck, think or hesitate. His arm snaked out to his side before Alex could get a shot off. The nearest man fell bleeding to his knees.

One down.

Not slowing even to ensure his own safety, Connor rounded the corner of the hangar with long and steady steps. Alex was out there somewhere, but Connor only had eyes for one person, and she damned well better still be breathing when he got to her.

His weapon spit lead as rage and pure muscle training assumed control. For this single moment in time, he was the avenging angel and hell better get out of his way. The second bastard fell quickly, then the third dropped, gurgling and whining his way to the concrete tarmac.

Three down. I'm coming, Izza. Hold on.

The fourth fled to the only chance at leverage left to him. The rear of the hangar. To Izza.

"You think I won't kill her?" he growled, crouched behind Izza, taunting Connor with his pistol stuck in her neck. The fool should've taken his one and only chance while he had it.

Connor didn't pause for a split second to reconsider probabilities or physics after he caught sight of what they'd done to Izza.

Red, hot fury flamed to life in the deepest depth of his soul. Never had he felt more righteous or more full of the power of an angry god. When the idiot cartel guard peered over Izza's right shoulder and pulled her ponytail to force her unconscious and battered face forward, Connor's wrist snapped the borrowed weapon to target.

He needed no spotter. No crosshairs. No conscience. He was judgment incarnate, the final horseman of the Apocalypse come to wipe the wicked from the face of the earth once and for all.

Reaction time diminished with every step.

Not once did Connor slow or hesitate.

He was sent to bring death and death he would bring.

Connor could hear the man's heart pounding. The idiot didn't get it. He was already dead.

"I'll do it," the stupid man declared like he had a prayer of living another ten seconds.

"No." Connor fired one quick killing shot in reply, and one only, with the celestial sneer of an archangel sent to earth on a divine mission. "You won't."

The cartel's finest jerked backward with the only headshot Connor had allowed. Bloody spray and brain matter smeared the wall behind him as his lifeless body slipped to the floor, the pistol grip caught in his limp hand.

Four down.

The men who'd beaten Izza were dying or dead. And it was good.

Connor holstered his weapon, the blessed fury in check once more. Alex stood suddenly at Connor's side.

"You shot them all," he declared with a twinge of awe, but Connor didn't care for shooting records. That day was done.

He knelt at her chair, his heart climbing out of his chest at the sight of Izza's bloodied face. Cradling her head tenderly in his palms, fear grabbed hold. Was he too late after all? "Oh, my God. What have they done to you?"

Alex pulled a knife from his pocket and sliced the ties that held her. She slumped forward into Connor's arms, her battered face against his chest, streams of blood running down her neck and arms.

Her swollen eyelids fluttered. She looked up at him through slits, her voice as faint as air. "They... kicked... me. My baby...."

Hot tears streamed down his face. He pressed his hand over her swollen belly, but nothing stirred beneath his fingers. No tiny elbows or knees. Nothing.

"You listen to me, Izza. You're both going to be okay, you hear me?" Easing her off the chair, he lifted her into his arms and stood. But Izza didn't speak again. Connor cradled her, weeping for the woman he loved and his unborn daughter as he strode out of the hangar.

Alex stood with his cell phone. "I need paramedics at—"

"No, Boss," Connor declared. With Izza safely tucked into his body, and his pistol in the other hand, he was ready to kill the bastards he'd left writhing on the tarmac. "Not for these guys you don't. They're mine."

"Connor. No!" Alex barked sternly.

"Yes," Connor hissed, his decision already made and clear as hell. These men deserved death for what they'd done to Izza and her unborn baby. Mad dogs had to be put down. Brutal men were no different. They needed to beg for their lives or pray to die. Either way, Connor intended to deliver the same hard truth. *Don't ever mess with my woman!*

"Boston." Izza's sweet endearment came to him on the breeze. He looked down at her. She hadn't spoken. She couldn't, curled up in his arm like she was. The word hadn't come from her. And yet....

Izza and this baby were everything. His world. His heart. These last two pigs on the tarmac weren't worth the kinetic energy of a wasted .9mm round. Connor holstered his weapon, wrapped both arms around his life and walked away. He had what he'd come for.

Let Alex make the call. Let Alex clean up the mess. Hell, let him shoot the sons of bitches if he wanted to.

He sat outside emergency surgery not sure he'd have a reason to smile again. Alex had just brought another cup of bad hospital coffee. It was just one of those things a person did while they were waiting and praying – and holding their breath. Connor didn't touch it.

Four men against one little woman were not good odds even for a tough Hispanic chick who could easily whip Connor's ass. And he'd give anything if she'd come charging out of surgery right now and do just that, all bent out of shape and mad as hell like she used to be. Somehow he'd known all along that behind that dammed up hate and anger was love. It was just hard for a girl to know how to love softly when all she'd known was how to fight to live.

He sat with his elbows on his knees and his face in his hands. He couldn't look his boss in the eye, his fear too close to the surface. He felt worthless on so many levels. His gut hurt. His head was dizzy one minute and throbbing the next. But his heart hurt the worst. And they wouldn't let him see her. They made him sit. With Alex. And wait.

"Izza's one of the toughest gals I've ever known." Alex sat with his arm across the back of Connor's chair. "She's one helluva shot, I can tell you that much. I watched her last firearms certification. She could give Zack a run for his money. I hired her because of that coin you showed Murphy. Remember?"

Connor nodded. Of course he remembered. It was the same one she'd accused him of stealing. But that day was another day to remember. She'd boasted she could take out that center palm tree on the coin no matter how far away it was. So he egged her on. Against the sun. An extremely tough shot for sure.

The girl had eyes like a hawk. Sharp. Angry. Loving. And he wanted to see them again. He knew now why he'd kept that stupid coin. It was all he had left of her and that perfect day. It was all he had left of Jamie, too. Connor raked his hands over his head wanting to pull his hair out or scream.

Alex kept talking and bugging the hell out of him. "You don't know this, but Izza came to me for the job. I've never had that happen before. Guess I'm a male chauvinist, but I was only looking to hire men until I met her. I've got to change that stupid mindset of mine. There are some damn good women snipers out there."

Connor couldn't speak. The conversation seemed so damned trivial while Izza and his baby's lives hung in the balance. Alex needed to shut up and leave him alone.

"You were her only reference."

"Say what?"

Alex nodded. "You were her single reference on her job application. She said you'd vouch for her."

"How'd she know that I—?"

Alex shrugged. "Guess you'll have to ask her, won't you?"

"Yeah, so move your sorry ass over."

Connor looked up at those unexpected words. There stood Roy Hudson, his hand gripping a walker. Connor stood to make room for his senior agent, but Roy grabbed him in a big ole bear hug instead, smacking his back as he suffocated him. Connor collapsed against him, the sight of another friendly face finally too much. He'd forgotten all about Roy's injuries in the crisis of finding Izza. "I'm sorry, Roy."

Roy straight-armed him. "You have got to stop saying that, you hear me, boy? You got nothing to be sorry about. You didn't shoot me anymore than you shot Jamie Ramos back in Iraq. You're not responsible for any of this. You listening, son?"

Connor stared at his friend, too emotional to respond.

"Yeah, I know all about Izza's brother. And I know that smart-mouthed little gal in there has been blaming you for what happened to her brother, ain't that right? It took me awhile to figure out why she was throwing up so much while we were in the canyon. She's pregnant, isn't she?"

Connor nodded.

"And that baby is yours." Roy's dark eyes glowed with concern, and maybe a little pride.

Tear welled up in Connor's eyes. "Yes. It's a little girl."

Roy hugged the young man again. "Well, I hope you and Izza got your differences worked out, cuz any daughter of Izza's is gonna give you one helluva run for your money. How's our girl doing?"

"Still waiting for the doctor to come tell us something. They've been in there for a while." Connor helped Roy sit and stored his walker next to his chair.

Roy turned to Alex. "I've never had more female trouble on an operation than this one. And damned if Connor wasn't smack in the middle of it like always." He had his hand in the middle of Connor's back as soon as he sat down again. "One minute I've got him and Cassidy making goo-goo eyes at each other. The next thing I know, Izza's square in between them and ready to fight everyone and anyone."

"That's Izza, all right," Connor said quietly, his voice tight and sad. *My Izza. My baby girl.*

Roy smacked his back. "She's damn tough. How are you doing?"

But Connor didn't have time to answer. The doctor at the door waved him into the next room. The minute he took Connor's arm in a firm hold, his heart stopped. The man's gray eyes were too serious. The hospital walls swayed.

"Ms. Ramos had a bruised spleen and a couple cracked ribs. She's pretty banged up, but she'll be fine. She's in recovery right now. We're treating her for dehydration. That's the real problem right now."

"How's the baby?" Connor tried to focus with the walls still weaving behind the doctor's somber face. Dry fear clutched his throat. It was difficult to read this man. Even now his face blurred. He shook his head, as if—

"I'm sorry, Mr. Maher, but we had to take the baby."

What? Connor's heart crashed to the floor in a thousand pieces. He choked, not exactly sure what he'd just heard. *Poor Izza. Does she know yet?* "So the baby, she's—dead?"

"Oh, no. She's six weeks premature. She's up in NICU, the Neonatal Intensive Care Unit on the second level."

"She's alive?" Tears sprang to his eyes. The doctor swayed. Lights flickered. Connor steadied himself with a palm flat to the wall and still the doctor swayed like a drunken sailor.

"Congratulations, young man." He grasped Connor's hand as if Connor had a clue what was going on. "You have a beautiful baby girl. She's going to be fine."

He sagged to the floor, his knees too weak to hold him up anymore. The doctor caught him by the elbow just in time. "Whoa, now. Up you go. Let's get you back on your feet. Can't have you passing out now, can we?" He assisted Connor back to the waiting room. "You go join your friends. The nurse will come by in a few minutes to take you to see your wife and daughter."

Connor looked at those serious male faces waiting for him in the waiting room, more serious because of the doctor holding him up. But all Connor could do was sit in his chair and cover his face. He sobbed at the doctor's word—*your wife and daughter*. His mother's smiling face came to mind. He wanted to tell her most of all. She'd be so happy. So proud. But first he wanted to hold *his wife and his daughter.*

Alex was at his side. Heck, even Roy stood in his walker. Both worried. Still waiting.

"Connor?" Alex asked, the alarm clear in his voice. He had his hand on Connor's shoulder, rock solid and ready for anything that might come. "Tell us, son. How is she?"

Connor raised his bleary tear-filled eyes. "Boss," he choked. "I'm a dad."

Twenty-Eight

At that very happy news, Alex grabbed a wheelchair and rushed Connor to the ER for his own emergency surgery. Connor leaned back onto the narrow bed with a groan as the nurse attached an IV line in his forearm. "Thanks, Boss," he muttered, closing his eyes.

"No problem," Alex said as he stood aside and watched. Somehow Connor's good looks always aroused the same curious behavior in women. It was an interesting phenomenon. Ladies seemed to go into some kind of high-energy, high-alert mode around him. The kid just seemed to have it, whatever *it* was.

Even now, this particular nurse gently washed his face and tried to make small talk. She was very pretty and happy to see him. Short blond hair, bright brown eyes, everything that Connor liked in an available woman, but his eyes had closed the minute his head touched the pillow. He lay on the narrow bed relaxed, finally ready to have his wounds properly attended to.

"You should have come in earlier with this kind of an injury," she scolded. "My goodness, where have you been?"

"Working," he answered, completely missing the gentle flirting going on around him. "Hope this doesn't take very long."

The nurse shot Alex a cool look. "Your boss must be a slave driver to make you work in this condition. You poor thing." She washed Connor's neck and proceeded to his arms while another nurse came in with a surgical tray. Watching her gentle administrations, Alex noticed again how gaunt his junior agent was.

"No. He's a good man," Connor said calmly, his eyes still closed.

Alex grunted. Connor had it wrong. He was the good man today. For as unsteady as he seemed on the ride there, he'd transformed into some kind of deadeye gunslinger the minute his boots hit the asphalt. He never really aimed, just pointed, squeezed off round after round, and kept walking until he'd saved Izza and shot everyone in his way.

Alex stepped away to make another call to Mark. No answer. He dialed his two guardian angel techies still on twenty-four-seven duty on the East Coast.

"Anything from Mark yet?" he asked Ember quietly.

"Alex," she bit out. "We've got a live satellite feed. It looks like a war zone down there."

"Is Libby in the air?"

"Yes. I have Rory's parents' number in Nebraska. Should I call them?"

"Not yet," Alex replied somberly. "DEA has a man inside the SC. He better be damned good."

"How's Connor?" Ember asked. "How's Izza?"

Alex glanced back at Connor. "He's out cold in the ER, finally getting his wound cleaned and stitched. Izza is in recovery. And their little girl is five pounds, two ounces, and breathing on her own."

A blinding explosion lit the gate of the hacienda, throwing several guards clear off the ground. Mark closed his eyes tight. Automatic fire roared to life behind his and Rory's position. *What the hell?* For a split second, he feared crossfire, that armed guards had circled behind them, that he and Rory were sandwiched in a meat grinder, a kill zone.

But then another rocket propelled grenade ripped over his head and hit the gate, aimed again from somewhere behind him. More guards flew. The cartel halted their forward march. Mark still couldn't see who was firing, but the men ahead of him suddenly turned and scrambled back behind the safety of the high hacienda walls. That much was a good thing.

He looked over to where his junior agent laid deathly quiet. Except for the blood smeared across his face, dark-haired Rory looked like a kid asleep, his face in the dirt, his arms still hugging his rifle and his baseball cap on backwards. Instant tears filled Mark's eyes. *God. Not Rory.*

He rolled to his back. A bright spotlight advanced toward his prone position, the glare in his eyes. He squinted. Three dark silhouettes approached. "Mark Houston?"

Mark didn't recognize the Hispanic male's voice.

"Mark Houston!" the voice boomed again. "Alex Stewart sent me. Is that you?"

He raised his left hand. "Yeah. Here. We're here."

The same man barked an urgent order into his headset as he crouched at Mark's side. "Send the medics up to the front. Two men down. *Arriba! Ándale! Ándale!*" A swarthy Mexican, his strong voice exuded authority and calm. "Stay down, Mark Houston. You and your friends are safe now. We have your Agent Dancer and the Ramirez girls in our custody. Let us clean up the rest of this rat's nest. Is that acceptable with you?"

Mark sagged limply against the dirt. A dozen or so heavily armed men marched past him on their way into the hacienda. "Who the hell—?"

"I am Carlos Santiago, a friend of your Governor Baxter. You and your team are badly outnumbered, I think." Carlos peered anxiously down at Mark. "Yes?"

"We had 'em... right where we wanted 'em," Mark muttered, surprised how weak his voice sounded.

Carlos smiled kindly. "Yes. I believe you did."

"My man." Mark pointed at Rory with is one good hand.

Carlos nodded grimly. "Medics are coming. You stay still. I will attend to this dirty business, but I will be back."

With that Carlos rejoined his men. They continued firing into the hacienda compound. Finally, the noise of the battery ceased. Mark listened to the strangers making several not too gentle demands of their prisoners. And threats. Harsh death threats. *Ahh. Music to a dying man's ears.*

Dozens of Mexican police poured around Mark and Rory. Medics followed close behind. A very kind man knelt beside Mark, several at Rory's side. They had tourniquets, compresses and whatever it was in that hypodermic that felt so—good.

"How is he?" Mark shouted to the medics attending to Rory. "How is...."

He never heard the answer. The medicine swept through him, a soft, sweet wave of pain free euphoria.

It was the middle of the night when he got out of the emergency room, but he didn't care. Connor went straight to Izza's room. She lay there asleep, wrapped in warmed hospital blankets, her normally olive skin pale against the stark white bedding. Black hair, all shiny and washed, lay in soft tendrils around her poor battered face. Between the butterfly bandages, bruises, swelling and stitches, it was hard to recognize the sweet woman he knew for sure lay beneath. He wiped his eyes and went to her side, afraid to wake her and yet hoping he did.

"Hey there, Papa." She smiled one of her half-crooked smiles as she squinted through two purpled blackened eyes.

"You look like you've been in one hell of a fight, Mama."

She gave him a weak snort. "You should see the other guy."

On most days Connor would've laughed, but he had seen the other guys and they were dead. Her rescue had been too close of a call. He couldn't stand there another minute. Connor pulled her carefully into his arms, tubing and all. "God, Izza. I'm so sorry."

She winced at the movement but burrowed into his shirt anyway, her trembling face pressed against his neck. He held her gently; once again that familiar wave of protectiveness was out of control in his gut. Choking with emotion, he whispered his failure into her hair. "I'm so damned sorry."

"For what?" She snuggled closer.

He held her tight, ashamed of always crying in front of this woman. "Because I left you. Because they hurt you. Because I—"

"Oh, stop." She pressed a finger to his lips. "You didn't hurt me, and I just need a couple days to rest up. Then I'll be ready to kick their butts for sure." She smoothed her hand down his now clean-shaven cheek, the look in her puffy eyes intent as she wiped the tears off his face. "I love you, Connor."

He gulped. "I thought I'd lost you. God, Izza, I came back as fast as I could, but you were gone."

"I'm here, baby." Her hand wrapped around his neck as she pulled him to her mouth. Gently he kissed her poor swollen lips. But Izza was not one for gentleness. She held him tightly, her mouth asking for more than just the chaste kiss he'd intended to give her. He maintained the careful contact as long as he could, but she was contagious and determined. Connor obliged, his tongue softly melting with hers as she pushed into his arms. He smothered her to him, for a split second willing to give her all she seemed to need. But caution overruled. This woman had narrowly escaped death and delivered a baby within the past few hours. He came back to his senses and pulled away.

"Izza," he breathed hotly in her neck. "You're the most gorgeous, wonderful, crazy woman in the world, do you know that?"

"Yeah." She sighed and relaxed, her eyes glowing softly up at him. Even back and blue and stitched, she was irresistible. "I am, huh? So, did you get 'em or do I need to go back to that hangar and clean house?"

"I got 'em," he answered without one iota of remorse.

Her eyes lit up. "All four of them?"

He nodded. The image of her bound and beaten flashed to his mind again. Killing was not something he was proud of, but he'd do it again in a heartbeat. "All I could see was you. They had to die."

"I was going to do that, you know," she declared darkly. Burying her face into his shirt again, Izza was suddenly hanging on for dear life. "You saved me."

She felt so small in his arms, so fragile. He made himself comfortable alongside her on the bed, still holding her carefully so as not to squeeze her ribs or hurt her incision. "So how are you feeling? Can I get you anything? Some rotisserie rabbit, maybe? Boiled tortoise? Rattlesnake steak?"

She sniffled. "A tissue would be nice."

"I can do that." He set the box of tissues next to her. Izza blew her nose and wiped her eyes. She looked exhausted and all he wanted to do was hold her for the rest of his life. When she looked up, she touched the side of his nose carefully.

"You have a bandage and you shaved." She traced his jaw with her fingertips.

"Yeah, some nurse in the ER took pity on me. And look at this." He lifted his shirt and twisted sideways to show off his bandaged gut and back. "I'm all stitched up, and these guys don't use whiskey to sterilize a gunshot wound, either. I didn't feel a thing."

She lifted her hospital gown to show him her taped midriff. "My scar's bigger."

"Does it hurt much?" He traced the C-section tape extra gently. His little girl had made her entrance through that incision. He wished he'd been there to see the birth, but Izza had been so badly beaten. No wonder the doctors made him stay in the waiting room. They must have been scared, too.

"Does yours?" Izza countered.

"Nothing I can't handle." Connor gave her a gentle kiss on her forehead as he played to her competitive nature. "I'll bet yours doesn't hurt at all, does it?"

Dark eyes flickered over his face, searching for what he didn't know. She must have found it, though. A gentle light replaced the dark. Izza smiled as she admitted, "It hurts like hell. I don't want to take anything for pain so I can nurse my – I mean, our baby."

He caught the course correction. "We have a beautiful little girl. Have you seen her yet?"

"They wouldn't bring her to me." The pout on her face made him smile again.

"She's beautiful. She looks just like you. I'll get the wheelchair. Are you ready?"

Izza smirked. "What do you think?"

He left the room to check with the nursing station to make sure he could fulfill his promise. The nurse gave him a warm smile. "I'll call the NICU and tell them you're coming. They're always happy to work with preemie parents."

Izza winced and groaned a little as he settled her into the wheelchair.

"Are you sure you're up for this?"

"Yes," she answered promptly. "Let's go."

Within minutes, they were at the NICU window, their fragile daughter only inches away in an incubator, attached to so many monitors and lines for such a little girl. Dark hair drizzled around the edges of the pink knit cap on her head. Connor held Izza steady as she leaned against the wall.

Her clenched fist went to her lips. "Oh, Connor. You named her."

He rested his chin in the corner of her neck. "You can change it if you want."

The baby's hospital information card proudly declared her mother to be Isabella Ramos and her father, Connor Maher. But the best surprise was written on the next line. Baby's name: *Jamie Maher.*

Izza leaned heavily into Connor and wept.

"I thought I'd let you pick her middle name." He kissed the top of her head and handed her another box of tissues.

She wiped her face and at last composed herself. "Bridgette. Her middle name is Bridgette."

That surprised Connor. He wanted to cry himself. His mother would be so pleased. Heck. His mother would be pleased no matter what they named her first granddaughter, but Jamie Bridgette Maher had an especially nice ring to it.

"I love you so much." Izza clutched his arms, pulling them tighter around her.

"I love you more than you know," he murmured. "I was hoping you and Jamie would move out to Alexandria with me when you're both able to."

"You were, huh?" She nestled against him, not taking her eyes off their perfect child.

"But if you don't want to, I'll move to Seattle."

"Alexandria. I want to live with you in Alexandria." The decision was made. "Look, Connor. Jamie's crying. Oh, I want to hold her."

"Let's see what we can do about that. Come on. Sit back down." He got her situated in the wheelchair again and rapped on the NICU door. Before long, they were both inside the neo-natal unit, but they couldn't hold their little girl just yet. They had to content themselves with only touching her while she lay in the heated isolette. The fragile infant squirmed when Connor covered her entire body with his hand. She was perfect in every way, but so very small. The enormity of fatherhood hit him.

"My God, Izza. What have we done?"

She smiled, her battered brown eyes glistening with the tender moment. And that's all he needed to check his temporary anxiety. Judging by the look of love on her face, he knew exactly what they'd done. They'd done damned good.

Jamie fussed. She made little coughing sounds and cried in her scratchy baby voice. They stared in wonder at every perfect thing she did.

"See. I told you she was just like you," Connor whispered.

Their perfect little girl had two black eyes. She was a fighter—just like her mother.

Twenty-Nine

"Hey, babe."

Bleary and medicated, Mark thought he'd died and gone to heaven at the sound of that sweet voice. A golden angel leaned over him, and she had the bluest eyes. He'd never seen such beautiful eyes. Never. Ever. Even full of drugs like he was, he was sure of it.

"How are you feeling, honey?"

A cool touch caressed his forehead. Was this a dream? He tried to focus, but exhaustion tugged him under and away from her. A sweetly persistent kiss brushed his cheek. He couldn't help but smile. Ahh. Her lips felt good. Wherever he was, he was never leaving this place. It had to be heaven because she was there. Again cool fingers soothed over his whiskered cheek. A sigh. A kiss. He fought the dark lure of sleep so he could stay with this angel. So she'd never leave.

"JayJay misses her daddy," the angel whispered against his ear, tickling him into a lighter level of sleep.

Hmm. JayJay. His baby girl had been named after his angel mother. She would've loved meeting her precocious granddaughter, both named after a bird. Hmm. It was hard to think which bird that might have been. His mother loved them all. Gray fog still roiled around him, enticing him to sleep. *Yeah, okay, but what's JayJay doing here?*

He twitched his eyelids. Blinked without opening his eyes. Tried again to focus so he could see that golden angel. Tried to think. *Where am I? What day is this?* One eye finally creaked open.

The angel leaned directly over him like a sentinel, those blue eyes piercing and loving. *Ahh. Libby.* He smiled to see his wife's face. She was the angel in his life, her blond hair a halo. Only she looked sad.

"How are you feeling?"

"Good." He croaked like an old man, cleared his throat and croaked again. Mark vaguely remembered the clean white room of a Mexican hospital and a bumpy flight. "Where am I?"

Libby brought the straw of a water bottle to his lips. "You're at Saint Mark's hospital in Utah, but don't talk. You've had a tube down your windpipe, so it's probably very sore." She smoothed her hand across his forehead. He nodded as he sucked down some water. Relief was instant. He wanted to sit, but she pressed him easily back to the sheets. It didn't take much. Libby sat at the edge of his bed, his hand grasped firmly in hers. "It's good to see your eyes again."

Mark pulled her weakly to his side. His right hand had been transformed into a pincushion with a lot of gauze, tape, and metal rods and pins sticking out of it. A monitor beeped quietly at his bedside, somehow in sync with the dull pain in his shoulder.

"Where am I?" he asked again, the fog lifting a little more.

"I already told you," she whispered. "You're in a Salt Lake City hospital. Saint Mark's of all places."

He stilled to absorb that piece of familiar information. It made sense. Alex would want all his men together after a difficult op. A frission of fear cruised through his body. He grimaced, anticipating the worst possible news. "Rory?"

Her fingers patting his collarbone diffused the gloom. "Calm down, honey. Rory's three rooms down the hall from you. He's a little worse for wear, but he'll be fine."

Gulping the spike of fear, Mark relaxed again. "So how many?"

"Three. One shattered your hand. One hit your collarbone, but it glanced off and didn't do much damage. The last one grazed the side of your head." She touched the tape on his head, her voice tight in her throat. "It's going to take you a while to recuperate this time, but I'm thankful for your hard head."

He gulped, grateful for the patience of this particular woman. Libby was a nurse. She knew exactly how hard his head was.

"I'll be fine." He smiled his best smile, hoping he could lift the gloom shadowing her pretty face. "Who's taking care of JayJay?"

"Kelsey."

Mark sighed. Alex's wife did have a way with children. "That means JayJay will be spoiled rotten by the time we get home, huh?"

"I guess." Libby looked away, but not before he saw the quivering lip. Changing the subject wasn't going to work this time. Plain and simple, he was lucky to be alive.

Someone knocked on the open door. "Is everyone decent in here?" Alex asked as he entered.

Libby stood to shake his hand. Mark watched her put on a brave front, but he knew her too well. She knew exactly how close he'd come to dying. He pushed the thought from his mind. He knew it, too.

"Are you still talking to me?" Alex gave Libby an instant hug despite Mark's look of warning.

"No." Her voice cracked. She tried to pull away, but Alex wasn't letting her go. "I'm still mad at you."

"Well, I deserve that after I got your husband shot." He said tenderly. "That's why I'm here, Libby. I know it's too soon, but I'd like to offer Mark another job if you'd let me."

"That's up to him," she said quietly.

Mark studied his wife. She wasn't looking at him or Alex, and it was easy to see how heartsick she was.

"The State Department needs a couple observers needed over in Afghanistan. I'd like Mark and Harley to take that on as their permanent assignment, but it depends on what their wives say. Your husband would be travelling back and forth to Afghanistan a couple times a year, but only to observe and not for months at a time. No weapons involved. No high risk operations, either."

Libby didn't answer, and she wasn't looking at Alex yet. Mark knew why. She didn't want to cry in front of his boss.

"We'll get back to you," Mark said. He just wanted her to look at him again.

"Well, of course. I have a Learjet on standby to take you home as soon as you're ready to travel, Mark. An ambulance will meet you at the airport and transport you to the hospital in D.C. unless Libby would rather take you home with her."

Mark shrugged, his eyes still on his unhappy wife.

"Thanks," Libby said quietly. "I'm taking him home."

Alex cupped her chin, his voice low and gentle as he tipped her head up to see into her eyes. "This is all my fault, Libby. Not Mark's. He's a hero. He could've told me to go to hell when I gave him this insane mission, but he didn't. Instead he saved two little girls and their nanny. I'm damned proud of him."

"Me, too." Her voice was so small and shaky. She bit her bottom lip. Mark ached to hold her. Any second now she'd fall apart, and he wanted her in his arms when she did.

Alex gave her a peck on the cheek and let her go. "Kelsey is going to kick my ass for hurting you. Take your man home, Libby. I don't want to see his face in the office until you can forgive me."

That did it. Tears breached the damn. Alex gave Libby a quick farewell squeeze before he nodded to Mark and left them alone.

Mark reached for his wife. "Come here, Libby. Please?"

When she came to the bedside, he pushed his blanket aside and pulled her close. Libby snuggled in carefully as the torrent continued. He was desperately tired, but this was the perfect medicine, his sweet wife in his arms, even if she was mad and crying her heart out.

"Mother called. She was crying and I—" Libby couldn't go on.

"It's okay. I'm going to be okay," he crooned, his good hand firmly around her waist and his nose in her hair. "Ember should've called. Mother's a drama queen. You know that. Yes, I'm a little shot up. It did get ugly, but I'm going to be okay."

"She said I had to come to Utah. She said that you were—" Again she choked. More tears soaked the front of

Mark's hospital gown. "All I could think of was that this time you might die, and I wasn't there and—"

He kissed the side of her head. "I'm here."

It was still plenty hard to focus on the hospital room spinning around him. Alex's job offer was unexpected, but that was the last thing on Mark's mind. All he wanted to do was comfort his wife. Her body alongside his was doing a good job of comforting him. Between the exhaustion and the hypnotic pull of the meds in his system, he fluctuated, one foot in dreamland and the other in heaven on earth.

"So you saved two little girls?" Libby asked, sniffing back some of her emotions. Her warm hand on his chest felt good. Absentmindedly, she twirled her finger through the chest hair that showed above his hospital gown collar. She did that simple intimate gesture often after they'd made love, and that's when he knew they were going to be okay. And she was asking questions. She cared. He buried his face in her hair and just breathed.

"Yeah. We did. Christina and Sophia. We got them out of there just in time," he said dreamily. "It was close."

She snuggled under his arm. "How old are they?"

"Christina's five. Sophia's nearly three, just a year older than JayJay. You'd have fallen in love with them. Dark black hair and eyes, they looked like two little china dolls. Little Christina kept trying to take care of her baby sister." Mark tried to focus enough to satisfy Libby's curiosity with intelligent answers. He kissed her forehead, wishing he could offer more than just a one-armed hug.

She sniffed a couple more times. "Who tried to kill them?"

"Their mother, Alejandra. She used them as human shields. It made me sick. She didn't deserve them." Either it was the drugs in his system or the miracle of what he and his team had accomplished, but it felt more like he'd saved JayJay instead of the children of a powerful drug lord. A single tear escaped the corner of his eye. Libby caught it with her fingertip.

"Oh, Mark. I'm sorry. I am proud of you. You know that." She eased her body up and laid her head on his chest. He sighed. This was all he'd wanted when he thought he was dying down there in Mexico, to be in the arms of his angel.

"It's hard to balance the good we accomplish when we have to live with the consequences, huh?" He smoothed his hand through her hair, hoping he made sense. The room swirled. Shadows of painkillers beckoned for him to let go and relax. He closed his eyes with, "I love you, Libby," on his lips.

She kissed him softly and he slipped back into a deep sleep.

Yeah. They were going to be o-k-a-a-y-y-y-y....

Connor stood behind Izza at the NICU window again, his arms wrapped around her as they gazed through the window. A nurse was bathing Jamie while the infant protested loudly.

"I have something for you," he whispered.

"Is it a flashlight?" she teased as she pushed her backside against him in play. Earlier, she'd tried to coax him into her hospital bed, but Connor had more restraint than she did which was probably smart. Her body did need time to heal from childbirth. Common sense didn't seem to stop them from wanting each other though.

"Besides that." He bumped her again with his, umm, flashlight.

"Is it more thank-you cards?" Izza couldn't take her eyes off their baby. Jamie had proven to be every bit the fighter her mother was. Her lungs strengthened daily, she slept soundly in between feedings, and she was by far the favorite among the nurses.

As tiny as she was, she was a force to be reckoned with. The nurses doted on her parents as much as they did her, their story of survival and rescue a definite human-interest story in the hospital as well as the local media. And they weren't the only ones.

Stores up and down the Wasatch Front donated gifts galore. Some kind person started an account at a local credit union for them. People sent cards and flowers until the hospital was forced to move the many pink bouquets and arrangements to the cafeteria for display. And baby blankets? Jamie had enough pink quilts, crocheted afghans and frilly blankets to stock her own boutique. Connor and Izza spent most of their mornings writing thank you cards to the generous people of Utah while Jamie grew stronger.

"I do have more cards, but no. This is better." Connor held a huge ruby ring in front of Izza. "I don't know for sure, but I think red is your color. You needed something full of fire, not something pasty white like boring old diamonds."

She turned to face him, her eyes brimmed with moisture. "Damn it, Connor. Mom had a ruby ring."

"Would you marry me?" he asked, his voice husky. He lifted the ring from her fingers and slid it over the knuckle of the ring finger on her left hand. "All I know is I can't live without you. I knew it the first time I saw you in Iraq. I'm done trying to."

All those mean words out of her mouth came back to her now. She searched his eyes for the slightest hint of hesitation or anger. He of all people should be at least a little bit mad at her. "Are you sure? I mean, after all I've said and done to you—"

"Yes. Please say—"

"No." She handed the ring back, shaking her head. Marriage scared her. It couldn't be. It wouldn't work. She'd seen what happened when people got married. People died and the ones left behind went crazy. "I can't marry you. We've only known each other a short time, and most of that was in Iraq."

Connor's eyes widened with disbelief. Shock maybe, but no, she couldn't put him through that.

"Just because we did something stupid in Iraq, and just because we were stuck in the middle of the desert for a few days doesn't mean we should get married." Her eyes swelled with tears. With each excuse her voice grew tighter and sadder. "And just because we made a baby together doesn't mean you have to marry me."

He tipped her chin up. "Marry me or not, I'm not leaving your side unless you tell me to go. Is that what you're saying? Do you want me to leave?"

"No." She blinked through the confusion in her heart. *God, no. Don't you dare leave.*

"Izza," he said sternly. "I'm not asking you to marry me because we made a baby, although I think that's a pretty damned good reason. I'm asking you to marry me because you're my life. Do you understand? You are not just a wild fling in the middle of a war. You are everything to me. My sun. My moon. And every last one of my stars. And I did see fireworks that first night. God knows I saw fireworks. That's how worlds are made, Izza, and that's exactly what we were making. Look at that little girl we made. She's our world, isn't she?"

She nodded, still blinking hard just to be able to see him clearly. It didn't make sense. How could anyone love her? Especially after—

"And I don't *have* to marry you, Miss Ramos. I *want* to marry you. With all my faults and failures, I hoped you'd want me, too."

"I do." With a crush she hugged him tight, her hard head pressed against his chest so she could hear his heart. Wow, it was pounding as hard as hers. "I just don't want you to feel like you have to. I don't want you to—"

"Shush." He squeezed her tightly. "You know me better than that. I've loved you since the first time I saw you. What's really going on here? I know you love me."

"I've been so mean." Now the tears really came. "I've hit and kicked you and—"

"Yes, you have."

"And I'm afraid."

He waited.

"I'm afraid I might be one of those abusers, too, like kids who turn out to be just like their parents. Like my dad. And I couldn't bear to put you through what I've lived through. And I'm scared I might hurt Jamie. And she's so little and—"

Her world caved in. Maybe Connor should be the one who raised Jamie. Maybe she was the unworthy one who didn't deserve the perfect child they'd helped create.

He wrapped his arms around her like a blanket. "Do you trust me?" he asked softly.

"Yes." Her instant answer came strong and unequivocally into his shirt.

"You don't want to hit me anymore, do you?"

"No."

"And I know for sure you would never hurt Jamie."

She gulped. There was no word for the depth of love in her heart for that tiny little girl.

He held her tight. "So here's the deal. I'll let you spend the rest of your life making it up to me."

She sobbed. "But I don't deserve you."

"Listen." He could hardly talk, his voice hoarse and low. "If you don't want to marry me I guess that's the way it is. Will you still come live with me?"

"But—"

Connor stopped asking difficult questions and just rocked her. Exhausted from her bath, little Jamie lay asleep in her isolette just feet away while her mother and father figured out what on earth they were going to do with each other.

"Think about it," he whispered. "I've got this gorgeous ruby ring—"

She pushed her hair off her face and grabbed a handful of nearby tissues. With a loud honk, Izza blew her nose and wiped her eyes. He held his palm out, the ruby hot and sparkling in his hand. She snatched it and stuck it on her ring finger, blinking another cascade of tears away. There was only one way this could go down. She had to have him in her life.

"I will marry you, Connor Maher." She drew in a huge breath. "If you forgive me."

He pulled her under his chin. Finally, she nestled quietly where she belonged.

"If that's what you need to hear, then yes, I forgive you. But there is nothing to forgive. We're still going to argue. We're going to fight. And I'm looking forward to our first round of make up sex. That's the way life is." He bumped her again with his, umm, flashlight. "I love you, Izza. I always have. I always will. One of these days, I'm going to be able to show you just how much."

A sigh swelled up from the soles of her feet, and Izza was finally free. "You already have."

Thirty

Finally Connor and Izza were allowed to hold their daughter. It was either the emotion of the moment or the fact they were both still recuperating from their surgeries, but both bawled like babies when they held little Jamie for the first time.

Connor wiped his face. "She looks just like you."

"But she's got your nose. And look at her feet." Izza pulled the blanket away from the baby's spindly legs.

"Are you saying they're big?" He kissed the tiny wrinkled feet at his fingertips. They looked like they belonged to a fairy child from another world.

"No, but look at her toes. They're long. Just like yours." Izza was all smiles through her tears. Tired and still healing, she couldn't contain her joy. It leaked from her eyes like a drippy garden faucet.

Connor was busy taking pictures with his cell phone, snapping one after the other when Alex knocked on the door and entered with a vase full of pink roses and a teddy bear. "How's the happy family?"

She beamed at her boss's kind attention. "Do you want to hold her?"

"Sure." Alex set the vase on the counter and washed his hands in the rest room before he scooped the tiny girl into his arms. His eyes were soft as he gazed down at the precious bundle. "My goodness. I forgot babies came this small. She looks like you, Izza."

"Nah. She's beautiful." Izza couldn't take her eyes off her daughter.

Alex settled on the couch. "I just hired Cassidy for the Seattle office."

"She'll do a good job." Connor glanced at Izza for a smart assed comment, but she just winked back at him with a smile and a shrug. He probably needed to speak with Cassidy in person someday, but for the life of him, he didn't know what he'd say. They'd only just met. Hadn't even been on a real date. Yet.

"She said to tell you congratulations on your new wife and daughter. What are your plans? Will you kids be coming back to Alexandria or moving to Seattle?"

"Alexandria." Izza's answer was quick and sure. "You don't have a rule about married agents working out of the same office, do you?"

Alex's brow lifted. "Wouldn't matter if I did, would it?"

"No, not really." Izza had no problem standing up to Alex. It made Connor smile. The Alexandria office would never be the same.

"She isn't coming back to work for a while, though." Connor had his arm around his intended wife's shoulders. "We're going to get married in Boston next month so make room on your schedule for a wedding. After that, she's staying home with Jamie."

"Take whatever maternity leave you need." Alex gazed down at the sleeping child in the crook of his arm. "Get your family settled. Make sure you take a honeymoon somewhere between all the diapers and midnight feedings. Work will always keep."

"Umm, Alex?" Izza's eyes were suddenly brimming with tears. Again. "Could I ask you a favor?"

"Sure. What do you need?"

"You look like the perfect grandfather. I was wondering. Connor said you would, but I'm not sure, and, umm, would you, I mean would you give me away on my wedding day? I don't know where my old man is, and I don't think he'd do it anyway, and I don't really want him to, and—"

"You bet," Alex answered quick and sure, blinking and smiling. And blinking again. "There isn't anything I'd love more, Izza."

She slipped out of her bed and made her way slowly across the few steps between them. With a tired huff she sat next to Alex. Izza looked up at her boss, her brown eyes full of liquid love. "You are a very good man." With that soft pronouncement, she gave him a big hug.

"That's what I'm here for," he said, pressing Izza to his side.

Connor's eyes teared up. Here was this feisty woman in her cotton nightgown, the same one who used to be so angry at the world, crying in his boss's arms like a little girl. He had to turn from the tender scene. With a cough, he sat on the edge of the bed and changed the subject. "Did you ever figure out who poisoned Ramirez?"

Alex released Izza and handed the sleeping infant back to her mother. "Yes. Quinones had family working in the jail's kitchen. He injected an overdose of bark scorpion venom into Ramirez's coffee. Miguel didn't stand a chance."

"Man, those people were blood thirsty," Connor exclaimed. "Their solution for every problem was to kill somebody."

"They're finished for a while. The Mexican government's going after the rest of Javier's business. They've been after him for years. Last I heard from Scott Sylvane, they'd burned both the Ramirez and Quinones haciendas to the ground. They found seventeen bodies at the quarry."

"If Ramirez didn't kidnap us, who did?"

"His wife. Alejandra was playing both sides, only she didn't know Ramirez was dead when she offered to trade Izza for him. You two were only kidnapped because she needed leverage in case things didn't go the way she planned with her brother. Ibarra was the linchpin. He stayed in touch with the old Ramirez guards as well as the Quinones army. With him on her side, either way, she was guaranteed to come out on top."

"She would have turned on her own brother?" Izza asked.

"Hell, yes. A mother who could kill her own children has no moral boundaries," Alex explained.

"Where's Ibarra now?" Connor wanted to know.

But Alex saw through his junior agent's question. "You shot four of them. Isn't that enough?"

"Just tying up a loose end," Connor countered, his voice steel. "Seems to me that's what you'd do."

"Leave it alone, Connor. Ibarra is in a deep dark federal hole. He'll get what's coming to him."

"Good. Maybe the cartel really is out of business then."

"For now," Alex answered. "Someone will try it again eventually. I've got to give Ramirez credit for one thing, though."

Connor's eyebrows lifted. "What the hell for? He's the reason Morgan's dead."

"Yes, but he also loved his daughters enough to ask for help," Alex said thoughtfully. "Drug lords are very proud men. Not many would've done that."

Connor glanced at his perfect little girl. Jamie's lips were squeezed together in the cutest bow. Izza had rubbed a drop of baby oil on the infant's tiny head and combed her hair into a peak. His heart melted at the sight of the women in his life. Yeah. He'd do anything for them, too. Maybe he did understand Miguel Ramirez after all.

"Another thing you'll be surprised to know," Alex said. "Remember Juanita? The nanny? Who do you think she was?"

Izza cringed. "Please don't tell me she was Alejandra and Javier's older sister. That would be just plain disgusting."

"Oh, no. She was Miguel's mother's sister – his aunt. After the smoke cleared, she took Christina and Sophia home to live with her and her husband in Juarez. She over-nighted a dozen chicken tamales to me."

"She did?" Izza asked. "Why?"

"Because I asked her to move to America," Alex said. "She turned me down with the tamales. Said there was no reason to leave the country she loves. Mexico has seen worse demons than Alejandra and her brother. If Mexico could endure them, so would she."

"Guess there's hope after all," Connor muttered. After all he'd heard about the battle at the Ramirez hacienda, he'd never have believed it. "What's next?"

Alex pushed to his feet. "I'm flying home in a couple days with Rory. How long until you and your baby are released, Izza?"

"Tomorrow. Connor's hotel room is nearby. We might spend a few days resting before we fly home."

Connor grinned. A very important word had just rolled off Izza's lips like it was no big deal. That bachelor pad of his was due for a definite makeover. Heck, maybe it was time to buy a real house. Ahem, home.

Alex pulled a gold chain out of his inside jacket pocket. "This was on the floor at the hangar where we found you. Thought you might want it back."

Izza laid Jamie across her lap and took the locket lovingly back into her fingers.

"Is that your grandmother's picture?"

"No. I don't have a clue who she is."

Alex raised a brow. "Isn't it your locket?"

"It is now. Connor and I found it when we were exploring our cave. Look at this." Izza showed Alex the simple declaration of love etched inside the locket cover. "I know it sounds really dumb, but it's like my brother sent me a message when I needed it most." She fastened the gold chain around her neck again. "Quite the coincidence, huh?"

Alex put his arm back around her in a fatherly hug, maybe the first she'd ever known. "I don't believe in coincidence. My wife taught me that. Everything happens for a reason."

Izza smiled across the room, her eyes aglitter with fresh tears. "I think she's right."

Connor bit his lip and blinked like crazy.

Alex stood beneath the hot Utah sun again in somber reverence with Connor at the Pines of the Wasatch Memorial Park. Izza couldn't attend because of the baby. Mark and Libby were already back east, but Roy insisted he could make it to the service. He also insisted on a motorized wheelchair, an excellent idea considering the rolling lawn and lush green grass of the cemetery.

"He would've been one of my boys," he muttered angrily when they'd first arrived at the carefully prepared gravesite. "Damn it. Morgan was already one too many."

Alex silently agreed. Losing agents in the line of duty was never easy. A gentle breeze filtered through the pines and honey locusts that lined the cobbled streets. The foray into Mexico had come at too high a cost. Morgan Humphrey's funeral at Arlington was hard enough. Alex had flown home with the body for that one. Another good young man laid to rest too damn soon. Listening to his sister cry at the graveside reminded Alex how valiant his men were. How brave. How rare.

They didn't have to do any of this. They didn't owe their country anything more than time already served, and yet they'd placed themselves in harm's way by joining a company that still fought the good fight, that still believed in uncommon truths like right and wrong. Truth. Justice. American dreams.

"The hearse is here," Connor whispered confidentially. Alex felt him stiffen when it rolled to the edge of the curb. Ordinarily, he and Connor would've been pallbearers. Not today. An army of young men in white shirts and ties advanced to the rear of the vehicle the same as a military honor guard would have done. They did things differently in Utah, but these young men looked the same. Standing tall to do their duty. Honorable. Proud.

The preacher or whatever he was stepped forward. "Ladies and gentlemen. Elder Coltrane will now dedicate the grave." Alex bowed his head as the prayer was offered. He had to give the Mormons credit. They did know how to find comfort and solace, even in the middle of heart breaking tragedy.

"But it wasn't me, Mom," a familiar voice insistently whispered behind him. Another glance back at the Dennisons and Alex caught Rory's dark eyes roll in semi-aggravation as he endured another emotion-filled hug from his thankful mother, Ruth. Rory was another who'd insisted on attending Brigham Coltrane's funeral. His mother hadn't stopped crying since she and Rory's father arrived at the hospital courtesy of Alex. Even now, Ruth stood hanging over the back of her son's wheelchair, her arms around his neck and her teary cheek against his. It could have been him in that lovely bronze casket beneath the pines, no doubt about it.

Sawyer Dennison coughed. Ruth sniffed. But Brigham Coltrane's mother and father wept. And Alex wished he were home with his wife in Alexandria, and this day was behind him.

It was newly hired ex-DEA Agent Brigham Coltrane who had caught a bullet as he and Cassidy fled with the Ramirez girls and their nanny. The round pierced his jugular. He never stood a chance. His last whispered words to Cassidy were simple and fast. *Keep them safe.* And another mother had no son to smother with hugs, no freshly pressed shirt to drench with tears of gratitude.

At the funeral service in the chapel, Alex learned Brigham had been a missionary for his church. Well, he'd fulfilled the greatest mission in the universe as far as Alex was concerned. Brigham had died to save another. Better yet, he'd died to save the children of his enemy, the very man who'd brutally ordered the killing of three of Coltrane's DEA brethren a year earlier. There had to be a pretty damned good reward in heaven for a kid like Brigham.

Alex winked at Rory. Ruth kept hugging her son, and Rory kept holding onto his mother's arm. Somehow, he didn't look very annoyed at all. He'd taken a hit to his left shoulder, left leg, and right elbow. The worst injury and the one that required the most extensive surgery was his leg, damaged in nearly an identical wound as Roy's. Yet here he was, honoring a fallen hero as if Brigham had already been one of The TEAM. Which he was. Alex just never got the chance to meet the heroic agent he'd hired sight unseen.

"Ladies and gentlemen," the preacher said. "The seventh ward has prepared a meal for you at their building. Directions are located on the back of your programs. We would certainly love it if you would partake of their compassionate service."

Alex glanced at Connor.

"Not me," he said. "Izza's waiting. I just moved them into my hotel today."

"Already?"

"I'm telling you, my little girl's going to whip the world some day. She's a fighter." Connor beamed, his face warm with fatherly love. Now there was a sight – the biggest womanizer on The TEAM wrapped around two little girls' fingers and their pinkie fingers at that.

"I'm out of here," Roy grumbled. "I've got company." Alex suspected part of Roy's grumpiness lay in the fact that Collette, his ex-wife, had shown up at the hospital. She'd become a permanent fixture at the hotel he'd been holed up in the last couple of days, too. He and Collette hadn't been together in years, and yet neither of them had remarried either. Interesting.

After a short word with Brigham's grieving parents, Alex and his men headed back to their respective vehicles, Rory Dennison with his doting parents while Alex loaded Roy's wheelchair in the back of the his SUV. Connor assisted in getting the grumpy senior agent settled.

"I'm not dead, you know," Roy grouched when Connor latched his seat belt for him.

"Damned good thing. I hear you and Rory were having wheelchair races in the hospital halls."

"Just one. The damned kid was up walking before I was. He came into my room and challenged me. Said I was old and lazy. What was I going to do? Turn him down?"

"Have you already started rehab?" Alex asked when they were all inside the SUV and ready to go.

"Couldn't. Had a damned staph infection. My leg's been in a damned brace. How do you expect me to workout like that?"

"Which hurt worse?" Connor asked. "Chest or leg?"

"Hell, why don't you tell me?" Roy snapped. "How's a bullet hole supposed to feel?"

Connor grinned at Alex. "Yeah, Boss. He's feeling better."

Thirty-One

Izza found herself humming a baby lullaby. With Connor at Brigham's funeral, she'd done nothing but hold her newborn infant. The rocking chair he'd positioned at the open balcony doors was perfect for the job. She'd made herself a cup of hotel room coffee, left the deadbolt unlatched so she wouldn't have to get up when he returned, and there she and Jamie stayed and played.

Nothing compared to the swell of love in her heart for this tiny little girl. Jamie was perfection come to earth, a ray of pure light from heaven. Motherhood. Who'd have thought it could change a woman so radically and make her so protective? Or so humble...

Connor's hotel room was a suite with a view of bustling Salt Lake City below and the Wasatch Mountains to the east. A sudden summer shower had quenched the last of the fires set by the cartel. Utah smelled fresh and clean and Izza was at peace for the first time in—forever. Not since her mother was alive had she felt so loved or relaxed.

Her memories strayed to the days when sweet Lucia would gather both Jamie and Izza to her lap in another wooden rocking chair in front of another open window just like this one. There were no scary monsters living in the Ramos house then, just a hard-working father named Pablo who truly loved his dark-haired wife and their children. Izza and Jamie didn't need hiding places or escape routes then. The coat closet in the hallway was simply a place where boots and coats were stored. It never had a padlock until....

Izza shivered the ugly memories away and vowed. Jamie Bridgette would never know a harsh word or a mean hand. She'd never cry herself to sleep or lie in her baby brother's arms too sweaty and beat up to move. Placing a kiss in her sweet baby's hair, Izza promised with all her heart to be Lucia. Never Pablo. God, no.

The prettiest yellow bird lighted on the balcony railing.

"See that songbird, Jamie?" Izza whispered. "He's singing just to you."

She closed her eyes as that tiny bird's joyful chirp heralded the start of her new day and with it, her new life. Connor did not have a mean bone in his body. She would know. She'd bullied him enough, but not once had he struck back when she'd stepped over the line. And she'd been so mean. All he'd ever done was take her crap, and Izza just plain did not understand how. He seemed to have an ocean of patience. And love.

Her heart ached to make amends. Tears brimmed in her eyes and Izza let them fall. Holding the tiny person she and Connor had created filled her heart with the oddest emotions. The oddest realization. More tears and Izza let her old life go so she could embrace the new.

"You're a good girl," she whispered to her baby—and to herself. "You never did anything wrong. It wasn't your fault Mama died."

She took a deep breath. "And it wasn't your place to make him happy. Papa was sick. He was a very sad man who should have gotten professional help. You were just a little girl who wanted something he could no longer give."

Jamie arched her back and stretched. Izza looked down into the darkest eyes and saw herself. She choked at the lovely truth staring back at her through dark, thick lashes and dreamy eyes. Now was her time to be a mother, to teach and to love, to protect and guide. With Connor at her side, she knew without a doubt that she could make the kind of home she and Jamie should have grown up in. She and Connor really could make their world.

Maybe he was right. Maybe she should let him locate her father if only to show him that she was nothing like him. That she'd made better choices. That she'd lived. That Lucia still lived through her.

"I'm going to marry your daddy," Izza promised Jamie. "And we are going to live happily-ever-after if it's the last thing I do."

An angelic smile flittered over Jamie's face. Her eyes rolled back into preemie dreamland once again.

"But first." Izza reached for her cell phone on the nearby desk. "Daddy's going to bring us girls some of the best fajitas north of the border."

Connor tapped his fingers impatiently on the display glass. For a girl who grew up in Seattle, Izza sure lived for Mexican cuisine. And for a boy from Boston who'd grown up on blue crab and Icelandic cod, he didn't mind the spicy menu at all.

"You want habaneras?" the clerk asked.

"Are they hot?"

"Oh, yes. Only one pepper is hotter. The Reaper." She lifted a brow. "You want that instead? It will make you wish to die after just one taste."

Connor deliberated a half-second. Izza did like the heat. He remembered the bottle of hot sauce she always carried with her in Iraq. "Sure, but on the side. Throw in a double order of guacamole, too."

"You bet," she replied as napkins, plastic utensils, and a large carton of salsa joined the nachos already in the carryout bag. "Have a seat. I'll call you when it's ready."

He took position on one of the many wooden stools lining the window and wall. Knowing Izza and Jamie were safely tucked in his hotel room should have made him happy. She had recovered enough to leave the hospital and Jamie was doing outstanding for a preemie. It had to be all those tough-girl attributes she'd inherited from her mother. The little thing didn't do much more than eat and sleep. Come to think of it, that's all Izza was doing right now, too.

But he wasn't happy. Maybe it was Brigham's funeral or waiting for his order that bugged him. Connor couldn't put his finger on that creepy sniper sixth sense poking at him. He glanced out the window to his right. The normalcy of the city streets only irked him more.

"Your order, sir." The very helpful clerk held up two bags of the best Mexican food in SLC.

"Thanks." He tossed a couple twenties on the counter and grabbed the bags.

"Wait. Your change."

"Keep it," he muttered, his hand already flat to the exit door. He knew what bugged him now. Izza was alone. His cell phone rang. Sweet Mother Mary and Joseph, it was

Izza's pretty face on his caller ID. That girl could read his mind.

"Hey, Mama," he answered in the deepest, sexiest baritone he could muster, already imagining her in his arms again.

But Izza did not respond. Connor listened to the racket over her phone, rapid words in Mexican, but nothing he understood. It was not her voice. Whoever was in the room with her was angry. Definitely not a man's voice either. Maybe a woman's? A young man's?

And then Izza said strong and clear, "Put the gun down."

"Izza?" Connor barked. Panic lengthened his stride. "Talk to me. What's going on?"

More noise answered as if the phone was being bumped and jostled. He ran, dodging traffic on the busy city street and a fire in his gut. Shoving through the hotel doors, he grabbed the nearest elevator and ran to his hotel room. The door was open. The same angry voice he'd heard over the phone could be heard in the hall. "No way! No way! You and your boyfriend are gonna pay. I'm going to do to you what you did to my mother and father."

Connor set the bags of food on the floor outside his door and peered cautiously at the stranger's back, his SIG drawn and ready. He could easily end this confrontation. It was a clear case of self-defense and intruder alert, but he also caught the slight shake of her head.

She stood against the open balcony door facing someone in a black hoody over baggy black jeans. Black running shoes with bright neon green laces, both untied and dirty, adorned his or her feet. The person's clothing looked new, but he or she was a lightweight, somewhere between a hundred and a hundred ten pounds. Connor could not identify gender, but he guessed male. The person had a speech impediment. He lisped when he talked.

But he also waved the gun erratically, not necessarily focused or aiming at Izza. If anything, he used it like an exclamation point. Just then the stranger turned on Connor. "I see you now. Get over here."

But Connor had already drawn his weapon. They stood locked in a standoff. And worse yet, he was face to face with a child. An angry teenager boy who handled his weapon as if it were a toy. And that was the problem with a kid and a gun.

"What's going on, Izza?" Connor asked calmly.

The kid exploded. "Hey, dumb ass, what are you asking her for? I'm the one you need to be talking to, not some stupid bitch. What! Can't you see me or something? I ain't invisible. Look at me. I'm the guy with the gun!" He lifted his weapon over his head in an erratic circle almost as if he were batting flies.

"Okay then. You tell me what's going on." Connor stared at the young man in his line of sight. "Who are you?"

"That's a good question, but you're a little late asking, aren't you?"

"So enlighten me. What do you want?" Connor eased inside the room and closed the door behind him.

"I want you guys to die. Both of you. You killed my father and my mother. I'm here to make you pay!" Again the gun jerked back and forth between Connor and Izza. By all rights, Connor should have shot him. Izza and Jamie's lives were in danger. He could have. Maybe he should have. But he didn't.

"You're Ricardo. You are Alejandra Ramirez's son."

"Alejandra Quinones!" the boy spat. "At least use her right name."

Connor drew a deep breath and calmed. "How about we both put down our weapons and talk for a minute before either of us does something drastic?"

"I ain't putting nothing down but you three pigs."

"So you're here to kill me, a woman, and a baby, is that right?" Connor verbalized the threat, hoping to get through to this young man.

"What? You don't hear so good? Yeah! That's exactly why I'm here, dirt bag."

Connor had no trouble reading this young man's body language. One second angry and the next afraid, he was obviously frustrated, hurt, and a whole lot of mad. Every emotion rampaging through his brain revealed itself through his dark brown eyes. Despite his threat, tears welled up, his nose dripped, and he was sweating like a prizefighter. Ricardo's lisp was the product of a mild harelip that lifted the middle of his upper lip and no doubt his palate. Connor would know. His youngest brother was born with the same condition.

Taking the first step toward what he hoped was a peaceful outcome, Connor raised his gun over his head in a sign of surrender. "I'm putting my weapon down, son—"

"I'm not your son!" Ricardo screamed. "You're the boss man. You're the big man who sent that guy to kill my father. And my mother, too."

Ah, so Ricardo thought he had entered Alex's room. That put a slightly different spin on the situation, not that it alleviated the danger, but it did reveal what little Ricardo knew. Did he even realize that he had two half-sisters? Did he know how his mother used two little girls as human shields or that she fully intended to kill them? But most of all, did he knew who his parents really were?

Now the gun was totally on Connor. He stared the young man down. "Have you ever killed anyone before?"

"Course I have. I've... I've killed lots of people. Most of them were American pigs just like you." The gun waved like a matador's red cape at a bullfight.

"It's pretty hard to take that first shot, don't you think?"

The kid's wild eyes narrowed. "What? Oh, yeah. But then it gets easier. What do you care?"

"I don't. It's just that a man has to get himself psyched up every time, doesn't he? It's harder in close quarters like this hotel room. You've got to look your victims in the eye. Women are harder. Children are hardest. But babies...." Connor paused to let the reality of shooting an infant sink in.

"Yeah, but... but...." Ricardo's false bravado wavered. His gaze drifted to Izza and the baby in her arms. Izza crooned softly into the top of Jamie's head, but her dark eyes never left the other child with the gun.

Connor continued soft and low. "I'm sure glad this isn't your first time, Ricardo. I'd hate to have to kill three people once I've looked them in the eye. They say it gets easier, but it didn't for me. By the way, that pretty lady's name is Isabella, and the baby in her arms is a little girl named Jamie. Jamie isn't even a week old yet. She was excited to get here so she's two months premature."

Ricardo blinked hard. The gun lowered a fraction before he caught his second wind and screamed, his hands covering his ears like a spoiled child, the pistol against the side of his head. "I can't hear you. I can't hear you."

Connor offered another quick nod of encouragement to Izza. She winked back.

"Okay. I get it. You're just here to kill us. Can you at least let Izza sit down while we're talking, I mean, before you murder us?"

Ricardo gulped. The kid's eyes widened at that stupid request in the middle of his insane plan for revenge. He waved his gun at Izza and then the chair. "I don't care. It's not like I said you hafta stand around all day. So sit."

She lowered into the rocking chair. "Thank you, Ricardo."

The poor damned kid looked confused. "'S okay," he muttered with a shrug.

"That was a very kind thing you just did. Thank you for being so polite to Izza and Jamie." Connor kept trying to breach the wall of anger.

"Shut up. I am not here to be kind and polite," Ricardo snarled.

Connor still held his SIG in his hand, but it was not aimed at the young man. "You're right. A man's got the right to be mad when his father and mother have been killed."

"You killed them."

"You loved your father, didn't you, Ricardo?" Connor ignored the young man's angry accusation.

"No, I didn't." The gun snapped back to Connor again. "That's the thing. I didn't love him. He was a pig. I didn't love my mother, either, if that's what you're gonna try next. She was worse than he was. You should've seen them together. You're all liars. You people are just like them."

Connor stared at the kid, wishing he could see what else was inside that angry head. He was missing part of the puzzle here. Why was Ricardo seeking revenge for the parents he hated?

"So what's the next question, cop? Huh?" Ricardo wiped his nose on the sleeve of his hoody. "You wanna know why I'm gonna kill you?"

"No, but you look thirsty. Can I get you anything to drink?"

Ricardo frowned, his head cocked as if he hadn't heard right. "You what? You want to get me something to drink? Are you stupid?"

"Probably." Connor holstered his gun and stepped toward Ricardo. "But I'm pretty sure you aren't going to kill anyone."

The young man's jaw dropped when Connor approached. He didn't stop until his chest pressed hard against the barrel of the lethal weapon.

"You don't really want to kill me, do you?"

"Yes, I do. What? You think you're so tough. You think—"

"No, but you are not a cold-blooded killer." Connor peered deeply into the young man's eyes. Dark brown, angry, and hurt. That was the color glistening there. "Are you, Ricardo?"

"But I... I...."

"You're all alone now, aren't you?"

"It's just that..." Ricardo blinked hard, the barrel of his gun still pressed against Connor's heart. "It's just that I... I...."

"Let's talk. Just for a minute. Then you can kill me if you still want to."

The angst left Ricardo's face in a heartbeat. He lowered his weapon. His shoulders sagged in defeat. "I'm not going to kill you. My father was right. I'm worthless."

"No, you are not." Connor steered the boy to the couch and away from Izza. She rolled her eyes in relief and hurried into their bedroom with Jamie. He felt certain she would call the police, but in a way, he hoped she wouldn't.

Ricardo's lips quivered. Tears shimmered in his eyes. "They took everything. The police came in and... I hated my father. He was mean. He called me fat and stupid. He said I was nothing. I'm the most worthless piece of crap on the planet! I can't even do what I came here to do."

"No, you're not," Connor said evenly. "You're a young man who's lost everything."

Ricardo wiped his face again. "He said he would arrange it so all I had to do was grow up and start acting like a man. That's all he ever said. Grow up. Be a man. Well, I don't want to be a man if I have to be like him."

Connor let the young man talk.

"He was a pig. I know they were sister and brother. I had disgusting pigs for parents. What does that make me?"

Izza padded silently out of the bedroom and into their kitchenette. In a tremendous show of courage, she brought a tray of refreshments to the coffee table in front of Connor and Ricardo. "Would you like some lemonade?" she asked, and Connor could have kissed her right then and there. That's why he loved her. She knew exactly what this poor damned kid was going through, and she was not afraid to reach out to him.

Ricardo looked up at her in shock. "Me?"

She stood over him for a moment, hesitated and said, "I have some really good fajitas if you're hungry. Come on. Let's eat."

He looked back to Connor, dumbfounded. "I don't get it. You folks are being nice to me. I... I don't know what to do!" He crumbled into the snot-nosed kid he really was.

Connor took a deep breath as he absorbed the troubled condition of Alejandra and Javier's only child. The product of an incestuous affair, the boy appeared to have had too many strikes against him to please his arrogant father. But the real problem seemed to be in Ricardo's head and heart. He was not cut from the same vulgar cloth as his parents.

"You're already a man," he said quietly, pondering his options. He had every right to turn this kid over to the authorities. "The real question is what kind of man do you want to be? Do you still want to kill the woman I love and our baby? For that matter, do you want to kill anyone?"

Ricardo shook his head and handed the gun over. Connor swiftly switched the safety on and stowed it on the floor beside him.

"I didn't really want to kill anybody. It's just that..." Ricardo wiped his face with the sleeve of his hoody. "My father always said that a real man must avenge his family. He must kill the people who murdered his loved ones. I was just... I was just...."

"You were trying to be a real man according to your father's definition, but that would make you just like him. Is that who you want to be?"

"No!" Ricardo buried his face in his arms. "I don't want to be like him. I don't."

"How old are you?"

"I am fifteen and a half, almost sixteen."

Connor sighed. He had a sixteen-year-old brother, but Ricardo and Matt had nothing in common. The Mahers were poor by Boston standards, but somehow, the son of a filthy rich cartel boss had less.

Izza brought a tray of the best Mexican food in SLC to the coffee table. She shrugged apologetically. "It's not much, but it's really good. There's more salsa if you want some."

Ricardo covered his face and sobbed, his shoulders shuddering at the change in events. Connor wrapped his arm around Izza when she sat beside him, her hand on his knee and the tenderest smile tugging her lips.

"Izza, this is my new friend, Ricardo," Connor said honestly. "He's one lucky kid."

"I am?"

"Sure," Izza soothed. "Look at you. You have your whole life ahead of you. Did you know you have two little sisters?"

He frowned. "I do?"

Izza left Connor's side to sit alongside Ricardo, and Connor fell in love with her all over again. She read this poor kid like a book. "Yes, Ricardo. Your mother had two little girls with Miguel Ramirez. Christina is five and Sophia is only three. They are your half-sisters."

Ricardo's blank look told Connor plenty. She'd just dumped another boatload of crap on this poor boy. He knew nothing about his mother's other life, only that she'd left him for – what? A contrived marriage? A plan so insidious she was willing to bear another man's children in order to take over his drug business? The depth of Alejandra's deceit astounded Connor. In the end, she had sacrificed all three of her children for worthless greedy power.

But the young man wasn't dumb. His silence was punctuated with blinks and sighs as Ricardo connected what he already knew. There was resignation and sadness in his voice when he finally spoke. "That must be why she left when I was ten. Mama said looking at me made her sad. She had to leave so she wouldn't have to see me every day. It's because of my... my...." He hiccupped so hard, he couldn't continue.

"You have a slight harelip," Connor intervened. "That can be corrected with a surgical procedure. I'd be glad to pay for it if you'd let me. My little brother was born with the same thing."

The revelations of the night proved too much. With an anguished groan, he leaned back into the couch and covered his face with both hands again.

Izza put her arm around the young man's heaving shoulders. "It's okay," she crooned. "It's going to be different now. You'll be okay."

Her words only made him cry harder. Connor's eyes grew a little misty too. In a way, their murderer was Izza all over again, mad as hell at the world and all alone.

He thumped Ricardo's knee with his fist. "I know a guy who can put you in touch with your sisters," he said. "They're living in Juarez, Mexico, with a very good woman and her family."

"No. I don't deserve any of this. Besides, I don't know them. I couldn't."

"Well, you sure don't deserve what's already happened, do you? Besides, everyone deserves a second chance, especially someone who has decided to be a real man. You have a tough job ahead of you. Those two little girls do, too.

They've lost their mother and father. They could use a good big brother to stick up for them when people start talking behind their backs and pointing fingers."

Ricardo dried his eyes. "But do they already know about... me?"

"Like what?" Connor asked softly.

"Do they know that... that I am so ugly?"

Izza gasped. "You are not ugly," she declared vehemently. "A real man is judged by his choices, not his looks. And I'll knock the jerk on his butt who says different."

Ricardo sat blinking furiously. "That would be my father," he said meekly. "You would have to travel all the way to hell to knock him on his butt."

"Listen." Izza scooted closer to him, her dander up and all those motherly, big sister instincts alive and well. "My father wasn't so nice either. He used to beat me and my brother like red-headed stepchildren. You want to know what I did?"

"What?" he asked shyly.

Connor could not help the smile tugging his lip. Ricardo had gone from a wanna-be tough guy to a shy young man with a no-kidding gorgeous woman talking to him. He seemed to be having a hard time making direct eye contact with Izza all of a sudden.

"I got the hell away from my old man the first chance I could and I never looked back. I joined the Marines, that's what I did." Izza bragged like the true jarhead she was. "My baby brother did, too. I haven't regretted it for one second." She shot Connor a tender glance. "My brother died a hero, Ricardo. We both had a mean SOB for a father, but Jamie still died a hundred times a better man than our old man was."

Connor leaned back into the couch. No matter which road he chose to follow, Ricardo would never forget the day he met Isabella Ramos.

"Do you really think I could be a hero?" he asked.

"You already are," Connor replied. "The minute you put that gun down, you proved what kind of man you are."

"Are you going to call the police?" he asked.

Connor pursed his lips in thought. That was a tough one. He should contact the authorities. Ricardo had committed a serious transgression.

Izza didn't seem to need any time to think about it. She interrupted his moment of silence with a pointed, "Hell no. We don't call the cops on heroes, do we?"

"It would be an honor to help you locate your sisters," Connor replied evenly. The juvenile system did not need another young man. He needed family. Not state.

The transformation took place immediately. Ricardo stiffened his back and blinked away his tears. "I would very much like to meet my little sisters. I think maybe they might like a big brother, don't you?"

"I know they would." Connor extended his hand, but Ricardo needed more. With a sob, he threw himself into Connor's arms, just another lost kid who needed someone in the world to care. Izza wiped her eyes. The would-be murderer had vanished, replaced instead by a humble young man. Connor thumped Ricardo extra hard on the back before he released him.

"Just because Izza joined the Marines doesn't mean you should," he said. "You'll have your hands full being a big brother. That's enough responsibility for now. Ask me. I've got six."

"I always wanted a sister or a brother," Ricardo said. "It has been a very lonely life being my father's son."

"Hey." Izza elbowed him. "You've got family now."

Connor grinned. Judging by the flush creeping up this young man's neck, he was not exactly thinking brotherly thoughts. "I think I heard Jamie," Connor interrupted all the sisterly love.

That got Izza out of earshot for a couple minutes.

"Listen, Ricardo. I'm keeping your weapon. You're damned lucky the way things turned out today. Not only did you break the law, but you picked the wrong woman to mess with. Izza's a trained USMC police sniper. She held the record while we were in Iraq for the fastest draw, too. That she didn't take your head off the moment you showed up tells me she sees something special in you. Don't let her down."

Ricardo cast a furtive glance toward the bedroom door where Izza had gone. "You are very lucky."

"Yes, I am," Connor agreed. "Now stop looking at my woman and dig in. You want some guacamole?"

EPILOGUE

Connor surveyed his handiwork. It was perfect. An ice bucket with a bottle of non-alcoholic champagne already chilled. A dozen candles lit and glowing. Mounds of bubbles. Two luxurious bathrobes. Fluted champagne glasses. Barely audible music. As soon as Izza finished feeding Jamie, he planned to whisk her away for a night of water sports and romance.

He hoped.

As soon as they'd returned to Alexandria, he'd housed Izza and Jamie at a first class hotel while he moved his bachelor's household into a larger and more family-friendly apartment. The baby's room was now decorated in peach and something called mint green at Izza's request. The antique baby bed and dresser his mother had shipped from Boston graced the wall beneath the window. Izza helped him select their new bedroom set, a cherry wood four-poster with a simple white comforter. They'd both been too tired for romance, but tonight was the night.

He hoped.

Besides, his mother would arrive next week to help out. Yes, she wanted to meet Izza, but Connor also knew Bridgette Maher couldn't wait to get her hands on her first granddaughter. Jamie was never out of one or the other's arms as it was. Tonight had to be the night.

He really, really hoped.

Connor stepped into the bedroom to see how his two favorite girls were doing. Izza lay in the middle of their bed, pillows propped around her and Jamie. Dressed in comfortable blue jeans and a pale blue button-down blouse, she looked the picture of contentment. Connor stretched out behind her, his fingers gently tracing Jamie's soft cheek as she suckled.

"How are my girls?" He placed a kiss at the side of Izza's head.

"Happy." She smiled all the time now.

Connor ran his fingers through her luxurious hair. She rarely pulled it back into a ponytail anymore, and she never looked prettier. He loved that he was a part of the simple act of her feeding Jamie, Izza's breast laid bare as the tiny child slurped like she was starving.

The little girl had a regular schedule. Sleep two hours. Eat like its going out of style. Sleep another two hours. Starving again. Even now her lip smacking noises while she suckled made him smile. She might be Izza's sweet little daughter, but she sounded like one of the Maher boys at chowtime. Between that and her cute way of passing gas, without a doubt she was Connor's girl.

"My mother will want to hold Jamie the whole time she's here." Connor pulled Izza's blouse back to place a row of kisses along her bare shoulder.

She shivered. "I feel like I know her already. Is her room ready?"

"Oh, yes. Everything is ready."

"You should see your face," Izza looked up at him, her dark eyes aglow. "You have the handsomest smile right now."

"I do, huh." He couldn't remember ever feeling this good, a tremendously sexy woman comfortable in his bed with his child snuggled in her arms. Could there be a more perfect picture?

"What do you think Boomerang is doing right now?" she asked.

"Probably wishing someone would toss him a few rabbit bones. That scoundrel had it pretty easy while we were there, didn't he?"

Her eyes lit up. "So did Homer. I still think he would've made a good turtle stew, though."

Connor chuckled. "Speaking of faces, you should have seen the look on yours that morning. I almost thought you might do it for a moment there."

"I could've done it until you named him. I was so hungry I thought I was going to die."

"The only time I thought I was dying was when you played doctor." He kissed her again.

Izza chuckled deliciously. "I'm just glad it worked."

"Me, too. You saved my life. That was good thinking."

"You saved mine, too." Izza rolled out of bed and moved the sleeping baby to her nearby crib. "I was starving until you snared those rabbits."

"And you didn't think I had any skills, did you?" He arched his eyebrow mischievously as he stood over the crib with her. Jamie hadn't budged when Izza transferred her to the crib, another sign she was a Maher—comatose after a full stomach. "I'd like to take you up on your offer," he said quietly.

"Offer? What offer is that? I don't remember making you any offer."

"Oh, yes. You made a definite offer in the cave when we went exploring. The one about a bubble bath, remember?" With that unanswered question, Connor scooped Izza over his shoulder and hauled her off to the bathroom.

"Connor," she whisper giggled. "Put me down."

He complied by depositing her into their over-sized tub, clothes and all. She came up sputtering and laughing, her hair wet and bubbles from head to toe. Grabbing him, Izza pulled him in with her. Water sloshed everywhere in the playful mayhem that followed, and within minutes, she had him pinned—right where he wanted her.

He grinned through the bubbles as he unbuttoned her shirt. "This has to go."

She pulled his shirt over his head. "So does this."

Before long, two shirts and one lacy bra lay in puddles on the tile floor. Connor had Izza in a lip lock that wouldn't stop. Her hands roamed over his shoulders and down the muscles of his stomach. She nestled on top of him. He cupped each breast, gently massaging as she lavished kisses over his lips, chin, and jaw. Moving against the light pressure of her lithe body, his hands wandered down her ribcage and over her hips until they came to flex on her jean's pockets.

She giggled. "Something in your way, Boston?"

He opened his eyes to the most gorgeous woman in the world. Izza rose steaming above him, her bare body spiking his feelings all the more. With a surge of foamy bath water all over the floor, he stood and pulled her up with him. Kneeling in front of her, he unsnapped and unzipped her jeans. Izza gazed down at him. Her wet hair straggled over her breasts, her eyes dark with desire.

Connor's breath caught. Never had he seen a more glorious sight. Here he was, nothing more than a humble man on his knees before an angel.

"There is nothing sexier than you in bubbles," he murmured while he peeled her jeans down.

When she stepped out of them, he stood slowly, kissing his way up until he reached her lips. She gasped when he pulled her hips against his. His fingers wandered. There was so much to this woman he didn't yet know. With just two hours to make slow passionate love before Jamie needed to eat again, he intended to make the most of his time.

Smoldering sparks arced between them. In one deft move, he pushed out of his own wet jeans and boxers and tossed them onto the sodden mass by the tub. Izza leaned warm and soft against him, wrapping an arm around his neck.

"Connor," she whispered urgently into his waiting lips. "I want you inside of me. Now."

He clenched her bubbly wet backside, sinking back into the tub, the ache in his groin suddenly out of control. The water splashed rhythmically around them as they melded together.

Izza gasped.

He growled softly as they climaxed together, "I love you so much."

She relaxed with her head on his chest, her eyes peacefully closed. The hot water tap trickled additional warmth into their liquid blanket of bubbles. Izza glowed down to her toes tonight, her olive skin rosy and blushed with the heat of the love they'd just made. And Connor had never felt so thoroughly at peace. He maintained a firm grip on her bottom while they chatted through the afterglow.

"This is a lot different from our usual romantic places, huh?"

He nodded. "Yes. No more making love on dirt. Only silk and satin for you from now on."

"Why? You'd just rip them off."

"You know me well," he whispered, his fingers tapping a gentle beat on her bottom. "Do you remember that day Jamie swatted your backside?"

"Yeah, the smart ass."

Connor smoothed the suds off her shoulder. "I was sure I'd be court-martialed."

"Nah, I wouldn't have done that." Izza folded her arms across his chest, her dark eyes glittering with a sexy smile as she kissed his chin. "I'd have tortured you first."

"Your brother was a pretty good con artist, Izza. I never suspected you two were related. He told me a lot of Hispanics have the same last names, but it didn't mean anything. I'm a white boy from Boston. What did I know?"

"You did look like you wanted to die." Izza was all delicious smiles and mischief. "Besides, you don't kid me. You were looking."

"Yeah, but I'm not sure I'd have done much more if Jamie hadn't smacked your backside like he did." Connor's heart pounded at the memory. "I've seen a few butts before."

She wiggled seductively against him. "Not like mine, you haven't."

"If you think about it, that's the first time we really noticed each other." Connor glanced around the drenched room. "Your brother brought us together, Izza. All of this is because of him. And he did it again by sending you that locket."

Izza stopped smiling. She scooted up closer to Connor's mouth. He thought she was going to kiss him, but instead she cupped both of her hands and pushed his head underwater. He came up sputtering to her wickedly delighted laugh. With a gentle boost of his knee to her backside, he pushed her up out of the water, his hands at her waist. The sight of her naked and glistening in suds spiked his heart all over again.

Dark eyes glowed down at him. "I don't want to talk anymore."

"I can see that," he whispered.

She settled back onto his lap. A more seductive smile was never smiled in all the history of Connor's world. His heart opened wide, then wider still as all his hopes and wishes came back to him a thousand-fold. His life was full. His heart and hands, too. The enormity of the exquisite treasure he held overwhelmed him. When one tiny tear crept out of his eye to mingle with the heat of sudsy water and bubbles, Connor knew to the innermost depths of his soul. Here was the lady he'd been searching for. His reason to live. To breathe. To dream.

Izza. It had always been Izza.

THE END

Sneak Preview of Rory

Book 6

In the Company of Snipers

"One!" A little boy's cheerful voice rang out across the gym floor.

Ember watched intently. She'd thought the man with the boy looked familiar, but now she was certain. There was no mistaking the Hollywood handsome guy she worked with at the best East Coast surveillance company out of Alexandria, Virginia—The TEAM.

Even sweaty and hard at work like he was, Junior Agent Rory Dennison was the epitome of eye candy. Lean muscles rippled beneath a sleeveless T-shirt while he completed crunch after crunch. He made them look simple. Smooth and easy. Steady and sure. The perfect trademark of one of America's elite snipers.

Only Ember didn't know he had a son—if that's who the little boy was. It had to be. The resemblance was unmistakable—black hair that might be curly if it were allowed to grow longer, deep blue eyes, and the hint of a cleft in both of their very masculine chins. The boy was a mini-Rory. A clone. Only a lot smaller. He looked to be maybe five or six. Never having been around little kids, Ember couldn't tell.

"Two!" He wiggled his backside on the basketball he was sitting on, and waved his hands as if shaking water off, only they weren't wet. Mini Rory couldn't seem to sit still.

His father performed another sit-up as easily as his other reps, never losing the rhythm of a well-oiled machine. Sweat glistened on his forehead, neck, and arms from the earlier sets of push-ups he'd finished. His gray shirt darkened in a line down his back and across his chest. And still he pumped. The boy had helped then, too – by sitting on his father's back and counting with as much gusto.

Rory smiled through another crunch, barely grunting as he lifted upward. "How am I doing?"

"You doing great!" Tyler beamed. "Go, Daddy, go!"

A seemingly perpetual smile tugged at the corner of Rory's lips—a most endearing sight for a man as tough and steadfast as he was. He truly seemed to be enjoying his son. *Wow. What a picture.*

"Then which crunch are we on now?"

"Six!"

"You mean eleven," Rory said, barely panting between repetitions.

The cute little guy shook his head, bounced three times on his basketball, and said very seriously, "No, I mean four."

"Okay then, four it is."

"Now is thirteen!" Tyler crowed. "I is your best counter, huh Daddy?"

"Always have been, always will be." Rory continued crunch after crunch with his son shouting random numbers in glee to urge him on.

"Eleven!" Tyler called out, but then he spotted something funny. "Look. That lady gots pink in her hair."

His patient father glanced in the direction Tyler had pointed. Ember gasped. She'd been caught. "Hey, Rory." She waved across the gym.

Sure enough, Rory looked directly at her. The smile faded. His brows scowled to an unhappy V. He returned the wave without enthusiasm, rolled to his side and pushed to his feet. Swiping his face with a gym towel while she approached, he said to Tyler, "Pick up your ball, son. It's time to go."

"Wow, it's a small world isn't it?" she asked enthusiastically. "I didn't know you worked out here, too. Who's this cute little boy?"

Tyler dropped his ball and wrapped both arms around Rory's thigh, proudly and loudly proclaiming, "I Ty-ler Den-ni-son," he crowed, "My number is—"

"That's enough," Rory cautioned his eager son. At the same time, he smiled at Ember with an uncharacteristically tight-lipped smile that didn't even hint at reaching his eyes. "You'll have to excuse Tyler. We're learning our phone number and address. He's excited to share."

"Wow. Kids are brighter than most people give them credit for, huh?" She grinned, a thousand questions pinging for answers. Rory and she had worked together for the last year or so. Why had he kept this darling little boy who was obviously his son a secret?

Rory nodded, his eyes guarded and his voice the same. "Yes, they are."

"How old is he?"

"Four."

"He speaks quite well for a little guy." She opted for small conversation.

"Yes."

"Wow." Ember couldn't think of anything else to say without coming across nosy. He already seemed perturbed, his one-word answers revealing little. "This is your son?"

She emphasized the words *your son*, hoping he'd offer conversation. There was a time he'd seemed friendly toward her, when she'd almost asked him to go out for coffee or a drink. Somewhere in the past few months, the easy going feeling between them had changed. She didn't know why.

He rolled his neck, ruffling Tyler's hair. "Tyler, I work with this lady. Her name is Miss Davis. What do you say when you meet an adult?"

Tyler stuck out his arm for a gentleman's handshake. "I glad to meetcha."

Ember shook his hand with a big smile on her face, impressed with his fairly perfect diction. The little guy spoke as good as some adults she knew. "Wow. Aren't you the polite one? It's very nice to meet you, Mr. Tyler Dennison. Is that your ball?"

"Uh huh," he replied, jumping out of his father's reach to scoop the basketball into both arms.

"Tyler," Rory said sternly. "How do we act in public?"

Immediately, the boy beamed a thousand-watt smile, dropped the ball and hugged Rory's leg again. "I did good, huh Daddy?"

"You did very good, Tyler." He winked down at his son.

The resemblance between father and son was amazing right down to the same straight and elegant nose. Rory's jaw was more square, but Tyler's gently arched brows were exact copies of his father's. He had the same handsome smile, only Rory had yet to offer one. She'd seen it often enough at the office. Why was he acting so odd now?

She knelt at Tyler's level to take the pressure off his father. "So, Mr. Tyler Dennison, do you come to the gym often?"

"Yep!" he said with gusto. "I Daddy's bestest counter. You wanna hear me? I know my twos and frees and tens."

"I do," Ember replied enthusiastically.

Rory frowned and tapped the top of his son's head. "Another time. Get your ball. Let's go."

Tyler scrambled after the basketball.

"He's adorable." She stood, her hands on her hips and her eyes full of unanswered questions. "I didn't know you had a son. Where have you been hiding him?"

"It's none of your business, is it?"

She blinked, totally speechless.

Without another word, he corralled Tyler and didn't look back as they headed toward the exit. But Tyler did. Turning with a little wave before his father hurried him through the double glass doors, he shouted in a big outside voice, "Bye, Miss Davis! See ya later, alligator!"

She waved at the precocious youngster. "Bye, Tyler. It was very nice to meet you. Bye Rory. See you at work tomorrow."

He didn't even turn around.

Thank you for reading Conner!

Be sure to check out the rest of the guys and gals of Irish Winters' series: *In the Company of Snipers*

Other Irish Winters' books:

King of Hearts, Deuces Wild Series, *#1*
Joker Joker, Deuces Wild Series, *#2*
Smoke, Hearts and Ashes Series, *#1*
Ash, Hearts and Ashes Series, *#2*

Coming soon!

Seth, In the Company of Snipers, #17
One-Eyed Jack, Deuces Wild Series, #3

YOU are the key to this book's success!

Please tell other readers why you liked Connor and Izza's story by leaving an honest review at the retail site where you purchased it. Recommend it to your friends. Lend it. Most of all, enjoy it!

The best way to keep up with my new releases, giveaways, and actionable intel is to sign up for my spam-free newsletter at IrishWinters.com.

About the Author

Irish Winters is an award winning, Amazon best-selling author who, when she isn't writing, dabbles in poetry, grandchildren, and rarely (as in extremely rarely) the kitchen. More prone to be outdoors than in, she grew up the quintessential tomboy on a dairy farm in rural Wisconsin, spent her teenage years in the Pacific Northwest, but calls the Wasatch Mountains of Northern Utah home. For now.

She believes in making every day count for something, and follows the wise admonition of her mother to, "Look out the window and see something!"

Connect with Irish!
On Facebook: https://www.facebook.com/author.irishwinters
On Twitter: https://twitter.com/irishwinters1
Or at www. IrishWinters.com